The Best of All
Possible Worlds

The Best of All Possible Worlds

A Novel

B. Steven Verney

Library of Congress Control Number:		2012901496
ISBN:	Hardcover	978-1-4691-5784-9
	Softcover	978-1-4691-5783-2
	Ebook	978-1-4691-5785-6

The Best of All Possible Worlds is a work of fiction. Apart from Maharishi Mahesh Yogi, who is an historical figure, all the characters, places, and incidents are the product of the author's imagination or are used fictitiously. The author has attempted, to the best of his ability, to present Maharishi's teaching in the spirit in which it was given in the specific context of this fictional story.

Transcendental Meditation, TM, and the Transcendental Meditation Program are registered trademarks to Maharishi Foundation USA, a 501(c)(3) non-profit educational organization. www.tm.org

Credit : From, The Upanishads, translated by Eknath Easwaran, founder of the Blue Mountain Center of Meditation, copyright 1987,2007; reprinted by permission of Nilgiri Press. PO Box 256. Tomales, California 94971, www.easwaran.org

Credit: Han Shan,[" Who takes Cold Mountain Road"] translated by Red Pine, from the Collected Songs of Cold Mountain, Revised and Expanded. Copyright c 2000 by Bill Porter. Reprinted with the permission of The Permissions Company., on behalf of Copper Canyon, www.coppercanyonpress.org

Credit: From Tao te Ching by Lao Tsu, translated by Gia- fu Feng & Jane English, translation copyright c 1972 by Gia-fu Feng and Jane English, copyright renewed 2000 by Carol Wilson and Jane English. Used by permission of Alfred A Knopf, a division of Random House, Inc.

A portion of the proceeds of the sale of this book will be donated to the David Lynch Foundation, whose purpose is to offer TM to underprivileged children in the US and around the world. davidlynchfoundation.org

This book was printed in the United States of America.

Rev. date: 03/07/2013

To order additional copies of this book, contact:
Xlibris Corporation
1-888-795-4274
www.Xlibris.com
Orders@Xlibris.com
72068

For my sons,
Michael and Jonathan

Dedicated to His Holiness Maharishi Mahesh Yogi
for bringing the Light of Pure Consciousness to the world

Table of Contents

PROLOGUE. xi

Part One

CHAPTER 1   Growing Up in Greenwich Village. 1
CHAPTER 2   The Meeting on Elm Street. 11
CHAPTER 3   A Trip to Concord 17
CHAPTER 4   The Law of Attraction 21
CHAPTER 5   The Call 27
CHAPTER 6   The River and the Ocean. 33
CHAPTER 7   The Master and Enlightenment 39
CHAPTER 8   The Seed of Change 47
CHAPTER 9   The Flow of Desire 51
CHAPTER 10 All You Need Is Love 63
CHAPTER 11 The Magic of the Moment. 75
CHAPTER 12 The Course. 81
CHAPTER 13 The Book 91
CHAPTER 14 The Storm Hits. 95
CHAPTER 15 The Aftermath 109
CHAPTER 16 The World Is Upside Down 115

Part Two

CHAPTER 17 The Game Begins Anew 121
CHAPTER 18 Julian Takes a Trip to the Library 133
CHAPTER 19 A Change in Direction. 139
CHAPTER 20 Nothing's Gonna Change My World. 149

CHAPTER 21   Dinner with the O'Connors 159
CHAPTER 22   The Appointed Time 169
CHAPTER 23   String Theory 175
CHAPTER 24   The Mystery of Enlightenment.................... 183
CHAPTER 25   Where Light Is Perpetual 195
CHAPTER 26   The Theory of Relativity 199
CHAPTER 27   Mums, Tea, and Muffins 205
CHAPTER 28   A New Life 211
CHAPTER 29   The Gathering................................. 219
CHAPTER 30   A Walk in the Woods 227
CHAPTER 31   The Petition.................................. 239
CHAPTER 32   The Meeting.................................. 249
CHAPTER 33   The Plan..................................... 257
CHAPTER 34   A Promise Made.............................. 271
CHAPTER 35   The Activity of the World 285
CHAPTER 36   The Holidays................................. 299
CHAPTER 37   The Divine Artist and the Lover of Art............. 311
CHAPTER 38   The Lecture 319

EPILOGUE   I Stop Somewhere Waiting for You............... 355

ACKNOWLEDGEMENTS 359
THE AUTHOR 361

Prologue

EVERYTHING WAS GOING SO WELL, Sam O'Connor thought to himself as he walked across the Amherst College campus from his afternoon class. *My life here as a professor is all I hoped it would be. My incredible family . . . How blessed I am to have them in my life! My students are excited. The discussions in class and the small groups are showing just how engaged they are. My consciousness course is a great success. And my book is on the Times' best sellers list. My, my, life is good and it's only going to get better,* the young second-year professor thought to himself.

Sam arrived at his office in Williston Hall to find a note tucked under his door. He picked it up and put it down along with the stack of notebooks and books he'd carried in. He took off his tweed jacket, hung it up on the hook, and sat down at his large wooden desk.

At the back of his desk to one side, Sam had a picture of his wife and two young boys playfully huddled together, smiling at the camera. Every time Sam looked up from his desk, he saw the three men who had the greatest influence on him. On a small shelf, he had placed white plaster busts of Socrates and Plato, and above them hung a large framed picture of His Holiness Maharishi Mahesh Yogi with a gray shawl draped around his shoulders. A few flower petals clung sweetly to Maharishi's long, dark, and graying hair and his full beard. He looked to the right with a far-seeing gaze, as if envisioning a new and peaceful world unfolding.

His most cherished books filled a mahogany bookcase the length and height of the wall. On one shelf sat a framed eight-by-ten picture of Jesus depicted as a yogi. He sat Buddha-like in half lotus in the middle of the forest, his face serene and full of compassion. Sam had been raised Catholic, and the teachings of Jesus formed the bedrock of his spiritual awareness. As a child, they nurtured his young heart, and his belief in God's goodness became the central point of navigation for his life. From his present perspective, Sam saw Jesus as a yogi, which meant he was one with God, a position Sam emulated.

Christ's teachings were deeply transformative, and as Sam's own awareness and understanding expanded, they beckoned him more and more strongly. When he discovered *The Cloud of Unknowing*, written by an unknown medieval monk, his heart quickened. This small book celebrated the mystical in Christ's teaching, the living relationship with God, rather than the dogma of the church. Sam recognized that the monk's description of slipping into the "cloud of unknowing" was just what he had learned to do through Transcendental Meditation: transcend the activity of the mind and dwell in the silence of pure consciousness. Repeated merging with that infinite inner silence led to a permanent oneness with it, the unfolding of unity with all that is. Sam was profoundly moved by this reconciliation between the spiritual tradition of his youth and the world of TM. He felt certain that the mystical aspect of Christianity, which was its heart from his point of view, also had transcending and the experience of pure consciousness at its core.

A framed photo of his parents in Ireland sat next to the picture of Jesus. His dad never looked so happy and relaxed; his mom beamed like a child. Their parents, Sam's grandparents, had left Ireland because of the famine, made America their home, and never looked back. Sam's own parents, Jimmy and Lilly, were brought up on all the Irish stories and myths, and within minutes of landing at Shannon Airport, they knew they were home. His parents felt so at home in Ireland that the trip to the Emerald Isle made them realize they had been living almost in exile in New York City their whole lives. Over the years, they had written at Christmas and Easter to their cousins in County Clare and arranged to meet them. The visit proved a grand awakening and a refreshing sense of fulfillment and belonging fell upon them like a gentle spring rain.

He opened the note. It had been hastily written.

> Sam,
>   I need to see you. I'm going to your house to see if you're there.
>
>   Albert

Albert? Albert Hill? Who else could it be? I haven't seen Albert since we were juniors here, Sam thought to himself.

The phone rang in his office. Sam picked it up. Before he had time to say hello, Amy, sounding desperate, said, "Sam, you must come home. There's a strange man here. He wants to see you."

"Amy, it must be Albert Hill. I just found a note under my door. He's an old friend."

"There's something wrong with your old friend then. Please come right home."

"Okay. I'm on my way."

Sam grabbed his coat and instantly left the office. On the short ride home, he wondered why his friend had arrived unannounced or why he was there at all. They hadn't spoken in over ten years. What was Amy sensing? Sam pulled into the driveway and saw Albert standing outside. Uncharacteristically, Amy had not invited him in.

"Hey, Al! What's happening?" Sam got out of the car and greeted his friend enthusiastically. Albert kept his distance.

"Hi, Sam. Your wife doesn't want me here," Al spoke bluntly in a monotone.

"Oh, nonsense. She just called. You surprised her, that's all. And me too for that matter. It's been years since I last saw you. How have you been?"

Albert only stared as Sam waited for a response.

Sam recovered. "Come on in. Would you like to stay for dinner?" Sam tried to warm the air.

"I don't think Amy would go for that."

"I'm sure it would be fine. Listen, we usually meditate before dinner . . ."

"I'll take a walk and come back."

"No, come in. I'm sure we can find something to entertain you while Amy and I meditate." Sam gestured to the porch stairs.

"Sam, I appreciate the invitation and all, but I'll just take a walk and come back in a half hour," Albert responded, "if that's okay."

"Sure, sure, and then we'll have dinner. It will be good to catch up." Sam watched Albert walk away. His shoulders were slumped, and his hands were stuffed in the pockets of a brown corduroy jacket that had seen better days. Sam also noticed that one of Albert's sneakers was untied as he walked down the driveway. He felt confused by Albert's arrival and behavior but thought all would become clear at dinner.

xiii

Sam entered the house and called to Amy, "Hi, I'm home."

Amy left the kitchen and came to the front door to meet him. She was obviously upset and jumped in before they had their usual hug. "Thank God you're here! I get a weird feeling from Albert. Something's wrong with him. Beyond telling me his name, he barely spoke. He just stood there and stared. He was clearly anxious. I told him I'd call you to come on home, and thank God, he seemed fine with waiting for you outside. And Rufus kept barking. He wouldn't stop, so I put him in your office."

"I'm sorry you're so upset. Look, Albert's taking a walk now. Last time we were together was in the spring of '67. We were juniors at Amherst. He dropped out that summer and went back to North Carolina. Maybe he's just tired. I haven't seen him for what, ten years? Let me liberate Rufus, say hi to the kids, and then we'll meditate. I invited him to stay for dinner."

"You did what?"

"Amy, it will be fine. Let me get Rufus out of my office and say hi to the boys."

Amy frowned as she walked back to the kitchen.

Sam opened the door to his office, and the five-year-old golden retriever greeted Sam with a lick to the hand and a wiggle in his hips. He then ran down the hall to the den. Sam followed, swooping Josh and Paul off the floor into his arms, and plopped down on the couch as Rufus jumped all over them. Josh was three with clear blue eyes, masses of brown curls, and a vast amount of mischievous energy. Paul was just over two with green eyes and gently waving hair. He adored his older brother and mimicked him constantly.

"How are my boys doing?"

"Good," said Josh.

"Good," mirrored Paul.

After a few minutes of wrestling, laughing, and giggling, Sam, feigning exhaustion, told them, "I love you both with all my heart, but you have worn me out." The boys giggled in response, and Sam continued, "I'm so happy that you are here with Mom and me. I'm going to meditate, and then we'll have dinner, okay? Now, what are you guys going to do? Did Mom help you pick out a tape?"

"Yeah, *Yellow Submarine*," Josh informed him.

"Yeah, *Yellow Submarine*," Paul repeated.

"Okay, let's set it up."

After getting the boys settled in with the video, Sam entered the softly lit meditation room. Amy sat among the multitude of cushions and pillows scattered about the room. Her eyes closed, she had already started. Sam sat down quietly beside her and closed his eyes as well.

The time passed quickly. Almost as soon as they opened their eyes, Amy declared, "He can stay for dinner, and that's it."

"All right, no problem," Sam easily conceded. He got up slowly, stretching and rubbing his eyes, and left the meditation room. He headed for the front door and out to the porch of the old farmhouse where he waited for Albert, who appeared within seconds.

"I heard about your book and your great success. You must be quite proud," Albert offered as he walked up the drive without saying hello.

"No, I wouldn't say proud, Albert, but excited, definitely. It makes me feel as if enlightenment is truly coming for the world," Sam shared eagerly.

With an unexpected directness, Albert asked, "What master do you serve, Sam? The Prince of Light or the Prince of Darkness?" Albert's deep-set eyes focused intently on Sam, staring out of a pale face.

"Now, that's a loaded question. We'll save that one for after dinner," Sam rejoined, trying to lighten the moment. "Come on, let's eat and catch up. It's been a few years."

The two men entered the house together, and Sam introduced Amy and the boys to Albert. Both he and Amy noticed Albert's disheveled appearance. Once inside, they also took in his strong body odor. Sam discreetly opened a few windows, hoping that neither boy would ask an embarrassing question. Albert made a small attempt to acknowledge Sam's family but kept his eyes down most of the time. Undeterred, Sam played the host well. Ever the Irish conversationalist, he tried to keep the exchange going among the five of them. Albert, however, remained aloof and quiet, hardly touching his food. He had made but one small attempt at conversation, and at the meal's conclusion, he politely thanked Amy.

After dinner, Amy stood and announced that it was time for her to give the boys their baths and get them ready for bed. Paul and Josh said good night to the mysterious guest before they clamored after their mother and passed her on the stairs.

Sam and Albert, left in private, migrated to the living room, where Sam began, "Albert, you haven't said much, and yet you're here, out of nowhere. What's happening?"

Albert's words tumbled out quickly as if he had been holding them for this moment. "Sam, from what I've read about you in the paper, ever since you came back from studying with Maharishi in Switzerland, you've gotten it all. You got the PhD, the girl, the professorship, this farmhouse, and now a best-selling book. Me, I got nothing material to speak of, but I discovered the Lord Jesus, who's given me everything."

"Well, Al, that's great. I'm happy for you," Sam commented with sincerity in his voice, hoping Al had really found spiritual fulfillment.

Sounding like a tape recording, Al went on, "Sam, the Lord will cast all nonbelievers into hell. He will force all those with pride in their accomplishments to be lower than the low. I'm here on behalf of the Lord to warn you, to help you."

"What the hell are you talking about, Albert? Warn me about what?"

"I asked you outside who you served: the Prince of Light or the Prince of Darkness." Al's voice had grown threatening.

"Albert, I don't live in the world that you're describing, the world of duality and judgment. I hear Jesus telling us that the kingdom of heaven lies within. First seek the kingdom of heaven, and all else will be added unto you. That's how I understand Christ's teaching."

"So why can't you say you serve the Prince of Light?" Albert challenged.

"I would say it, but I'm not sure it would mean the same thing to both of us," Sam explained patiently.

Albert asserted, "Sam, this is simple. Do you serve Jesus Christ, the only begotten Son of God, or your self-serving ego with its pride and conceit?"

Sam felt the anger in Al's voice and rejoined, "Albert, this is ridiculous. You haven't even been in my life for seven years, and now you show up with this kind of judgment. How do you think you can possibly know my motives? This book is to help bring about a synthesis in our collective consciousness. Enlightenment, the unfolding of full potential, belongs to all people everywhere. This is not about me. It's about opening people to fulfillment. It's about saying that for all these years, we've had a shitty deal, but now we can let go of the ignorance and suffering."

"So you're saying you serve Jesus Christ?" Al was glued to one track and one track only.

Sam hesitated. "Albert, we're all sons and daughters of God the Father." He attempted to lighten the conversation. "I have that on high authority, by the way. You can check with Mother Superior over in Petersham. Now that woman lives the life of devotion to the Lord."

"I don't believe in Jesuits."

"Well, that's fine, but she's Benedictine," Sam shot back, growing annoyed.

"Roman Catholics, they're all the same," Al sneered.

"You're starting to be boring. Why are you here?" Sam finally asked, exasperated.

"I told you why. I've come to warn you." Al was almost shouting this time in frustration. Things had not gone as he envisioned.

"Well, I consider myself warned. And you, my friend of yesteryear, need help."

"The Lord gives me everything," Al said, his hands tucked between his knees and his eyes gazing at the floor once again.

"Oh, is that so? Then why so gloomy? Really, Al, what's going on?" Sam probed.

"You have the pride of Satan," he insisted.

"And you, my friend, are blind to the truth."

"Oh, and what is the truth?" Albert was virtually interrogating Sam. He was starting to sound like a throwback to a Spanish inquisitor, Sam thought.

"Listen, friend, I saw *Jesus Christ Superstar* too," Sam said flippantly, wanting to bring the fruitless conversation to a close. Albert merely frowned.

"Okay, you say you want the truth. Here's some truth. Humanity is made in the image of God. Humanity was not born to suffer, and humanity can find the lost paradise and be one with God again."

Albert merely muttered, "I reject Satan and all the temptations of this world."

Sam, annoyed and losing any sense of compassion, proclaimed sarcastically, "Hallelujah, brother! Bully for you."

Sam stood up and Albert followed suit. Without a word from Sam, Albert walked out of the living room, down the hall, and out the front door. Sam followed him to the door, relieved to see him go. Albert strode down the dark driveway and into the night while Sam stood on the front porch watching. After half a minute, he heard a car engine start and a car drive away. He waited a moment before entering the house.

This was not the conversation Sam had wanted to have. What had happened to his friend? He was not the funny, curious, self-assured undergraduate he once knew. What in the name of God just happened here?

Upstairs, Amy heard the door open and close. She came down and joined Sam in the front hall, surprised that Albert had left so quickly. She took Sam's arm and asked, "Sam? Are you all right? Where did he go?"

"I'm fine. Albert left, drove off to who knows where. Everything's okay, except for the fact that Albert Hill is seriously out of balance, and it's really sad to see him that way. He needs professional help," Sam observed, shaking his head.

Sam and Amy made their way back upstairs and to their bedroom. "I'm afraid of him, Sam. He's unhinged. He's dangerous, and we've got to do something," Amy said as she sat in bed with her arms locked around her knees drawn up to her chest.

"Look, Albert's obviously upset about something. But I don't think he's dangerous. We were friends at one time."

"That was a long time ago. People change. Something's not right."

"He's gone. I love you, honey, but let's turn the lights out and go to sleep."

"Did you lock the doors?"

"We never lock the doors."

"We never had one of your deranged friends show up either. Please lock the doors. I'll check on the children."

Sam got up and reluctantly went back down the stairs and locked the doors. He took a quick look around and, satisfied, climbed the stairs back to their bedroom.

"The boys okay?"

"Fine. Paul wanted to sleep with Josh tonight. And Rufus is at the foot of the bed. He'll be on the bed in a matter of minutes," Amy said, shaking her head at the events of the day as she climbed into bed. Sam kissed her, and they both laid their heads down.

As the O'Connors drifted off to sleep, Albert drove off into the deepening darkness.

Part One

Poets to come! orators, singers, musicians to come!
Not to-day is to justify me and answer what I am for,
But you, a new brood, native, athletic, continental, greater
than before known,
Arouse! for you must justify me.

I myself but write one or two indicative words for the future,
I but advance a moment only to wheel and hurry back
in the darkness.

I am a man who, sauntering along without fully stopping,
turns a casual look upon you and then averts his face,
Leaving it to you to prove and define it,
Expecting the main things from you.

—Walt Whitman,
"Poets to Come," from *Leaves of Grass*, 1860

Chapter 1:
Growing Up in Greenwich Village

SAM GREW UP IN GREENWICH Village, the oldest and only son of Jimmy and Lillian O'Connor. His sister, Susan, was born seven years later. Jimmy and Lillian were hardworking Irish Catholics, born in Brooklyn to Irish parents who had sailed as newlyweds to America to create a new life. Jimmy and Lilly grew up two blocks from each other and met when Jimmy was seven and Lilly five. By the time they were teenagers, they were going steady. When they were twenty and eighteen respectively, they were married in the same church where they were baptized and where they had their first Communion and their Confirmation. Jimmy worked numerous jobs. In fact, he worked sixty hours a week most of the time but always took Sunday off. He always rested on the seventh day. His father-in-law approved.

Eventually, with Lillian's father's help, they were able to buy a bakery café in Greenwich Village, which they called the Dublin Café, where Jimmy specialized in fruit tarts, long hours, and conversation. Lilly specialized in the rosary, taking care of her family, friends, and customers, as well as paying bills, counting the day's receipts, and handling the banking.

They lived above the café in one of four apartments. Family life played out as much in the café—a well-loved neighborhood institution—as in the upstairs apartment. From the time they were six or seven, both Sam and his best friend, Kenny Murphy, spent time at the café after school and on weekends, relishing the adult conversation and the opportunity to take on small jobs that made them feel grown-up. Sam's parents were delighted that their son had such a strong interest in learning and reading but also had a concern since working in the family business, not in higher education, had been their priority for their oldest son.

In recognizing Sam's gift, Jimmy and Lilly went to see Father Mike, the local priest and educator at the neighborhood parochial school. Father Mike couldn't miss Sam's intelligence and curiosity. He encouraged Sam's parents not to put limits on their son. Father Mike then began to introduce Sam to local writers and thinkers as he moved into his teenage years. Sam became an avid reader of Homer, Plato, Aristotle, Marcus Aurelius, Plotinus, Joyce, Shaw, and Keats, along with the New Testament. Sam especially loved the Gospel of John. He became an idealist and a romantic at an early age. His love of the classics fueled his intellectual life.

His best friend, Kenny, lived down the block. His mother, Mary, was a sweet, hardworking woman. When Kenny was a year old, his father went out for a pack of cigarettes after dinner one night and did not come back. He disappeared and was never seen again by the people in the neighborhood, and certainly not by Kenny or his mother. No foul play was ever discovered. It appeared he'd decided to just move on. Jimmy became Kenny's father, and he looked after him as if he was his own son. And anyone looking from the outside would have figured that Jimmy and Lil had two sons and a younger daughter named Susan who was born with Down syndrome. Jimmy, and especially Lilly, were in denial of Susan's condition at first. But as she grew older, her condition became more evident. It had the effect on them of pouring all their love into that child. And everyone in the neighborhood did the same.

Sam didn't always have his nose in a book. He was good at basketball and street ball. In fact, he could hit just about everything pitched at him. As school got back into session in September, Billy Sobestski, a ninth grader, started to taunt Sam, who was in seventh grade, about his "mentally retarded" younger sister for two days running.

Kenny counseled, "Forget it, Sam. He's got an arse a mile wide, he's dumb as a stone, and he's most likely as strong as a horse. He's got two years on ya and a good thirty pounds. Let it be. He's just a big Pole. He'll quiet down after a while."

"He's got no right to call my sis names. He does it again, I'm taking him down. I don't care how big he is."

"All right, if you're so determined, I'll cover your flank," Kenny had stated flatly, staring straight ahead.

Sam had looked at Kenny with a feeling of benign amusement and appreciation. He couldn't help chiding the slightly smaller and younger boy.

"Kenny, you're like a brother, but what the hell are you going to do, punch him in the kneecap?"

"Hey, don't worry about me. I'll hit him in the stomach so hard he'll lose his lunch."

"Oh, great. So now he's going to be puking all over us. I don't know if that helps," Sam had said with a laugh, giving Kenny a playful shove.

Sam challenged Billy amid a flurry of insults flying back and forth at lunch. After school, Sam, Kenny, Billy, and some other boys filed out to the asphalt-covered playground and walked over to the basketball court. Books dropped; coats were shed. The boys formed a ring around the two combatants. Sam knew he had to strike Billy first and hard to have any chance. The two fighters moved clockwise, slowly circling. Sam covered both sides of his face with fists held high. Billy held his fists in front of his chest, confident of victory. Billy taunted Sam one more time, calling his sister, "a retard of the highest order." Sam pounced and hit him hard with a right to the head, followed by a left and then a right to the nose. Billy, caught by the suddenness of the assault, put his two large hands over his face. His nose was bleeding. As Billy realized he was hurt, fury overtook him. He cocked his right arm back and let it fly. It landed straight on the bridge of Sam's nose. Sam went down like a sack of potatoes, and the back of his head hit the pavement. Billy moved forward to stomp Sam into the blacktop, but before he could, Kenny came in from his left side and landed a punch into Billy's breadbasket. The hit was surprisingly hard, and the older boy doubled over. As Billy staggered, Kenny threw a nice cross-body block at Billy. As both boys went down, Billy ended up cushioning Kenny's fall. After a few seconds, Kenny jumped up, looked down at Billy, and said, "You're the retard, you big bastard."

Kenny then looked over to where Sam was lying and realized he had not gotten up. Some of the other boys checked on Billy. Kenny knelt next to Sam, who asked with a grin and a grimace, "Is he going to puke on us?"

"Nah, he's down. He broke your nose good though. Come on, I'll help you up." Kenny pulled Sam into a sitting position, but Sam felt dizzy and wanted to close his eyes. Kenny saw his dazed look and decided it would be best for Sam to walk it off. He helped Sam to his feet.

Some other boys were helping Billy to stand. His nose was also bleeding.

"Father Mike is going to hear about this for sure. You and big Billy over there are going to be in a heap of trouble," Kenny commented.

"Yeah, I know," Sam said with a sigh. "What about you?"

"I was never here is the short answer."

"Yeah, right, as if that's going to fly."

"Don't worry about me. You better worry about yourself. You got blood all over your tie and white shirt, and that means you're gonna have to face Lillian."

Sam looked down at himself and realized Kenny was right. He suspected he could reason this out with Father Mike but realized there was no way he could do that with his mom. "Maybe we could go to your apartment and I could clean up a bit?"

"No good. My mom's home, and I'll get blamed for this crime scene. Besides, she's going to call your mom right off the bat. No, bro, you're going to have to face the firing squad on this, so you might as well get it over with."

"I hope Billy has some blood on his shirt, too," was all Sam could muster. Both boys looked over to see Billy finally on his feet.

"You can take a little satisfaction in that," Kenny allowed with a faint smile as he witnessed Billy's bloody nose and the blood-spattered white shirt.

Growing up, Sam took some pride in his crooked nose. The story of the fight was embellished over the rest of his teenage life. Billy turned out not to be a bad guy after all and became a plumber like his dad.

Sam thought about going into the priesthood as a young teenager. But Alice, an older girl from the neighborhood, erased any consideration of that vocation. Alice lived around the corner and up the block from Sam. She had a womanly, curvy figure at fifteen that males of all ages noticed. Alice's father, Joe, had known the O'Connors for twenty years.

Joe's wife had passed on eight years earlier, and Joe was devoted to Alice but spoiled her. For the last year, she had hung around the Dublin Café and flirted with Sam shamelessly. Everyone saw it, especially Sam's mother. She told Jimmy more than once, "That girl needs her mother. Her mother would have taught her not to be acting like this." Jimmy only nodded in agreement.

The summer when Alice turned eighteen and was out of school, Sam was just sixteen. He never exactly dated Alice. Rather, on a warm, humid summer day in July, Alice educated Sam in a subject he couldn't learn from a book. Sam got off work at the café at three o'clock, and Joe wouldn't be home until six. Alice had it all planned out. She invited Sam up to the apartment after work with the promise of a cold beer. Sam had just opened the beer and

4

taken one sip when Alice started in, saying, "It's so hot. I think I'm going to take my clothes off."

Sam had never seen a woman naked before, except in pictures. Those women looked friendly, and so did Alice, who wore a big smile as she removed her clothes piece by piece. Sam just sat and watched, not really knowing what to do. Down to just her panties, Alice walked over to Sam, bent over, and started kissing him. Before he knew it, his shirt was off, then his pants; finally, his white briefs were around his ankles. Sam stepped out of his briefs and pulled down Alice's panties. She led him by the hand to her bedroom. He never thought of the priesthood again.

Unbeknownst to the two young lovers, Joe decided to come straight home instead of stopping in at Paddy's Bar and Grill for a couple of cold ones and some protracted conversations as was his custom. As Joe unlocked the apartment door, Alice shushed Sam.

"Holy Mother of God," she exclaimed, "my dad is home!" Sam bolted upright and began quickly looking around for his clothes and then realized they were all over the kitchen floor. He ran for the kitchen and arrived just as Joe did. Alice grabbed her robe and was attempting to tie it when she too arrived at the threshold of the kitchen. It didn't take Joe but a second to see what had transpired.

"You little bastard, I'm going to kill ya" was all that Joe could manage to say.

Sam grabbed his pants off the floor and managed to blurt out, "Hey, she invited me . . ."

When Alice saw her father's face and neck turn red and the vein in his forehead pop out, she knew what was coming next.

"Daddy, it's true. It's my fault. Let Sam go. Daddy, let him go," she cried out.

Joe looked at his daughter, kicked a hole in the kitchen wall, and walked out and into the parlor and plopped down in his chair, cursing up a storm.

Sam wasted no time in putting on his pants, shirt, and sneakers. He grabbed his underwear and socks, looked at Alice, and said, "I'm sorry. It was so great."

Alice kissed Sam. "You better get going."

"You'll be all right?"

"Yeah. He'll calm down."

Sam gave Alice a quick kiss. He then reached for the knob on the front door and ran down the two flights of stairs and out the main entrance. He tossed his underwear and socks into an empty garbage can sitting on the sidewalk near the street and continued running up the street home.

Later, Joe called Jimmy to tell him what had happened. Jimmy hung up the phone without saying much. The two men agreed to meet at Paddy's. But not before Jimmy told his wife what transpired between Sam and Alice. Jimmy called Sam into the kitchen. Sam knew he was in for it. Lilly took her rosary beads out of her purse and prayed, but not before hitting Sam twice, though he was a head taller than her. Sam tried to explain what had happened. After he was done, Lillian turned to her husband and said, "I've been saying that girl needed her mother all these years, and this proves the point."

Jimmy and Joe met at Paddy's regularly over the years. This warm summer evening made for a long night as they drank one Guinness after another. In their minds, their children had lost their innocence and were in dire need of confession at the very least. Joe was confused and angry. He was angry with his daughter and upset that his wife had passed and left him alone to raise her. He wasn't sure what to do with his daughter. After discussing many options, Joe realized that his little girl had grown up. It was the first step in seeing her in a new light. She needed an opportunity to safely get on with her life.

Jimmy's shock at the news wore off on his walk back to the apartment. He then had a feeling of being a bit proud of his son. He kept the thought to himself, knowing he'd have to face his wife when he got home. On Saturday morning, Sam and Alice went to confession. Father Mike heard both of them and gave them as penance a dozen Our Father's and an equal number of Hail Mary's.

Kenny was wild-eyed with envy when Sam told him what happened. Sam's experience was a true inspiration for Kenny. He never considered becoming a priest and had no interest whatsoever in Greek philosophy. However, he was very interested in learning about Alice in bed. At first, he tried charm. No go. Then he tried being extra cool. Alice wasn't moved. He then bought Alice some flowers from Mr. Kelly's shop. Alice accepted the gift with a smile and even gave Kenny a kiss on the cheek, but nothing more. Kenny then practically got on his knees and begged Alice for a chance at love. Alice eventually conceded after weeks of Kenny's advances but made doubly sure nobody would walk in on them. Kenny was sworn to secrecy and kept his word to Alice for several years before he told Sam what happened. He was overwhelmed by the experience of being with a woman. The impression of that first blissful event lasted his entire life. His gratitude to Alice was heartfelt.

After the confessions and the penance, nothing more was said until Alice had her period. Joe called Jimmy and said, "It happened."

Jimmy replied, "Right," and hung up.

Jimmy and his wife Lilly went to the church, put money in the offering box, lit candles, and prayed with great thanks that no baby was coming. As they were leaving, Joe was coming in to do the same. They hardly spoke as they passed one another. Jimmy and Lillian never said a word on the way home. Once they said that final prayer, none of them mentioned it again.

Joe, with Father Mike's advice, sent Alice that fall to finishing school in Providence, Rhode Island. Best to get her out of the Village and into a new place, Father Mike counseled. It turned out to be good advice. There, Alice met her future husband, who was attending Brown. She went on to have two children and a happy marriage, settling in Morristown, New Jersey. Her father began seeing Hattie O'Leary, who had been widowed the year before. Jimmy and Lillian stood up for them at a quiet private ceremony. Sam, Alice, and Kenny were not in attendance.

Sam dated a few girls in high school, never quite getting as far as he had with Alice on that steamy July day. At Amherst College, he had a long relationship with a woman he loved. It was passionate and physical but had no real future, and by the time they graduated, they both knew it. A year later, while living in Boston, they separated. It was painful to be sure, but she was more practical than Sam and wanted a career, traditional home, and family—sooner rather than later. To her, Sam was a dreamer, trying to figure it all out. She grew impatient with his philosophical musings. The fact that Sam was meditating twice a day fueled his girlfriend's doubts. The idea of settling down had not even dawned on him. He was too busy chasing a deeper understanding of himself and the world. So having finished his master's at Boston College, Sam decided to move back to Amherst for his PhD program in philosophy at UMass.

There he saw Amy for the first time in late May of '73. Sam saw her walking across the Amherst commons. He stopped in his tracks and just looked at her. He felt as if she had emerged from a mist. Amy's appearance grabbed and startled him, yet she also felt deeply familiar. She was tall, maybe 5'8", with long legs, thick blond hair, and blue eyes. She had a face of kindness and remarkable beauty. It seemed as if Amy had stepped out of a dream that had been floating just below the surface of his mind. His mind could make no sense of it, but somehow his heart recognized that a long-running vision of love was suddenly becoming real. Sam attempted to start a conversation, but Amy was distracted. Her eyes never met his, and she walked away, lost in her own thoughts. Sam believed in his heart's urging and trusted his intuition. He felt so strongly connected with and attracted to this woman. Why didn't she acknowledge him? Bewildered, he didn't know what to do, so he decided to walk over to see Kenny.

Kenny had moved to Amherst after Sam's freshman year. They shared an apartment in town. Now a café owner in his own right and a pursuer of love, Kenny sensed Sam's confusion as he walked in the door.

"What happened to you?"

"I just saw the woman of my dreams, and she completely ignored me."

"My God, Sam, get it together, brother. Maybe she was having a bad day. Maybe someone died. Maybe she just couldn't take one more guy hitting on her."

"She didn't even look at me."

"Well, she was right. You are an ugly son of a bitch. Maybe she peeked at you, saw that crooked beak, and thought, 'This guy? Please!'" Kenny said with a grin.

Sam smiled despite himself and said, "Kenny, if you weren't my best friend, I'd take you outside for a beating."

"Well, lover boy, who'd be giving who a beating is the question here. I, for one, say you're in no position to answer." With that, he gave him a playful punch on his shoulder.

"Don't push your luck."

"Sammy, there are many fish in the sea. Maybe she slipped out of the net. But if it's destiny and really meant to be, you'll catch up with her again, and then maybe both of you will be ready."

There was a pause as each one looked at the other. Sam noticed Kenny's angular jaw, deep-set blue eyes, and his ready smile. Sam continued, "How the hell did you get so insightful all of a sudden?"

"Well, buddy, if you didn't have your nose buried in all those books, you might've noticed I've been insightful and giving meaningful advice for years," Kenny observed with his own certain cockiness.

Though Amy showed no interest in Sam, his mind took a sudden romantic turn. He started writing poetry and taking long walks through the New England countryside. In time, he barely remembered Amy's face. She retreated into the mist, and Sam was left alone to unravel the web of his thoughts. After several months, Sam became himself again, but a bit more cautious, a bit more uncertain, and a bit more humble. All of which pleased the gods who were rooting for him all the way.

Just over a year later, on a late spring day in 1974 when the yellow-spotted newt had already made its way to its mating and nesting wetlands, Sam almost literally ran into Amy again. She was walking slowly and deliberately down a forested path of worn brown earth. A tall man with a thick mustache walked a full step behind her, lost in some passionate discourse. Amy, with head down and an ear cocked in the man's direction, listened like someone who had heard enough but needed to remain polite.

Much to his surprise, Sam's heart leaped when he saw Amy. Numerous thoughts ran in rapid succession through his mind. *Turn around. Hide. Run. Put your head down. Walk past, not noticing.* None of the thoughts took hold. Instead, Sam waited for his feelings to emerge like a batter waiting for the right pitch. They came: wonder, then happiness. When Amy was only three strides away, Sam smiled. With a start, she was suddenly aware that a stranger was moving toward her and they were close to colliding. She looked up, met Sam's sparkling eyes, and smiled back. They stopped moving for the briefest moment to avoid the collision. Sam nodded, his smile grew into a grin, and they both walked on. The man with Amy barely caught their interaction.

Sam walked briskly and confidently. Instinctively, he knew that the current of his life had shifted and taken on new momentum. Sam's logical and penetrating mind had surrendered to the illogical and unrealistic experience of falling instantly in love, and every cell in his body sang with hope.

Sam realized years later that he had not been ready to meet Amy the first time. However, his year of self-exploration had opened his heart, and he was now ready to receive one of life's most precious gifts: love from a full heart. Like a soft, warm spring rain, love washed through and around him, nourishing new life.

Three weeks later, Sam saw Amy on Elm Street. She was standing in the doorway of a professional building, kissing the tall man with the thick mustache.

Chapter 2:
The Meeting on Elm Street

SAM SAW AMY IN AMHERST for only the third time in all those years he had lived there. She was kissing the man with the thick mustache good-bye while Sam was walking down Elm Street toward them. The tall man turned around and walked into the building. Meanwhile, Amy descended the steps of the professional building, and just as she reached the sidewalk, she felt something. She looked up to see the man from the woods strolling toward her, smiling. Amy said hello and stopped, and Sam did the same. Both paused; both had the same question: what now? Sam let the moment linger, and Amy looked down at the sidewalk for a second before she glanced back up into his eyes.

Sam reached out. "So did you enjoy your walk through Hampshire Woods? It was a lovely day for it."

"Well yes. Yes, I did. Do you often walk there?"

"I do, especially in the spring. I love the color of those first budding leaves, that tender, vibrant green color all around you."

"Ah yes," agreed Amy, "that spring green makes everything feel special." Meanwhile, her mind was running a much more excited commentary, something like, *Wow! Maybe he's an artist like me. He's so gorgeous, and those amazing eyes . . .*

Sam introduced himself, "I'm Sam O'Connor," and he stuck out his hand.

Amy, a bit startled, said, "I'm Amy Sanders."

"Well, Amy Sanders, have you got time for a cup of joe and a pastry? There's that little café on the next block that I know well, the White Oak."

"Yes, I know the place. The owner is interesting."

11

"That's an understatement. Kenny, the proprietor, is my best friend."

"Oh. That is interesting," Amy said, eyeing over this unknown man. She carefully considered before answering, "I don't drink coffee, but a cup of tea would do me good."

Though he managed to maintain outward equanimity, Sam was finding Amy's beauty and grace almost overpowering. It looked to Sam as if Amy glowed from the inside and loveliness emanated from every pore.

Sam ordered the coffee and tea at the counter while Amy found a table. They settled in across from each other. Each shared their academic histories. Amy was also a graduate student. Her undergraduate degree in art was from Smith College. She loved "the Valley," as the locals referred to the area, and had decided to do her MFA at UMass.

After the introductory history lesson, Sam took a chance and shot, "Who's the man in your life?"

Amy, shocked but impressed by the directness, disclosed, "Oh! You mean Gregory. Yes, well, I've been seeing him for six months. He's a lawyer. Just passed his boards."

"Oh, I see," replied Sam. "You like him?"

"Yes, I do. He's wonderful, really."

"Yes," Sam returned, encouraging more.

"Well, I'm not sure I love him the way he loves me. And then, I'm going to Switzerland to study. Naturally, Gregory doesn't want me to go."

Sam didn't swing at the first pitch but took a poke at the geographical description and asked, "You're going to study art in the Alps?"

"No," Amy revealed, "meditation."

"Ah, meditation. That is somewhat familiar territory," Sam mentioned casually.

Amy jumped at the statement. "You meditate then?"

"Yes."

"Do you do Transcendental Meditation?"

"Yes, Kenny and I saw a poster of Maharishi in the Student Union at UMass in the fall of 1970 announcing an intro lecture. We went and we started four days later. When did you start TM?"

"I started over the Thanksgiving break at the Cambridge Center, also in 1970. I loved it. There was such a feeling of going home."

"I agree. Both Kenny and I felt the same way. Does Greg meditate?"

"No. Gregory doesn't get it," Amy sighed.

"Most people don't, Amy," Sam stated with some confidence.

"But we're going to change that," she said with zeal. "Oh, listen, I have to go," she interjected, noticing the time.

"You're going to Europe today?" Sam pretended shock.

"No, I'm leaving a week from Wednesday." Amy got up, and Sam rose alongside her.

Taking a chance, he proposed, "Can I call you for a dinner date before you cast off?"

"Yes, I'm in the book, but call soon. Time, the tide, and a woman with airline tickets wait for no man. Thanks for the tea." *Boy, I hope he calls*, she thought as she walked out of the café and onto the sidewalk.

Sam sat and watched her walk past the window. She turned and smiled, and his heart melted and collected in a pool at his feet. *Here I've been waiting all these years to meet this woman*, reflected Sam, *and she's off in only one week for the other side of the world.* As he sat with that piece of information, a six-year-old boy shot him with a water gun square in the face. The boy's mother immediately grabbed and scolded the child and apologized profusely. Sam looked into the boy's clear brown eyes and thought he saw God laughing at him. *Okay*, thought Sam. *I need to learn to play along in this cosmic game with no guarantee of the outcome.*

"Don't worry," Sam comforted the mother. "I needed the wake-up call." Then, "Good shot, kid," Sam said with a wink to his small assailant. He could have sworn he saw the boy wink back at him just before the mother shuttled the giggling child out the door.

Three nights later, Sam and Amy met at Amherst Chinese, or Am Chi, as the locals knew it. They talked and laughed and shared a delicious array of dishes. They tossed episodes from their life stories back and forth across the table and described their desires for the future. Sam tried to soak in the whole of the experience so he wouldn't forget any of her: the personal magic, the facial expressions and vivid language, the elegant features, the grace and light, the easy laughter. All felt precious to him.

Amy, in turn, loved watching Sam's hands participate animatedly as he told quirky, affectionate stories of New York City and his Irish American family. She especially liked his hands—strong, lifesaving hands. She began to think she should postpone the trip but realized she couldn't. She needed more time with him before she left but knew it wasn't possible. There was Gregory, and her parents were expecting her in Concord. She found herself silently contemplating sleeping with Sam that night but thought better of it. It would be unfair to Gregory, and beyond that, Amy realized she might want far more than one night with Sam, maybe even a lifetime. She felt happy and complete, and she wanted it to last.

After dinner, they walked around the town, covered by a light mist. Before they knew it, they found themselves in front of Amy's apartment. It had been a perfect evening. Impulsively, Amy reached inside her bag, found a pen and an old receipt, and scribbled down her parents' address and phone number in Concord. She asked him to call her there.

"Phone you? I think I'll buy the house next door."

Almost before she knew what she was saying, she beckoned, "Kiss me, Sam."

Sam obeyed her command with a long, warm kiss that would live in his memory until the end of his life. A sense of unadulterated bliss overtook them, and they embraced for what felt like something close to forever.

When they started to separate, Sam grinned and professed, "I want you to know, I'm a 100 percent robust, healthy male, and I really love kids and the idea of being a father. In case you didn't notice . . ."

Amy smiled acknowledgement then turned and walked up the stairs. Her heart pounded, and she had to check the impulse to shout with joy. Sam ran blindly up the street with no destination in mind, but an internal homing signal brought him to the White Oak Café, which was just closing.

"Kenny, my bosom buddy, I just came by to see if I'm walking on earth or have made it to heaven."

"I'd say you remain a mere mortal except that cupid's arrow is sticking out your backside. So how was the date with fair Amy?" Kenny asked.

"To say it was my finest moment on Earth would be an understatement."

"So it went okay then. Is that what you're saying?"

"Aren't I making myself clear, man? It was divine. She's exquisite, intelligent, creative, and I think she loves me."

"Oh, I see, she loves you now. Well, you did have a good night. So what's next?"

"She's flying out in nine days for Switzerland. Going to study TM with Maharishi," Sam said, not believing it himself.

"You gotta be kidding." Kenny guffawed.

"No, I wouldn't be kidding about that," Sam conveyed sadly. "But I think I'll have one more go at her before she flies off."

"Listen, let me buy you a cold one before we head home," Kenny offered.

"If you're buying, I'm drinking," Sam quipped, and the two friends sauntered up the street.

"Listen, old friend, does she have a sister?" Kenny poked.

"No, she's an only child."

"A best friend then?" Kenny persisted.

"Not sure, but then again, everyone has a best friend. So yeah, I imagine she does," continued Sam.

"We may not marry a pair of sisters and live happily ever after, but maybe we'll marry best friends? That could be nice," Kenny concluded with a sigh.

"You know, Kenny, we were twelve years old when we started this 'marrying sisters or best friends' business."

"I know, but it could happen. It doesn't have to be sisters. Best friends would do, don't you think?

"Yes, it would be nice," Sam concurred.

Sam helped Kenny shut down for the night and lock up the café, and they made their way to the pub, ordered their pints, and clinked "Saliente" like the good Irishmen they were. After a second round, they embraced like the true friends they were and strolled home contentedly to the apartment they shared.

Alone in her apartment, Amy slowly changed and got ready for bed. She felt elated about what the days ahead might bring but also sad and concerned for Gregory. She realized change was afoot, and her relationship with Gregory was limited. She had had her doubts all along but had tried to push them aside. Her parents liked Gregory and encouraged her to trust that he would make a fine husband, but it was her life after all, and she was the one who had to marry him. How could she feel so clear so quickly about such a momentous change? Yet she did and could not deny it, crazy as it all looked. She began to prepare herself for a difficult and painful conversation with Gregory that suddenly appeared inevitable.

When she took off for Switzerland, she would leave their relationship behind. It probably would have happened anyway, Amy realized. She sensed she would be learning and growing in a different direction on her TM course and that they would have trouble connecting when she returned. And now there was Sam, so full of promise, so spiritually and personally attuned to her, curiously appearing at just this critical junction point in her life.

As Amy appeared to be sailing on calm waters with a steady breeze, Gregory was asleep in his apartment across town, lost in a restless dream. He tossed and turned like a small boat, taking on water in heavy seas.

Chapter 3:
A Trip to Concord

AMY'S START IN LIFE HAD been considerably different from Sam's. She came from what some New Englanders call good stock and, physically speaking, she embodied that ideal to an almost unreal degree. Amy was blond and blue-eyed, with high cheekbones and a dazzling smile. She had athletic long legs and a graceful slim figure that made her look taller than she was. She often seemed to be in perpetual motion, ate salads with alfalfa sprouts daily, loved Indian food, and avoided dairy except for yogurt and the occasional Italian dinner or a slice of pizza; she had stopped eating meat at seven. Her parents were perplexed but went along with her new direction.

Amy's family had lived in Concord, Massachusetts for four generations. Her parents had lived there their whole lives. Mary Sanders inherited the family home built by her great-grandfather, George Henderson, in 1872 at the age of thirty-five. George Henderson had known Emerson and Thoreau and had been a successful merchant and a leading citizen in Concord. It therefore wasn't surprising that his great-granddaughter worked at the Concord Historical Society and had completed a BA in history from Boston University.

Ed Sanders had met his future wife in the third grade, and they had married shortly after earning their respective BAs. Ed attended Harvard undergrad on a half scholarship and later Harvard Law School. He worked two jobs over the summer months to help make ends meet. He then joined the largest law firm in Boston right out of law school and eventually worked his way to partner, specializing in torts and contracts.

Amy invited Sam to drive to Concord two nights before her flight to Switzerland. She felt uncharacteristically restless while she waited for Sam.

She watched and listened to the grandfather clock and felt as if five o'clock would never come. She badly wanted Sam to get there before her parents, fearing that the combination of the stately house, her folks, the cook, and the seemingly rarefied air of generations of wealth and privilege could do in Sam O'Connor on the spot. When his yellow VW bug finally rolled up the driveway, Amy's heart nearly burst. In her mind, Sam had crossed the equivalent of deserts and oceans to arrive at her door.

As Sam approached the house, he saw a spacious, century-old colonial home with perfectly groomed grounds. Giant maple and hickory trees that appeared older than the house graced the property and neighboring streets. Usually, this would have been a source of delight for Sam, but the grandeur unsettled him and gave rise to a feeling akin to seasickness. "Wrong address," he mumbled to himself. However, the number on the mailbox was correct. He then thought, *Wrong girl, wrong socioeconomic bracket, and wrong world*, before Amy appeared at the front door, hurried across the porch and down the steps. With a wave of her arm and a smile from her face, the world stopped spinning, and Sam, taking a breath, saw the situation anew. He got out of his car and returned the smile.

His smile set off fireworks in her heart. As they moved toward each other and hugged, the angels sang and the gods beamed with joy. They saw only each other; the surroundings melted away.

Just minutes later, Edward Sanders drove up the street and saw Amy embracing a young man. He commented to himself, "That's definitely not Greg. Well, here we go. I hope Mary is not late getting home."

Mary Sanders was just rounding the corner in her own car, and she watched her husband reach the end of the driveway. She had planned to catch Amy before her mystery date showed up, but she was too late. Ed had gotten home first, and Amy was introducing him to an attractive young man. She might need to intercede.

"Here's Mom now," exclaimed Amy. "Hi, Mom!"

Sliding out of her car, Mary noticed Ed had that look on his face. It was not easy to be the father of a young woman in 1974, and the confusion showed. "He's forgotten that we were once young," she observed silently.

"Hello, darling," she called. "Glad I caught you still at home. I so wanted to meet Sam. Ed, you've met Sam?"

"Yes," Ed replied politely. "We were just introduced."

Mary continued without as much as a glance at her husband. "Sam, please come in for a few minutes and relax. You must be thirsty after that long ride on Route 2. Amy, I'm sure Sam needs a cool drink, maybe lemonade. Can you two spare a few minutes before heading out for the night?"

The house and the furnishings were impressive, mostly antiques, and the lemonade cold. Sam and Amy sat on the couch, and Mary and Ed in the two floral-printed wing-back chairs. Mary placed four coasters on the coffee table.

Ed then launched into the standard interview: Where was Sam from? What did his parents do? What was he studying? What were his plans once he graduated? Sam delivered the answers with a philosopher's acumen, giving just enough information to be truthful, but not too much.

"I'm from New York City. Oh, my family owns a bakery café in Greenwich Village. I'm a philosophy PhD student, and I have no definite plans yet except to finish my doctorate and perhaps teach at a college someday."

Ed tried hard not to like Sam. He had approved of Gregory, and Sam was clearly competition.

Mary asked about his parents and if he had any brothers or sisters.

"I have a younger sister named Susan."

"And what is she studying?" Mary asked.

"She was born with Down syndrome, and right about now, she's most likely in the kitchen with my mother studying what's for dinner." Sam laughed. Amy smiled. Ed and Mary sat emotionless.

"Oh," Mary managed and then recovered. "Amy, remember Judy Maynard on Maple Street? She had Down as well. A very sweet child."

"Yes, Mom, she was very sweet. And I'm sure Susan is too."

"Susan is that. But she also reads and writes at a sixth-grade level, has a good sense of humor, knows everybody in the neighborhood, and is well-adjusted. She's just wonderful," Sam concluded.

Before Ed could comment, Amy jumped up and said, "Mom and Dad, we've got to go." After a hurried good-bye, Amy hustled Sam out the door and across the porch.

"Thanks for the lemonade, and nice to meet you both," Sam managed to get out as she pulled him down the porch stairs.

Mary and Ed called good-bye from the porch and watched Sam and Amy cross the lawn toward Sam's car. Mary turned, looked at Ed, and said, "I think he may be the one."

"What do you mean?" Ed shot back. "What about Gregory? He just passed his boards." He seemed to feel as if that achievement somehow tied the marriage knot.

Mary replied, "A mother's intuition."

"Oh, for Pete's sake!" Ed rolled his eyes and retreated into the house.

Once safely outside, Amy confided, "My mom likes you."

"Yeah, maybe, but your dad sure doesn't."

"Dad doesn't like anyone at first, but if Mom likes you, Dad will fall into line."

"Is that the way it works around here?"

"Pretty much. Dad is a brilliant man in certain ways, but Mom holds the power."

"Sounds like the royals. So you must be the princess?"

"What does that mean? Is that a put-down?" Amy began circling Sam like a boxer in the ring. "Come on, Sam O' Connor, you Irish thug. I'll take you down in the first round."

Sam laughed. "No doubt, Amy, you'd take me in less than a minute. All right, woman. You've already won. Now let's eat. I'm half-famished."

Jumping into Sam's VW Bug, they drove toward Cambridge. Over dinner, Amy stared into Sam's green eyes and again found herself noticing his large and expressive hands. Energy, strength, and spirit poured out of this man to whom she felt deeply drawn. Sam faced Amy across the table and saw her as a blessing from on high. He was filled with gratitude and knew he'd never be lonely again.

As the conversation over dinner developed, Sam learned about Amy's family tree stretching back to the time of Emerson. In her teens, Amy had read Emerson, Thoreau and Louisa May Alcott, the transcendentalists of Concord. Sam explained that shortly after learning to meditate, he picked up Walt Whitman's *Leaves of Grass*, another transcendentalist from the same era. Sam said he continued to read Whitman every day, and he was enthralled with the native New Yorker's cosmic vision.

After dinner, they wandered along the Charles River, holding hands. The spring night conspired with their already heightened emotions. Above the lights of the city, an almost full moon glowed, a celestial source of human dreams. The scent of new life emerging from the earth filled the air, and the river, swollen with spring rain, seemed to whisper ancient songs. Sam turned to Amy and with a soft kiss whispered that he loved her. Amy, as if in another world, confided her love for him. That moment was etched in their hearts and duly noted by the angels in heaven.

Two days later, she left for Switzerland. An ocean lay between them, but their hearts knew something different. Their hearts had merged. Separation was a mirage, fostered by time and space, the biggest illusion of all.

Chapter 4:
The Law of Attraction

MAHARISHI MAHESH YOGI LEFT INDIA in 1958 to teach what he came to call the Transcendental Meditation technique and to create an enlightened world. He traveled around the planet many times, drawing increasingly larger crowds wherever he went. His message was simple: The purpose of life is the expansion of happiness. In fact, every human being is born to enjoy life, not suffer. All people have to do is enliven the unlimited potential for fulfillment that already dwells inside them, and since that infinite potential is within everyone, it is easy and natural for everyone to experience.

Maharishi offered the world a truly simple and effortless technique to transcend all activity, even the mind's subtlest thoughts, and become one with the limitless awareness at the source of thought, the source of life. Contact with that infinitely lively field of Being for a short time twice a day produced a host of benefits. TM meditators experienced increased energy, heightened intelligence, and enhanced creativity, as well as more happiness and the peace that had eluded so many of the globe's modern residents. Maharishi predicted that over time, regular practice of the TM technique would make that unlimited potential a permanent reality. He taught that enlightenment should be understood as a natural state, a real possibility for anyone.

Because Maharishi was so alive, sharp, energetic, and blissful, the messenger matched the message, and he became enormously popular, especially among college students. The Beatles, Beach Boys, and Donovan all sat at his feet, learning to meditate and listening to Maharishi lecture on the unfolding of higher states of awareness. Maharishi began offering one-month courses on various college campuses and thousands of newly meditating students began attending.

Now, four years later, Amy was on her way to study with Maharishi and become a TM teacher. As Amy's plane took off for Switzerland, Sam was on his way to visit his family in New York. He was traveling sixty miles per hour down I-91 in his yellow VW Bug, and Amy was flying in a British Airways jet at five hundred miles per hour over the Atlantic. Amy was going to spend sixteen weeks meditating and doing yoga for many hours a day, eating vegetarian food, and attending meetings with Maharishi. Sam was going for bagels and cream cheese, great pizza, and good movies. While Amy spent time with a contemporary master in the Swiss Alps, Sam would be passing part of the summer living with Jimmy and Lilly and engaging with the characters that make up Greenwich Village. What could be better? As far as Sam was concerned, a life with Amy Sanders at his side was a good beginning.

Sam loved his parents and his younger sister, Susan. They were good to him, always encouraging, always supportive. Jimmy and Lilly worked hard and taught Sam to do the same. However, they decided long ago they didn't want their son to run a bakery or a restaurant. They wanted to see Sam become a doctor or an educated man with a PhD. They wanted him to have a different kind of life, a life that would express his God-given gifts.

Sam's parents knew he had started meditation, but not much beyond that. They remembered that Sam had always been full of questions and thought about things deeply. They also recalled his tendency to be restless and moody, and that underlying it all, he was idealistic and optimistic.

At age twenty-seven, Sam was young. When Jimmy was twenty-seven, he was married and working dawn till sundown. He saved everything he could to open his own place. With his father-in-law's help, Jimmy secured a long-term lease on the bakery café. In time they bought the building, which included the storefront and the four apartments above. At twenty-seven, Jimmy was getting used to being tired from the responsibilities he shouldered. Not that he minded. His satisfaction came from providing well for his family, creating a successful business, and getting ahead.

Sam loved walking into the café and seeing his parents behind the counter, absorbed in their work. He would walk up to where they were standing and, with a disguised voice, complain, "Can't a person get any service around here?" His father would consistently react, ready for a verbal battle. His mother would always know it was him. When all eyes met, smiles and shouts of joy would erupt, along with greetings all around and a few "God bless you's" to boot. Coffee would be poured, pastries selected, and Maria called from the back to stand at the cash register while the three of them slipped off to a corner booth. Lilly would catch Sam up on the home front and Jimmy on the business, the mayor, the president—who, by the way, according to Jimmy, was a lying, no-good son of a bitch. Lilly, at that point, would remind her husband that it was always best to forgive and forget, to which Jimmy would reply, "When this president is out of office and gone maybe." Sam would marvel at his parents' capacity for news and controversy. Behind all that was a constant love that shone in their eyes, a love they couldn't conceal from anyone.

On this particular day, Sam revealed that he had met someone special. That quieted both parents down.

"I'm in love," Sam confessed. "She is beautiful, intelligent, kind, and spiritual."

"And she's Catholic?" they asked in unison.

"Ah no, but she's wonderful."

Jimmy and Lilly wanted Catholic grandchildren, baptized and confirmed.

"So she wouldn't mind converting and being married in the church?" Lilly smiled.

"I don't know. I didn't ask. Besides, we just met, and we only had two dates."

Jimmy and Lilly were immediately relieved.

"Oh, you only just met," said Jimmy. "Oh, that's different. Why didn't you say so in the first place, son? Your poor mother is all upset and excited. Now, Lilly, calm yourself, dear. They only just met," Jimmy counseled.

"Jimmy, my dearest, I'm sitting right here and can hear with me own ears what my own darling son's been saying," Lilly stated calmly and slowly. "Thank you very much just the same, Jimmy."

"Oh well, if you're going to be that way about it, I'll just sit here and not try to help you calm yourself in any way," Jimmy countered, turning slightly away. Lilly looked to heaven and briefly mumbled a prayer for strength and patience.

"Ah, James Patrick O'Connor, you are so gallant to come to my rescue," she announced, and then she gave her husband a quick peck on his ruddy-pink cheek, which cheered Jimmy considerably.

Sam looked on in amused admiration along with a bit of horror. *Ah, the Catholic question rears its head for the umpteenth time*, he thought.

"So where is this young woman now?" inquired Lilly.

"Oh, I'd say she's getting ready to land in Geneva any moment."

"Geneva? Like in the convention? Like in Switzerland?" Jimmy piped in.

"Yes, like in Switzerland."

"Oh, she's the mountaineering, outdoors type," his dad offered.

"No," said Sam. "She's the meditating, spiritual type who's searching for enlightenment."

"Oh," acknowledged his parents, not really knowing what type that was.

Amy arrived in Seelisberg with a hundred and fifty or so other women. They all had comfortable rooms in the Bellevue, a hotel that lived up to its name. It overlooked calm, translucent Lake Lucerne and faced the powerful, sculpted mountains. It was just down the hill from Maharishi's residence and the TM organization's international administrative center, formerly a large turn-of-the-century hotel. Every evening, the group walked slowly up the steep road to the lecture hall, breathing in the clear, crisp air and feeling awed by the vista. At about 7:30 pm, Maharishi came into the lecture hall, beaming joy. A large painting of his master, Brahmananda Saraswati, affectionately and respectfully called Guru Dev, was placed behind the small sofa where he seated himself. The couch was covered with white silk and surrounded by luxurious bouquets of fresh flowers. Maharishi began each evening with a hearty, heartfelt, "Jai Guru Dev," offering deep gratitude and all credit for TM's success to his master.

One evening, Amy had the opportunity to sit up front for Maharishi's lecture. He gave an inspiring talk on the development of the heart and the expression of love. After the talk, one of Maharishi's young assistants asked Amy to wait where she was until the other students left. It seemed Maharishi wanted to meet with her. Amy was excited, curious, and nervous. What did it mean? Her mind raced with possibilities. *Maybe he wants me to use my art skills, teach in another country . . .*

When everyone had filed out of the hall, the assistant ushered Amy to a chair not ten feet away from Maharishi. For what seemed a long time, Maharishi sat with closed eyes. After some moments, Amy closed her eyes as well. She felt herself settle into silence.

After a few more minutes, Maharishi coughed slightly and said, "Jai Guru Dev!" and asked Amy how she was enjoying the course.

Amy slowly opened her eyes and answered, "Maharishi, the course and the knowledge are so profound. Thank you for creating such a fulfilling experience."

Maharishi chuckled. "Yes, yes, it is fortunate for the world that you are here. Now I have a question for you. Who is the man with the green eyes and expressive hands?"

Amy was stunned by the question. *Wow!* she thought. *That was definitely unexpected. Maharishi must mean Sam, but how could he know about him?* Amy felt foolish trying to explain Sam to Maharishi when he somehow, impossibly, knew about him—but she had to say something! "I did meet someone a few weeks before I came to the course. He's a meditator, working on his PhD in philosophy. His name is Sam O'Connor."

When Amy mentioned Sam's name, Maharishi sat up a little straighter and moved his head from side to side with a certain excitement. Then he shut his eyes and became still for several minutes. With eyes still closed, he whispered, "It would be good to invite him to the course." Now, Maharishi opened his eyes wide and added, "Please call him and ask him to join us here in the Alps. He deserves to have this precious knowledge. It would be very good for him to come. Very good, very good. You will call him and help him make arrangements? Hmmm?"

Even more confounded, Amy managed a response: "Of course I will, Maharishi. I'll call him right away."

Turning to his assistant, Maharishi said, "Help her with the call."

"Jai Guru Dev," Maharishi said, getting up and bringing his hands together in the form of India's traditional humble greeting. Amy replied with the same salutation and gesture.

"Yes," Maharishi said, "this is a fortunate day for the world." With that, he turned to leave the room, walking with the lightness and grace of a king.

Chapter 5:
The Call

AMY EXPLAINED TO THE ASSISTANT that she needed to go to her room to retrieve Sam's parents' number. The young man asked her to meet him on the second floor, room 202, where she could place the call. Amy was beside herself with wild imaginings, trying to understand what this all meant. Amy half ran, half walked back to the Bellevue. She felt dazed, a million thoughts and a swirl of feelings moving through her. It would have been a lot just to integrate her first personal meeting with her master. Add to that the meeting's astonishing content and the anticipation of talking to Sam, and Amy could barely think enough to stay on her unlikely task. She allowed herself to simply be with the confusion and recognize that she probably wouldn't understand all this for a while, maybe never. The important thing was just to make the call. It was after 11:00 pm in Seelisberg, and that made it just after 5:00 pm in New York. Amy didn't know if Sam would even be home, but she would place the call immediately as requested.

Walking quickly through the mist-filled mountain evening back to the Hotel Sonnenberg, Amy grew increasingly eager to talk to Sam again. They had been together so briefly; they hardly knew each other in any material sense, yet the connection was real and powerful enough for Maharishi to have recognized it, something that Amy was still trying to comprehend. Amy wondered how in the world Sam was going to receive this sudden invitation, how he would feel when he heard her voice. She rehearsed softly, "Hi, Sam. It's Amy. By the way, Maharishi just invited you to join our course. Can you pack your bags and be here in a couple of days?" It sounded surreal coming out of the blue like that.

Amy entered the now quiet hotel and walked along its broad, high-ceilinged hallways to the wide stairs that wound up from the lobby. She barely saw the fading red carpet that spoke of past elegance as she climbed to the second floor. Arriving at the phone room, Amy voiced her concern to the assistant, a rosy-cheeked German, who could not have been more than twenty. He smiled and offered her the advice, "Just close your eyes for a minute and then focus on what words to say to bring about the desired effect. Just be natural and let the words come to you. There's no reason to strain."

Amy sat for a minute to collect herself. She thought, *Don't go crazy on this guy. Be simple and direct. Feel free to convey at least a tinge of excitement, but don't overwhelm him.*

She dialed. On the fourth ring, Lillian picked up the receiver.

"Hello."

"Yes, hello. This is Amy Sanders calling for Sam. I'm calling from Switzerland. Is Sam at home?"

Aha, this is the girl, and she's calling from Switzerland. She must like him very much, Lillian thought. "Yes, Sam is here. Just walked in. Hold the line."

Lillian trotted down the hall and opened Sam's door without knocking. Sam was surprised at the sudden intrusion. "Sam, that girl is calling long distance from the Alps."

"You mean Amy?"

"Yes, Amy Sanders from the Alps."

Meanwhile, Susan, who had the ears of a fox, overheard everything in the apartment. She walked down the hall from her room and into Sam's room. "Hey, Mom, what's up?" she asked as Sam quickly squeezed past both women to get to the phone.

Lillian responded, "Honey, Sam's new girlfriend is calling from the Alps. It must be something important."

"Must be," Susan said, not knowing anything about the Alps.

Sam quickly traversed the hall to the phone on the kitchen wall. He had never expected a call from Amy, maybe a letter or two or a postcard, but not a call. Susan laughed as she saw Sam bounding past her toward the phone. "Boy," she said, "that was fast!"

Lillian handed Sam the phone and said, "Come on, Susan, let's go into the den and give your brother some privacy."

"Bingo," Susan replied.

Sam picked up the receiver. "Amy?" he asked with a certain disbelief.

"Yes, Sam, it's me."

"Oh, Lord, is everything okay?"

"Yes, yes, everything is fine. How are you, Sam?"

"Good, good, I'm good."

Yes, you certainly are, Amy thought. "Listen," Amy began, "an extraordinary thing happened tonight after Maharishi's lecture." She went on to explain that Maharishi had asked her to stay behind and wanted to know who the man with the green eyes was. She described how once she had said Sam's name, Maharishi had become kind of excited. "Then," she continued, "Maharishi sat for several minutes, seeming to meditate on your name, but really, I have no idea what was passing through his awareness."

Sam intervened and said jokingly, "I thought I felt someone's eyes on me."

"I know this must sound crazy, but Maharishi wants you to come to Switzerland to join the course. He said that you deserve this precious knowledge and something about the world being a better place for it."

Sam wanted to say at least he wouldn't be in the bakery burning the bagels, and that would help several hundred New Yorkers, but thought better of it. At that moment, calmness settled over him, and his mind was quiet and clear.

"Okay, Amy, I'll look into it. You know I have to talk to my folks, look into travel, and take care of the usual mass of practical stuff."

The words he uttered surprised him. Yet Sam's destiny had come knocking, and he intuitively knew the sound. Of course, he didn't understand why. He didn't know what a turn his life would take. He really didn't know anything except that Amy was asking him to come. He trusted her. He trusted his destiny.

He asked Amy at what number he could reach her. She explained that he'd only be able to leave a message. Sam acknowledged that he understood, and holding the phone between his ear and his shoulder, he wrote down the number she dictated. "Okay, got it," he confirmed. "Call you in a day or so."

Sam's mother was in the hall listening to every word, trying to piece it together. Susan listened too. Sam swung the kitchen door open and saw his mother and sister standing there.

"Mom, I'm going to shower and meditate, and then I need to talk to you both. Go ahead and start dinner. Susan, save me something to eat okay?"

"Maybe, maybe not," Susan said with a giggle.

"Well, why did she call long distance? Just to ask how's the weather?" Lilly made a small attempt to find out what was happening.

"Mom, I'll explain it all later." Sam went back to his room, wondering how he was going to explain this.

Jimmy came in the front door, looking frazzled from a long day at work. Lillian greeted him with Susan standing right behind her. Jimmy was surprised that Lilly and Susan were standing right by the front door just as he opened it. "What's up with you two?" Jimmy queried. "Lilly, you've got that strange look on your face." Before she could answer, Jimmy probed, expecting the worst. "It's not my crazy cousin again, is it?"

Lilly shook her head no and simply informed him, "She called."

"Yeah. She sure did," added Susan with a chuckle.

Jimmy, now following them into the kitchen with a feeling of relief, asked, "Who's she?"

"You know, the one in the mountains, yodeling for enlightenment."

"Yeah, boy, can she yodel, Dad!" Susan contributed.

"Oh, the mountain girl that Sam is stuck on. She called?"

"Yeah, and it looks like she's carrying him up the mountain."

"Well, it could be worse. They could both be tumbling down like Jack and Jill," Jimmy quickly replied. Susan giggled at the image.

"I don't know. They didn't talk long, and Sam seemed serious when they hung up," Lilly revealed.

"Bingo," Susan added for effect.

"What do you mean serious? Serious like in a problem serious, or serious like in love?"

"I don't know, just quiet and serious."

"Lillian, you're not making any sense. Where is he anyway?"

"In the shower or meditating. You don't think she's pregnant, do you? Oh, Mother Mary and Joseph, pray for us!" Lillian shouted, making the sign of the cross.

"Oh, Mother Mary and Joseph," Susan echoed.

"Don't know. I suppose that could be it."

"He said he'd explain everything. We'll just have to wait until he's done with all that other stuff."

"Yeah, we'll have to wait," Susan repeated as she slumped down on a kitchen chair.

"All right, Lil, we'll wait then. What's for dinner? Susan must be hungry. Right, dear?"

"I'm always ready to eat," Susan confirmed.

"That's my girl!"

"James Patrick O'Connor, how can you eat at a time like this?"

"Well, Lillian Mary O'Connor, because I'm hungry, and if I'm to be getting bad news, I don't want to hear it on an empty stomach."

"Well, if it's bad news, I'm going to be upset," Susan added somberly.

"Jimmy, you go out to the parlor and read the paper. Susan, dear, you set the table."

"Yes, Mom." Off the two went to their assigned tasks.

Sam entered the small dining room, where he found his mother sipping a cup of tea, his father with half a plate of shepherd's pie, and Susan with her plate scraped clean. He sat down at the table.

"Hungry, huh, Susan?" Sam asked. He added in a familiar and loving way, "Sweetie, you were born hungry. I remember when you were born."

"I remember when you were born too," Susan retorted for the thousandth time.

"Well, that's not technically possible, but if you say so," Sam affirmed.

"Okay, that's enough, you two. Aren't you the one getting a PhD in philosophy?" Jimmy asked.

"Sadly, Dad, it's true. I don't think my advisor believes it either."

"All right, just checking," Jimmy came back. "Sam, your mother told me you have something to discuss."

"Yes, I do need to talk with you about something," Sam conveyed.

His mother shifted uneasily in her chair; his father started clearing his throat. Susan sat relaxed, awaiting the entertainment that was sure to come.

"Son," Jimmy broached what he thought might be a delicate matter, "you can always come to us, and we will do what we can."

"Thank you, Dad. I don't want to let you and Mom down. As you know, Amy called me from Switzerland."

Lillian could hardly contain her anxiety. "It must have been important for her to call. She could've written I suppose."

"Well," Sam replied, "I guess it couldn't wait." Sam noticed his mother was saying a Hail Mary under her breath. "Mom, why are you praying?" he asked.

"Whatever happens, I just want the baby to be healthy. Do her parents know? Did she call them from the Alps too?"

Jimmy saw the puzzlement on his son's face and attempted to come to the rescue. "Sam, the world is a different place now. When your mother and I were young, we waited, you know, for the honeymoon."

Sam couldn't believe what he was hearing. *They think she's pregnant and I'm the father.*

"Good Lord, Amy's not pregnant!"

"She's not!" Jimmy and Lillian exclaimed.

"Bingo!" Susan added.

"Goodness, no! We haven't even had a good make-out session yet. Definitely no. She called to say I've been invited by Maharishi to join the course she's on."

"Oh, thank you, Mother Mary, Joseph, and baby Jesus," Lillian burst forth.

"Oh, I'm so happy!" mimicked Susan.

"Lord, son, you gave us a scare," his father added.

"Dad, let's be clear, I didn't give you a scare. You and Mom did that all by yourselves."

"True, son. You got me there. So what's this all about?"

"I'm not completely sure, but I think it's a good opportunity to really learn from a master from India. Though I don't want to leave you short at the café, Dad."

"Don't worry about that. That's not important. If you think the course is important, Mom and I will back you up." Jimmy and Lillian were so happy to be relieved from their own imaginings that they were glad to support Sam and his trip to Switzerland although they had no idea who Maharishi was and what kind of course their son might be talking about.

Later, Lilly questioned Jimmy, "What's all this about?"

"Lil, it's simple. The boy's in love. I wouldn't put too much into the other stuff, the Maharishi and all," Jimmy declared confidently.

"Jimmy, I don't know. I hope you're right."

"Sam said it was a course and he'd be learning a lot. So that, coupled with love—what choice does the boy have?"

They decided Jimmy's logic was good enough for them. Two days after the call, Sam was on standby with Swiss Air. They drove him to Kennedy Airport, and off he went. Jimmy and Lilly rode home in silence, pondering how they would explain his sudden departure.

"Here's what we say: An opportunity came up to study in Switzerland, and Sam couldn't pass it up. Naturally, we supported him. No bakery business for this boy. He's going places," Jimmy said with obvious pride.

So as customer after customer asked, "Where's Sam?" Jimmy and Lilly said, "He's studying in Switzerland. Some big philosophy course, even got an invitation. No bakery for this boy."

"Bingo!" added Susan.

Chapter 6:
The River and the Ocean

SAM ARRIVED AT MAHARISHI'S HOTEL in Seelisburg early in the afternoon. Amy had alerted the reception desk to Sam's schedule, and the man on duty warmly showed Sam to his room on the fifth floor. The room was spacious and painted a light golden yellow, while the substantial furniture reflected the gracious, turn-of-the-century European style. Sam walked to the window and drew the heavy velvet curtains to find that his room looked out on an inspiring vista of lake, sky, and mountains. The light filtering in made the room glow. A letter from Amy waited for him on a large oak desk next to the window.

> *Dear Sam,*
>
> *I'm so thrilled that you are here. I can't wait to see you. Sorry I couldn't meet you at the airport, but I love you. Maharishi knows you are arriving and wants you to rest. You must be exhausted. I'll be finished with my evening meditation at six thirty, and, if you're up and about, I'll meet you in the lobby at seven. The roses are for you to give to Maharishi, but take one for yourself from me. You have a nice room, and you should be comfortable. See you soon.*
>
> *Love,*
> *Amy*

A large vase filled with red roses sat on the bedside table. All the thorns had been carefully removed. They were accompanied by a second note.

My Dearest Sam,

I'm so proud of you for being here, that you trust me enough to drop everything and fly halfway around the world means so much. Maharishi will be so pleased to see you, and I can hardly wait until seven. Try and get in some rest and meditation.

Love You,
Amy

Sam moved restlessly around the room, saying to himself, *She loves me. Wow! She loves me! All right, ole' boy, steady now. You've got five hours to shower, nap, meditate, unpack, and change clothes. Don't keep her waiting. Never keep a lady waiting, or a rishi for that matter. My Lord, my God, you do love excitement!*

At ten minutes to seven, Sam was in the lobby waiting for Amy. She came through the front door, and Sam was amazed by her light. She seemed like a goddess on a cloud. For the first moment, Sam was struck dumb. They looked into each other's eyes and embraced.

Sam found his voice. "Amy, how could I have let you go? My God, it's incredible to see you!"

Amy returned emotionally, "Well, we're both here now, and that's what matters."

Amy took Sam's arm and led him outside. Still fatigued from his journey, Sam felt as if he had entered a walking and talking kind of a dream. His attention was entirely focused on Amy; he barely noticed the towering mountains and the placid lake below.

Sensing his vagueness, Amy spoke, "Time for a short walk, and then we'll meet Maharishi."

They strolled out into the warm mountain air that would turn chilly after sunset. They moved lazily, relishing every moment of their time together and keenly aware of each other's bodies and closeness. Sam was gliding along with his right hand full of roses destined for Maharishi and Amy on his left arm.

"Sam," Amy began, "I'll introduce you to Maharishi. You'll give the flowers to him and say, 'Jai Guru Dev.' Maharishi will answer the same. Then we'll sit down and wait for him to start the conversation. It's probably hard for you to imagine how special it is to get this personal welcome from Maharishi. It's not the way things usually happen."

"Glad you have it all worked out. I'll do my best not to disappoint," Sam replied, suddenly reminded of the other big reason he was in Switzerland and not brewing coffee in New York. It felt so absolutely natural to be meeting the master. Somewhere inside he knew it was always meant to occur. He had a deep sense of perfection.

"Don't worry. Maharishi's going to love you," Amy said encouragingly. Sam was in fact not worried—not yet.

They returned to the hotel and climbed the stairs to Maharishi's suite. Maharishi's cheerful assistant greeted them and asked them to sit while he announced their arrival. They sat waiting in comfortable, wing-back chairs, covered in gold-toned fabric. As the minutes ticked by in the rich silence outside Maharishi's room, Sam's self-possession started to dissolve. He began to feel intensely curious about all this. After all, it really was a bit odd to be in the Alps with a woman he loved yet barely knew, waiting to meet a great rishi from the Vedic tradition. He started to get nervous. *What am I doing here? Holy cow! I can't believe this is happening!*

"Amy, are you sure I'm supposed to be here? This could all be a mistake," Sam said, feeling stranger by the second. She reached over and squeezed his hand.

"I don't think Maharishi makes mistakes. And my heart tells me you are here because you're meant to be here," she quietly reassured him.

"Well, strictly speaking, none of this is good, logical thinking, but I guess I'm used to that. You know my mother leaps all over the place when it comes to thinking and making decisions. With her, everything is done with a nod and a prayer. Drives my dad crazy, but he has a bit of that in him as well. He can't show it too much because Mom can be such a loose cannon. So I guess I'm used to this, though I shouldn't admit it in public," Sam babbled nervously.

"It sounds as if your mom is a very intuitive woman. Maybe some of that gift rubbed off on you. I look forward to meeting her."

"Well, I'm sure Lilly won't let you down. She's as lively as they come."

Sam paused. "Amy, I'm not sure about this. I don't want to let you down. Maharishi could take one look at me and say to himself, 'Wrong guy. Would somebody please drive this man back to the airport? Don't call us. We'll call you—in around a thousand years.'"

"Sam, you are an interesting man." Amy laughed.

While Maharishi sat with eyes closed on his dais, Sam and Amy were ushered into the room and guided to sit in two comfortable chairs. Maharishi kept his eyes closed, so Sam and Amy shut their eyes as well and began to meditate. After about ten minutes, Maharishi opened his eyes and said in a voice just above a whisper, "Jai Guru Dev."

Sam opened his eyes, but it took a few seconds to come out of the all-absorbing silence of his meditation and focus. He found himself looking into Maharishi's deep brown eyes. They were bottomless pools of bliss and unconditional love, brilliant as the morning star. At that moment, something deep inside of Sam awoke.

"Jai Guru Dev! Welcome to the course."

Sam immediately jumped up out of his chair. "Jai Guru Dev, Maharishi. Thank you for inviting me," he said as he handed Maharishi the roses. Maharishi admired the flowers for a moment, selected three, and laid the rest on the small table in front of him.

"Maharishi," Amy said, "this is Sam O'Connor. He's studying philosophy and is a PhD candidate at the University of Massachusetts." Sam and Amy sat down.

"Very good. You are studying philosophy. Very good."

"Yes, Maharishi. Thank you. I finished my course work, and I'm writing my dissertation," Sam responded.

"Very good." Maharishi laughed softly. "My field is the field of Being. What I teach is not in a book. Knowledge from books tends to stay in books. This is a problem when you need it. More important, knowledge from books cannot relieve a man from suffering. Only direct experience of Being can do that. I teach direct experience of eternal Being, Bliss Consciousness. This course will give you the chance to immerse yourself in Being, to dive deep into your own reservoir of pure, unbounded Bliss. All that you learn here comes from Guru Dev and the Holy Tradition of masters."

"Thank you for this precious opportunity to study with you," Sam spoke humbly.

"While on the course, you only need to go with the routine," Maharishi continued. "No decisions to make, just follow the routine. It will be very, very interesting for you. We will go into such profound knowledge. The knowledge and the experience together will transform anyone's life for the better. Suffering will be a thing of the past when the knowledge and experience of transcending goes to every corner of the world.

"*Yogastah kuru karmani.* Established in Being perform action. This was the advice from Lord Krishna to Arjuna on the battlefield of life that we find in the *Bhagavad Gita.* Just this one phrase for you both: Yogastah kuru karmani. This is the theme of the course for you. Establish yourselves in your own unbounded nature, and then enlighten the world." Maharishi now addressed Sam directly. "For now, take some rest. In two or three days, you can join the course. For now, just sleep, meditate, take some warm food, then you'll join the course. Yes?" Maharishi concluded.

"Yes. Thank you, Maharishi."

Sam and Amy bowed their heads slightly and put their hands together, saying, "Jai Guru Dev." They turned to leave, when Maharishi started to share a verse from the Upanishads:

> You are what your deep, driving desire is.
> As your desire is, so is your will. As your will is, so is your deed.
> As your deed is, so is your destiny.

Maharishi's destiny was to enlighten the world. Sam and Amy's destiny was to help him accomplish it. Along with thousands of others, they did not know how or when this new enlightened society would appear, only that they felt strongly called to support the possibility for a better world, a peaceful world.

Maharishi knew his role. Sam and Amy would come to discover theirs. They didn't know what ups and downs lay ahead. They didn't know that some people would hail them as heroes, while others would see them as representatives of the devil. They didn't know about fame or rejection. They only knew they were in love, and somehow they had stumbled into the path of an enlightened master from the Himalayas. As they walked out into the cool mountain air, the world seemed fresh, and their happiness knew no bounds.

Chapter 7:
The Master and Enlightenment

MAHARISHI RADIATED JOY. HIS PLAYFULNESS and bliss were evident to everyone in his presence, and his energy seemed boundless. He never seemed to tire, and he outworked all the young people around him. His eyes twinkled and emanated compassion. They seemed to see both measureless depths and unbounded horizons. Whenever Sam was with Maharishi, he found himself smiling. Whatever concerns he felt melted away. He had never met someone so full of wisdom, peace, and bubbling happiness all at once. Maharishi's fullness was infectious.

Sam joined the men's TM teacher-training course in the Hotel Sëeblick, magnificently situated high above Lake Lucerne in the small town of Emmetten. He began each day with three rounds of meditation. A round consisted of a period of meditation framed between a set of yoga postures or asanas, ten minutes of a special breathing exercise called *pranayama*, and rest. When he completed his morning rounds, he showered, dressed, and proceeded to a spacious dining hall, lined along one wall with windows that looked out over the lake far below. He usually ate a light breakfast, fresh fruit and some yogurt, but now and then his appetite swelled and he indulged in delicious warm bread and fresh, sweet butter from the local bakery, which reminded him of home and his parents' bakery. In the beginning days of the course, he had time for exploratory walks after he ate. One path took him through the charming town with architecture that had largely escaped the twentieth century. Another trail followed the outline of the cliff and provided clear views of the lake. Each day he marveled at his exquisite surroundings. To be in the Swiss Alps with Maharishi was like being in heaven; he felt full and complete.

Sam returned from his walks to a morning meeting, which usually consisted of a video tape of Maharishi and a short group meditation. Then came lunch. The men's course had 188 participants, mainly Americans, but also representatives from almost every country in Europe. After lunch, everyone took up to an hour for a "walk and talk" before the afternoon meeting, and that was Sam's opportunity to call Amy. They tried to talk several times a week, though they were dependent on pay phones, which were few in number and much in demand. Sometimes they talked about a point of knowledge, sometimes about their meditations, and sometimes they just laughed and talked about nothing sensible. It didn't really matter.

After the afternoon meeting, all the course participants filed back to their rooms for more meditation rounds. Within a couple of weeks, Maharishi increased the number of rounds he wanted everyone to do until the course participants were doing up to six rounds a day.

Around 6:30 pm, Sam and his fellow students ambled slowly down to dinner. Appetites fluctuated unpredictably from ravenous to minimal from day to day. The vegetarian food was generally warm and nourishing and always included salads and a range of lightly cooked vegetables and grains. The men's group was blessed with a professional Spanish pastry chef among the kitchen staff, and the desserts were uniformly over the top. Sam's senses were highly enlivened from all the meditation—everything tasted and smelled wonderful—and he sometimes found himself enjoying the freshly baked breads and farm fresh cheeses a little too much.

After dinner, some of the men took another short walk if time allowed, but everyone met again for an evening meeting that lasted until ten o'clock. If Maharishi joined them, the meeting might continue until one or two in the morning; he tended not to notice time. Maharishi visited the men's course several times a week to answer questions on their meditation experiences and explain higher states of consciousness. Many of the best lectures evolved from a particularly discriminating question, and Maharishi actively encouraged such probing thoughts. "Good questions bring out the knowledge," Maharishi often said, and the men became almost competitive in their attempts to frame compelling queries.

Sometimes Maharishi's answers appeared to wander from the question, and he took everyone on a journey though whole new cities, even nations, of knowledge. He could speak for an hour or two, drawing on an endless continuum of inspiration. Then, almost suddenly, he would bring the spellbound listeners back to the original destination, tying everything together. The answer to the question was not only complete, but also full, deep, and multidimensional.

Like everyone there, Sam wanted to know more about the nature of Being and enlightenment, but the philosopher in him also wanted to ask Maharishi about the limits of the mind and whether one can have absolute certainty about truth and non truth. If so, how? Is something true only for the experiencer, or is truth something universal on which everyone can agree? How does the human mind evolve? Are the principles of evolution the same for all cultures and societies everywhere?

At some point in the evening, Maharishi always wanted to hear about how meditation was going. Many a night, when Maharishi called for experiences, Sam went up to the microphone to describe his and ask Maharishi his pressing questions of the moment.

"Maharishi, Jai Guru Dev," Sam began one evening.

Maharishi beamed back, "Jai Guru Dev. It feels so good to say these three words, 'Jai Guru Dev.' By Guru Dev's grace, we are so fortunate to have this knowledge. Yes. Now, what would you like to ask?"

"Sometimes in meditation, I am clearly absorbed in the transcendent. The mantra has disappeared along with all other content, yet I remain fully awake inside. Other times it's as if I've fallen asleep, yet I'm not sleeping. What's happening?"

"There is transcending, but also some smoke, some fog. We can call this cloudy transcending, but we really shouldn't call it that. Transcending is transcending, but we have it along with some cloudy perception, due either to fatigue or release of deep-rooted stresses. As you now know well, when the mind transcends, the body and nervous system rest deeply. Whenever we get deep rest, the nervous system normalizes. We release some deep-rooted stress. When we transcend, the rest is so profound, so complete, it allows a big cloud of stress or fatigue to dissolve.

"Eventually, with enough meditation, enough deep rest, the nervous system is totally free of all its accumulated stress and supports the experience of infinite awareness twenty-four hours a day. We never lose our infinite status. We call this state cosmic consciousness. On a sunny day, a muddy pool can only reflect a small value of the light, while a clear pool reflects the full value of the sunlight. Like that, in cosmic consciousness, the nervous system has become so pure that it reflects the full brilliance of unbounded consciousness, along with the waking, dreaming, and deep-sleep states. Day and night, we never lose the Self. That is why we call it Self-Realization. We never lose pure consciousness. It is such a beautiful thing. Pure consciousness is never overshadowed by any experience ever again. Like the sun, it is always shining."

"So, Maharishi," Sam continued, "the smokiness is just the result of purification of the nervous system?"

"Yes. When the mind settles down, the nervous system and the body spontaneously shift into a profoundly restful state. Such deep rest—all this new research shows that it is deeper than sleep—allows the body and nervous system to normalize, to throw off the deep-rooted stresses and strains accumulated during the whole lifetime. When the body releases stress, some thoughts arise in the mind, some emotions or physical sensations, or some dullness, even sleep. These are all indications that some stress was neutralized and now we are free to dive deeper than before into the transcendent.

"It is important to understand that cosmic consciousness is the normal state of awareness for men and women everywhere. Now the full potential of the individual is available." Emphasizing his words by tapping the microphone with a rose from the table, Maharishi reminded everyone, "Jesus told the people that the kingdom of heaven is within. First seek that, and all else will be added. The kingdom of heaven, infinite Being, established within. Just like that, Lord Krishna said, 'Yogasta kuru karmani.' Established in Being, perform action. First transcend, be established in the Self, then perform action. With this, everything goes right for the individual, the society, and the universe. When we act from that infinite level of life, all that we do spontaneously supports life. We act in accord with all the laws of nature, and what we do upholds evolution for all beings.

"With the grace of Guru Dev, we are going to create an ideal society, heaven on earth. What great accomplishments we will see in every field! No one will suffer. Just remember: Go with the routine, go deeply into the Self. Don't worry about smokiness, just go deep. Transcending brings up and then clears the smoke. Both effects. Just keep meditating. Transcend, transcend. Now it's time to rest."

With that closing, Maharishi stood up, slipped on his wooden sandals, and said, "Jai Guru Dev," and walked off the stage. Everyone responded, "Jai Guru Dev," and the hall of students emptied behind him.

Sam noticed more and more whenever he was in the hall with Maharishi that his thoughts quieted down and his mind became still, just as in his meditations. The silence continued even when he slept. He began to find that as he fell asleep, some part of him remained awake, and he witnessed his dreams and even his deepest level of sleep. He was somehow asleep and yet awake. He then noticed that the witnessing continued seamlessly into his waking moments. He was watching himself gesture and talk, watching his mind think. It felt like activity seemed to occur on its own. He was a silent, non-moving, non-doing, transparent presence. *This must be what Maharishi has been describing, what cosmic consciousness feels like,* Sam thought.

As the days passed, Sam enjoyed his first taste of this new state of consciousness, or CC. One evening, Maharishi asked if anyone was witnessing. A few hands went up, including Sam's, and Maharishi asked them to come to the microphone and share their experience. As each person talked, Maharishi sat and listened intently with eyes closed. When the student finished, Maharishi acknowledged him with a "Very good, very good" and asked the next person to share.

Finally, it was time for Sam. As he came up to the microphone, Maharishi began to talk. "We've heard some descriptions of witnessing. These are the beginning of our stabilization of pure consciousness. The Self has always been there, and when I say always, I mean always. It is eternal Being, pure unbounded consciousness, only we lost awareness of it. Our attention focused outwards and Being lies deep within, transcendental to all activity. It is pure existence, one without a second." Maharishi nodded to Sam and asked encouragingly, "Yes, what is your experience?"

"Maharishi, I began witnessing about a week ago."

"All the time? Even in sleep?"

"Yes, Maharishi, even in sleep."

Sam expressed the changes he had noticed, and when he finished, Maharishi responded, "Very good. CC is the fifth state of consciousness. When we start TM, first we experience a fourth state of consciousness, transcendental consciousness or TC, the infinite Silence that is transcendental to all activity, even the finest level of mental activity. When TC becomes permanent, then we have CC. Sometimes symptoms of CC arise for a few days and then disappear. When this happens, it means the nervous system needs more purification, and the mind needs to become more familiar with the transcendent. So we go with our routine. We meditate and act.

"Each time we alternate meditation and activity, TC becomes more permanent. It is like dyeing a cloth. In the villages of India, people dip some cloth into a vat of dye—say, yellow dye—and then they put it out in the hot Indian sun to dry. Most of the color fades, but some tint remains. Now the villagers put the cloth back in the dye and put it out to dry again. Once more, the sun fades most of the color, but this time a little more remains, and it is permanent. Like that, they continue to dip and fade, dip and fade, until the full value of the yellow color remains and it is permanent. It's just like that when we alternate meditation and activity. The mind dips into the transcendent during TM. When we go into activity, we appear to lose the transcendent, to fade the cloth, but we actually hold on to a little of it, and that is permanent. So we keep meditating and acting, meditating and acting. Meditate and dip into infinity, act and integrate or stabilize our ability to live more and more of that unbounded consciousness. Eventually, the full value is there. We never lose it. We are one with the limitless ocean of Being no matter what life brings.

"Now we know about a fifth state of consciousness, CC." Without hesitating, Maharishi asked, "Can consciousness expand beyond this?" and began to answer his own question.

"In the state of cosmic consciousness, we know who we are: Self, infinite, and eternal. However, we have a new kind of duality now: Self and non-Self. I know my Self, but what is all of this?" Maharishi's hand swept the hall. "All the rest of life appears to be something less than unbounded. So we are left with a paradox. Certainly the ultimate reality can have no duality. Inwardly, the Self cannot expand further. It is already infinite, an all-time, infinite reality. However, the world of the senses remains just that, a relative world of complexity, variety, and qualities. We appear to be left with the infinite and the finite.

"Now, how to create unity? Hmm? Love comes to our rescue. The heart cannot tolerate separation, and love begins to flow to dissolve it. Before CC, love flowed but in small waves. Now love becomes more powerful. Love is an extreme value of appreciation. Tidal waves of love begin to rise up, and each wave brings a deeper appreciation of the world around us. This refines our senses, and life is more enjoyable. This, in turn, inspires yet greater love in the heart, greater appreciation for the world, and more joy from our perception. This back-and-forth between more love and more refined perception continues until our perception opens to the finest level of reality in every object. The world appears to be made of divine Light. We experience everything as shimmering golden divine Light. Then we call this a new state of consciousness, a sixth state, God consciousness, GC. We see everything in terms of the first or finest expression of consciousness, as Light. Here we find the personal aspect of God. Here we can shake hands with God.

"But still we have some duality: the Absolute infinite silence and the finest level of the manifestation of creation. Some very slight duality still exists. How do we unify them? In time, living in GC, unity happens almost by itself. The tidal waves of love produced by the bliss of GC overcome the last faint remains of duality. Now the senses interpret everything as Self: I am That, thou are That, everything is nothing but That. It's very, very interesting. We merge with this infinite ocean of awareness in CC, and then, through love, our senses awaken to that infinite reality in the world. Everything is Self. The object as something separate drops off. Only the infinite ocean of Self remains. Infinite fullness meets infinite fullness everywhere. When this ocean meets that ocean, something tremendous happens. When the Atlantic meets the Pacific, something tremendous happens. Two infinities become one infinity. It's tremendous, impossible to imagine, but everyone can experience it. We call this unity consciousness, UC, eternal oneness.

"Now we have seven states of consciousness. This is the total range of human awareness. This is the full potential of the human nervous system. Human beings were made to live infinity. This is natural life, and anything less is not natural. Transcending is the way. TM is the way."

A palpable stillness filled the hall. The course participants were stunned into silence by Maharishi's description of unity. Sam had stood at the microphone, transfixed, through the entire explanation. Feeling as if he was coming back from a long journey, Sam broke the silence in the hall and asked, "Maharishi, surely some individuality remains? Otherwise, how can we function?"

Maharishi breathed in the fragrance of the flower in his hand and replied, "Yes."

"How does it happen?"

Maharishi stated, "Two words: *lesha-avidya.*"

"Can you please clarify that?"

"When you have a butterball in your hand and you throw it off, some feeling of the butter remains. You've thrown it off, but a film remains. Like that, with UC we have thrown off ignorance once and for all, but some trace of ignorance, just a trace of individuality, remains. The reality is infinity everywhere, but some tiny trace of separation, of boundaries, is there, just enough to allow us to function in the world of form. We call this tiny remains of ignorance lesha-avidya."

"How does a person go into unity and then go about his daily life?"

"When it first happens, it would be a good idea to take some weeks off." Maharishi roared with laughter.

"We are so blessed to have this knowledge of life. We thank Guru Dev for this good fortune. The journey of life is from Here"—Maharishi used a carnation to point to a space in front of him—"to Here. We seem to pass through there, but it's actually all Here." Maharishi continued to move the flower to illustrate what he was teaching. "From the level of the Self, nothing actually happens. It is like a dream. When you are in the dream, everything seems so real. The tiger is about to pounce, and then you wake up and realize that nothing happened. It was just a dream. The same thing happens in unity. You wake up to the oneness of life. You realize that you, that everything, has always been this oneness. Individuality was just a dream.

"Now, since we are not yet in unity, we should go by our common sense when dealing with daily life. We must do some activity between meditations, so we should choose to do great things in the world. And we should continue to meditate every day, twice a day. When possible, come to long rounding courses for extra deep rest and to stabilize unboundedness," Maharishi continued, "and always enjoy your life. Just enjoy. Live a balanced life and transcend. It will be enough to enjoy unity.

"Now it's time to rest." Holding up his hands, he pressed them together gently and gazed lovingly at everyone present. He concluded reverently, "Jai Guru Dev," and put the flowers between his hands carefully down on the table. He stood up, slipped into his sandals, and descended from the stage. He moved slowly down the central aisle, smiling and accepting offerings of ever more flowers.

Chapter 8:
The Seed of Change

IN THE FINAL DAYS OF the course, Maharishi made Sam and Amy and the other course participants teachers of TM. It was truly a gratifying moment. Before leaving for the airport in Zurich, Maharishi had been particularly kind, inviting them to a private meeting.

"How was the course? Mmm? Were your expectations met?" Maharishi inquired, smiling.

"Yes, Maharishi, the course was beautiful. The knowledge and the experiences, just beautiful. It's hard to find words for it," replied Amy.

Sam added, "Yes, Maharishi. Thank you for inviting me. My life is changed forever. Now I'm thinking about what I should do. I need to finish my PhD, but then I'm wondering whether it's better to teach philosophy at a university or teach TM."

"Finish the PhD and teach at the university," Maharishi answered without hesitation, "and teach TM when you have time. This will be the best way."

Maharishi paused and looked at them with great happiness. "Only now," he continued, "you should look for the transcendent in Western philosophy. It is there. Socrates, Plato, they knew about pure consciousness. Bring out the knowledge of pure consciousness so that the students realize it is not some foreign idea from India, but something universal. Many Western philosophers, writers, and scientists have experienced and expressed the transcendental value of life. Have a course bringing together Eastern and Western thinking. Create a universal appreciation of pure consciousness from both perspectives. The students will find it so fascinating to find the transcendent, their own Self, in their own tradition of knowledge."

Sam was a bit taken back. He had not anticipated Maharishi charging him with such a project, or any project for that matter.

After a short pause, Maharishi continued, "Because of your experiences these last months, you will find pure consciousness lively everywhere and in everything. Without the direct experience of pure consciousness, readers do not recognize it when the writers and scholars refer to it in their books. They are not familiar with the transcendental level of life, so they just pass over the descriptions of it. It is like a family enjoying their house without awareness of its foundation, which remains hidden from view. But the architect knows that the house could not stand, let alone be enjoyed, without the foundation. In the same way, now you own both the experience and understanding that will shine the light for you on the foundation of Western philosophy. That transcendental foundation has always been there, but it has been forgotten for a thousand years, two thousand years. Without awareness of its own foundation, Western philosophy has had little power to influence the people. Now you will change that.

"Life is always seeking more and more: more knowledge, more growth, more happiness. Pure consciousness is infinite. It is the source of creation and knowledge and also their goal. Being unbounded, it is the one experience that brings permanent fulfillment to that natural yearning for more and more. Even if the philosophers and thinkers recognize pure consciousness, if they cannot give people direct experience of that infinite basis of knowledge, people will naturally feel the teaching is incomplete. They will remain unfulfilled.

"Just knowing about pure consciousness is not enough. Knowledge alone will not change the life of the student. The great Western thinkers knew about and described that eternal reality. Only their followers were left wondering about its value for daily life. So now you have something to do in between your meditations," Maharishi concluded, chuckling.

Sam immediately began to see the possibilities and agreed, "Yes, Maharishi. I'll think about how to do it."

"Don't think about it much." Maharishi said with a laugh. "You have everything you need. Just plunge into action."

"Yes, Maharishi. Jai Guru Dev."

"Amy," Maharishi went on, "you should be happy and create beautiful art that will inspire people everywhere. And teach other artists to meditate so that their senses become so refined that they can see the finest relative aspect of creation. This is where the Creator creates, and they should be on that level also. TM has so much to offer everyone. Whatever you do, you become better. Better artist. Better businessman. Better scientist. Even better philosopher." Maharishi rocked with laughter again.

"Storms may come and storms may go. We remain anchored in eternal Being. Sometimes clouds come and try to hide the sun. The sun is unconcerned. The clouds come and they go. The sun is always there. Like that, pure consciousness is always there, shining brightly. Everyone is born to live life from that level. It is natural to do so. Only the knowledge of TM and the ease and naturalness of transcending was missing. Now we add this one thing, and everyone and everything becomes better.

"Over so many generations, the knowledge has been revived and lost many, many times, and it will be lost again. When many people live in fulfillment, they forget the suffering of the past and lose interest in the path to enlightenment. When someone lives in a palace for some years, he forgets the hut that he came from, and the path from the hut to the palace becomes overgrown with weeds. And that is all well and good. No need to hang on to suffering or its memory. But now we are not concerned about that. Now the path is clear. Now is the time to spread the seeds of enlightenment. So enjoy, enjoy all of life. Live each day fully. Mediate twice a day, morning and evening, and let people know your experience. You are both so full of light and happiness. People will be curious about you. Tell them and invite them to begin TM. Remember that what you radiate is as important as what you say. Live and radiate the full light of life. Jai Guru Dev." Maharishi reached out and offered flowers to both Sam and Amy.

"Thank you, Maharishi, and Jai Guru Dev," Sam and Amy responded in unison. The couple walked slowly out of Maharishi's suite, down the hushed hallway, and down the stairs to the lobby. They picked up their luggage, left the Sonnenberg, and boarded the bus to the airport. As the bus pulled out, they took a last fond look at the mountains and lake that had been their hosts and companions on this incredible journey.

Sam and Amy had spent less than three months on the course, but they felt profoundly transformed, light and blissful, and they were in love. With the sun shining brightly and no sign of clouds or storms, they rode on with the innocence of newborns into a world that was often terribly stormy, cranky and resistant to change.

After Sam and Amy left Maharishi's suite, Maharishi closed his eyes and sat very still. Time and space are no barrier for a rishi.

He began to see and remember.

Chapter 9:
The Flow of Desire

*D*EVENDRA WAS THE FIRSTBORN SON *of Vishvakarma and Himani, members of a Brahmin family. He was both intelligent and pure of heart. As he grew, his interest in spiritual matters mushroomed, and he soon devoured all the knowledge his father could give him. By the time Devendra reached adolescence, his father recognized that this son needed the instruction of an enlightened master.*

Within six months, Swami Krishnamurti came through the village, and Vishvakarma brought Devendra, now fifteen, to meet him. After the devotional prostrations and the offering of sweets, fruits, coconuts, flowers, and coins, Vishvakarma presented his son and respectfully asked Swamiji to accept him as a student.

Swamiji turned to Devendra and inquired, "Are you ready to leave your father and mother, your brother and sisters, your friends, and your village to become my student?"

Devendra answered, "I will not leave all that I love. I will carry it all in my heart."

The master saw that the boy's feelings ran true and that his devotion to his family was deep. This gave him pause, but he also saw that his devotion to family and friends was the same devotion needed to become one with the Supreme.

Balram, Devendra's younger brother, sat outside the hut where the meeting was taking place concerning his brother's future. Balram deeply loved and admired his older brother and did not want to be separated from him. Balram was not a potential scholar like Devendra, but he had a heart full of devotion and courage. He prayed to Krishna for His help, asking to accompany his brother to the Swami's ashram.

51

As the meeting was concluding, Swamiji casually mentioned if there was another son he should also consider for discipleship? On impulse, Balram opened his eyes, got to his feet, and politely knocked on the door. The door opened, and Balram stuck his head inside and asked if he might enter.

Swamiji laughed to see the small boy. "I see I have my answer."

Before his father could admonish the boy, Swamiji welcomed Balram to join them.

Balram immediately prostrated himself at the feet of his master. Swamiji saw the great devotion of the child. He realized that he could not separate these two souls, for one supported the other, like the two legs that support the body.

With Vishvakarma's consent, he agreed to take both boys with him. Thus, early the next morning, Devendra and Balram said good-bye to their parents, younger sisters, and ancestral home and traveled with their new master to a new life.

Swami Krishnamurti was a great saint. He carried the wisdom of the illustrious Shankara, who had revived the truth about Vedanta, the fullest value of enlightenment, throughout India. He had unconditional love and compassion for all the people, and the people revered him wherever he went. He honored them with his blessings and his talks on dharma. He didn't have to speak much; his silence was even more powerful than his words. Everywhere Swamiji journeyed, people's hearts opened and they knew peace.

For the next month, the young entourage traveled with their master, walking along the dirt roads that meandered through the rural villages. In every village they visited, people greeted Krishnamurti with joy and celebration. Everyone, young and old, gathered at his feet, and he recounted ancient tales from the Puranas, India's epic poems full of stories about gods and heroes and their interactions. From these sagas, the people learned about right and wrong, dharma, devotion to God, and the nature of enlightenment. He taught with warmth and authority, and people were certain that he was like the ancient rishis who cognized the Vedic teachings thousands of years earlier. After a few days, the Swami and his students would return to the road before rosy dawn lit the darkness.

Eventually they came to the master's ashram. They joined the master's twenty disciples who lived, worked, meditated, and studied there. Krishnamurti's house was small and set apart toward the rear of the compound. Two larger buildings comprised the disciples' residences. The kitchen with its surrounding dining room was the hub of the compound's activity.

It was here that Devendra and Balram were asked to work with the cook. His name was Aseem, but everyone referred to him as Cook. He was a good-spirited *man who loved his part in ashram life. He barked orders at the young disciples to do this or that, but always with compassion. Aseem was Swamiji's chief disciple and had served him for over thirty years, longer than anyone else. Aseem was so close to the master that he knew his heart and mind and could anticipate his every need or desire without so much as a word from anyone. While the master was quiet, soft-spoken, and retiring, Aseem was loud, direct, and commanding. Both were enlightened; both played their respective roles. Swamiji would always be the master, and Aseem would remain the head cook. However, they shared one unbounded, eternal consciousness.*

Though Devendra and Balram could have been offered no higher position than to work day and night with Aseem, they didn't see it that way. Devendra and his brother, Balram, did not understand why they were relegated to the cook's supervision, asked to do work they found demeaning, and only saw the master for a few minutes each day. They had not come so far just to chop vegetables, stir dal, and wash dishes. Their month of closeness with the master while they traveled to the ashram had created the expectation of more of the same. They felt frustrated and confused.

After two months, the master sent for his newest disciples. Cook knew what was about to happen, so he pulled the boys aside and said, "Quickly! Wash up and put on a clean dhoti and then come back here. Quickly now!" Both boys jumped at the chance to break their daily routine.

They returned washed, with their hair neat, and in clean clothes. Cook had prepared two baskets for them to carry to Swamiji's hut. Each held a bright-orange mango and two ripe bananas, a coconut, a piece of white silk, and a handful of freshly picked and colorful flowers from the abundant ashram garden. He handed both boys their baskets and sent them off. When they tried to ask him what was going on, he hushed them in a dramatic fashion.

They arrived at the master's house—an unpretentious rectangular whitewashed building with windows on four sides and an intricately carved wooden door at the east entrance. A covered veranda surrounded the house with flowering vines along the supporting timbers and scattered plots of brilliant blooms. Devendra entered first, and the master invited him into a room simply furnished with wood and bamboo chairs and a tea table. On the eastern side of the room sat an altar with sandalwood incense that sweetened the air, bowls of rice and water, and a painting of Swamiji's master. Though he had explained it before, Swamiji told Devendra that the knowledge he taught had been handed down from master to student in an unbroken chain extending back to the first day of creation. Krishnamurti performed a puja, a ceremony to honor the tradition. Then he gave Devendra a mantra, a Vedic sound with known benefits, and a technique to use it properly so that his awareness would open to infinity and peace.

Both Devendra and Balram learned how to meditate that day, how to transcend the senses, mind, intellect, and emotions and slip into pure unboundedness. Even a brief glimpse of That transforms a life forever.

In time, Devendra's awareness expanded through meditation and his master's teachings. Inner peace and silence rarely dimmed, no matter what challenges the day brought. He noticed that his senses were keener and his mind was sharp and quick. Nevertheless, he still carried the seeds of unfulfilled desires. He had taken a vow of celibacy but wondered at the happiness he witnessed among the couples he saw. He loved children and enjoyed their innocence and playfulness.

Devendra also noticed Jyoti, a lovely, shy fifteen-year-old who lived in the village that served the ashram. She was the only daughter of Janak and Poonam, both of whom studied with Swamiji. Normally, they would have arranged Jyoti's marriage by the age of twelve. However, she was so bright and devoted to her mother and father that she persuaded them, or so she thought, not to start marriage negotiations. She argued that it would be better to let her stay at home and take care of them, something highly unusual in those times—but Jyoti was unusual. She was drawn to learning, and her father had taught her reading and basic mathematics. Jyoti would later teach the younger students at the village school.

Jyoti also noticed Devendra whenever he entered the village. He was friendly to everyone, particularly kind to children and elders, clearly intelligent, and definitely attractive despite his celibate mind-set. She found herself daydreaming about him but, well aware of his vow of celibacy, tried to restrain her thoughts. Jyoti's mother also observed the handsome young man from the ashram and sensed her daughter's budding feelings toward Devendra. Despite her deep respect for ashram life, she found herself wishing for a miracle: Devendra would be released from his vows and service to the master and marry her daughter. None of this escaped the notice of Cook or Swamiji.

Devendra had been in the ashram for nearly nine years. He had studied, meditated, worked in the kitchen, and received twice-daily darshan from his master. When someone becomes one with his divine nature, his presence embodies and radiates that reality to all around him. The term darshan refers to the gift of basking in the divine light of a fully realized teacher. Simply sitting with Swamiji enriched Devendra's awareness. Eliminating ignorance and all its complex causes and components can be a momentous task. However, just as turning on the light in a dark room instantly dispels the darkness there, turning on the student's inner light dissipates his or her inner darkness or confusion. Sitting in the divine light of *the master's presence ignites the disciple's inner light. Darshan is the enlightened person's silent, automatic blessing for the world.*

Daily life in the ashram followed a regular routine. In the morning, after meditation, chores, and breakfast, all the disciples gathered to sit with Swamiji. In the evening, he first gathered with the ashram students, then with the men of the village, and finally with the women. He sat in full lotus on a small wooden dais covered with a few cushions. Sometimes he spoke, and sometimes he kept his eyes closed and maintained total silence for the entire meeting. When the master became silent, all who gathered did the same. Everyone benefited from these meetings, but it was more apparent to some than to others. Those who could turn inward and surrender to their inner silence reaped richer fruits.

The master knows that everyone is pure awareness, a divine expression, but that most people see themselves in limited terms—qualities, goals, and possessions to which they are often strongly attached. From compassion, great masters make themselves available to help people transcend those limiting beliefs and wake up to eternal freedom. The master sits like the unbounded ocean, but the disciple must lay a pipeline to the ocean to receive its fullness.

Devendra, then approaching his twenty-fifth birthday, had benefited much from the ashram routine. He loved his master for his warmth, clear, gentle guidance, unconditional love, and unfailing wisdom. He loved Aseem the cook for his demanding yet compassionate nature. He would sharply shout his orders in the kitchen one moment and the next take Devendra aside with avuncular concern and give him the encouragement he needed to keep going.

Jyoti turned twenty-one that same year, and the fact that she was not married and still home with her parents was odd to say the least. She taught the younger children in the village school to read and write and looked after her aging parents. Swamiji had arranged both the opportunity to teach and the permission to put off marriage. He wanted all the village children to gain basic literacy. Although men and women had different roles in family life and society, Swamiji encouraged educational opportunities for everyone, reminding them that everyone was a child of God and equal in God's eyes.

Shortly after Jyoti was born, her parents brought her to the master for his blessing. He sat quietly with eyes closed and then recommended that her parents raise her with special love and attention. They should not work her too hard but rather help her learn to appreciate the beauty of the world. They should educate her and teach her to worship properly. When her father, Janek, asked when she should marry, the master informed them that she would not marry early and they should not arrange a marriage. The right husband would come at the right time.

Janek immediately began to object, but one look from his wife quieted him down. Swamiji softly reassured them, "You have brought a bright light into the world. Cherish her and all will be well."

This message gave her father the pride and strength he needed to resist the tradition of marrying his daughter off at the age of thirteen, the custom of the day. Her mother felt only joy to know that her daughter would stay with her for many years to come. Both parents doted on Jyoti while doing their best not to spoil her. They instilled in her a level of self-esteem unknown to most women born at that time and place. Jyoti proved to be gifted with intelligence, quiet happiness, and kindness. She was loving and caring to everyone in the village, irrespective of who they were, and she soon won many hearts. In time, people accepted her delay of marriage.

Jyoti's mother, Poona, taught her bright and inquisitive daughter not only to cook but also to heal and maintain balance and health through the use of food, spices, and herbal compounds meticulously described by Ayurveda, the five-thousand-year-old science of health and immortality. Aseem, an Ayurvedic expert, had generously taught Poona. With his vast knowledge and experience, he could have easily taken on the title of vaidya, but titles did not interest him. Being the ashram's cook was enough. Twice a week for many years, Poona spent two hours or more with Aseem. Her fondness for her humble teacher grew as she gratefully absorbed all the knowledge he shared, and the two grew very close over the years. She, in turn, taught other women in the village how to cure many common and serious ailments as time and circumstances allowed.

With the master presiding over the village, the inhabitants enjoyed peace and balance in their lives. Even the local raja was the master's disciple, and he felt genuinely responsible for the welfare of those he ruled. Harmony and comfort were the norm; the seasons and the rains came on time. On this small piece of earth, something close to heaven appeared to have descended.

However, change is one of life's only constants. Despite his love for Swamiji and ashram life and despite his spiritual progress, Devendra was becoming restless. His mind wandered, and he found himself remembering his family and wondering how they were doing. He also found himself thinking of Jyoti. She was so lovely and graceful. He kept these thoughts private, but the master and his faithful cook knew the young man's heart. In fact, they had long foreseen the love that was unfolding. The same destiny that had brought Devendra and his brother Balram to the master and the village was drawing Devendra and Jyoti together.

One day, Jyoti's father became seriously ill. All the medical wisdom of Poona and Aseem could not prevail against his fate. Janak died quietly one morning before dawn; his wife and daughter were beside themselves with grief. That evening, Swamiji gently reminded the women that the soul is eternal and they should not grieve too much.

Word of his death came to Janak's older brother, who was now entitled to inherit Janak's property. Jyoti and her mother became anxious. Would the brother force them from their home? Would he force Jyoti to marry? Whom would he choose for her husband? Would Jyoti and her mother be separated?

Poona brought her burdens to her trusted mentor Aseem. He listened with complete attention, not saying a word, as Jyoti's mother poured out her fears. Only after she finished did the cook gently take her hands in his and say, "There is no need to worry yourself sick over this. You still have many weeks of mourning to complete and rituals to perform for your dear husband's departed soul. The master will fix everything. He always does. He has that skill of silently persuading all parties to do the right thing. Just stay focused on the present moment, and handle each concern that arises with full awareness. Now go home and rest. You will see everything is as it should be."

Aseem took Poona's hands in his and encouraged her, like a parent with an infant, to stand up and walk. His eyes never left hers. She felt comfort from those eyes and strength from his hands. After a few minutes, she thanked him and began to walk to the eastern gate of the ashram and back home.

The cook had not held a woman's hand since he was a boy of twelve and said good-bye to his mother. He chuckled to himself as he strolled up to the master's small house. Krishnamurti sat writing in his front room when his friend knocked gently and entered. The cook sat quietly for a moment then suddenly broke the silence and told the story with his usual flourish. When he was done, he ended the tale as abruptly as he began it. Both men simply gazed at one another. Finally, the master said, "The situation is in God's hands, and he never lets down his devotees. Thank you, my friend, for bringing it to my attention."

The cook bowed from the waist, and the master in turn bowed his head to the cook. Aseem left, and as he crossed the courtyard, the master heard him softly singing a song of devotion to Mother Divine.

The next day, Swamiji sent Devendra to the school with a message for Jyoti. Devendra was excited for any excuse to see her, and he strode energetically through the town. He knew that the future was uncertain for both Jyoti and her mother. However, as a disciple, he could not get involved in their troubles. When he was just yards from the school, he saw Jyoti through the classroom window and stopped in his tracks. She looked radiant as she smiled encouragingly at her young students. He paused to watch her and listen to her sweet laughter drifting out the open *window, feeling as if he was in another world. Meekly he approached the door and knocked. Jyoti asked one of her students to open it, and there stood the handsome young brahmachari with a scroll in his hand. Devendra immediately came back to himself and smiled at all the children. "Good morning!" he greeted them.*

The class responded in unison, "Good morning!"

"What are you studying this morning?" Devendra asked.

"Teacher is reading us a story," came the reply.

"Oh, wonderful!" Devendra exclaimed. He moved purposefully toward Jyoti, holding out the scroll and informing her that he brought a message from the master.

Jyoti thanked him, took the scroll, broke the wax seal, and began to read it to herself.

"Dear one," she read, "please don't be concerned. All will be well. God is with you now and always." It was signed Krishnamurti.

She closed her eyes to thank God for her life and his blessing. When she opened them, she found herself looking directly at Devendra, whose eyes were filled with love. An eternity passed. Suddenly the children exploded with shouts and laughter, shaking Devendra and Jyoti out of their daze to find themselves at the front of the schoolroom. Despite their embarrassment, they could not hide their joy. They laughed with the children for a few seconds before Jyoti stirred and regained control of the class. Devendra announced that he needed to leave, and Jyoti thanked him for bringing the message.

The brahmachari left the one-room school accompanied by coos of delight and the enthusiastic clapping of small hands. Elated, Devendra ran the short distance back to the ashram, where he found his brother, Balram, in the kitchen preparing the noontime meal. He liked working in the kitchen, whereas Devendra merely endured it. Up to that moment, Devendra had lived to study the Veda, the ancient texts that were a virtual encyclopedia of creation, as well as a guide to enlightenment. Balram was dedicated to his meditation and the master but not to studying. When Devendra burst into the kitchen, all the workers looked up, curious about why he was so excited. Suddenly he became self-conscious and tried to hide his emotions. Balram, however, wasn't fooled by his brother's attempt to cover up.

"What god, or should I say goddess, have you just come across?" Balram questioned.

"Listen, let's go outside for a moment," Devendra said urgently.

Balram instructed the young chelas, "Stir the soup, and stir the butter gently with great love, and then let it settle and boil. But be careful to watch it. It must be removed from the flame at the precise moment. Remember what I have taught you about how to make ghee. You must only have kind, loving, and grateful feelings when cooking ghee. The butter is so sensitive that it absorbs your feelings as you cook. The ghee is much more beneficial if you tenderly stir your love into it."

Having completed his duty with the chelas, Balram turned back to Devendra and told him, "All right, brother, let's go outside and you can tell me your tale."

The minute that they were beyond the ears of the kitchen staff, Devendra, who was usually calm and reserved, blurted out passionately, "Balram, I'm in love with Jyoti! I just saw her at the school when I ran an errand for the master. Without intending it, we found ourselves lost in each other's eyes. I felt like something erupted inside me and flooded me with waves of ecstasy. I didn't know what to do. I ran back here. I've never felt this way before. I want to be with her, but I don't know what I'm saying."

"Wait! Wait! Be careful," Balram warned. "You are a brahmachari, a committed celibate. You are a disciple. You chose your life many years ago."

"No, our parents chose our life," Devendra argued.

"No. Though young, you wanted to do this. You wholeheartedly agreed to follow the master. You took vows and now you are bound," Balram corrected him.

"But, brother, isn't it our duty to dissolve what binds us?"

"Yes, and that is why we are here. We are breaking the bonds of ignorance so we can experience liberation. We are so fortunate to have a perfect master and this life," Balram insisted.

"I don't know what to do," Devendra agonized. "I feel such a stirring in my heart. Everything has changed. I'm not the same person I was when I woke up this morning."

"Get hold of yourself and let go of these disturbing emotions. Be calm and let's discuss this more later."

Suddenly a shout came from the kitchen: "The ghee! The ghee! It's ready! Balram, come quickly!"

Balram jumped up and ran inside to the cooking fire. One must know the precise moment to remove the butter from the fire to create ghee. Ghee is the foundation for both cooking and certain herbal medicines. It is a precious substance that nourishes both body and mind. Balram didn't want to lose the batch of ghee and the time he spent making it and face Aseem. He approached the boiling pot and saw the clear amber liquid. Taking the pot off the stove, he blessed the contents with a Sanskrit chant.

"You did well," he praised the chelas. "We'll let it cool, and then we'll carefully strain it."

Balram left the kitchen again and walked over to where his brother sat, sad and confused. He had never seen his brother look like that, and he realized the situation was serious. He put his hand gently on Devendra's shoulder and advised, "Talk to Aseem. He can help clarify this and give you the insight you need if anyone can."

"Maybe you're right. I'll approach him tonight before we sleep and ask him for his advice."

Later that evening, Devendra found Aseem. He pressed his hands together and bowed slightly. "Namasté," he said softly.

"Namasté," Aseem answered. He looked at the young man who held so much promise but now stood before him looking downtrodden. "Devendra, what has overtaken you?" he inquired with concern.

"I need your help. I feel shaken to the core, and it is making me sick and feverish though I have no illness."

"Tell me what has happened. Start from the beginning, and leave nothing out," Aseem responded kindly.

Devendra described in great detail his meeting with the master and the errand on which the master had sent him. He confessed his long-term interest in Jyoti and the fact that this troubled him quite a bit. Finally, he portrayed the errand's unforeseen result. When Jyoti and he found each other's hearts in their eyes, they surrendered fully. "I was absorbed in her," Devendra explained. "She was all I saw. I forgot everyone and everything, everything in the room and everything I had ever known. It was as if I had disappeared in the depths of her eyes. Seeing us like that, the children exploded with laughter like roaring tigers."

"Or like thunder perhaps," Aseem added.

Aseem knew the time had come and that the master had set the inevitable into motion. He addressed Devendra, "The best way to explain what happened to you is in relation to the monsoon."

"The monsoon?" Devendra, bewildered, cocked his head.

"Yes, the monsoon. You see, when Jyoti and you looked into each other's eyes, lightning struck. In a flash of brilliance, your heart revealed itself to you and to her. Then the thunder rolled—the children's laughter. Laughter from such innocent hearts is a good omen. Rain followed, and you were completely filled with joy. This was good, but soon flooding began and broke the dam. You felt overwhelmed. Your happiness vanished and panic set in—thus the confused state of mind in which you find yourself. I have seen this before. It's nothing new. Sometimes life changes in

an instant, and your life just did. Somewhere you know this, but the uncertainty and newness of it all have made you afraid. It's all understandable."

"I don't find any comfort in your words," Devendra protested. "My life hasn't changed. I've . . . I've taken vows that cannot be broken. I've vowed to serve my master and God. I've vowed to reach enlightenment and help humanity, to teach the Veda when the master says I'm ready. I've vowed to be celibate. My life can't change. I'm happy here." Devendra was practically shouting.

Aseem listened quietly. "All this is true. You have made certain vows to the master and God. However, neither God nor the master gains anything from their fulfillment. They do not need you to keep these vows. The vows are tools, meant to serve you. Chelas make vows to support their path to enlightenment. Their purpose is enlightenment. Even when life alters dramatically, the seeker finds a way to keep his vows and carry out their intent, which is to live in fulfillment. Heartfelt vows to God are always kept, and over time, life will provide opportunities for you to keep yours. No, in this case, you're not breaking your vows, just finding a different way to fulfill them."

"I still don't understand. What am I to do?" Devendra was almost in tears.

"The flood recedes with time, whether it is water or emotions. In time, all will become clear."

"What do I do until then?" he beseeched Aseem.

"Follow your heart. You may not know the way, but your heart does. Each soul knows its destiny. And naturally, continue to meditate."

"Oh, Aseem, how do I face the master? I don't know my destiny. I feel lost."

"No. I wouldn't say you're lost. We can only find our way one step at a time. For now, don't make any major decisions. Let your confusion recede. Go about your routine and be alert to your heart's knowing," Aseem counseled.

"What do I tell the master?" Devendra begged.

"Always tell the truth. He knows your heart better than you do, and he is wise and understanding. He is also very kind."

"Does he see the future?" Devendra pressed.

"What we do in this moment always creates the next. Each of us has many innate tendencies, many desires, and many influences. The confluence of these factors creates the content of this moment and the next moment and so on. All of this is surely beyond the capacity of my mind. After all, I'm just a cook," Aseem reminded Devendra.

Aseem continued, "Each of us is responsible for our own destinies. I think the master can see the tendencies of time, but they are just tendencies. Nothing is inevitable. Life's circumstances change as we grow and shed one layer of ignorance *after another. Perhaps I'm being too honest here with you, but I don't want you to think that the master is like a fortune-teller. Now it's time to retire. Rest well, and I think you'll find that the floods have receded in the morning and you'll see things more clearly."*

"Everything feels so uncertain. Everything is upside down," Devendra complained.

"Yes, my dear Devendra. The best stories always are," Aseem smiled encouragingly, got up, and departed for his room. He sang as he walked.

For her part, Jyoti was at peace. Her grief for her father and the concern for her mother had retreated into the background. She was no longer worried. She would not marry her aunt's cousin; she would marry Devendra. Of that she was certain.

However, it was not a certainty in her mother's mind. "Jyoti," Poona argued, "Devendra can't marry you. He is brahmacharya. This is no time for delusions. I must deal with your father's brother. He is ignorant, and his wife is more like a jackal than a human being."

"But, Mother, the master sent him to me. Why send Devendra? He could have sent anybody."

Poona stopped and sat down. "Yes, that was unusual. Well, he must have had a reason."

"Yes, he did. He wanted to give me a sign," Jyoti spoke confidently.

"It's funny. I met with Aseem yesterday," Poona revealed. "I hardly spoke. I cried more than talked. He took my hands and looked into my eyes, and I felt a great sense of peace. Before I left, he told me not to worry, that the master would take care of things. And today Devendra brought you a message."

Poona leaped to her feet and exclaimed, "Quickly! We must go to the temple and pray and make offerings to Krishna and Divine Mother."

Poona and Jyoti hurried out, both now sure that something good was unfolding.

Chapter 10:
All You Need Is Love

SAM AND AMY EMERGED HAND in hand from their flight from Switzerland. After the pristine beauty of the Alps, the effulgent atmosphere of the course, and the many hours spent in inner silence, the hustle and bustle of Logan Airport was startling. Everywhere they looked, people were moving about, greatly determined to win the race with time. Three months of rounding had imbued them with undisturbable inner stillness. They felt quiet but more alive than ever before.

The last thing either Sam or Amy wanted was to part ways, so they planned on meeting in Amherst in a few days. Sam needed to visit his folks and pick up his car in New York, and Amy's parents were home in Concord waiting for her arrival. From Logan Airport, they both jumped onto the train, or T, as Bostonians call it. Sam planned to take the T to the Back Bay Station and connect from there to an Amtrak train to New York. Amy called her folks and arranged to meet them at the Alewife Station. When Sam's stop was coming up, the two kissed passionately, and after a long embrace, they separated with reluctance. Sam barely made it off the train before the doors closed behind him.

He was on top of the world. How much his life had shifted! "Love, love, love. Love is all you need," the Beatles lyric played in his mind as he skipped and danced his way to the Amtrak ticket office. The ticket seller took one look at Sam's glowing face and said, "Honey, whatever you got, I want it." Sam caught the 10:15 am out of Boston and arrived at Penn Station by 1:30 pm. From there he took the subway downtown to the village. It was Sunday, so he knew Jimmy, Lilly, and Susan would be home.

Amy met her father at the Alewife Station and was home in Concord in twenty minutes. Her dad greeted her warmly, delighted she was back and satisfied that she would now settle down. He was relieved to see her dressed in a light linen suit and even wearing nylons. The initial evidence showed that she had not become a flower child despite her time with the bearded giggling teacher from India. Her mom was overjoyed to see her daughter looking so radiant and didn't notice much else.

After the homecoming celebration, both sets of parents felt their children looked a bit thin but also had to admit that they looked positively blissful. They didn't know yet that Sam and Amy were in love. If they did, it would explain all that luminosity to their satisfaction. This talk about consciousness and creating an ideal society was way beyond their way of thinking, so they didn't pay it much attention and simply dismissed it as the overzealousness of youth.

They couldn't fully grasp the light that their children emanated. To acknowledge that light would have strained their well-established beliefs about life and how it worked and opened up a gulf too wide to cross. Jimmy and Lilly noticed the light around Sam right off but didn't know what to make of it. Jimmy kept saying, "By god, Sammy boy, you look great! Much younger, and for Christ sakes, you're already young!"

When Lillian couldn't come to terms with a situation, she reverted to the basics. Her first comment was something like, "Jimmy, he's skin and bones! My god, didn't they feed you, Sam?"

Susan echoed, "Yeah, didn't they feed you?"

"Of course they fed us, and very well. And it looks like my darling little sister hasn't missed a meal since I left."

"No way, José. I haven't missed a single one," Susan proudly announced.

"I'm fine, though I admit I am a bit famished," Sam conceded.

"Well, you don't have to say it twice to convince me of that," Lillian declared. "From the look of you, you haven't had a proper meal in ages." With that, she headed into the kitchen and got busy cooking for her son.

Lillian was never happier than when she was in her element in the kitchen. As she cooked for Sam, she was so delighted that she started to sing. Sitting in the parlor with his son, Jimmy heard his wife singing in the kitchen and sank a little deeper into his chair with a smile on his face. Susan, ever the mimic, sat and smiled also.

"I'm so glad to have my boy home," Susan inserted.

"Good to be home, sis," Sam confirmed.

"Well, son, how were the Alps and that girl you hadn't kissed who likes to yodel?"

"She's not much of a yodeler, but she's a great kisser. I'm in love, Dad. I think this is it," Sam broke the news without hesitation.

Jimmy reacted with some alarm. "You don't want to rush into anything, son. That's a big commitment you're making."

"I'm not rushing into it," Sam protested. "I'm just in love. I feel so close to her. We agree on almost everything, but more than that, I feel so relaxed, so at ease with her. She's warm, beautiful, smart, and spiritual. Only problem I see is that she's a Red Sox fan."

"Oh well, that won't do. I'd end the whole thing right now if I was you," Jimmy said with a wink.

Sam thought about that and replied accordingly, "Yeah, gee, what was I thinking? I'd better call her," and he started for the phone and winked back at his father.

"On second thought," Jimmy philosophized, "there's probably not a chance in hell that they can win the pennant, let alone the World Series, in the next thirty years. By that time you'll be in your fifties, your marriage will be solid and secure and I'll be six feet under. No, I don't think the Red Sox are going to affect things too much." Both men laughed.

"I give up," said Susan, and she went into the kitchen to help her mom.

"Have you met her parents?" Jimmy asked.

"Yeah, Dad. They're real nice. Her father is a lawyer."

"Ah, that's too bad."

"And I don't think that he cares for me much," confided Sam.

"Well, Sam, I have a story about that," Jimmy mused.

"I'm sure you do." Sam grinned.

"You see, son, my father-in-law, your grandfather, God rest his soul, didn't exactly take a liking to me either." Sam had already heard this story numerous times, so he settled in for the retelling.

"Never gave me a look or the time of day, so it was an awkward moment when I had to ask him for your mother's hand in marriage. I was never so nervous before in my life. I quite remember pacing back and forth in front of your mother's two-family house over in Brooklyn. My god, it must have been more than an hour, walking back and forth. Lillian kept opening the window and asking me when I was coming in. I kept telling her to give me another five minutes. Meanwhile, the old man starts asking what the hell was going on. Lilly put him off for a while, but finally he was getting so upset about her dillydallying around the living room and calling out the window to me that he yelled, 'For Christ sakes, it's Sunday afternoon. I'm trying to relax, Lillian. What's going on?'

"She told him that I'd been outside for an hour and a half, too nervous to come in.

"'What the hell's wrong with that boy?' her father shouted.

"Well, Lillian told him that I was all nervous about asking him for her hand. The poor man was so stunned that his cigar almost fell out of his wide-open mouth. He had been reading the paper, so his hands just dropped on his lap. His only daughter stood there, a bit fearful, but also determined. He put the paper down, took the cigar out of his mouth, and put it in the ashtray. He then asked her in a calm voice if she wanted to marry him, meaning me.

"'Yes,' Lillian told him, with her whole heart. Lillian's mother, your grandmother, knew all about it, and she came into the living room looking smug and satisfied. He looked at her standing next to her daughter and knew the jig was up.

"Lillian told me her father asked a second time how long 'he,' meaning me, had been out there.

"'Almost an hour and a half,' your mother repeated, her foot tapping and her arms crossed in impatience.

"'All right, if he doesn't come in on his own in the next ten minutes, go out and tell him to come in and have supper with us. After we eat, we'll come out here and talk.'

"Your mother comes out to the porch and tells me, 'Pops has invited you in for supper, and you'd better not keep him waiting.' So I hustle in, say hello to everyone, and take a seat at the dining room table. Your grandfather didn't say much, but every once in a while, he would stare at Lillian and me sitting side by side. I thought later he was trying to imagine us married and all the nights, birthdays, and holidays we'd all be together sitting at the table, one big happy family. So he'd stare for a while and then he'd look back at his plate or take a drink. I started wondering if maybe he was as nervous as me in his own way.

"Finally the meal was over, and he turns to me and says, 'Come on in the other room. We've gotta talk.' I looked at Lil and then your grandmother, and they both nodded, like 'Go ahead, it will be fine.' So I did.

"We had a great talk. I was surprised. He even offered to help set me up in business. Naturally, he agreed to give me his daughter's hand in marriage.

Your grandfather was a smart man when it came to business. He was as smart as they come." Jimmy paused, looking almost embarrassed. "Ah, listen to me. If I've told you that story once, I've told it a dozen times."

"It's still a good story, Dad, and I don't ever get tired of hearing it," Sam reassured him.

"At the end of our talk, your grandfather says, 'I'm going out for a walk and to inspect my sidewalk. I hear you just about wore it out. I'll send you a bill for the damages.' Then of course, I realized he knew I'd been out there walking back and forth for almost two hours. When Lillian heard him leave, she came running up the hall, burst through the sitting room's swinging door, and ran into my arms.

"'What'd he say?' she asked excitedly.

"'He's checking for damages to the sidewalk,' I told her. I held her at arm's length and gave her a look that said, 'I know that he knows I was out there for hours and why I was out there. And he said yes. He also informed me in no uncertain terms that he expected me to take good care of his only daughter.

"Your grandmother, who always liked me, was beaming joy from the doorway. 'I'll put the tea kettle on,' she said and was off to the kitchen."

Suddenly Jimmy's story, heard so often before, took on unexpected significance in Sam's mind. He found himself contemplating how he would approach Amy's father on the subject and was not totally at ease with it. His mother called them for supper, rescuing him from further imaginings.

Meanwhile, Amy was riding home in the car with her father, looking out the window fondly and appreciatively at her neighborhood as they drove the short way to town. It was as if she was seeing Concord for the first time. She loved the tall, thickly-leaved, long-standing trees embracing Concord's homes with all their history. She felt grateful to her parents for giving her the privilege of growing up in this special place.

The car pulled up to the driveway, and her mom was out the door and waiting on the porch to greet her. Her dad popped opened the trunk and grabbed her bags.

She was thrilled to be home. She told them over lunch how amazing the course was, how Sam had ended up attending as well, and finally, that she was in love with him. Her mom gasped inwardly, and her dad sighed outwardly.

"You're in love with that student you met just before you left?" her father questioned just to cover his shock. "What about Gregory?"

"I ended our relationship before I left. We had a good talk, and I think he knew it was coming. Our goals are so different."

"Why?" her father continued as if he hadn't heard her brief explanation. "He's a catch, as they say. He has an excellent career ahead of him as a litigator, comes from a fine family, and he's good-looking. What's not to like?"

"But I'm not in love with him," Amy asserted flatly.

"Darling, she's not in love with him," Amy's mother repeated pointedly.

"What's love got to do with it?" Ed almost shouted. "Gregory's a good man, an excellent man, and would make a fine son-in-law."

"Yes, he is a good person. I'm sure he'll make a fine husband and a good son-in-law for someone, just not me," Amy countered firmly, strangely unmoved by her father's reaction. She felt so still and sure inside.

"Yes, dear, after all, Amy is the one who would have to marry Gregory, not you. You might be very pleased with the idea of Amy and Greg, but Amy is in love with Sam," Mary stated strongly, looking directly at her husband.

"But what does Sam have to offer? His family has a bagel store in Greenwich Village. He may or may not get a PhD in philosophy. He may or may not get hired as an assistant professor in a small college in Kansas or someplace like that. Greg's family is established. His father is a CPA with a large firm in Boston. His wife is on the board of directors at the MFA. This is a family to marry into," Ed argued as if he was litigating.

"First of all, Dad, it's a bakery café, not a bagel store, and secondly, Maharishi thinks Sam is special," Amy countered.

"Maharishi thinks Sam is special? And that's it? So we're suddenly off to the altar because Maharishi thinks Sam's special?" her dad asked incredulously.

"No, Dad. I think he's special. Sam's kindhearted, exceedingly smart, and he will be very successful."

"Darling, I think you're getting upset over nothing. Amy's just gotten home. She's tired. I'm sure this will all work out fine. Did you have enough to eat, Amy?" her mother interceded.

"Yes, Mom," Amy said, quite content to change the subject.

"Good. Let's get your things upstairs, and you can tell me all about it. Ed, darling, would you be a dear and clear the table?" As Amy excused herself, Mary raised her eyes to her husband and, glaring, shot off a warning: "You best be careful, mister. You are on thin ice."

Three days later, Amy was driving along Route 2 west back to Amherst and her apartment. Sam was simultaneously heading north, picking up I-91 to Route 9 east through Hadley, and heading to Amy's place. When he arrived, Amy had been home only a couple of hours. Incense was burning; candles were lit. She was waiting for him in shorts and a Red Sox T-shirt. Her long blond hair was flowing and golden in the late afternoon light. They kissed gently at first, and then passion began to build. Sam, a little out of breath, muttered, "This T-shirt must go. A Sox tee? I don't know if I'm ready to join another team."

Amy replied, "You've already been traded, buster." And then she pulled off her shirt.

"My God, Amy, you're beautiful," Sam gasped.

"And you're mine, Sam O'Connor." She took his hand and led him into her bedroom where they made love and fell asleep exhausted.

In late August 1974, soon after Sam completed his PhD, Sam and Amy married. They held the ceremony in a farmer's field outside of Amherst. Sam's family had expected to be standing in a church, as had Amy's. However, rather than negotiate which denomination would govern the ceremony— Catholic or Unitarian—Sam and Amy resolved to marry in the beauty of the outdoors. Amy's minister, Reverend John Cole, presided, along with Father Mike Sullivan, who came up with the O'Connors from the city.

Amy was dazzlingly lovely in a white gown that flowed gracefully to her ankles. Delicate lace and beadwork covered the bodice and hemline, and a wreath of fragrant white gardenias crowned her head and held back the veil. Sam was dressed in a beige linen suit with a light blue silk shirt and tie.

Kenny, also formally decked out except for his sneakers, stood up for Sam. As part of the ceremony, he read the last verse of Walt Whitman's "Song of the Open Road."

"Camerado, I give you my hand! I give you my love more precious than money, I give you myself before preaching or law; Will you give me yourself? will you come travel with me? Shall we stick by each other as long as we live?"

When Sam and Amy were pronounced husband and wife, they kissed tenderly. Both mothers began to cry; both fathers sought one another out and shook hands. Jimmy began to weep and hugged Ed as if they were long-lost brothers.

Having completed the ceremony, the newlyweds, along with their families and friends, drove over to the Lord Jeffery Inn for the reception. Sam and Amy danced as if there was no tomorrow. They also made the rounds to all the tables and received everyone's well-wishes. Jimmy and Ed got good and drunk and started talking to each other in louder and louder voices as late afternoon proceeded into early evening. Fortunately, they had rooms at the inn. With the help of their wives, the two fathers stumbled up the stairs to their respective rooms and into bed.

Lillian and Mary thrived on every minute of the day: the moving ceremony that the couple helped to write; Father Mike singing and playing his guitar; the soft late-summer sunlight; the maple trees, thick and green, rustling in the wind. Lillian reflected to herself that only God in all his goodness could have created this exquisite day, and only God could have brought her Sam and Amy together.

Mary was overjoyed for her daughter, and she loved Sam. She couldn't have been happier with her new son-in-law. They were such a striking couple; it was obvious they belonged together.

Sam and Amy had the inn's suite for their first night together as a married couple. They slipped into their own world, a cocoon of love, a realm of mutual adoration. As they lay naked and entwined, they heard the rain begin, gently at first, and then more steadily. A unity had settled over them; the two had become one. Without speaking, both felt as if they had entered heaven. Though they didn't know it, the angels all around them agreed. Eventually they drifted off to sleep, wrapped in each other's arms.

When morning broke, the rain had ended. Only a few wispy clouds remained, and they dissipated in the full sunshine of day. Sam and Amy awoke fresh and rested; the air around them felt pure and vibrant. Heaven had not vanished while they slept. They made love, not with the previous night's passion, but with great tenderness. They showered, meditated and dressed, and went down to the dining room for breakfast.

Father Mike, Jimmy, Lilly, Susan, Ed, and Mary had already found their way to the breakfast table and were drinking coffee and talking among themselves. Amy and Sam walked over to them with expansive smiles, kissing and greeting each person. Jimmy and Father Mike relished their kisses from Amy. Jimmy remembered his romantic side that flourished in his youth, and Father Mike allowed himself to recall the path not taken just for an instant. There were shared exclamations on the perfection of the previous day's events. As breakfast began to arrive, Father Mike offered a prayer.

"Oh, Lord, we thank you for the blessings of this day. We thank you for bringing Sam and Amy together in holy matrimony. We thank you for bringing these families together to share in all the good times and to support one another through the times when they will be tested. These two families have been united through love. May you, Father, strengthen that love and union, and may they all be in harmony with one another and with thee, forever and ever. Amen."

"Amen," the group affirmed.

"Forever and ever," echoed Susan.

"I was afraid, Father, that if you had kept going, me eggs were going to be getting cold, and I don't like me eggs cold," Jimmy turned up his best Irish accent.

"All right, Jimmy, I knew what you were thinking, so I kept it short and sweet," Father Mike responded in kind.

"You're a good man, Father. An extra blessing on you," Jimmy toasted, and the table erupted in laughter.

"Why aren't you taking your bride to Ireland?" Father Mike asked Sam.

"Well, we just came back from over the pond, and we thought a pleasant drive through New England and up into Canada would be nice."

"Yes," added Amy, "Dad and Mom suggested Quebec and staying at Chateau Frontenac."

"Well, I've never been," Father Mike owned, "so I can't give an opinion one way or the other."

"Father Mike, not knowing the subject at hand has never stopped you from giving your opinion before," Jimmy submitted with a twinkle in his eye. "I mean no disrespect, but where have you been besides New York and Dublin?"

"You're a fine one to talk, Jimmy. At the café that Lillian runs, Jimmy is known as the Opinionator. Isn't that the truth, Lil? And I don't recall you being a world traveler. In fact, I'd go as far as to venture this is the first time you've been out of the city in a dozen years."

Lilly jumped in, "Oh, but, Father, Jimmy complains of gas pains whenever he flies. That last trip to Ireland, my God, I had to listen to him for two days."

"Now that's a helluva of a thing to be talking about in front of our new family," Jimmy objected. "Besides, a few Guinness's usually take care of that. No, I generally like traveling. It's the business that ties me down."

"Well," Mary ventured, "Ed and I love France. The countryside, the wine, and my goodness, the food—and Paris! I just adore Paris—the Louvre, the outdoor cafés. You know what they say about Paris in the spring!"

Ed cleared his throat. "Yes, France is wonderful, but Quebec, particularly Old Quebec, has a similar ambiance. We first explored Quebec before we went to France, and we loved it. Since then, we've made six trips to France over the last eight years," he stated with some pride.

"Well, you must really like the place," Jimmy commented, genuinely impressed. "I'll tell you what. We'll take you folks to Ireland, and you take us to France. What do you say, Ed?"

The offer took Ed by surprise, but he managed to return, "Yes, fine, Jim. We'll do that."

There was a brief pause as the rest of the wedding party sat quietly, trying to imagine this foursome traveling together. Amy and Sam exchanged a dubious glance.

Not wanting to exclude his priest, Jimmy continued, "And, ah, Father Mike, you should come with us too. Having an Irish priest with you in Ireland assures you of good service and the best seats anywhere. It's like traveling with royalty, if you know what I mean, Ed, or like a good-luck charm."

"Ah, Jimmy, you're always the one I can count on to reduce me down to one of the little people, a good-luck charm indeed," Father Mike protested.

"Oh, Father, he's just playing with you," Lillian added for the Sanders' benefit. "You probably already guessed that the two of them are referring to Ireland's magical wee people, the leprechauns. They're a legend that never leaves us, and they bring good luck."

"Yes, I've heard of them," Ed said, raising an eyebrow and wondering what this marriage had gotten him into.

Sam changed the subject. "As you all know, I've been hired at Amherst College as an assistant professor, and," Sam reminded the gathering, "Amy and I will start looking for a house next summer. We're envisioning an old farmhouse outside of town. We'll be putting the gifts you gave us towards the down payment. So thank you, Mom and Dad, Ed and Mary. It will really help."

Amy quietly looked at her parents and said, "Thank you, Mom. Thank you, Dad." She thanked Jimmy and Lilly as well.

"So we need to get packed and ready to hit the road. Thank you, all, for making this celebration possible," Sam shared from his depths and eased his chair from the table.

"Yes, thank you for all the help in making our wedding day so completely fantastic," Amy added.

"Amen to that," Father Mike chimed in.

"Hallelujah," offered Susan.

Kenny strolled into the dining room. "Good morning, everyone," he said. "Trust everyone slept well?"

"Hey, Kenny boy!" exclaimed Jimmy. Jimmy had a fatherly love for his son's childhood friend. "Come join us. I'll find the waitress and get you some coffee."

"So how're the love birds doing this morning?" Kenny inquired.

"Just grand, Kenny. We're off to Quebec shortly."

"I'll hold the fort down here. Don't you worry," which confused everyone except Sam.

"Good man. I knew I could count on you."

"You've been counting on me for more than this lifetime."

"Yes, I owe you big-time."

Finally, Jimmy said, "What the hell are you guys talking about? For Christ sakes! Pardon me, Father," Jimmy added softly.

Kenny and Sam just smiled.

Amy spoke up, "Dad, it's just something they do. A leftover from childhood, I think."

Sam and Kenny laughed. Ed frowned and Lillian prayed. Susan smiled and said, "I love them both just the same."

Father Mike had the final word. "You boys haven't changed much since the fifth grade. Don't worry, Amy, they're harmless."

'Thanks, Father Mike. I'm sure you're right." Amy smiled weakly.

Everyone stood to leave except for Jimmy and Kenny. "I'll sit with ya, Kenny, whilst you eat your breakfast."

"Good of you, Jimmy, good of you."

"So how's the café? How many cases of cups are you going through in a month?"

Father Mike, Jimmy, Lillian, and Susan traveled back to New York together. Ed and Mary drove back to Concord. Sam and Amy, with the open road before them, headed north on I-91 to Montreal and from there on to Quebec.

Sam and Amy savored every minute of their honeymoon. They made love, ate fine French food, explored old Quebec, attended chamber and bluegrass concerts, visited museums and galleries, and dreamed together of the days to come. They both felt more alive than ever before and open to the abundant gifts each moment held. Without knowing why, they knew they were blessed, and for that, their gratitude knew no bounds.

Chapter 11:
The Magic of the Moment

AS A NEW ASSISTANT PHILOSOPHY professor at Amherst College, Sam taught Introduction to Philosophy and Ethics 101 to the incoming freshmen. The classes were big, with around forty students each. They were required courses, so many students took them in their first year to get them out of the way. However, most students hadn't had a teacher like Sam before. He brought an energy with him that was both disarming and engaging, and his teaching inspired dynamic discussions, an unexpected bonus for many of the students. Attendance was unusually good. One month into the semester, word got back to the dean of faculty about the student enthusiasm in Sam's classes. Intrigued, the dean asked him out to lunch.

"I hear things are going well," Dean Griffin began. Before he became dean of faculty, Griffin had been a comparative literature professor for twenty years and department chair for seven. He loved the college and felt honored to be one of its deans. He saw the role of educator as hallowed and singularly important work.

"Nothing is more important than educator, nothing. The transformational power of education is truly miraculous," the dean often stated. He was interested in Sam for many reasons, but most of all, because he knew Sam would be a brilliant teacher. He had recognized Sam's gifts, even during the first interview.

"It's early in the semester, but things are going well. The students are coming to class, so that's a start." Sam laughed.

"Yes, that a good start, all right," the dean joined him.

"And we're having some good, lively discussions," Sam added.

"Excellent! I know the first year can be challenging. The students have high expectations of their professors. These are bright young men and women and future leaders in their respective fields. So I'm pleased to hear talk of such a positive reaction to you and your teaching."

"Thank you. It's nice of you to tell me this." Sam hesitated before he continued. "Dean Griffin, I've been thinking about a course I'd like to teach that synthesizes Eastern and Western philosophy, based on their shared foundation in what I'll call Being. I think we can discover their commonalities by looking at their source. We can explore unifying aspects of Plato's Forms and the East's understanding of pure consciousness, Martin Buber's I-Thou relationship, and the Vedic state of enlightenment, and so on. Students these days are tremendously interested in meditation, higher states of consciousness, and enlightenment, and Western philosophy has something to offer in this area. It's all there in Western thought—it's actually the foundation. However, we've overlooked it for a long time, centuries. I think there is a way to do this that will be both stimulating and academically sound. I've been working on a series of lectures."

"It sounds like an interesting idea," Dean Griffin interjected. "What does Frank think? As the chair, you'd have to get his support for this to be considered."

"I haven't spoken to him yet. I thought I'd run it past you first," Sam explained.

The dean sat for a moment thinking it over. Normally, he wouldn't consider getting involved this early on in the process and most especially with a new assistant professor. On the other hand, he realized that he had an unusually promising young man sitting before him.

"Sam, why don't you drop off the first two lectures along with an outline of the course, and I'll look it over. I will get back to you next week. Sound okay?"

"Absolutely! Thank you! I'll do that," Sam responded with a mix of relief and exhilaration.

"If I like what I see, I'll have a word with Frank, sort of clear the way," the dean offered.

"Great! Thanks again. I'm excited about this, and well, the department hasn't offered a new course in a number of years. I don't know how they'll feel about my venturing forth with this idea at this point, but I think it's timely, and I think the students would be enthusiastic. It might interest faculty members as well."

"All right. I'm looking forward to reading your work. Now, what about lunch and telling me about that lovely wife of yours?"

Dean Griffin was impressed with the thoroughness and scholarship of Sam's initial efforts. He arranged to meet with Frank Barnes, the head of the philosophy department, and told him how the course had come up in his lunch meeting with Sam. "Sam just spilled it out. He was too excited to hold back. It was quite innocent. I'm sure he'd have come to you first if I hadn't asked him to lunch."

"Maybe. Anyway, I guess no foul, no harm."

Frank Barnes was a man of sharp intellect, but also a man of heart. He had been instrumental in Sam's hiring and consistently supported him. It was unusual that a first-year assistant professor would attempt to originate a new course, but Sam obviously had a passion for the subject.

Frank invited Sam to a meeting where Sam outlined his ideas. Frank made a couple of organizational recommendations, but all in all, he was impressed. He arranged an opportunity for Sam to present his concept to his colleagues at the next department meeting.

Afterward, Frank and Dean Griffin got together to talk.

"I was truly impressed by the scope of Sam's thinking and the preparation he's put into this new course," Frank observed.

"Yes, definitely impressive," Dean Griffin concurred. "I think he'll get the support from the other department members. However, I'm a little troubled by the lab fee—seventy-five dollars for learning Transcendental Meditation—and the fact that it goes to an outside organization, even a nonprofit. I may have to get our legal department to look into that."

"I thought about the legal aspect too, but I do see the significance of the idea. Include real experience, not just intellectual knowledge," Frank remarked then added, "the department is meeting next Wednesday at four o'clock, in case you want to stop by."

"Well, that's good of you to put it on the agenda, and thanks for the invitation. I will definitely join you. I'm curious to hear what the department members think."

It was therefore no surprise to Frank Barnes when Sam walked into the conference room with Dean Griffin, and their entrance had the effect the Dean anticipated. The faculty members sat up a little straighter, and the gathering acquired an air of greater formality. Drs. Frank Barnes, Janet Smith, Henry Watson, and Robert Harris exchanged pleasantries with the latest arrivals. Frank introduced Sam's idea for a new course and asked him to make a brief presentation to the group.

Sam was more than eager to share his proposal but knew he needed to strike a detached, professional tone to be taken seriously. His nervousness surprised him as he looked around the table at the familiar and intellectually distinguished audience.

Sam began, "The course I'm developing will explore the commonalities of Eastern and Western philosophy based on both knowledge and experience of a field of pure Being. This field of Being, as I choose to call it, is the source of thought, and therefore knowledge, but intriguingly, has no content within itself. We could describe it as a field of pure, infinite potential. Certainly, any number of Western philosophers have insisted that if we are awake or conscious, we must be conscious of something. Yet Eastern philosophy and some important Western thinkers, including Plato, have described an alternative understanding: it is possible to experience a state of pure inner wakefulness, to wipe the mental slate clean of content, and to experience the very consciousness, in and of itself, without which we could not be conscious of anything."

Sam was quiet for a few seconds, allowing the abstract concepts to sink in. He drew a breath and went on. "I want to compare and contrast Eastern and Western understandings of this transcendent reality and discover their commonalities, assuming they have some. The old refrain, 'East is east and West is west, and never the twain shall meet,' may be true on some levels, but on the level of the preconceptual source or Being, I believe that the differences dissolve. I suspect we'll find confirmation of this in both streams of knowledge."

Sam paused again, this time to hand out some printed sheets. "Here's the first lecture, course outline, and reading list. As you can see, instead of a textbook, we'll use selected readings from various sources, East and West. You'll also see that I've included a lab fee of seventy-five dollars to learn Transcendental Meditation, something I consider essential to the success of the course. We'll have a ten-minute group meditation at the beginning of every class. The students will discuss, read, and think about Being. However, most importantly, they'll experience Being, and that part will make all the difference."

Dr. Robert Harris had earned his PhD at the University of Chicago, and Amherst's philosophy department had hired him just two years earlier as an assistant professor. Bob was intellectual, energetic, and not afraid to state his opinion.

"Make all the difference?" Bob Harris asked with an incredulous tone that was not lost on the group. "What does that mean? How can you presume your students are going to experience Being? My God, if it's that easy, why isn't the whole world experiencing Being? And aren't you getting dangerously subjective? Are we contemplating navels here, or are we at a world-renowned college studying serious subjects?"

Before Sam could answer, Frank Barnes interjected, "Well, Bob, honestly, my first reaction was somewhat similar to yours. However, after careful study and reflection, I think introducing meditation into a class and making a serious study of Being from the Eastern and Western point of view is a brilliant and timely idea. From what I've learned, TM is not a religion, doesn't impose any heavy baggage of beliefs, and doesn't require any lifestyle changes. Sam himself has been using TM for five years now, I believe."

Sam cleared his throat and clarified, "Actually, it's closer to seven."

"In any case," Frank resumed, "students are, in large, part searching for new answers, and if this meditation feels relevant to their young lives, all the better."

"I see," Bob Harris mused. "Next we'll be introducing astrology and its relevance to the ancient and contemporary world." Coming on the heels of the chairman's endorsement, the remark was followed by an uncomfortable silence.

Dean Griffin spoke up, "Bob, to be honest, I agree with Frank. I've considered it at length and made some inquiries. I know we sprang this on you without warning, and you haven't had the time to review Sam's lectures and course materials."

Having attempted to relieve some of Dr. Harris' concerns, Dean Griffin turned to the group. "Now, we have a responsibility to our students after all. It wouldn't be right to offer something that was a far cry from our academic standards or destabilizing for that matter. However, I've looked into it and also had the school's attorney look into it," the dean revealed. "The TM teaching organization, the Students' International Meditation Society, checks out as a nonprofit educational organization. Some serious scientific research on TM has been conducted, and the results are remarkable and promising. Students practicing TM apparently improve their grades; score higher in moral reasoning; have less stress, greater mental clarity, and higher self-esteem; and voluntarily stop or reduce alcohol and drug use, even cigarettes. The college's attorney has signed off, and I've even had a discussion with the president. He has also agreed to give the course a go. Naturally, we'll be observing and monitoring."

After the dean's statement, any misgivings Henry and Janet had were laid to rest, and both concurred it all sounded fine to them. Bob did what he could to hide his jealousy and embarrassment, but of course, it was obvious to all present. Sam, less than two months into his first semester of teaching, had already created a new course and won the dean's and the department chair's approval—and their full blessing.

"Well, I guess it's done then," Bob Harris conceded. "I expect only majors will be allowed to take the course?"

"Yes," Sam agreed. "The material they'll discuss and the commitment they'll need will require the students to be serious."

"So, for whatever it's worth, I support the idea but suggest this course have a formal review at its completion," concluded Dr. Harris.

In February 1976, Sam began teaching his course, From Here to Here: The Pathless Path to Being, to sixteen students. To say that the course went well would be a huge understatement. To say the course was timely would be a grave disservice to Mother Nature. The course was life altering for the students who took it, and word spread around campus that this course was a must-take. In the fall, 124 students signed up, much to the displeasure of the registrar. The philosophy faculty, the dean, and the unhappy registrar all met to see what to do. Sam welcomed the idea of adapting the course for a larger group. He would need at least three students from the last class to act as TAs, and of course, he would need the auditorium in Converse Hall.

"But what about the non majors who want to take the class?" the registrar pressed.

Sam replied, "With the dean's permission, it would be okay with me. Besides, we could use a few new majors in the department." He was convinced that after taking his course, inspired students would sign up with the philosophy department. This idea did not exactly go over well with Henry, Janet, and Bob, but they couldn't argue. The formal review had satisfied them on the course's academic merits, but the philosophy department had never had a rising star in their midst before, and it was unsettling to some of them, most particularly Bob Harris.

Chapter 12:
The Course

SEPTEMBER 7TH ROLLED AROUND, AND classes began. The students had arrived over Labor Day weekend when the cooler air already hinted at the fall weather to come. The campus that had been so quiet over the summer was now teeming with life.

Sam left the farmhouse earlier than usual to be ready for his class on consciousness and meet with his four teaching assistants. They were all philosophy majors and had taken Sam's class during the spring semester. Dan, Jim, Shelly, and Elizabeth, who had changed her name to Ananda over the summer, were waiting for him when he arrived at his office. They extended a hearty welcome to their mentor and exchanged hugs as they celebrated their reunion.

Sam sat down at his desk and asked each of them how they were. He also wanted to know how their meditation was going and whether they had any questions. All briefly described their meditation experiences as Sam listened with full attention. When they were finished, he simply said, "Very good. We'll meet on Wednesday afternoons at two fifteen right here in my office. We'll have a chance to discuss your meditation experiences, the upcoming course, and anything else you might want to talk about. I appreciate your willingness to work as TAs this semester. Each of you will lead two different hour-long discussion groups, with fifteen to sixteen students weekly. One group will meet Monday and the other on Friday. You'll also be expected to attend the classes on Tuesdays and Thursdays, from ten fifteen to twelve thirty. It's going to be a great class, and I'm sure you'll get even more out of it this year than last. Here's the course syllabus. Look it over and get familiar with it. You'll notice a few changes from last year. Okay! Let's head over to the lecture hall and set up."

Converse Hall held a large amphitheater-style lecture hall with 180 seats. One hundred and twenty-four students had signed up for the fall class. As the morning progressed, the students began to file into the hall, and a mounting crescendo of voices filled the air. After greeting several students who came up to the stage, Sam walked over to the lectern and fastened his microphone to his shirt. The TAs were all seated in the first row. Ananda was smiling—no, beaming at Sam. Sam acknowledged her with a faint smile and nod.

"Welcome. Welcome. Please find a seat so we can get started. That's right, find a seat. Don't be shy. Come down and fill in the front seats. This is not the class where you want to sit in the back row. That's right. Move down. Good."

Sam began the first talk. "You may have heard from last semester's students that this course is unusual. In fact, you might be tempted to call this class the Magical Mystery Tour." A wave of giggling spread through the room. "We'll be going into some of the most powerful, influential, and sacred texts that human culture has ever produced. We'll discuss concepts that were the foundation for major civilizations and religions. Finally, we'll explore the inner worlds of mystics, masters, and saints."

One student raised his hand and asked, "With all of this, we only earn three credits?" More laughter echoed through the hall.

"Technically, you will only earn three college credits, but cosmically, you will earn great renown. Good karma credits all around, I can assure you." More laughter ensued.

"By studying several Eastern wisdom traditions, we're going to discover some underlying unifying principles that our Western traditions of knowledge also have as their basis although they have been obscured for hundreds if not thousands of years. We'll look at Jesus and Buddha as teachers and philosophers rather than as founders of religions. We'll read Lao-tzu, Plato, Shankara, Plotinus, Meister Eckhart, Maharishi Mahesh Yogi, William Blake, Walt Whitman, Ralph Waldo Emerson, Henry David Thoreau, and others.

"In addition, you'll all learn Transcendental Meditation next week, thus your lab fee. TM will allow you to enliven the full potential of your mind and become familiar with more expansive levels of your own consciousness quite effortlessly. You'll open to the transcendental source of thought at the foundation of your mind, an experience that is essential for you to connect with the minds of history's most important thinkers. You'll be meditating twice a day on your own for twenty minutes, and we'll start each class and your small discussion group with a ten-minute meditation—hence, I request that you enter the hall quietly in the future.

"The schedule for your TM course is posted at the back of the hall. You'll attend two introductory lectures, one session of individual instruction, and three follow-up meetings, all on consecutive days. The two introductory lectures will take place in this hall. The personal instruction will take place at the TM center on Lincoln Avenue, and the three follow-up meetings will take place in your small-group meeting rooms. Meditating twice a day is essential to get the most out of this course for which you all so eagerly signed up. This will become clearer to you in the days to come.

"Let me introduce our four TA's: Dan Keller, James Farber, Shelly Perkins, and Ananda Smith. Each of you will be in a discussion group with one of them. Rest assured that they are all gems. They all took this course last spring and are cosmic in nature. So are all of you, so don't trouble yourselves with any thoughts to the contrary. The only difference is they already know it and you will soon know it." Smiles and laughter swept the room one more time.

"Enough organizational chitchat. I see many hands have gone up already. All questions will be answered in time. Many of them are answered in your syllabus, which the TAs will start handing out." Sam paused and nodded to the TAs, who began to distribute the booklets.

"I assure you that none of you will be left behind if you keep to the rules of the game. And what are the rules? Come to class on time so you can enjoy the group meditation. Meditate twice a day. Do the readings. Come to your discussion groups on time and participate in them. Ask questions. Don't waste time. Learn to focus on what's happening in the moment. Simple and straightforward enough? All right, let's begin, shall we?

"Ontology, the study of Being, is one part of the study of philosophy. This course is a course on Being, and we are going to look at Being from many angles or points of view. By practicing the TM technique, you'll come to know Being directly. The focus of this class is knowledge and experience. Real progress in life and study requires both. Reading or discussing the *Tao Te Ching* or Plato's dialectic without also practicing TM would be a waste of our time, and none of us can afford to waste time.

"Merely studying the writings listed in the syllabus without actually experiencing Being is like studying the shadows on the walls of Plato's cave without ever knowing their source. While we can certainly gain some value from intellectual inquiry alone, it is a small fraction of what is available and has far less ability to transform our lives. Yet the works of men like Plato and Lao Tzu are nothing if not life changing. Their teachings were not purely intellectual. Both men were intimate with the field of infinite Being; both directly experienced infinite Being within their own awareness. Once you begin to experience Being, or pure consciousness as Maharishi calls it, you will open to the full transformative magic of their wisdom.

"The field of Being has no content and therefore no qualities. Words cannot describe it. We cannot know anything about it. We can only become it, merge with it, and be it. The Taoists say that the Tao that can be described is not the eternal Tao. 'Water cannot wet it, fire cannot burn it, a cleaver cannot cut it.' Why? Because the Tao or Being is transcendental to creation. It lies beyond speech, feelings, and even the finest level of thought. Yet we can each find Being in the depths of our own awareness, as the source of thought and all creation. Pure consciousness, or PC, just is. Being just is—infinite, self-sufficient, pure existence.

"Words cannot capture Being, but words are what we have to work with, so they'll have to do. Notice the large scrolls of paper and colored markers here and there around the lecture hall. Each class we'll have a ten-minute share. What I mean by that is, when you come across a quote in your readings you like, I want you to stand up and share it. Describe what resonates with you and why. If any more of you resonate with those words, please stand up and explain as well. Then the whole class will decide if that quote should be written on the scroll and hung up. By the way, last semester, with just twenty-four students, we lined the walls with 120 quotes. It was very powerful.

"So this Tuesday and Thursday, we'll meet here for the lectures on TM, at the end of which you'll schedule your appointment for private instruction with a teacher, and that will happen on either Saturday or Sunday. Then you'll have three additional consecutive nights of instruction in small groups, about thirty per group. This will be your homework for the beginning of next week.

"The packet handed out by the TAs contains the list of course materials, some of which you'll need to buy at the bookstore. Start reading the excerpts from the *Tao Te Ching* and Maharishi Mahesh Yogi's *The Science of Being and Art of Living* for next Tuesday. No other homework until then. See you tomorrow for the lecture.

"I promise that if you meditate regularly, that is, twice a day, and you stay focused during the lectures, which I guarantee will be absolutely brilliant," Sam said with a smile as a ripple of laughter filled the hall, "and if you do the reading and participate in the group discussions, the class will be very transformational. As with the microcosm, so with the macrocosm. As you go, so does the universe. Maharishi likes to say, 'The world is as we are.' I see a question has arisen. Pray tell us."

"Dr. O'Connor. You've mentioned Maharishi a couple of times. Who is he?"

"Good question. Maharishi is a contemporary teacher and philosopher. In the Vedic tradition of India that he represents and teaches, he is considered a *rishi* or seer. *Maha* means great, so he is a great rishi or seer and embodies the pinnacle of that tradition. Maharishi has revived the knowledge that the experience of pure consciousness is meant to be a natural part of everyone's life, not something fantastic or just for a few spiritually gifted people. Through the TM technique and its absolute simplicity, he has made it possible for anyone and everyone to experience their infinite source and live in fulfillment. It may sound implausible today, but by next week at this time, it will seem more credible. We'll read some of his writings as well.

"The rishis of old were the scientists of their day, and they gave humanity techniques that support our capacity to live our full—which is infinite— potential. *Enlightenment* is, of course, a word commonly used to describe this state. Maharishi sometimes points out that since pure consciousness is already within us, a part of us, it should not be difficult to experience. Hence, the TM practice is totally effortless."

"Is this a course in enlightenment?" one student queried.

"Yes and no," Sam responded. "This is a course on Being and an attempt to reconcile the Eastern and Western approaches to Being. It also includes a meditation practice, which, if continued and used regularly, can lead to enlightenment. We'll explore various traditions and their views on enlightenment or human fulfillment towards the end of the course, so stay tuned. There will be a pop quiz," Sam said with a smile. "Another question?"

"There's a rumor going around that you're a disciple of Maharishi and you're enlightened. Is it true?"

"I have studied with Maharishi, and he is a most extraordinary man. However, when Maharishi was asked how many followers he had, he replied, 'I have no followers. Everyone follows his own progress.' Each of us will progress in our own unique way. Each of us will discover our own path to fulfillment, to understanding who we are and our relationship with the world, and to realizing our greatest potential.

"As Socrates said, and you will hear me repeat this more than a few times, 'The unexamined life is not worth living.' What does that mean? It means in part that we have the ability to be self-aware. We are aware of ourselves as living beings, and we are aware of our surroundings. We can think and question, comprehend, decipher, and decide. We can enter into relationships, communicate our needs, and express our ideas. We can solve problems, create, envision, and expand our inner and outer horizons. With all these abilities and many more, we can rigorously examine our lives, our thoughts, feelings, and beliefs and evolve an increasingly profound understanding of and insight into our own nature and the nature of the universe.

"Thus, philosophy is born. Socrates is the father of Western philosophy. Many of our ideas—on ethics, morality, art, music, mathematics, beauty, law, and government, on knowledge itself—harken back to Socrates and his disciple Plato, with whom we will get acquainted this semester.

"We'll have time for more questions and discussion over the coming weeks. As for rumors, my advice is not to believe them. Thank you for signing up for the class. See you next Tuesday."

With that, the students started collecting their notebooks and syllabuses and started talking among themselves. The air was fused with all possibilities and considerable excitement. Sam admired the students, so full of promise, and felt a great sense of satisfaction. As he collected his notes, his thoughts turned to the department meeting coming up.

The first full department meeting of the year had a tendency to be formal and businesslike. Sam, however, was brimming with excitement about his first class as he entered the meeting room. This kind of enthusiasm was not the norm for a group of philosophers. They tend to be a rather serious lot. However, Sam's inspired presence was infectious and could not be ignored. The philosophy faculty found themselves relaxing and verging on lightheartedness. More students were interested in the major than ever before. Their discussion was lively and friendly, and the hour passed quickly. Even Dr. Harris relaxed and enjoyed the camaraderie.

Afterward, Sam headed into town to see Kenny at the café, which was hopping with students swirling about with hot cups of coffee, pastries, and sandwiches. Much conversation and laughter, mixed with the energy of anticipation, floated in the air. Kenny stood at the center of the swirl, sharing a joke with several students. Kenny noticed Sam and acknowledged his friend with a nod. Sam headed to Kenny's small office off the kitchen since all the tables were taken. Kenny arrived moments later with two cups of coffee and two turkey, swiss, and coleslaw sandwiches garnished with Russian dressing.

"Hey, the place is jamming. Congratulations. What a difference with the students back in town," Sam cheerfully observed.

"Yeah, the drought is over, and the milk, honey, and cash are flowing in once again as God intended," Kenny concurred. "So how did the first class go?"

"Really well. To have so many students interested in consciousness! They'll all start meditating this weekend. The center is bringing in more teachers. They need more than the four already here. I've heard through the grapevine that Maharishi has heard about the course and is very pleased."

"Well, if he's happy, we're all happy, or something like that. These guys are going to owe you big-time."

"Well, Kenny, not everything is about business."

"Au contraire, my friend, it's all business."

"Ah, I thought it was all knowledge. Anyway, the class went well. I've got four great TAs from last year's students. Each one has continued meditating, and they're all pretty happy. One of them, Elizabeth Smith, actually changed her name to Ananda over the summer."

"Cool."

"Yeah, well, we'll see. I think Elizabeth is a fine name."

"Hey, brother, you sound very old-fashioned."

"I guess I do. Anyway, she might have a schoolgirl crush on me."

"How can you tell?"

"Just the way she kept looking at me," Sam replied, looking despondent.

"You better start getting used to that, my man. You're young, bright, successful, good-looking from a certain angle, and on the cutting edge. If it gets to be a problem, you bring Ananda around here sometime soon, and I'll take her off your hands pronto," Kenny asserted.

"First of all, she's not on my hands, and secondly, how do you propose to do that?"

"First, I'll try the approach of taking you down a notch or two, and then I'll charm her myself. You know, the old misinformation and deception routine. The government does it all the time. Seems to work for them," Kenny rambled.

"You are totally insane! Why my father backed you in this business I'll never know."

"Well, the place is full, and it's by far the most popular café in town."

"Yeah, well, I guess you have a point," Sam concurred.

"By the way, is she pretty?" Kenny brought the conversation back around.

"Kenny, I'm not going there."

"Ah, that's a shame. Best go home to lovely wife." Kenny paused. "Hey, why don't you have another kid? That would help nail your coffin shut."

"Honestly, Kenny, I have no idea why I talk to you, and one child for the moment is enough. Besides," Sam shifted in his seat, "Amy's pregnant."

"Oh, I see. So you are nailing your coffin shut." Kenny took a long look at his best friend. "I thought there was a glow about you," Kenny continued with a chuckle.

"Kenny, sometimes you are rather bothersome."

"Some people call it charm. When is the due date?"

"Beginning of March."

"You've been keeping this under your hat. So let me think. If I'm doing the math right, Josh was born in April, and Amy's due in March, which means you're having Irish twins." Kenny sat back with a big smile on his face.

"Well, this isn't exactly a science, picking the due date. Dr. Goldberg's best guess is March fifth."

"Good. I'm glad that's settled. Irish twins. So what about Ananda?"

"Forget it, Kenny."

"Well, you don't have to get huffy."

"I was just making conversation."

"Now you sound defensive."

"All right, maybe I am."

"Sammy, you better get used to all this attention. I got the feeling you're going to get a lot of it from this point out."

"God, I hope not. I like things simple."

"If you stay simple, all will be well. But, brother, you've caught a wave whether you know it or not. And things could get complicated fast."

"How's that?"

"You've thrown your hat in the ring is all I'm saying."

"Kenny, I have no idea where you're going with this."

"I know, and you're the one with the PhD," Kenny paused and smiled. "Still, Sam, I think your life's going to change. With this course that Maharishi asked you to do, you're stepping up."

"Look, it's just a course."

"No, it's more than that. You said so yourself. It's potentially life changing, a game changer. That's a big deal. That's all I'm saying."

"All right then. We'll take it one step at a time. Thanks for the sandwich and coffee. I've got to get back for my next class," Sam said with some exasperation.

"Anytime, brother, anytime. The door is always open. Congratulations and love to Amy," Kenny offered magnanimously as Sam stood up and walked out the door.

Chapter 13:
The Book

IN THE FALL OF 1975, information about Transcendental Meditation had started to flood the media. Maharishi had appeared on TV's *Merv Griffin Show* once in 1975 and again in 1977. Maharishi's smiling face adorned the cover of *Time*. *The TM Book* had been published and landed a spot on the *The New York Times* bestseller list. Over 350 TM teaching centers had sprouted up across the United States, many near major colleges and universities. Sam and his course had hit a vein of great excitement.

Sam was swept along by the current, but he didn't know about the white water ahead. He didn't know when he had proposed the course that channel 22 out of Springfield, Massachusetts, was going to carry a story on the course's popularity and the angle that TM played in its burgeoning success. He didn't anticipate that the article in the Springfield *Republican* on his course would make it to the desk of Jack Abrams, a publisher from New Horizons in New York. He didn't know that when he answered the phone one morning in late October of 1976, the call was going to change his life forever.

"Hello," Sam said picking up the phone.

"Hello. Am I speaking with Dr. Sam O'Connor?"

"Yes, this is Dr. O'Connor."

"Great. This is Jack Abrams. I run a publishing house in New York, New Horizon. Dr. O'Connor, this course you're teaching at Amherst College on consciousness and meditation sounds very interesting."

"Thank you, but how did you hear about it?"

"Read the article in the *Republican*."

"You're in the city and you read the *Republican?*

THE BEST OF ALL POSSIBLE WORLDS

"Actually, I have a friend in Springfield, and I try to keep up on interesting stories, and well, what you're doing at Amherst College is interesting. I wanted to ask you if you'd be willing to write a book based on the course you're teaching. I think it could be very timely and popular. The Maharishi is everywhere these days. He's captured the imagination of America. A book like yours could do very well."

"Well, I guess anything's possible, although I don't have much time."

"I have a great editor who could work with you. It could be as simple as adapting your lectures into book form. I sense a great opportunity for you. We can work out all the details, your contract, and your advance, how it will all work. For now you just have to say yes."

"Let me think about it for a day or two and get back to you. Where can I reach you?"

"Wonderful. Take a few days. My direct number is 212-228-3475. I look forward to your call and discussing this more with you."

"Thanks. I'll get back to you. I'm sorry, what publishing company are you with?"

"New Horizons Publishing. I'll send you some information on us by overnight mail."

"Good. Thanks for the call, Mr. Abrams."

"My pleasure. So can I expect a call on Thursday?"

"Yes. Thursday afternoon. Does that work?"

"That would be great. Look forward to hearing from you. Good-bye for now."

"Okay, good-bye."

Sam walked up the hall from his home office and found Amy in the kitchen.

"Amy, you won't believe who that was on the phone. A publisher from New York. He read the article from the *Republican* and wants me to write a book about the course," Sam said in disbelief.

"Sam, that's incredible. What did you say?"

"I asked him for two days to think about it. I'm teaching a full load. I'm not sure how to do it."

"Sam, I can't believe it. What's the name of the publishing company?"

"New Horizons."

"They're big. Oh, Sam, I'm so proud of you. Maybe I should call my dad to work out the contract?"

"Well, I haven't decided to write the book yet."

"Sam, you have to write the book. You can't say no. This is a great opportunity."

"Yeah, you're right. How can I say no? I have to think how to structure the book. Jack Abrams, the publisher, suggested I adapt my lectures. I could do that. Okay, give Ed a call. I'll check in with him tonight. I have a ten o'clock class this morning," Sam said looking at his watch. "I have to get going."

Amy moved to kiss Sam. "Sam, I'm so proud of you."

"Thanks, honey. See you around five."

Sam's father-in-law took care of the book contract negotiations, and Sam wrote the book based on the lectures from his course starting over Christmas break and into early spring. The first copies were printed in June of '77.

Jack Abrams had a gut feeling that the book would create a stir, just as Sam's course had done at Amherst College. The book was good, he thought, but the timing was perfect. The first printing of the book, thirty thousand hardback copies, sold out in a matter of weeks. The *Times* gave it a very favorable review, as did other major newspapers around the country. The second printing was one hundred thousand copies and sold out in only a few months. A third printing of one hundred thousand sold out in five months. The publisher decided to print a paperback and ordered 150,000 copies for April of '78. He also organized a twenty-city book tour that Sam would do in thirty-two days starting in mid-June. He arranged for book reviews and press coverage at every stop. Sam would offer readings, sign books, and give lectures. Jack Abrams expected the 150,000 copies to sell out by the time the tour was over, and he was already contemplating another printing and translations for overseas sales. Jack was very pleased with his ability to pick up on the trend.

Sam was thrilled with the success and all the attention it brought. He had catapulted onto the national stage. He couldn't quite believe it, but he sure liked the feeling. Ever since Sam had that last meeting with Maharishi, when he suggested Sam create this course on Eastern and Western knowledge traditions, Sam wanted to play a larger role in ushering in the Age of Enlightenment. In his mind, his desire was being fulfilled.

Chapter 14:
The Storm Hits

SAM HAD, WITH GREAT RELUCTANCE, agreed to do the tour. Albert Hill's visit a mere six weeks before had unnerved him. He hardly wanted to be separated from Amy and the boys, but both Jack and Ed thought the tour and the ensuing coverage would create the momentum for the book's success. Amy, also concerned about Albert and seeing Sam so down about the tour, suggested he ask Angel Hernandez, former chief of security at the college, to accompany him. Sam called him, and Angel happily agreed. A road trip with Sam and all expenses paid by New Horizons wasn't a bad deal, Angel thought.

So the two started off in Boston, then to New York, next to Philadelphia, and onward to DC. From there, they flew to Chicago where Amy was to join them for four nights while her parents watched the boys.

Once Amy felt settled that her parents knew about Josh and Paul's routines, she eagerly packed her bag to join Sam in Chicago. Sam arranged for a car from the Drake Hotel to pick Amy up at the airport since he was otherwise occupied with a radio interview. When Amy and Sam met up at the hotel, it reminded them both of their meeting in the hotel in Seelisburg. Sam even had a vase of long-stemmed red roses waiting for her.

Readings, book signings, and an evening lecture made their two days in Chicago hectic. Every event was packed, and Amy was amazed at the openness and receptivity of the people who gathered to hear her husband speak and buy his book. Amy found herself reflecting on Sam's masterful grasp of the knowledge of consciousness and Maharishi's intuitive recognition of Sam's innate ability despite the fact that Sam was three thousand miles away and Maharishi hadn't even met him when he invited him to the TM teacher-training course.

Sam was delighted to be with Amy again. Her presence completed his happiness, although she also reminded him of his two young sons at home. He felt the pang of separation when he thought of Josh and Paul.

At the University of Chicago lecture, Sam thought he spotted Albert Hill in the back of the auditorium as the public was filing in. The perception brought a wave of fear through him. He looked away for a moment to greet a well-wisher, and when he looked back, Albert or whoever the person he took for Albert, was gone. With his lecture before him, he motioned to Angel to come to the podium.

"Angel, just a minute ago, I thought I saw Albert Hill in the back of the auditorium."

"Really? What was he wearing?"

"Hard to say, baseball cap, beige short-sleeve shirt, maybe wearing a day pack."

"All right, I'll have a look around. Why don't you hold up a few minutes? I'll give you a wave from the back as an all clear sign."

"Okay."

Amy, sitting in the front row, saw the two men discussing something. Angel left quickly and headed to the back of the auditorium. Professor Gilbert from the university's philosophy department was approaching the podium to introduce Sam, who had taken his seat. Amy came up to the stage and asked, "Sam, everything okay?"

"Yeah, everything's fine," Sam said as he smiled weakly.

"Where's Angel?"

"He'll be right back. He's checking on something. Oh, there he is now." Sam pointed to Angel, and Amy turned to see Angel waving. "Amy, time to get started. Wish me luck."

"All right, Sam. Best of luck, though you hardly need it."

"Thanks, love."

Amy went back to her seat in the front row. Partway through Sam's lecture, she realized Angel never came back to his seat beside her.

After the second busy day of interviews by the *Chicago Sun-Times* and the local CBS TV station and an afternoon book reading, Sam and Amy had a free evening. Angel had made plans to visit friends, allowing Amy and Sam to enjoy a quiet and delicious dinner in the Cape Cod room in the Drake.

Sam was eager to show Amy the initials of Joe DiMaggio, a childhood hero of his, and Marylyn Monroe carved into the bar. Afterward, they strolled arm-in-arm along Lake Superior, feeling grateful and serene before turning in for the night.

Next morning they caught a commuter flight to Minneapolis. The publisher had arranged a comfortable rental car at the airport. After studying a map of the city, Angel drove Sam and Amy to a local radio station, arriving in time for an 11:00 am interview. After the show, they checked in at their hotel. In less than an hour of downtime, they changed clothes, relaxed for all of fifteen minutes, and ate a quick snack before heading over to the Barnes & Noble downtown location. Sam was growing tired of the tour, and the tour still had a long way to go. After Minneapolis, they would fly to Denver, Seattle, Portland, San Francisco, Los Angeles, Phoenix, Atlanta, and finally Raleigh before heading home. Reflecting on what lay ahead, for the first time, Sam felt an impulse to wrap things up, cancel the rest of the tour, and just go home.

They walked into the bookstore just before 2:30 pm. Readers, potential readers, and fans filled twenty-two of the thirty-five seats available, patiently waiting for Sam. This was by far the smallest turnout of the tour. Sam sat down in front of the group while the store manager announced over the PA that Dr. Sam O'Connor would be reading from his book on consciousness. That brought another seven customers, who had been milling about the bookshelves, to the audience.

The store manager introduced Sam enthusiastically and reminded audience members that Dr. O'Connor would be available after the reading to autograph any copies they purchased. He turned toward Sam, and everyone clapped briefly. Sam began with an introduction to his book and himself. He read excerpts for about twenty minutes and then invited questions. In Boston, New York, and Chicago, these exchanges had been animated and lasted almost an hour. However, the Minneapolis audience posed only two questions, both of which required little discussion. The assembled group was polite and happy but almost shy. When it was clear that no more questions were forthcoming, Sam thanked the audience for coming. He and Amy then moved to the book-signing table, where he signed all of the twenty-four books purchased. In Chicago, he had signed several hundred.

Sam finished placing his signature in the last book and looked up to find Albert Hill approaching the table, looking intense and serious. Sam rose to greet him. Amy was already standing, talking to the customer who received

Sam's last autograph. When Albert met Sam's gaze, he paused for a moment. Then he reached behind him and drew a handgun.

Sam, reacting instantly and instinctively, grabbed Amy and pushed her to the floor. In that instant, Albert hastily took aim and pulled the trigger. The first bullet missed, and Albert shot again. The second bullet caught Sam in the left shoulder and knocked him back and onto the carpeted floor.

The catastrophic succession of events took only seconds in real time, but for those involved, everything seemed to unfold in slow motion. During those few seconds, Angel, sitting in a chair in the audience, leaped up and covered the distance to Albert in a burst of speed. He tackled Albert like a blitzing linebacker from behind. When they hit the floor, Albert was flattened and the wind was knocked out of him. The gun popped out of his hand, landing a few feet away. Next, Angel, now lying on top of Albert, sat up from the waist, grabbed Albert's right arm, and pulled it hard to the center of his back. With his left hand, he pressed Albert's face into the carpet.

Hearing the shots, the store security guard and manager came running from the front of the store. Angel shouted at anyone who would listen, "Call 911 now! Shots fired! Tell them a man is down and we need an ambulance. Someone do it now!"

The people close to the shooting, initially too stunned to think or act, suddenly came to life. One woman fell to the ground and cried; several others screamed and scattered, running desperately from the scene. The store security guard helped Angel keep Albert immobilized, and the manager gave his attention to Sam. Amy had crawled over to Sam and lay next to him with the left side of her face on the carpet. She was crying softly as she whispered, "Sam, Sam, stay with me. Do not go like this. Hang on. Help is coming. Please, don't go."

Sam opened his eyes and asked quietly, "Are you hurt?"

"No, I'm all right. Sam, you've been shot."

Knowing Amy was unhurt, Sam closed his eyes again.

The first police officers arrived only minutes later. They raced to the back of the store and cleared the crime scene area. Only a couple of customers lingered nearby; most had fled. One officer swiftly handcuffed Albert and ordered him to stay on the floor while a second checked Sam's condition and connected with the ambulance and EMT group on their way. Relieved of his captive, Angel turned and knelt by Sam. Angel had focused on subduing Albert and did not realize how seriously Sam had been hurt. Then he saw his friend lying on the floor, eyes closed, and bleeding badly. Angel was angry and blamed himself for his failure to protect Sam. He knelt next to him, feeling helpless.

More police officers ran into the store, followed immediately by the emergency medical team. They needed to stabilize Sam quickly. He had lost a significant amount of blood and was unconscious. They rapidly assessed his condition and wound. Sam's pulse rate kept dropping. The EMT staff knew they needed to stop the bleeding and keep his pulse rate from falling any further. At least he was breathing remarkably well with no sign of blood in his lungs. They gave him a shot of adrenaline to keep his heartbeat steady then taped thick gauze pads over the wound.

Angel stood up and helped Amy to her feet. He led her away so the emergency responders had room to work.

Amy hugged Angel, who held her tightly. She buried her face in his chest, softly repeating, "He can't die. He can't die."

Angel, fighting back his own tears, consoled her, "He won't. He'll be okay. I know he'll be okay."

Two of the EMT staff brought in a stretcher from the ambulance, and the four-member team now arranged themselves around Sam and carefully lifted him onto it. They covered Sam with a sheet and blanket and rolled him through the store to the waiting ambulance. By this time, five more police cruisers had arrived and blocked off the front of the store, holding back the curious crowd that had gathered. The press and TV news teams had quickly assembled. Two photographers snapped photo after photo of Sam being lifted into the ambulance, and the video crews taped every detail they could. The ambulance crew helped Amy and Angel into the ambulance and sealed the door. Sirens blaring, the ambulance raced toward the emergency room at Saint Paul's Hospital.

Inside Barnes & Noble, the officers pulled Albert to his feet and led him through the store and out the door to a waiting police car. Meanwhile, other officers secured the crime scene with yellow tape and began marking the evidence. The crime lab arrived and continued the process, noting the gun, the two shells, the bloodstained carpet, and the single bullet hole in the back wall, a few feet from where the victim fell. Other detectives were interviewing the witnesses who remained.

As the investigation staff collected information, Lieutenant Beale of the Minneapolis Police Department entered the store. He immediately sought out the chief detective at the crime scene and asked with his usual directness, "Okay, Harry, what do we have?"

"Well, Lieutenant, we have a professor on a book tour with his wife and a friend who happens to be the former security chief of Amherst College. And we have a shooter—from the sound of him, he's a bit of a nut. Anyway, the professor is Dr. Sam O'Connor, his wife is Amy O'Connor, and their security man is Angel Hernandez. The professor took one bullet to the upper body from a .38 at close range. Before he was shot, he pushed his wife out of the way and onto the floor, and she appears to be unharmed. We were able to ask Hernandez, who brought down the shooter, a few questions before they took him to the hospital, and I have a man at the hospital now waiting to continue the interview. It appears the professor and his wife know the shooter. The shooter may have even been in Chicago stalking them according to Hernandez. We found one slug in the wall, and we have several witnesses that heard only two shots. We have the weapon. The suspect dropped it when Mr. Hernandez tackled him. As to possible motive, the shooter may be psychologically unstable. He rambled on about protecting people from false gods, but he was clear enough to demand a lawyer."

"For Christ sakes!" the lieutenant barked. "This is Minneapolis, not New York or Chicago. We don't settle differences of opinion, religious or otherwise, with a gun. I want to know why they brought the security officer with them. Did they know about a threat against this man's life? If so, why weren't we notified? Get some answers. I'm going outside to give a statement. Keep me informed."

Beale stepped out the door, where the local print and TV reporters were waiting for him, recorders and cameras ready. He stepped up to the microphone and cleared his throat. "At approximately 4:00 pm, Dr. Sam O'Connor, an author and professor from Amherst College in Amherst, Massachusetts, was shot. The assailant was disarmed and subdued just moments after the shooting. He is Caucasian, about 5'10" tall and probably in his early thirties. We have not yet determined his motive. We are drawing up formal charges, and they will be filed shortly. That's all I have."

A TV reporter demanded more. "What hospital has Dr. O'Connor been taken to? What is his condition?"

"He was just admitted to Saint Paul's minutes ago. They haven't released details about his condition yet."

"Anyone else wounded or hurt?"

"No. From early witness testimony, we know that Dr. O'Connor pushed his wife out of harm's way before he was shot. A private security guard tackled the shooter and secured him until the police arrived. That's all I have for you." Lieutenant Beale turned firmly around and strode back into the store.

At Saint Paul's Hospital, Dr. John Beckman and his team were in scrubs, waiting for the ambulance. The operating room was being prepared for surgery. As the ambulance pulled up, a triage team ran out to meet it. They had received a phone message about the incoming patient and his condition only minutes earlier. The patient was in his earlier thirties, Caucasian, and had sustained a gunshot wound to his upper body. In addition, the patient was unconscious with shallow, quick breathing, a slow but steady pulse, and stable blood pressure. This information did not fit the usual pattern for gunshot victims, and Dr. Beckman doubted its accuracy. However, all that was irrelevant until he and his team could examine the patient themselves.

The ambulance drew up to the ER entrance. The EMT people opened the doors and began lowering Sam's stretcher to the ground, where hospital staff stood ready to receive him. The triage staff quickly lifted Sam onto a mobile hospital bed, hooked him up to an oxygen source, and checked his vitals as they simultaneously rolled him toward the OR. His clothes had already been cut away, and he was covered up to the waist by a sheet. Once in the OR, the surgical team lifted him onto an operating table, cut away the blood-soaked gauze pads and bandages, connected him to various monitors, and examined his wounds, everything happening more or less all at once. They identified his blood type as O, replaced the plasma bottle with a blood bag, and began transfusion.

Near the emergency room entryway, an evaluation team greeted Angel and Amy.

"How is Sam?" Amy demanded adamantly.

"He's already in the OR," one of the nurses reported. "Dr. Beckman is in charge, and he's in very good hands. Now come with me," the nurse directed. "We want to clean you up and be sure you're not hurt." Amy now realized she had Sam's blood on her hands, blouse, and skirt.

The nurse placed Angel and Amy in separate rooms and checked their vital signs. Both had elevated pulse rates and increased blood pressure. Nevertheless, they had largely overcome the initial shock and were beginning to think about what had happened and what to do next.

Amy asked for a phone, and a nurse ushered her into a small office. She took a deep breath and called her parents. On the third ring, her mother answered. Amy's faint composure deserted her, and she began to sob.

"Mom," she managed, her voice choked by tears.

"Amy, what's wrong?"

"Mom, Sam's been shot!" She started crying hard.

"Oh, God, no! Ed, come quickly! Pick up the extension."

Ed picked up the phone in the den. "Amy?"

Hearing her father's voice calmed her a little enough to speak. "Dad, someone shot Sam."

"Amy, where are you?"

"I'm at the hospital in Minneapolis. Sam's in the ER. He's in surgery."

"Are you hurt?"

"No, I'm okay."

"Who's with you?"

"Angel, Sam's friend from the college."

"Is Angel hurt?"

"No, he saved our lives." Amy sobbed again for a couple of minutes and then tried speaking again. "This man . . . we knew him. His name is Albert. Sam knew him in college. We were at a book signing, and he just started shooting at us. Sam pushed me to the floor before Albert shot him. Angel must have tackled Albert, so he dropped his gun. Then everyone started screaming or crying. I crawled over to Sam. He was barely conscious. He was bleeding. It was terrible." More tears flowed.

Ed and Mary were shocked and frightened. Ed, however, put his feelings aside and gathered his thoughts. "Honey, we're glad you're okay. We'll pray for Sam. Now we need to know how to get in touch with you. I have a good friend who's an attorney out there, and I'm going to call him and ask him to go right over to the hospital."

"Dad, we're in the ER at Saint Paul's Hospital. He should just come here."

"Okay. His name is Joe Hemming. We were in law school together. He'll help you until I can get a flight."

"Amy," said Mary, "do Jimmy and Lillian know?"

"No, I'll be calling them right after we hang up. It feels like this all happened only seconds ago."

"Would you like us to call them?"

"No. Thanks, Mom. I want to talk to them myself."

"All right," Ed chimed in. "You call the O'Connors, and I'll call Joe."

"Thanks, Dad. Mom, how are the boys?"

"They're fine, they're fine. Don't worry about them."

"Okay, thanks. Don't tell them please. I'll call you when I know anything more," Amy added and hung up. She sat for a moment, sighed, and picked up the phone to call Jimmy and Lillian but then decided to call Kenny.

Amy realized she needed to call Kenny next. She knew Kenny would help Jimmy and Lilly to make arrangements to fly to Minneapolis. She asked to use the hospital phone again and dialed Kenny's café.

Kenny picked up the phone and said, "White Oak Café. How can I help you?"

"Kenny, it's Amy," she answered, her voice trembling.

"What's wrong, Ame? You sound terrible."

"Kenny, Sam's been shot. Albert Hill shot Sam . . . in the bookstore in Minneapolis." Amy started to cry harder.

"Oh my god! How bad is he? Is he going to make it?" Kenny's heart raced with fear, an emotion he rarely felt.

"I think so, but I don't know. He's in surgery. He lost consciousness moments after the shooting. He lost a lot of blood," Amy confided amid sobs.

"All right. Okay. I'm coming. I'll be there as soon as a plane can get me there. That son of a bitch Albert Hill. Cops get him?"

"Yes. Angel tackled him to the floor."

"Thank God."

"Angel saved our lives," Amy clarified.

"Divine protection," Kenny mumbled. "Do Jimmy and Lilly know?"

"I'm going to call them next. Give me a few minutes, and then you give them a call, okay?"

"Okay, will do. Listen, Amy, we'll be there as soon as we can. You let Sam know we're coming. No sudden exits on his part."

"All right, I'll tell him."

"I'll call you when we land. Hang in there."

"All right, Kenny. See you then. It's good to hear your voice. I'm so glad you're coming."

"Hey, blink your eyes three times, and I'll be standing in front of you. Hang in there. Sam will be okay. He and I have a deal."

"What deal?"

"Neither one can make a big move without letting the other know. And since he didn't inform me, he can't make the move."

"Kenny, is this another one of those childhood things?" Amy smiled slightly.

"No, we were about eighteen at the time."

"You guys are amazing! A bit crazy, but amazing. Hey, how come I'm not in this deal?" Amy asked with benign amusement.

"Good question. I'd say you're definitely in the club though."

"Kenny, where would we be without you?" Amy replied with some amusement.

"Another good question, but we don't want to contemplate such a situation right now. Remind Sam about our deal. Love you, Ame."

"Love you too. Thanks for being so supportive of me—ah, us."

"It's all right, just part of my Vishnu nature."

"Vishnu nature?"

"You know, Vishnu. One of the big three, he supports creation, and I help him out with this small piece of it."

"Kenny," Amy started to feel impatient, "I have to call Jimmy and Lilly."

"Yes, you do. I'll give you ten minutes, and then I'll call them myself to arrange our travel times. Bye. See you soon. Sam will be okay. Don't worry."

And Kenny hung up. Amy felt better after talking with him. *He's crazy,* she thought, *but a good crazy. I'll never understand how my husband and his best friend are best friends though.*

Dismissing the thought and feeling grateful for Kenny in their lives, she once again picked up the phone and dialed Sam's parents' number. Lillian answered the phone on the third ring.

"Hi, Amy, hold on a sec. Jimmy, pick up. It's Amy." When she heard Amy's words, Lillian immediately made the sign of the cross and began praying, "Mother Mary, please save my son."

In shock and disbelief, Jimmy kept asking, "They shot my son? They shot my boy?" It didn't make sense. "They shot Sam?" Finally, he came to his senses. "Amy, how is he? How are you? What the hell happened?"

Amy replied, "He's lost a lot of blood, but he should survive. I'll tell you the story when you get here." Lilly quietly hung up and started to think about what she needed to do to get ready for the trip to Minneapolis.

"Oh, thank God in heaven." Jimmy exclaimed, "Look, we'll be there as soon as we can. I think Lilly's already getting the grips from the back closet. We're coming. I'll call you back. What's the number? Where are you?"

"Dad, we're in Minneapolis at Saint Paul Hospital. I've already called Kenny, and he'll be calling you next. Anyway, Dad, here's the number."

"All right, I got it. Well, thank God you're at a Catholic hospital. So Kenny knows?"

"Thank God we're at any hospital, Dad. And yes, he'll be calling you shortly."

Jimmy continued, still somewhat breathless, "Yeah, right. Look, we're on the next plane. If we miss that one, we'll catch the one after that. God bless you. We're coming." And with that pronouncement, he hung up.

"For Christ sakes, Lillian, pack some clothes." *All right, Jimmy, think,* he said to himself. "I'll call Clem. He'll open the café," Jimmy thought out loud. "I'll call Larry. He'll take care of the bank. I'll call Umberto. He'll put the orders in. I'll call the airlines and get some tickets. What about Susan? Lillian," Jimmy shouted, "what about Susan?"

"I'll ask Mrs. O'Brien to look after her," she yelled back.

"Okay. Hey, where is she anyway?"

"She's with some friends," Lillian called out from the back room.

"Oh, all right."

"Jimmy?" Lillian shouted from down the hall.

"Yeah, Lil?"

"Call Father Mike."

"All right, Lil, I call him."

"Jimmy?"

"Now what is it, Lilly?"

"Jimmy, say a prayer for your son before you start on all those calls."

"Oh yeah," Jimmy began as he made the sign of the cross and prayed out loud, "Lord, please, they shot me boy—in Minneapolis of all places. Please, Lord, watch over him in this time of great need. He's my only son. I know you gave up yours for the good of the world, but I don't want to give up mine. I'm sorry, Lord, if that sounds a bit selfish, but I can't lose him now. He's got a wife and boys of his own. His mother would never forgive and forget, and there'd be no living with her. So please, Lord, I don't ask for much. I haven't bothered you for a while about anything. Lord, just make him well. I'm forever grateful, Lord. You know I am. Amen. In the name of the Father, the Son, and the Holy Spirit," he finished and crossed himself again and started making his phone calls.

After Amy hung up the phone with Jimmy, she sat quietly for a moment. Then she thought of another call she should make—David Roberts, Sam's buddy from teacher training in Switzerland. She pulled out her address book, found his number, and dialed. After three rings, David picked up.

"David, its Amy Sanders."

"Jai Guru Dev, Amy! How's everything?"

"David, something terrible just happened." And the tears came again.

"What is it?"

"Sam was shot. We're in an ER in Minneapolis. He's in serious condition. Could you call Switzerland and ask someone to tell Maharishi? He took such a deep interest in Sam. I know this isn't something people usually do, but I have a strong feeling that Maharishi would want to know."

"I agree. I'll call right away. What hospital are you in?"

"Saint Paul's."

"What number can I reach you at?"

"Call the main number, and ask to be put through to the ER waiting room."

"All right. My prayers are with you both."

Amy hung up the phone and thought of Maharishi.

David lost no time in calling one of Maharishi's assistants, a young man from England called VJ. He described what had happened and Sam's serious condition and asked gently, "Can you let Maharishi know?"

"Yes. Yes, of course." VJ hung up and walked down the hall to Maharishi's sitting room, where Maharishi was visiting with a world-renowned physicist.

"Excuse me, Maharishi," VJ spoke softly but firmly. "I'm so sorry to interrupt, but I just received a call from the States. Sam O'Connor was shot during his book tour. He's in surgery right now in a Minneapolis hospital."

Maharishi sat straight up, looking alarmed. He turned to his visitor and said, "Please excuse me, but I must put my attention on this." He directed VJ to call the Minneapolis TM center and ask the teachers to go to the hospital and meditate in Sam's room or in the hall outside. He then closed his eyes and joined Sam in awareness.

Sam remained unconscious to the world. Inwardly, he kept experiencing a sensation of tumbling and whirling through darkness. Suddenly he started to feel more centered, and the whirling diminished. He saw a glowing golden light. As it intensified, his confusion and the swirling sensation evaporated completely. He found himself sitting across from Maharishi. Sam beamed at the sight of his radiant teacher. Maharishi beamed back and assured him that he would be okay; his wounds would heal in time.

"Does everyone have to go through this?" Sam asked.

"No," Maharishi replied. "Everyone's path is different. Everyone's lessons are different. Your life will be quiet for a while. Rest and let everything go, everything. The clouds come and go, but the sun is always shining, unaffected by the clouds. Don't resist anything. The clouds will pass, and you will find the sun again."

Sam's surgeons successfully removed the bullet, which had gone through his left shoulder and shattered his clavicle. He would need a second surgery to reconstruct the bone, but most importantly, the bullet had missed his major arteries. The surgery lasted just under three hours, ending a little after 8:00 pm. Close to one in the morning, Sam unexpectedly woke up. He tried to remember what had happened. Where was he? Suddenly, it all flooded back like a hideous nightmare. He had been shot. Amy had been there. Albert had shot him. He opened his eyes with a start and realized he was in a hospital room. Then a faint memory of a dream about Maharishi showed up. He couldn't recall the details, but he felt deeply comforted.

Amy saw Sam's eyes open and then close again.

"Nurse, he's awake! He's awake!" she cried.

Chapter 15:
The Aftermath

JIMMY AND LILLY TOOK THE first flight out of JFK the next morning after a night of little sleep. Amy had called them after the surgery to tell them that Sam was going to be all right, but that hadn't brought them much comfort. They arrived at the Minneapolis airport at 10:30 am. Kenny had arrived an hour earlier and waited for them. The three had an emotional meeting, hugging one another and crying. Then they moved swiftly through the airport, exited, and hailed a cab at the arrivals curb. As the cab pulled up and the trunk popped up for their luggage, Jimmy and Kenny didn't wait for the cabbie. They hastily loaded their bags in the trunk and then slammed the trunk closed.

Kenny got into the front of the cab, and Jimmy and Lilly slid into the backseat. "Hey, pal, we need to get to Saint Paul's Hospital right away," Jimmy instructed.

"No problem, friend," the cabbie replied. An older man, he had heard and seen it all in his career as a cabbie. The need for speed didn't concern him at all.

"How far is the hospital from here?" Jimmy inquired anxiously.

"Maybe forty-five minutes, depending on traffic," the cabbie informed him.

"Listen, if you can get us there in thirty minutes, I'll throw in an extra fiver for your trouble," Jimmy offered.

"I'll do my best, sir. Can I ask what all the hurry is about?" the cabbie asked, trying to be discreet.

"Our son was shot and is in the emergency unit. We're just coming in from New York," Jimmy explained curtly.

"Is your son the professor in the bookstore?"

"Yeah. How'd you know?" The question made Jimmy nervous.

"It's all over the radio, the shooting and all. Last I heard, your son was in stable condition."

Lillian wept quietly.

"Oh, Christ," said Jimmy. "It's okay, Lil. We'll be there soon."

"Are they saying anything else?" queried Jimmy anxiously.

"Well, they caught the guy who shot him. A friend of your son's tackled him."

"It was Angel Hernandez," Kenny filled in.

"He must've been an angel. According to the news, this wacko guy was about to shoot your son again and then go after his wife. They say the shooter knew your son. The word's out that this guy is a nut case," the cabby revealed.

"I don't want to hear any more, Jimmy. This isn't helping. I just want to see my son," Lilly almost whispered.

"All right, Lil, all right."

"Listen, folks, I'll get you there as fast as I can," the cabbie offered kindly. "And the fare's on me."

"That's good of yah. Thanks, pal," returned Jimmy. They rode on in silence as the cab maneuvered through the morning traffic.

As soon as Ed hung up from Amy's call, he dialed his friend Joe Hemmings in Minneapolis. They hadn't talked in years, and Ed hoped he still had the same number. Ed felt relieved when Joe picked up the phone. After a warm but brief greeting, Ed quickly got down to business.

"Joe, my son-in-law, Sam O'Connor, was shot earlier today in Minneapolis. My daughter was with him."

"Oh my god, Ed! I saw part of that story on the evening news tonight. I had no idea your family was involved. I'm so sorry. How can I help?"

"Sam and my daughter are at Saint Paul's Hospital. Amy is waiting in the ER while Sam undergoes surgery. The press is going to go after this story in a big way. Sam was in the middle of a national tour promoting his best seller. He's also associated with the Maharishi, you know, the Beatles' guru. This could end up being a media circus, which is the last thing they need right now. Would you go to the hospital and act as their spokesperson? You know, shield them from any kind of aggressive media. Handle any legal issues that might come up? I've talked to Amy, and she's expecting you."

"Okay, Ed. I'm on my way. I can be there in thirty minutes."

"Great! Thanks so much, Joe. I'll try and get you some information from the publisher. I may have to stay here with my wife and grandsons for a day or two. I'm sure the press is going to show up here as well. Call me when you get to the hospital. I owe you big-time, old friend."

"I'll take care of it, and you don't owe me anything. What's the phone number where you're staying?"

"I appreciate that, but you may be putting some time in on this. We'll discuss that part later. The number here is 413-254-1008."

"Don't worry about the logistics on this end. I know the chief of police here, and I'm familiar with the hospital. It's a good hospital, by the way. Rest assured your son-in-law is getting excellent care. I'll call you as soon as I know anything."

Joe hung up. He explained the situation to his assistant and asked him to reschedule all his appointments for the next two days. Joe grabbed his coat and headed down to the office parking lot.

Chief Taylor walked into his headquarters and asked the desk sergeant, "Sergeant, would you get me the chief of police in Amherst, Massachusetts, on the line? I need to brief him on the situation here."

As soon as Amherst's Chief Swanson picked up the phone, his Minneapolis counterpart jumped in and described the shooting, including an outline of what they now knew about Albert.

"The shooter is Albert Hill from Rocky Mount, North Carolina," Chief Taylor clarified. "He and Dr. O'Connor knew each other as undergraduates at Amherst College. He says he had, and I quote, 'a religious awakening' a few years back. He claims he shot Dr. O'Connor because the professor was doing the devil's work. He confessed to the shooting, and we have twenty eyewitnesses. We have a team of psychiatrists standing by to do a preliminary psych evaluation. We're also trying to reach his minister in Rocky Mount and his family.

"Dr. O'Connor is in stable but critical condition at Saint Paul's Hospital. Mrs. O'Connor informed us that Mr. Hill visited the O'Connors' residence in Amherst two months ago in May. Mrs. O'Connor felt that Hill's behavior was strained and hostile, but Dr. O'Connor dismissed it. The O'Connors also spotted Hill in several book-signing audiences earlier in the tour. According to Mrs. O'Connor, they were surprised but too busy to think about it. That's what we have."

"Thanks for the report," Chief Swanson responded. "Sam O'Connor is well-known and well liked in this community. This news will come as a real blow. I know Angel Hernandez personally. He's a good man. Ran security at Amherst College. Thank God he was there."

"Another thing," Chief Taylor added, "we can't rule out a threat to the O'Connor children since we don't know yet if Mr. Hill acted alone or had accomplices. He may be connected with a fanatical religious group. We're still investigating. Also it looks to us like the press is going to be all over this."

"I got it. I'll send a squad car to the O'Connor residence to keep an eye on things right away, and thanks for your call. We'll be in touch. Whatever we can do to assist you, let us know."

"Thanks. I'll make sure you get all of our updates promptly as well."

John Swanson immediately dialed dispatch and ordered a squad car. After that call, he dialed the O'Connor house. Ed Sanders answered, identified himself, and told the chief his daughter had called soon after the shooting.

"I'm sorry for the news," Chief Swanson sympathized then asked, "is everything all right there?"

"Yes. It's quiet. The children are upstairs with my wife. Thanks for checking on us," Ed responded, happy and impressed that the chief was so concerned.

"Sam and your daughter, Amy, are well liked here. We want to make sure you're all okay. I just sent a car and a couple of officers over there to check the premises and keep an eye on things. They should arrive any moment."

"Do you think there's a threat to the children?" Ed inquired anxiously.

"We don't have any indication at this time of a threat, but we want to take precautions. Then you'll have the media to deal with. They're going to descend on this story big-time. We'll have officers there to help keep that bunch in line, but you should expect a crowd. I'll be over myself after I make a few calls. Are you comfortable making a statement to the press? If not, I can do it for you."

"I'm a lawyer. I suppose I could make a statement."

"Well, Mr. Sanders, you can think that over. This may turn out to be a big story. We'll establish an information center for the press at police headquarters. Sergeant Bolin would make a good spokesman. Anyway, I'm going to take a ride over and stop in. Should be there in a little bit."

"Thanks, Chief. I'll let you know. And thanks again for your help and concern."

"You bet. I'll see you shortly," the chief concluded.

While her husband related his conversation with the police chief, Mary Sanders sat down on the sofa and closed her eyes; her awareness began to drift. She began thinking about her daughter and her grandchildren, seeing their energetic smiling faces. Sam's face popped into her awareness too, smiling. Strangely, she felt as if he was talking to her. At first she couldn't understand what he was saying, but then she thought she heard Sam speak. "It's okay, Mary. Everything is going to be all right. It's resurrection time. The Lord loves the one who loves the Lord."

Ed's emotional voice suddenly brought her back to the living room. "The whole thing is appalling! I wish we could be there with Amy and Sam, but I know the boys need us."

Mary turned her head and looked at her husband. She said confidently, "Ed, it's going to be all right. Sam will recover, and everyone will be fine."

Stunned, Ed countered, "I don't know where you're getting this certainty, Mary. Things look pretty damn bleak to me."

Mary took her husband's hand and gently continued, "I don't understand it, but I know. Sam just came to me and reassured me. 'Everything is going to be fine,' he said, and I believe it."

Ed thought to himself, everyone acts differently under stressful situations, but he didn't expect this from his own wife. Shrugging off his self doubt, he bent over and kissed her saying, "Mary, if you say so."

Word spread swiftly through Amherst that Sam O'Connor had been shot. Quite spontaneously, a little over a hundred or so of town residents and what few summer students were in town began to gather on the Amherst Town Common. At one point, someone in the crowd suggested they all sit and have a moment of silence. A feeling of peace embraced the group. More people kept joining. A couple of students arrived with a hundred candles, which they passed around. The light spread from person to person. After a moment, someone began to sing Dylan's "Blowin' in the Wind." Slowly, everyone joined in, "How many roads must a man walk down . . ."

When the song was over, people began to hug one another and talk quietly among themselves. Some were still sitting with eyes closed, some were praying. Sam had no idea how much he had affected people, and the gathering would have surprised him. Many thousands of prayers were heard that night in the highest of heavens, all of them asking for one thing, for Sam O'Connor to live.

Chapter 16:
The World Is Upside Down

SAM HAD BEEN HOME SEVERAL months recovering from his wound and surgeries. He had declined an initial offer from the college to return to teaching and had given up early on trying to respond personally to the hundreds of well-wishers who had sent cards and flowers. He had even started refusing the flowers as they arrived at his front door, accepting only the cards. The publicity from the shooting had elevated him to celebrity status.

The legal system declared Albert mentally ill, schizophrenic, and he therefore did not stand trial for the shooting. The court committed him to a state-run psychiatric hospital, where he would most likely stay for the next decade of his life pending a review process.

Amy was greatly relieved and delighted to have Sam home. Josh and Paul were thrilled to see their dad again. Sam was equally happy, especially in the first few months after the shooting. He was grateful they were together and apparently safe, yet he was nagged by doubts about the latter. How safe were they, really? How could he keep them safe? The questions went round and round in his mind. On top of that, he seemed to have lost any vision or direction for his life, except for the role he played for his wife and children. Sam saw nothing beyond the present moment, the present day, and by late fall, he felt moody and restless. He kept trying, without success, to push away his concerns about his family's security and the emptiness that came with a loss of meaning and purpose.

The holidays came and went. He did his best to put up a cheerful front for his parents and in-laws. Everyone gave him the benefit of the doubt and kept their concerns to themselves. However, the signs of Sam's depression were clearly visible. He had stopped shaving and grown thin, quiet, and withdrawn.

Amy asked all of them to give Sam time. Lillian doubled her prayers. Since in Jimmy's eyes, the law had failed to punish Albert adequately, he dreamed of revenge, though he knew he could never act on those fantasies. Christ's teachings had vanquished the warrior in him long ago. Ed and Mary maintained a thin veneer of disbelief, never fully accepting that such a tragedy could have befallen their daughter and son-in-law.

Sam was uncommunicative, confiding only in Kenny. A couple of times a week, he walked up the road, took the bus into town, and visited the White Oak Café. The two would sit in Kenny's small office, drink coffee, and talk. Like a priest sworn to the secrecy of the confessional, Kenny kept all Sam's thoughts in confidence.

It was a long, cold, and melancholy winter. In early spring, Sam stopped at the Jones Library and took out a few books on gardening. He created a small plot by digging up the part of the lawn with the most southerly exposure. He turned over the soil, added some seasoned manure, and mixed it in well. At the end of May, he turned the soil one more time then planted in early June his first tomato plants, along with bell peppers, string beans, zucchini, and yellow squash.

In the summer, he began taking long walks through the woods that surrounded the valley, sometimes wandering for half a day or more. He always brought *Leaves of Grass* with him, Sam and Walt Whitman tramping a perpetual journey together. Sam would stop along the way, usually at a brook where he found a good-sized rock to sit on, and read some verses out loud. All these things seemed like signs of hope, but Sam remained gloomy, as well as distant and reserved toward everyone except Kenny. Amy did her best to accept this. She knew Sam was struggling with the shock of being shot and that he had lost his identity in the process. She knew Sam needed her and needed Kenny too.

In July, Dean Griffin called again to see if Sam was ready to rejoin the faculty and start teaching again. Sam declined. He entered the kitchen. Amy stood over the sink, rinsing the lunch dishes. "Who was on the phone?" she asked without turning around.

"Dean Griffin," he answered tersely.

"Oh?" Amy said. She turned off the faucet, wiped her hands on her apron, and turned to face Sam. She caught Sam's eye, letting him know silently that she demanded more.

"I told him I wasn't coming back," Sam replied coldly.

"Sam, don't you think we should have discussed it?" Amy queried, clearly upset.

"No, why would we do that?" Sam spoke vaguely, avoiding looking at Amy.

"For God's sake, Sam, because I'm your wife. And you have a family to think of. What you do and don't do affects the boys and me. I need to know what we're going to do. I need to know what you're going to do. Is that so hard to understand?"

Amy felt frustrated and sad. She took a deep breath and tried to speak calmly. "You've shut me out, Sam. We don't talk about anything anymore, and there's a lot that needs talking about. This is not the man I fell in love with. "

Sam sat in silence wanting to shout a thousand different things, but instead he stated, "Amy, that Sam is gone."

"Sam, I'm going to be blunt because I see you disappearing into a morass of self-pity, and I know you're so much better than that. What about everything you learned from Maharishi? Doesn't anything he said provide some comfort or insight?"

"Maharishi led me to believe that getting shot was not possible."

"Sam, he never said anything like that. I was there too you know."

Amy spoke emotionally, while Sam's voice registered numbness. "No. Not in so many words, but everything he said implied that."

"What Maharishi told us was that everything that happens happens for good, and that truth is different in different states of consciousness. We all see life, all life's events, through lenses colored by our own beliefs, our own state of mind. Do you remember that part of the teaching?" Amy continued without waiting for an answer. "Your lenses are colored gray and sad right now. You're feeling victimized by life, by Albert, by Maharishi, so you see everything as sad, hopeless, depressing, and you're looking for someone or something to blame." Amy began to feel both relieved and stronger. She had wanted to say this to Sam for months.

"Yes," Sam tried to argue, "but . . ."

Sam had opened so few doors to her over the past year. Amy took advantage of the moment and jumped in before Sam could finish his objection. "Sam, it's been a year since you were shot. Your body has healed, but the rest of you has not. Right now, you're only looking at things through the eyes of your pain and disappointment, so you feel betrayed by life and even by Maharishi.

If there is a silver lining in all this, it will be nearly impossible to find it until you decide to pull yourself out of gloom. I hope you'll find a way. I'm always praying that you'll find a way. The boys and I love you. I miss you. Lots of people do, and we all want you to find your way back to life."

"Amy, I need time. I'm empty inside. I'm angry and I'm scared. I can't find the energy or will or inspiration to do what you're asking right now."

"How much time? Maybe you should go and talk to someone."

"I'm talking to Kenny. I don't know. Honestly, I don't. I have to rethink everything. I have to let go of everything, everything I ever felt sure of."

"Me? The kids?"

"No, you're a part of me. It's the world I've known, the things I've learned. It's all meaningless right now. I can't find the meaning in anything. Except that's not true. You and the kids are the only thing that's real, my only anchor, but then I don't seem to be able to hold on to anything else. I just need more time."

Amy walked out of the kitchen and into the living room. She sat down and started to cry. Hearing her cry, Sam wanted to follow her, sit down next to her, hug her, and kiss her tears away. But he couldn't. His emotions were rising, and he felt the rage in him building. So Sam walked down the hall to his study and shut the door. There was nothing he could do to comfort Amy. He hardly knew what to do to comfort himself.

Part Two

One should not give up, neglect, or forget for a moment his inner life, but he must learn to work with it and out of it, so that the unity of his soul may break out in all of his activities.

—Meister Eckhart

Chapter 17:
The Game Begins Anew

JULIAN DRISCOLL THOUGHT ABOUT LEIBNIZ. Since God is the creator and he is good and has all possibilities within himself, and since he could create any world he wanted and, with all of that, he created this one, it must be the best one that he could have created. Why would God not do his best work?

Creating the best of all possible worlds was Leibniz's argument. Julian wasn't sure if he understood the fullness of Leibniz's argument, but after all, it was Friday afternoon on a lovely September day. Besides, he suspected his grandmother was closer to the truth than many of the great philosophers. As a boy, Julian had often asked his Grandma Betty, "Why did God make the world?"

Ten years later, he recalled her answer as if it was yesterday—but it wasn't just the answer; it was the way she had said it. And it wasn't just that. It had been the look on her face, especially the brightness in her laughing, shining eyes that had captured him. Grandma Betty had said, "Well, I don't know for sure, but I do get the feeling sometimes that God made the world and us humans because he likes stories."

Julian was just over 6′2″ with room to fill on his lanky frame. He saw the world through sky blue eyes that gave the impression of an intellect in a perpetual state of inquiry. However, a dimpled chin and wavy brown hair with a reddish tinge, worn fashionably long, hinted that he liked to play almost as much as he liked to figure things out. To the twenty-year-old philosophy student at Amherst College, his grandmother's answer just felt right. Everyone likes stories, and everyone is creating his or her own story every moment of every day. While the bus rambled down the avenue, Julian

121

looked around at his fellow passengers, and a thought bubbled up inside: *Yes, we are all story makers, creating drama and reacting to drama, playing a role in someone else's story while starring in our own.* With that thought, Julian's mind went inward, like a boy chasing a tadpole into deeper waters. It felt as if he fell into a gap, a split second without thoughts, a moment of silence.

When Julian slipped into perfect stillness for an instant, Sam O'Connor, former professor, was sitting across from him on the bus. Sam assumed the young man was a student. He looked the part, and his shoulder bag of books pretty much confirmed the role.

The Boston Globe lay on Sam's lap, open to the sports section. Years earlier, Sam hadn't had time to read the paper or ride the bus. He had become an important man. However, the last eight years of Sam's life had been one long retreat from the events of July 14, 1978. His life had become quiet and contemplative. He had resigned his teaching position and lived in North Amherst with his wife and two sons, gradually sinking into relative obscurity. His shoulder had healed well but had lost some of its range of motion and his arm some strength.

The Yankees, Sam read, took two out of three games from the Sox in a crucial fall contest. It wasn't the pitching as much as the hitting. *It looks like the Sox will once again be left in the dust,* Sam thought, *but this kid just got hold of a change up and hit it out of the park. This one I need to keep an eye out for.*

Sam's face had taken on lines that overstated his age, some from being outdoors in all seasons, some from carrying a burden that he couldn't measure but felt deeply. His once thick dark hair—his Irish pride, along with his round green eyes—had thinned and silvered into a salt-and-pepper pattern. He had stopped shaving after the shooting. At first, his beard had grown in lighter than his hair, and his chin hair had shown up reddish blond. Over the years, his beard had lost its reddish tone. It was now almost white on his chin, with the salt-and-pepper color spreading across his cheeks and filling in his mustache.

Inadvertently, he caught Julian's eye. "Nice hit, kid," said Sam softly.

Julian, snapping back from his inner voyage, couldn't clearly make out what this silver-haired, bearded man had said, but he did notice his vivid green eyes. He nodded slightly to Sam in recognition. Taking in a little more of Sam, Julian noted his work boots, aged and faded jeans, stained flannel-lined shirt, and crooked nose, and he concluded he must be a farmer or wood cutter. The rugged image seemed somehow at odds with eyes that had a soft quality approaching kindness.

The next stop was Julian's. He picked up his bag, swung it onto his shoulder, nodded one more time to Sam, and stepped to the front of the bus. His thoughts now drifted off to seeing Katy. What video should he bring home to watch with lovely Katy? He had never loved anyone as much as he loved her. True, he loved his old Irish grandmother and his parents, of course, but this was decidedly different. The nearest he had come was his love for Freckles, his dog and constant companion through childhood and adolescence. Loving Katy was like that, only better. He hadn't known how soft was soft and how sweet was sweet until Katy had shown up in his life. It seemed as if that simple, tender, loving relationship held all the answers if only one could think of the right questions.

Pizza and a movie, Julian thought. Snuggling up with a warm and beautiful woman on a Friday night. Could anything be better? Maybe this is what led Leibniz to declare that this was the best of all possible worlds. Then Julian's mind turned to the topic of what movie to pick up. A comedy? A love story? A psychological drama? So many possibilities . . .

Sam watched Julian jump off the bus and thought about him for a minute more before turning back to the *Globe*. Sam liked riding the bus. The PVTA was a free bus service for the Five College area. Sam, being from the City, was a fan of public transportation. He had sold his car almost seven years ago after not using it since the events in Minneapolis and bought a '74 Ford pickup a year later. Very helpful on a small farm, that.

Meanwhile, Amy had graduated to a light green Nissan minivan with a bike rack permanently fixed to the rear hatch door. It functioned as the designated family vehicle. Amy kept daily life running. She drove her two sons to school when they missed the bus, did shopping of all kinds, transported half the team to soccer games, and made weekly Sunday visits to her parents' home in eastern Massachusetts. Sam barely drove his pickup, but it was there if he needed it.

Sam had made a mental note to keep an eye out for "the kid on the bus" and promptly forgot all about him. The following week, he went into town on the bus to do some errands. Amherst was bustling anew with the return of the college students. The downtown businesses were all relieved that the students were back, even if it meant the tranquility of the summer months abruptly ended. Sam knew Kenny was delighted to be back to the hustle of the café. "You can take the boy out of the city, but you can't take the city out of the boy," as the old adage goes, and it applied directly to Kenny, less so to Sam.

As Sam walked up on the other side of the street, Julian spied him. *Hey, that's the guy from the bus*, he thought. He hesitated and weighed in on whether he should try to meet him now or let him go. He decided to cross the street. At that moment, Sam stopped and turned around, looking directly at the young student. Surprised, Julian again hesitated, like a boxer trying to size up his opponent, but he continued in Sam's direction.

"How ya doing?" Julian asked sheepishly.

"I'm fine, and you?" Sam replied.

"We were on the bus together last week," Julian explained helpfully.

"Ah yes, I believe you are right about that," Sam acknowledged.

"Yeah, I'm Julian Driscoll." He held out his hand.

The older man took up the offered hand to shake. "Ah, Driscoll, a fine Irish name. Well, Julian Driscoll, I'm Sam O'Connor. As one fellow Irishman to another, I should be offering to buy you a Guinness, and if we were in the fair city of Dublin, I would do just that, but today a coffee will have to do. My best friend owns the White Oak. Come on, I'll buy you a cup."

For some reason, Julian felt at ease with this man, and he had time for a coffee. They made their way to the White Oak, where Sam helped himself to a couple of pastries and coffees, all of which was added to his tab. The two of them slid into a booth.

"Come here often?" Julian inquired.

"Ah, I've been here so often, sometimes it feels I've hardly been anywhere else," Sam observed as he slowly looked around.

"I see. So you live in town then?" Julian asked.

"No, just outside of town, North Amherst. My wife and I have a house, a garden, a few acres, two children, a dog, and a few goldfish. You know, the New England package for aspiring forty-something-year-olds. And you, Julian? Where dost thou lay thy head at day's end?"

"My girlfriend and I have a small apartment on Sycamore Street. We have geraniums and mums in a few clay pots, a tiny front yard with crabgrass, and a cat. You know, the student package," Julian explained good-naturedly.

"Ah, Julian, well-done. You are an Irishman, not in name only." Sam continued quietly, almost as if he was thinking aloud, "I suppose I've been living this dream so long, I've gotten a bit cynical." He looked up and engaged Julian again. "So a student you are. And what are you studying?"

"Philosophy."

"Oh, I didn't think anyone studied knowledge anymore."

"There are a few of us left. Not everyone's gone over to big business yet."

"Ah, I see. I'm an old philosophy major myself, but I thought the study of philosophy had gone out of fashion like the turtleneck."

Julian couldn't help himself and shot back, "Okay, Obi-Wan Kenobi."

Sam looked up, feeling as ancient as the stars seeing this young man with the sparkling eyes, sensing his lively awareness. He said, "Ah, Julian, yes, *Star Wars*." Sam looked across the table at the young man. "By the way, I'm here every Friday about this time. If you'd like, we could get together and talk philosophy over a good cup of joe."

Julian, sensing this was perhaps an extraordinary opportunity, jumped in. "Sounds great."

"Good. I'm glad. Are you studying at Amherst College?" Sam inquired.

"Yes, I'm a senior."

"What classes are you taking?"

"This semester I'm taking the great philosophers seminar. We just finished Plato, and now we're on to Leibniz. I'm also taking philosophy of science."

"You must have Bob Harris for great philosophers. He's been teaching that course forever and a day."

"You know Dr. Harris?"

"Yes, I do know him. He's a good man and a good teacher. You know, Plato is the key for all of Western philosophy. As Whitehead stated, 'Everything after Plato is just a footnote.' In order to understand the Western world in which we now find ourselves, we need to have the proper starting point. Do you agree?"

"Yeah, sure, that makes sense."

"The senses, dear boy, often lead one astray. The intellect is only a little bit better. The emotions can be wild, like the dry Santa Anna winds or like tidal waves in the night that strike with little warning. Plato believed that we can only acquire true knowledge one way: his Dialectic, the beloved concept that almost nobody understood from the first day he described it. Why, you might ask? It's simple. No one understands consciousness. Although everything *is* consciousness—the stars, the sun, the earth, the trees—even the rocks have consciousness. Everyone has it, and everyone is looking for it, usually without much success, though it exists everywhere, inside and out. Plato knew this. It's the old story of the man looking, looking everywhere for his glasses, not realizing he's already wearing them."

"I see. That old story," remarked Julian, not sure that he did know that one.

"Ah, my new friend, we all see like the blind. So here we go. You and I are apparently sitting in a café in a liberal New England college town having a pastry and coffee."

"I wouldn't say apparently. I would say it is true from an empirical standpoint."

"Good. Nevertheless, I maintain we can't know for sure. We could be dreaming, you in your bed and me in mine."

"Perhaps, but we know that isn't the case. For one thing, the table is solid, the coffee hot, and I already got up this morning."

"Julian, this table is not solid. Physics tells us that it's 99.99% empty space, and quantum physics tells us that it only exists as a probability until we focus our attention on it. The table's solidity is an illusion, reinforced by the beliefs, assumptions, and expectations we collectively maintain despite the basic science we all get in high school. In fact, our science classes tell us that the table is made of atomic and subatomic particles whirling at tremendous speeds. We continue to see it as solid because we've been conditioned to do so, but really, we'd be better off describing this table as waves like the quantum guys do. Solidity is an illusion. All of this"—Sam gestured—"is energy, impulses of energy, fluctuating waves of energy. Your coffee, my friend, tastes and feels hot because it's full of excited molecules.

"In truth, only part of you woke up this morning. The rest of you is still deeply asleep. Our brains get wired to perceive the world in a certain way. In Blake's words, we see the world through cloudy lenses, and if we want to see clearly, we have to clean our windows of perception. In the Eastern spiritual teachings, they call this cloudy perception *maya*, which means 'that which is not.' Our limited or programmed perception means that we continue to see the world in fixed ways. We see the world we expect to see rather than the world as it truly is. Most of us, therefore, live in an illusion. Plato knew it, and now quantum mechanics has described it, although almost nobody understands it, really."

Julian was puzzled, and he began to feel anxious. He thought to himself, *Who is this guy? What have I gotten into?*

Sam saw the young man's expression change from deep interest to uncertainty.

"Julian, don't be concerned. I felt the same way when I was told that I didn't have a leg to stand on in this world. And yet I've been standing, walking, and even dancing ever since just the same. As my ol' auntie used to say, 'You see, the world is both real and unreal at the same time.'

"What makes ignorance so tough is that few people recognize their ignorance. Most people are pretty attached to their own version of truth. Ignorance of the true reality, our inability to see the deepest truth about life, gets built into the brain physiology through a complicated filtering process. Our brain and senses interpret our experiences: good, bad, safe, dangerous, fulfilling, damaging, etc. The brain filters and processes information taken in from the senses, and this helps us survive and learn—which is positive, especially if you have a saber-toothed tiger to contend with. However, it can also make uncovering the truth of who we are in the biggest and most profound sense extremely challenging. But as the Buddhists say, 'Without Maya, there is no enlightenment,'" Sam concluded.

"Well, that's why education is so important," Julian said, trying to keep up with Sam's argument. "In my mind, education is a progressive force. The ability of the mind to grasp concepts and understand complexities is what makes us different from any other creature. It's our source of strength."

"Good, Jules, good, but we continue to be plagued by the same age-old problems. Suffering of all kinds is still rampant in the world. The intellect is limited for all its ability. It is not up to the task of figuring out the game or helping us know who we really are, without which collective progress can only limp along.

"As I see it, the Western educational paradigm fails to consider and educate the whole person. It does not address the whole brain or the whole person. We only aim to educate part of the person, mostly the rational, linear part. What we like to call higher education increases specialization and narrows the focus with not much time spent on context, on the big picture. Not only that, information in all fields multiplies so fast these days that no matter how much we learn, it can feel like our ignorance is growing as fast as our expertise. We need to enliven the vast potential in people everywhere, expand intelligence and creativity, expand and enliven the container of knowledge, not just the quantity of knowledge we ask ourselves to hold. If we keep functioning with a small fraction of our potential, if we do not become fully awake, it's unlikely that our quality of life, inside and out, will change much. Poverty, disease, hunger, fear, hatred, and suffering will continue. The few will live better. The many will be left far behind. The question really is how to educate the whole person everywhere. The academic world hesitates to acknowledge the scope of the problem because the solution is not apparent to them."

"So you obviously believe it can be done," Julian challenged, sitting against the back of the booth with his arms crossed.

"The knowledge and techniques are there, but not the courage and political will. Two forces seem to sway our thinking and sometimes battle for dominance. One force promotes stability, tradition, resistance to change. Staying with what we think works makes us feel safe. The second force recognizes that change is inevitable and supports progress, creativity, new ideas—in short, moving the pile forward."

"Why don't we adopt both approaches?"

"Ah, you catch on quick. You're a tribute to your Irish heritage. Yes, when these two forces function together in balance, then we have the best of both. The English language has no good word to describe this kind of deep balance, but the sages of India call it *dharma*. *Dharma* loosely translates as 'that which upholds,' that which supports life. India's wise men consider dharma to be alive and well in the individual and the world when the three basic forces governing all life maintain their natural equilibrium. They call these forces the three gunas and describe them as the forces of creation, maintenance, and destruction at work everywhere all the time. When humans are in touch with dharma, their thoughts and actions support that fundamental balance, and we can make great leaps of progress. Dharma is the key."

"All right, so there's a concept that describes this natural balance. Let's say it's true. Now what?"

"Do you mean how do we achieve it?"

"Yes."

"Well, Julian, it first has to take place on an individual level. A great sage once said, 'A green forest is made up of green trees.' Each one of us needs to be whole, needs to be fully aware, needs to be enlightened. It's that simple."

"That doesn't sound simple. You've just introduced three terms that need to be defined or explained in the context of your argument," Julian protested.

"Good. You're asking for a long and interesting story, but you're right. We can look at all this from numerous points of view, but it involves asking some outsized questions. How can people actualize their full potential and eliminate suffering from their individual and collective lives? Can a few affect the many in this regard? And by the way, how much time do you have?"

Julian looked at his watch and became aware of the time and the fact that his coffee was no longer excited. In fact, it had become quite cold. "I'm out of time!" Julian announced.

"Good for you," said Sam.

Julian looked momentarily puzzled but then said, "Listen, this is interesting stuff, but I'm going to be late, and my girlfriend Katy hates that. You mentioned you're here every Friday?"

Sam nodded.

"Good, I'll look for you next Friday around four, and perhaps we could continue the conversation then. I don't know what dharma is, but it sounds like an interesting concept."

"Julian, dharma is an omnipresent, life-sustaining force in the cosmos. It's always at work maintaining balance in every life, in every corner of the universe."

"Sounds brilliant." Julian swatted one more backhand across the net. "But if it's always at work, what's the problem? Why all the suffering?"

"That's a big topic. Could take up a few Fridays."

"Well, fair enough then. Dharma, glad somebody thought of it besides George Lucas. You know, *Star Wars*, the Force? See you next week. Dare I say, 'Same time, same place?' "

"I'll have to remember you're in the Star Wars generation. Yes, though 'same time, same place' is not exactly clear and precise language, particularly since time and space are not exactly what they appear to be."

"How do you know Dr. Harris?" Julian abruptly changed the subject.

"We're old friends. See you next Friday then. Please give Dr. Harris my warmest regards."

"Will do. Take care. Good talking with you." With that, Julian slung his backpack over his shoulder and headed out to the warm light of the fading day. *Another Friday night, another pizza, and another movie,* he thought as he strolled up the street and floated back into his satisfying dream of life.

Sam watched him move past the window and disappear from view. *I haven't spoken to a student like that in years. Everything just flowed. Interesting. We'll just see what happens.*

Kenny sat down and joined him. "Well, Sam, you look particularly animated. Had a good conversation, did you?"

"Yeah, Kenny boy. Short in some regard, but sweet. That young man is a philosophy major at Amherst."

"Really? The past is becoming the present. No wonder you're a little teary eyed."

"I think it's the coffee. Nothing fresher in the house?" Sam zinged.

"That pot was just brewed," Kenny protested, a bit defensive. "Maybe it's starting up again?"

"I think that bridge has been burnt."

"Maybe Mother Nature has other plans for you, my friend."

"Maybe," Sam shrugged. "When it comes to Mother Nature, you never know for sure what's up. As John Lennon sang, 'Life is what happens to you as you're busy making other plans.'" Sam paused and then said, "Kenny, my dear comrade-in-arms, that kid's got a lot going for him."

"Yeah, Sam, another Irish kid gifted with intelligence. Maybe it all starts again with him?" Kenny repeated, trying to get Sam to concede the point.

"Lord knows I've been warming the bench for many a season, waiting to get back into the game."

"I don't see it quite that way. You had a long run. Like Ted Williams. But no matter how glorious a season, it comes to an end. All the players take a rest. Before you know it, spring training rolls around and a new season begins. No, Sammy, you weren't really benched. You were on the injured reserve list. The season just ended, and now it's turned spring again," Kenny pontificated.

"Kenny, you're using my own material on me, spring training and all. Baseball analogies? Is that how I sound?"

"Yeah, I've been waiting for a chance to throw some baseball stuff your way. Sounded pretty good too. Now home with you to Amy and those wonderful boys."

Kids, a dog, a few goldfish, and Amy, Sam contemplated. "Ah yes, home beckons the weary soul."

From the way that Julian described Sam, Katy imagined that he was either a terrifically bright man who had spent a lot of time thinking or a slightly mad genius type—or perhaps a burned-out PhD candidate who enjoys preying on undergraduates in back-room cafés. However, all Katy offered was, "Sounds like an interesting character. You might want to get the scoop on this guy from Dr. Harris, seeing that they were friends and all."

"Yeah, I'll check with him on Monday after class," Julian agreed.

Julian felt restless all night. He couldn't enjoy the movie, although it was pretty good. He didn't feel romantic, didn't feel like reading. "Hey, Kate, I'm going to take a walk around the block."

"Okay, go ahead. I've got a few things to finish up."

The sky was clear, and the moon was almost full. He knew there was something about Sam he couldn't quite describe—his liveliness and his bright penetrating eyes. Sometimes, for a moment, Sam gazed at him with a slight smile on his face. That gaze was a knowing look, a look in which one could rest, the same look that Grandma Betty gave him from time to time as a child. A wondrous feeling came over him. Julian realized that in meeting Sam, he had found a genuine human being, and his heart quickened. With that thought came the feeling of hope, hope that something magical could happen, that his life could be transformed, that he could put his doubts about himself and the world to rest. Nothing was definitive enough for him to hang his hat on at that particular moment, but it was a start, and he was intrigued.

At evening's end, Julian and Katy snuggled with each other in bed and drifted off to sleep. Julian began to dream. He was striding again on a bright sandy beach with turquoise water lapping on the shore. Sam, dressed in white flowing robes, was ambling toward him.

"Ah, Julian," Sam greeted him. "The question is, are we awake or are we dreaming? Are time and space fixed or fluid? Are we stuck in a prison or free to explore the whole creation? Is our conditioning our undoing or just the platform for leaping into the unknown? How we answer these questions determines to a large part how we'll participate in the divine play of creation."

Then Sam dove into the water and rose into the air. There he sat in full lotus, hovering above the water like the sun in the sky. "Come on, Julian, dive in," he urged. "It is refreshing beyond imagination."

Julian ran into the water and dove. The water was both warm and cool. He emerged floating in waist-deep water, light, buoyant, and laughing. Sam grinned at him. The warmth from that smile penetrated his body like the sun on a July day at the Jersey shore.

Julian awoke feeling deeply relaxed and wide awake. He heard Katy in the kitchen. He imagined she was already showered, dressed, and ready to go. *Darn Vermont farm girls who rise with the sun.* Then he remembered his dream. *Wow! Who is this guy Sam O'Connor anyway?*

"Katy, Katy, I had the weirdest dream."

"Well, lover boy, you've got exactly one-half hour to get ready if you want a ride in this morning. Coffee is on, English muffin's in the toaster ready to go down."

Boy, Julian thought, *she's better than Mom.* "Okay, honey pie, I'm in the shower."

"I can't be late, Julian, so no fooling around."

Just then, Julian made a grand entrance into the kitchen with Katy's robe on and his hair wrapped in a towel. "Madame, I never fool around. I'm always serious, proper, and on time."

"Julian, get out of my robe. You're going to wreck it."

"If you insist." Dropping the robe, he stood naked and proud.

"Julian, get in the shower, or I'm going to burn your muffin and you're on the bus."

Off to the shower he went. Katy thought, *This is like living with a puppy.*

"For goodness sakes," she muttered as she bent over to pick up the robe.

Julian showered, dressed, grabbed his backpack, poured his coffee, peanut-butter-and-jellied his muffin, and made it to the truck two minutes late. Katy was in the driver's seat, sitting with the motor running, waiting for Julian impatiently. As he swung into the passenger seat, she sighed dramatically and complained, "Late again."

Julian defended himself. "You know what, my love? Your problem is you take this time and space stuff too seriously. You know, all of this is just a whirling mass of energy anyway. There's no such thing as early or late since time and space, at a deeper level, don't really exist."

"Yeah, tell it to Professor Radisson. He hates when his students show up even a few minutes late, even on a Saturday morning field trip," she protested, missing Julian's brilliant observation, which she just couldn't see at the moment.

"I might just do that," Julian said with an air of defiance. Julian decided to keep the dream about Sam O'Connor to himself. It was neither the time nor the place to share his dream with the woman he loved as she barreled down the road in her dad's clambering pickup truck toward campus.

Chapter 18:
Julian Takes a Trip to the Library

O N MONDAY MORNING, JULIAN SAT through his great philosophers class with one question in mind for Dr. Harris: "Who the heck is Sam O' Connor?" However, Julian had to wait until after class to have the professor to himself. Finally, Dr. Harris gave the reading assignment and ended class for the day. Julian waited for his classmates to leave the room before going up to speak to his professor.

"Dr. Harris, good class," Julian began.

"Glad you enjoyed it, but it seems to me you were rather preoccupied through most of it. You hardly said a word, Julian," Dr. Harris observed.

"Well, you're right about that. I do have something on my mind. I ran into an old friend of yours, and he asked me to give you his regards."

"Really? Who?"

"Sam O'Connor."

"Oh yes. Sam. And where did you meet him?"

"First, I sort of met him on the bus."

"Sort of? Now, Julian, in studying philosophy, we are attempting to sharpen the intellect and the power of persuasion. Let's try that again, shall we? "

"I first saw him on the bus, and later I met him on Elm Street, and we talked at the White Oak Café," Julian clarified.

"I see. Well, yes, Sam O'Connor and I share a bit of history," Dr. Harris offered.

"He said you were colleagues."

"Yes, that's true. What did you think of him? An interesting, charming person, no doubt?" the professor probed.

"Well, yeah. He's fascinating. Good guy. I really liked him, and he seemed to have such great insights into how things work and why. What's the story on him?"

"Julian, let's walk together if you have time." Dr. Harris gestured with a sweep of his arm.

"Okay. Yeah, that will work. I've got a break between classes."

"Good. Sam O'Connor was a brilliant philosopher and teacher. He was a professor at this college eight years ago. He was different from the rest of us. He was restless, not content with studying traditional Western philosophy. He wanted more. He was looking for something like absolute truth in a deeply personal way," Dr. Harris disclosed.

"But the pursuit of the truth is something all students of philosophy get involved in."

"True. Sam, however, didn't want just to study and understand Plato and Socrates in a significant way. He wanted to become them, live their truth. He wanted not only to understand the knowledge, but also to embody it more or less," Dr. Harris continued.

"Isn't that the goal of everyone who loves philosophy?"

"Yes and no. Some feel that one must maintain a certain objectivity when teaching. Teachers can't be so wrapped up in themselves that they forget their academic purpose. All of us wish to emulate Socrates and Plato, but we don't all wish to become them. We wish to ponder their works, gain insights into their vision and knowledge, and teach it to others. This business about consciousness that Sam went on about, it was an interesting theory, but to lose oneself in it—it showed a nonprofessional attitude towards his work," Dr. Harris concluded.

"Well, from what you said so far, I'm not getting it. Are you saying he got on the wrong side of things?"

"No, I'm not saying that exactly. Sam suddenly got interested in Eastern philosophy, studied with a guru with some belief that the deep pursuit of those ideas would help to illumine Western thought. In the beginning, it sounded good, but Sam got so caught up in it that he didn't seem to know where he was headed or why he was doing it anymore. The academic motive seemed to disappear. Excitement is a good, positive energy, but taken too far, it turns to chaos. Sam's life, in my opinion, went into chaos, and he crashed and burned in a manner of speaking."

"Okay. For the sake of argument, I'll accept that. But what actually happened?"

"Sam wrote a book and became famous," Bob Harris stated and smiled thinly.

"And that's it?" Julian exclaimed.

"Yes, in a nutshell. Naturally, there's more to the story, but really, Julian, you have no idea what fame can do to you. He took himself so seriously, you see. As I said, he got involved with an Indian guru and all that went with that. He joined the pop culture and tried to call it holistic philosophy. Sam stopped doing rigorous philosophy. The rest of the story is all in the library. I can't tell you what to do, but I strongly suggest you not get too involved with him. Talk with him, yes, but leave it at that," Harris cautioned.

"Why would you say that?" Julian asked defensively.

"Sam O' Connor was a friend. He could have been great in his field. He gave it up to chase a dream. You have a good mind, and you're a good student. Stick to your studies and don't get distracted. That's my advice to you."

"Sam told me to give you his warmest greeting."

"Ah. Yes. He would do that. He's a good man—a dreamer, but a good man. Yes. Tell him hello if you see him again. I'm curious, now that we're talking about him, how things are turning out for Sam."

"Okay, Dr. Harris, I'll let him know," Julian said half-heartedly.

Julian sauntered through campus, head down, digesting the conversation with Dr. Harris. Suddenly, he said out loud to no one in particular, "Wow, he was famous! Wow! Wait till I tell Katy. That's so cool. The guy was famous!" He ran across the campus to the library to see what he could find out.

Once there, he quickly found Sam's book, *From Here to Here: the Pathless Path Home.* As he was checking it out at the circulation desk, he asked the librarian if there was any information on Dr. Sam O'Connor. Mrs. Cranston, the librarian, looked up, curious to see who was asking about Dr. O'Connor. It had been years since a student had requested information about the once famous professor.

"Well," she replied, "I can help you pull up the microfiche. Dr. O'Connor was a wonderful man. So kind and intelligent, so dedicated to his students. What happened to him was tragic."

"What happened?"

"You are about to find out. It was written up in the *Times*, the *Globe* and, of course, the local *Gazette*. Give me a minute and I'll have it for you to review. It's funny. Nobody has asked me about Sam O' Connor in years, and yet he had this campus in a tizzy."

"I just met him in town," Julian shared.

"Really? How is he?" the librarian's voice reflected genuine concern.

"Seems fine to me. He definitely has some ideas worth exploring," Julian responded.

"He didn't mention what happened?" Mrs. Cranston inquired anxiously.

"No. I didn't even know he wrote a book until Dr. Harris mentioned it," offered Julian.

"That's interesting. Come with me and I'll pull that microfiche. I personally thought Sam O' Connor was the best thing to happen to this college in years. What happened to him was a tragedy. It was a tragedy for all of us."

Within a few minutes, she pulled the file that contained the news articles and handed it to Julian. He sat down at the viewer and started with *The New York Times*. "Dr. Sam O'Connor," he read, "was shot at a book signing in Minneapolis yesterday."

Julian thought, *Oh god! He was shot!*

He read the rest of the article in a state of shock. He didn't know what to make of it; he didn't know what to do with the rage he suddenly felt. All at once, he detested Dr. Harris for his lack of concern and compassion, his air of superiority. Why didn't Sam mention this?

As Julian read on, he became more sober and resigned to the events of that awful day in Minneapolis. Other scholars, writers, artists, and musicians rallied around, arguing that intellectual and creative expression was under attack. Everyone had a point of view, an opinion, but nobody fully understood what happened and why.

Julian's enthusiasm to tell Katy about Sam's fame was overshadowed by the weight of what he had learned. When he got home, he told her about his conversation with Dr. Harris, his trip to the library, and what he had discovered there. He also showed her Sam's book.

"Wow," Katy said softly, "and you met this guy on the bus, on the PVTA?"

"Yeah, and the thing is, he's really an amazing man."

"He's certainly a unique thinker. I'll give him that," Katy came back.

"You don't understand. This shooting and this man, it was a real big deal. My god, the world press reported on this for days. It continued to resonate for months afterwards, causing debates about religious extremism and secularism, about freedom of expression and the threats to it. After a while, it wasn't even about Sam anymore. As a public figure, he just sort of faded away. He was forgotten. Even the college forgot him, and the community. Sam was a great man with a rare vision of the world. It's hard to understand how everyone could just forget."

"Maybe Sam wanted to be forgotten," Katy ventured. "As you just said, it wasn't just the shooting. There was all the attention afterwards. Maybe it was too much for him."

"You might have something there. The librarian who helped me thought it was a great loss for all of us," Julian added.

"She's probably right. I hear what you're saying, Jules. I don't know. I guess you're going to have to ask Sam what his perspective is," Katy suggested. She turned away and started to prepare dinner. Julian slipped into the living room, sat down on the lumpy couch with Sam's book, and opened it to the dedication page.

"To His Holiness Maharishi Mahesh Yogi for bringing the light of Pure Consciousness to the Western world."

Who's Maharishi Mahesh Yogi? Julian wondered. He perused the introduction while Katy bustled about in the kitchen, and after ten minutes or so, she called out that dinner was ready. Julian put the book down and joined her at the table. They started to eat and talk about their classes, the day's other conversations, and the work they needed to finish. And they both forgot all about Sam O'Connor.

Chapter 19:
A Change in Direction

*A*SEEM WALKED OVER TO THE *master's house. He was smiling inwardly at the unfolding drama he knew was taking place. He announced himself as he approached the open door.*

Aseem left his sandals outside the door and then came in. He bent his ample frame to touch the master's feet and said, "Namasté, Swamiji."

The master was sitting on a small platform in the front room. "Namasté, my old friend. Please sit," he greeted Aseem. The master gestured to a carpet covering the stone floor in front of the platform.

Aseem sat down and crossed his legs, adjusting his dhoti. The cook was approaching fifty-two, and he had grown more about the waist with every passing year. Nevertheless, he could still slip nimbly to the floor and back up again due to a lifetime of practice.

Aseem looked up into his master's shining face. Despite the master's nearly seventy-five years, he had an almost youthful appearance. The master's face remained almost completely free of lines, reflecting his tranquility. True, his hair and beard were gray. True, he was thinner and less robust than he had been in days gone by, but his eyes were brighter and clearer than ever, and visitors could lose themselves entirely in their depth. Aseem recalled when he first saw those eyes as a boy of thirteen. He had succumbed instantly to the boundless love and kindness that emanated from the master's countenance.

Aseem offered, "Master, Devendra came to see me. It appears he is quite taken with Poona's daughter, Jyoti."

"Yes," the master confirmed. "Now with the passing of Jyoti's father, things are set in motion. The lives of Poona, Jyoti, and Devendra are all about to change. Balram too may get caught up in all this."

"Devandra will seek you out tomorrow, perhaps after morning meditation," Aseem informed Swamiji.

"Yes, and Poona will want to talk to you."

"She's already spoken to me concerning her brother-in-law," Aseem revealed.

"I see, and what advice did you give her?" Swamiji's face remained unreadable as he asked the question.

"I simply listened to her story and feelings and reminded her that you would have everything in mind and not to worry."

"Not me, Aseem. God has everything in hand. Now, when Poona comes to see you again, invite her to come and sit with me after the evening meal. When her brother-in-law comes to you, he'll ask to see me as well. I'll see him in a day or two," the master carefully instructed.

"It could be difficult to put him off for two days. He is an insistent man," Aseem observed.

"My dear Aseem, a young elephant is no match for a bull elephant, no matter how much noise he makes or dust he kicks up." The master laughed heartily at his own joke.

Aseem raised an eyebrow. "Master, are you implying that I'm gaining more girth than height?"

"Your stature reflects how good a cook you are."

The two men shared an affectionate laugh.

"Aseem," Swamiji continued, "life is a mystery. Each life is a miniature universe. All lives are infinite. The individual life only appears more bound than the vast display of the stars and planets. Yet, it's all the same infinite. The Self unfolds Itself through Itself, by Itself. The story of creation is the story of the Self unfolding. Of course, it is just that: a story. Nothing, including the entire creation, ever really happens. It is all an appearance, a dream, and that's what we call lila shakti, the divine play of creation. This you already know very well.

"We simply bear witness to it while we play out our human roles—in our case, I as master and you as the cook. Someday, Aseem, you will become the master, and I will move on to the next adventure. But we both know that what appears on the surface of life is a mirage. In truth, we are the same unbounded, eternal consciousness. This is the mystery solved by few. Millions of souls play their roles without realizing their true nature. They take the mirage seriously. They get lost in complexity and stories and the suffering they bring."

"And my present role is that of a bull elephant?" asked Aseem, wide-eyed like a child.

The master burst into laughter. "Yes, my friend, you play the role of the wise bull elephant, stomping and trumpeting. Now be like Ganesh, the remover of obstacles, but in reverse. If Ganesh can remove obstacles, he can just as easily put a few in the way. Now, my dear friend, please send me two trustworthy young chelas to carry an important message to the raja. Pack them some food and water, for they must leave at first light."

Aseem rose from the floor, bowed, and departed quickly for the kitchen. He looked over the chelas busy preparing food and considered which ones to send. He knew that carrying out a direct instruction from the master was a valuable spiritual training exercise for the student. His intuition helped him make the selection, and he sent the two chelas he chose to the master's house.

The two young disciples arrived in good haste and found the master waiting for them, holding a scroll secured with his personal wax seal.

"Namasté," the teenage boys said in unison then quickly prostrated themselves at his feet.

"Namasté," the master responded. "Please carry this scroll to the residence of the raja. You must give it to no one except the raja himself. Announce yourselves as my disciples, and explain that you carry an important message from me to be read only by him. The palace servants will challenge you and demand that you turn over the scroll to them. However, insist on giving the scroll only to him.

"Leave at sunrise. You will need to walk steadily and take no more than two short breaks to reach the raja's palace by nightfall. The raja will offer you an evening meal and a room in which to sleep. Break your fast early the next morning, and be prepared to carry a scroll from him back to me. Return quickly so you'll arrive back before dark. Understood?"

"Yes, Swamiji."

"Take this scroll and take care of it. Now go to the cook and take your evening meal and rest. Aseem will pack some food and water for your trip. See him in the morning before you leave. He will explain the best route to take. Namasté."

"Namasté," responded the young chelas, who bent once more to touch his feet before departing.

Once outside they exploded with excitement. A trip to the Raja's palace on an important mission was a major event in their quiet, well-ordered lives. They sped back to the kitchen, where Aseem admonished them to take care of the scroll and follow the master's instructions explicitly. "I will wake you before dawn, and you have a long walk ahead of you, so rest early this evening. When the birds rest, you rest. When the birds wake up and begin to sing, get up, wash, and dress in *a fresh, clean dhoti. It's simple. To be sure you are on schedule, I'll come as the nosiest bird and wake you up."*

"With all due respect, Aseem, what type of bird would you be?" asked the older of the two disciples, setting the younger one off into giggles.

Aseem saw the joy in their eyes and responded, "I would be a fat bird."

The two chelas erupted into laughter. Aseem continued, "I would be so fat, I couldn't fly, but I'd also be so strong that no snake or wild cat would ever dare cross my path."

The chelas laughed even harder as Aseem began walking about like a fat bird, flapping his arms, bobbing his head, and craning his neck like a stork fervently looking for its next meal.

"But, Aseem, would you be a beautiful fat bird or a plain bird?" they asked.

"I would be an ugly bird to some, but to he that created me, I would be the most beautiful bird in existence." Aseem pranced away but called back to the boys, "Remember, get your rest, for I promise you tomorrow will be the longest day in your young lives." He bobbed his head and strutted out of view.

The next morning, well before dawn, Aseem gently shook the two chelas awake. "Wash up and meet me in the kitchen," he whispered. After about ten minutes, they bounced enthusiastically into the kitchen. Aseem drew a map for them and gave them instructions about where they could rest, through which villages they would pass, and whom in those villages they might meet. "I have packed you chapatis, warm rice with saffron, and peas. I wrapped them delicately in banana leaves, so take care when you open them."

"But what about our morning meditation, Aseem? It wouldn't be right to miss it."

"Today you are too busy to meditate."

"What will the master think?"

"He will be happy if you can complete your assignment. Life with the master is attuning our will to his. Now take some chai and fresh curd and be on your way."

Aseem had made this journey numerous times himself at the master's request. He knew many people along the way. Everyone wanted to feed him, and he stopped frequently along the way to eat. Most often, someone with an ox and cart would offer to take him to the next village. There, another farmer would offer him a ride, and on and on he would go. When he came close to the ashram on his return, he would ask that his ride drop him off a mile before he reached it. Thus, he would walk into the village fresh and energetic.

The master, of course, knew Aseem was being fed along the way and had numerous rides in both directions. He always asked the cook, "How was the journey?"

Aseem would reply, "At times it was hard, but I persevered."

"It appears, Aseem, that you have gained even more weight on this trip than the last," Swamiji would observe with a straight face.

"You tease me so." Aseem would look at the floor and blush. "Some kind, generous people did feed me some sweets along the way," he would admit reluctantly.

"Some people? How many is some?" The master would pretend to be stern.

"I never thought to count. My only intention was to get to the raja's palace to give him your message."

"And you fulfilled my request?"

"Yes, Master, and here is his reply," he would say and hand the scroll to Swamiji with a glow of pride.

"Thank you. Go and rest now," Swamiji would conclude the interaction. After Aseem would leave, Swamiji would chuckle to himself.

In time, he asked Aseem to visit the villages on his route and tell them stories from the Mahabharata and Ramayana. Aseem was always welcomed as warmly as if he was Ganesh himself, and the grateful villagers indulged him with sweets as he shared his tales with great relish.

Once the young charges were on their way to the raja's palace, Aseem roused the ashram's other boys and young men. Every morning he made a big pot of chai and placed an abundance of fruit on the kitchen's plain wooden table for everyone. The chelas helped themselves to a piece of fruit and a cup of chai and went back to their small, cell-like rooms to practice yoga, asanas, and meditation. After meditation, they sat with the master in the garden outside his house to receive darshan. They spent the rest of the morning performing daily chores: tending the gardens, caring for the cows, and working in the kitchen to prepare the main meal of the day.

This particular morning after darshan, Devendra waited until the other disciples departed and then approached the master, who sat beneath the verandah on the north side of his house. After greeting him traditionally, he spoke with emotion, "Master, I find myself in a most difficult place."

Swamiji nodded for him to continue.

"I'm so embarrassed. I don't know how to tell you."

"Close your eyes for a moment and calm yourself. The words will come easily then," Swamiji advised.

After a few minutes, Devendra's mind became quiet. He opened his eyes and began to speak. "In my heart, I have broken my vows. I am in love with a young woman from the village," Devendra finished and looked at the ground.

"Who?" Swamiji feigned surprise.

"Jyoti." Devendra looked up again as he spoke her name.

"I see. Many young monks go through this. It's natural."

"But I feel so ashamed." Devendra's face grew red. He was holding back his tears.

"You shouldn't. Shame has no place in your heart. Devendra, when I first met you more than nine years ago, I saw your great capacity to love. I also saw your brilliant intellect. For a moment, I hesitated to take you on as a disciple," the master disclosed.

"You did?" Devendra was stunned.

"Yes. I knew you would benefit from the discipline and routine of the ashram. I knew you would have good experiences in meditation and that your keen intellect would devour the knowledge. However, I also knew that you were not born to be a monk. You are a householder." The master paused, knowing that his next words would shock his disciple. He spoke kindly but firmly, "Your time here is up. You have spent it wisely and gained much."

Devendra was shaken. "But what do I do? Where do I go?"

"As your master, as your spiritual father, I will speak to Jyoti's mother and see if she will agree to your marriage." The master spoke calmly as if the news were not momentous.

"My marriage?"

"Yes, your marriage." Swamiji paused again, letting the information settle in while carefully monitoring its effect on his disciple. After a minute, he continued, "In the Lord's divine plan, this union was arranged before your birth, so I'm sure all parties will agree. Of course, you will have to leave the ashram, and your brother will go with you."

Devendra was speechless at first. Finally, he summoned some words, "Where shall we go? Should we go to my village?"

"For a visit perhaps. I will know more by sunset."

"I don't know what to say," Devendra mumbled.

"Then it would be best to say nothing," Swamiji stated. "Now I have other people to meet. We'll talk more tonight."

"Namasté," Devendra managed. He touched the master's feet and left.

Devendra sought out Balram and told him everything. Balram didn't say a word. When he had heard his brother out, he asked to be alone with his thoughts.

Balram knew in his heart that he should leave the ashram with his brother, but he longed to stay. He sought out Aseem for advice.

He found him on a bench outside the kitchen, singing to himself. "Aseem," he began, May I have a word?"

Aseem stopped singing, looked up at Balram's troubled face, and nodded. "Sit," he said, pointing to a place on the bench beside him.

"Aseem, Swamiji is arranging for my brother to marry, and both of us must leave the ashram," he reported emotionally.

"I see," said the cook, who seemed barely moved by the news. "And what are you going to do?"

"The master said my brother and I are householders and not cut out to be lifelong monks. If it was up to me, I would stay longer, but the master wants me to leave with Devendra."

"I will miss you," said the cook sincerely, for he was fond of Balram. "And the younger chelas will also miss you."

"Are you a recluse by nature, Aseem?"

"Hardly."

"But you've been here for forty years or more."

"My nature is to be active like you. When I met the master, I was thirteen years old. I knew I was meant to be with him. He was a young man himself, maybe thirty years of age. I became his first disciple. I cooked, cleaned, washed the clothes, milked the cow, everything. I had to be active to take care of him. My path is that of devoted service. I meditate only now and then. I am always thinking about what more I can do for him.

"Others became disciples, and the master put me in charge of their daily activities. I have seen many come and go. Very few stay past ten years, but their lives are changed forever as yours and Devendra's have been.

"You are like me, Balram, in that your path is one of service. In doing service, you find your joy. To us, all are God. Everyone we meet is God, and we serve all of them with gratitude."

The two men were quiet for a moment. Balram opened to the cook's insight and recognized its truth. He turned to the cook and said softly, "Thank you, Aseem, for everything you have given me. Namasté," he said with great feeling and bowed.

Aseem responded gently, "Namasté, my son."

The next day, Poona's brother-in-law, Arun Malhotra, came to see Aseem. He was a well-dressed slim man in his mid-forties. He began politely by introducing

*himself and handing Aseem a carefully arranged bowl of colorful fruit. "Namasté,"
he greeted Aseem. "May the Lord of Creation grant you health and long life."*

"Namasté," returned Aseem. "How can I help you?"

"I wish to see the master," Arun requested.

*"I see. What business do you have with him?" Aseem inquired as if he knew
nothing.*

*"I want to make marriage arrangements for my niece, and I know that nothing
gets done in the village without Swamiji's approval," Arun explained. "My wife's
cousin just lost his wife and is interested in marrying my brother's daughter." Such
complex marriage arrangements were common, and Arun described the situation
without hesitation. "We would also welcome my sister-in-law into our household."
Arun watched Aseem's face for some response. Finding none, he continued. "I also
want to sell my brother's house. Since my brother created only a meager dowry for
my niece, I will add to it when I'm paid for the house and its contents, minus, of
course, a commission."*

*"You have figured out everything," Aseem noted. "Very impressive. How old
is your wife's cousin, may I ask?"*

"Forty-eight," Arun supplied.

*"Jyoti is educated and can read and write. Does your wife's cousin read and
write?" Aseem queried.*

*"My brother was a fool to educate her and a bigger fool not to marry her at
thirteen," Arun answered irritably.*

"I take it he doesn't read or write," Aseem persisted.

"No, but he is a good man."

"How so?"

"He's honest and works hard." Arun stood his ground.

*"Is he a religious man? Goes to the temple?" Aseem continued his
interrogation.*

"No, that is the wife's duty."

"Does he have children from his first wife?" Aseem asked without let up.

*"Yes, he has several sons, two daughters, and two grandchildren." Arun felt
confused and increasingly angered by the long list of questions from the cook.*

"He is an older man. Has age brought him wisdom?"

*"When he was young," Arun disclosed, "he had a bad temper, and on occasion
he beat his wife and children, but now some of his anger has gone. I suppose my
niece could benefit from an occasional beating, hey, Aseem?"*

"No, I don't feel any benefit comes from beatings," Aseem stated strongly.

"But you are famous for yelling and ordering these young chelas about," Arun tried to defend his obvious error.

"Every word I yell is coated in reverence and love. My young chelas know this. Now, back to the business at hand. You must first put your proposal in writing, and then I'll give it to the master for his consideration."

"In writing?" Arun asked, surprised.

"Yes," Aseem spoke firmly and crossed his arms.

Not used to being asked to wait, Arun pronounced arrogantly, "That's ridiculous! Why don't you just arrange an audience and we'll talk it over?"

"By tradition, this type of affair is best approached by writing out the proposal. It requires some thinking to write it out, and the better written, the more consideration the master will give."

"But I can't write!" protested Arun.

"Oh, but you can count?" Aseem asked. He was thoroughly enjoying this interview but kept it well hidden.

"Yes, and I know if I'm being cheated!" Arun's face was now red with anger.

"No one here is going to cheat you out of what is yours. You'll find a man by the village vegetable shop who can write out the proposal for you. His fee is reasonable. But wait a moment. I just remembered he is visiting a sick relative. He should be back tomorrow. Come back with your letter in two days, and I'll present it."

"Aseem, if you are causing me an unnecessary delay, you'll pay," Arun exploded.

"My friend, you'd be wise to remember I'm the gatekeeper to the master. No one goes through the gate without my permission."

"If I don't gain satisfaction, I'll go to the raja."

"I hope you have a pleasant journey then," Aseem concluded and walked calmly back to his kitchen, where he finally allowed himself to break out into a huge grin.

Chapter 20:
Nothing's Gonna Change My World

THE FOLLOWING FRIDAY ROLLED AROUND, and Julian kept his appointment with Sam at the White Oak Café. Sam sat at a table toward the back, sipping a cup of coffee. He waved at Julian from his seat. When Julian was about to join him, he offered, "I've already paid for a cup of joe for you, so help yourself and pull up a chair."

Julian left his backpack with Sam, walked to the coffee counter, and poured himself a cup. He rejoined Sam and thanked him. He then began abruptly, "I spoke to Dr. Harris about meeting you."

"Did you, now? Did you give him my greetings?"

"Yeah. He seemed surprised when I mentioned I met you."

"Academics are surprised by a lot of things."

"He seemed to have mixed feelings about your academic career. He mentioned things got offtrack a bit," Julian threw out.

"Yes, well, he would. The world is an abiding mystery. Dr. Harris tries to keep that mystery at bay, so he needs to stay on track."

"Well, my girlfriend thinks you might be a bit of a nut," Julian shared frankly.

"Does she? Hmmm . . . Tell her by certain standards she's half-right. I like her already. But, Julian, in the face of these warnings, you came to see me anyway. Why?"

"Yeah, well, you are a pretty unique character, and I figured, what the hell. I could learn something from you."

"You may or may not. Depends on you and how interested you are."

"Dr. Harris said you were a great teacher, very passionate about knowledge, and then you got famous and it went south." Julian continued to put his doubts right on the table.

"Did he say, 'It went south?'" Sam asked, astonished.

"No, not really."

"That didn't sound like Bob. No, it didn't go south. What happened happened. The inner work of waking from the dream is not for the fainthearted. As Don Juan said, 'It requires a warrior of impeccability, who lives each moment as his last, knowing that death is just behind him over his left shoulder.'"

"Well, that sounds overdramatic. Death over my left shoulder . . ." Julian's voice trailed off.

"Well maybe, but Don Juan is making a point that, as a whole, we all live life unconsciously. To quote Socrates, 'The unexamined life is not worth living.' When we start looking at our lives and examine our beliefs and thinking, life can get extremely exciting," Sam countered.

"Yes, but 'death over my left shoulder?'" Julian repeated a little sarcastically. "I can see Darth Vader maybe."

"Ah yes, *Star Wars* again. Well, I guess in my youth I had the Lone Ranger and Tonto and Superman."

Julian wondered if he should express his next thought aloud. "But you also got shot, and the bullets didn't bounce off."

"I see you've been doing your homework. It is an interesting story, but what if I told you that that story is not important. Not now. It's more like a distraction than anything else."

"I would say it was a definite twist in the plot. I don't understand how you can just shrug it off. That event changed your life. From what I learned, it changed everything," Julian argued.

"For one thing, you have to let go of the past. Otherwise, you can't live life. It took me years to come around from what happened. Eventually I realized that what happens on life's surface is not important. Something much deeper makes our lives meaningful."

Sam looked Julian directly in the eye and asked, "What happens when you read someone's obituary in the paper? Mr. Charles Smith died at home after a long illness. He was born April 10, 1915, and all the basic facts of his existence follow. After you finish reading, if you finish at all, how long does it keep your attention? A minute? A half minute? No, you move on to the sports section. Why is that? It's not because you're coldhearted. It's just that a paragraph's worth of facts about a person's life by themselves is rarely compelling. Knowing where someone was born and went to school, how many children he had, and the nature of his career are not enough to hook our attention. Yet if you had spent even an hour with that person with genuine openness, curiosity, and compassion, that person and his life might have revealed much to you. You might have seen into his heart, his humanity, and caught a glimpse there of your own."

"Yes, I get it. But let's be realistic," Julian jumped in. "Getting shot in a Barnes & Noble in Minneapolis is a pretty big attention grabber in anybody's history."

"People get shot all the time, especially here in America. However, I will grant you it was a moment of high drama that I'd rather not repeat. And you see it is a distraction even now. So look, I'll make a deal with you. Someday we'll take a walk in the woods on a brilliant October morning and I'll tell you that story, but you must agree to take it as only a story and not as something of ongoing significance. Deal?"

"Yeah, deal. But what about the professors who were your friends and colleagues—how could they abandon you?" Julian pressed on, determined to get all his questions answered while he had the chance.

"They didn't. I dropped out. I abandoned them, really. Now, we're wasting our time together today. The spell of maya is difficult to break. It takes a lot of commitment to see through the veil of ignorance that drops when we are born."

"Well, I don't think it's a waste of time. You got shot, you dropped out, you walked away from your chosen career. And besides, I didn't know we were born into any such ignorance," Julian contended.

"No one is completely immune. Besides, I always wanted to learn about gardening, and that's what I decided to do with my time." Sam watched Julian's face carefully to see his response.

"Gardening? You gave up teaching for gardening?" Julian inquired incredulously. "There's something here you're not telling me. But okay. I can accept that. That was your decision to leave the academic world and become a gardener. Fair enough. I started reading your book. It's pretty good, actually. It must have been an interesting course."

"Yes, it was at least that." Sam switched gears and took over the role of questioner. "Julian, why did you decide to study philosophy?"

"My father is a businessman and wanted me to study business, but I took two philosophy classes, one in my freshman year and another as a

151

sophomore, and I just got hooked. I would have to say philosophy chose me, really. Dad's disappointed but still has hopes I'll find my way to getting an MBA or even become a lawyer."

Sam paused as he looked at Julian. "Many times a father can have aspirations for his son that say more about him than about the young man standing before him. I see your father's view of philosophy is that it contains nothing practical. He may be right for himself but probably not for you.

"To your father's point, however, philosophy does lack practicality, in that it generally doesn't ground knowledge in experience. We cannot know reality by merely thinking about it or studying it. I believe that Einstein once said that it was the nonthinking that was important, not the thinking. The Indian rishis, the ancient seers of the Vedic tradition, used both direct experience and understanding when they taught their students. When I was a doctoral student, I found a powerful source of both that my teacher called the Holy Tradition. I suppose a few exceptional human beings are born so highly evolved that they grasp the fullness of reality while just living life. However, most of us need something, a technique, a teaching, to propel us into truth.

"I learned that feeding the intellect with knowledge, no matter how profound, is not enough. We also need to experience the infinite source of knowledge, of life itself, which my teacher called the transcendent or pure consciousness. One glimpse of That and there's no going back. Life begins to blossom from the inside out. Life in the world goes on, but now we can also transcend it, go beyond every thought, every judgment, every individual and collective belief, and become one with their unbounded source. The mind is freed of any limited identity, and we start to feel the joy that comes with that stirring of freedom. Transcending allows the light of our own awareness to burn brighter. Turning on that light is the simplest way to banish darkness from every corner of life."

Sam sat with his eyes focused on Julian's. Julian held his gaze and then looked into his coffee cup. He sensed he was approaching a slippery slope and started to feel cautious. He fended off his descent with another question. "If I start down this path, is there any guarantee I won't get shot?" Julian asked, tongue in cheek.

"Ah, an astute question if there ever was one. Let's just say everything happens for a reason though we often don't see it except with hindsight, and sometimes not even that helps us understand. Just think of life on earth as a marvelous schoolhouse. We sign up to learn certain lessons, master certain aspects of the human experience. We sometimes have to repeat parts of the curriculum many times over and in different formats before we go on to the next class. However, the final graduation gift is lasting fulfillment.

"So we all have to live our lives. Class attendance is not voluntary, just the rate of matriculation. In the end, we find it's all just a wild imagining, a creation of our own minds, nothing more. Remember the old song, 'Row, row, row your boat gently down the stream. Merrily, merrily, merrily, merrily, life is but a dream,'" Sam sang with a big grin on his face.

"My grandmother and I sang that song when I was a kid," Julian acknowledged. "So you are saying that life is a dream. Let's say for the moment, yes. On some level, it is a dream." Julian was quiet for a moment then went on, "I must be having a good dream then, but I suppose one could drift off into a nightmare just as easily."

Sam concurred, "Yes. Sure, it can happen. It's called having a human life. Human life is a spiritual path, and everyone is, therefore, already on it, whether they know it or not. The circumstances along the path are different for everyone. Let me say that I rather doubt your path will include a shooting," Sam assured Julian.

Sam was on a roll, and he carried on before Julian could say another thing. "All life is evolving. Everyone and everything is evolving—or returning, depending on how you look at it—towards wholeness, the wholeness from which the universe emerged. That wholeness, the Absolute or Being, or whatever we want to call it, has neither content nor qualities. It just is.

"Most everyone has heard of the big bang theory these days. A singularity, a tiny point of infinite potential so compact that scientists say it had no dimensions, appeared. Time and space didn't exist yet. Time and space appear within the universe that the big bang releases when it explodes, creating a new world that grows with unimaginable speed. The question is from what did the singularity appear and how long was it around before it exploded? And what exists beyond the boundary of the world it generated? No one has yet been able to answer these questions scientifically because the singularity simply showed up. It did not show up in time and space because they were not yet created." Sam paused and then continued, "It is part of the mystery for which there is no good scientific answer. We only know that it appears that everything exploded out of a singularity, a point. Maybe millions of singularities are exploding all the time, yielding universes we can barely imagine. But infinity has burst onto the scene, and as Joyce put it in *Finnegans Wake*, HCE."

"What does HCE mean?"

"Here comes everybody."

"So we have infinite wholeness giving birth to incredible diversity on a cosmic level then the evolutionary journey back to wholeness—that's the path. However, on the return journey, we consciously experience that wholeness and realize we have always been that infinite Being.

"So you, I, and everyone else are on the path to unity, but life gets interesting when we consciously decide to make the journey rather than just getting pulled along. 'Living is easy with eyes closed, misunderstanding all you see.' John Lennon wrote that—'Strawberry Fields.'

"But life really isn't easy with eyes closed, misunderstanding everything. It may appear to be so on the surface, just floating along, but the fear, pain, and uncertainty that people live with is overwhelming. One just needs to scratch the surface, and it all comes bubbling out. But we all try to keep a stiff upper lip and push on, not really knowing where we're going."

Julian, while remaining fully attentive, looked as if he was approaching overload, and Sam moved to end the discussion. "Listen, that's probably enough carrying on for one sitting."

"Yeah, I have much to think about," Julian said, trailing off.

Julian looked a bit confused and uncertain as to what was next. So Sam made an offer.

"Why don't you and Katy come to the house on Saturday night and have dinner? It will be my pleasure and my wife's, when she hears about it, to feed you. She cooks a wicked spinach lasagna. I swear I don't know what secret herbs she puts in it. Ah, but it's good. Here's my card with our phone number and address."

Julian looked at the card and brightened.

> *Sam and Amy O' Connor*
> *Strawberry Fields*
> *101 Maple Street*
> *North Amherst, MA 01235*
> *(413) 254-1008*

"So you're a really big Beatles fan, huh?"

"Isn't everybody?"

"I don't know. I guess so."

"Julian, did you know what John Lennon answered when someone asked him what his favorite Beatle song was?"

"No idea."

"'Across the Universe.' You know." Sam sang softly, "'Nothing's gonna change my world. Nothing's gonna change my world. Jai Guru Deva, Om.' John and George, for that matter, spent two months in Rishikesh with Maharishi. It was a happy and peaceful time for them both."

Julian sat with no reply.

Sam finally jumped into the gap. "Julian, your homework assignment is to listen to 'Across the Universe' a couple of times before dinner on Saturday. By the way, it's my favorite Beatle song too. Sometimes I feel John wrote it for me. Of course, I know that's not true, and he'd probably be disturbed at me for saying it. Too many people piling on, you know, but it's my dream also. Filtering through my mind all these years, the song has, in its own sweet way, reminded me of what is true. It's become a kind of personal anthem. And of course there was George with 'My Sweet Lord' and 'All Things Must Pass.' George was the major spiritual force in that group, though Paul and Ringo were both profoundly influenced by Maharishi as well."

Sam's eyes were blissful as he gazed at Julian. Julian felt self-conscious.

"Well, Sam, I've got to go. Good to see you. I'll call you about Saturday."

"Call Amy, not me. She's the one cooking the lasagna. If you can manage it, we'll see you Saturday around five. I can show the garden while there's still some light."

"Okay." With that, Julian grabbed his backpack and swung around to leave. "Oh, thanks for the coffee."

Kenny, who was standing behind the counter, shouted out, "Don't thank him, thank me. He hasn't paid his tab in months. You no-good Irish scoundrel, parading as a man of knowledge!"

"Pay no attention to that man behind the counter, my young Jedi. Anytime, you're always welcome."

Sam knew he better get home soon to tell Amy they'd be having company on Saturday night. Kenny had his own interpretation of the meeting. "Yeah, Sam, you better let her know it's starting," Kenny quipped.

"What's starting?"

"The whole thing is starting up again for you to see."

"What in the world are you raving about?"

"You didn't quite get it last time even though you got it, so it's starting up again. Well, don't worry," Kenny went on, "it will come out all right this time. And there'll be no need for violence. You can reassure Amy of that."

"You're as mad as a hatter, Kenny boy."

"And you're my best friend and my worst customer in that you haven't paid your tab in who knows how long. And now you're bringing friends with you," Kenny said with a frown.

"When the bank comes to close you down, have them call me. I'll make it right."

"Oh, will you, now? That's a fine thing to say."

"Kenny, we've been through thick and thin together. I won't let you down," Sam grinned.

"No, I suspect you won't, but remember, as the sign says," Kenny pointed to the cash register, 'In God we trust. All others pay cash.'"

"Yes, I have seen the sign. Cash you want and cash you'll have. Meanwhile, I'll gladly pay you Tuesday for a hamburger today," Sam said as he held up his cup for a refill.

"Ah, you're the bastard, aren't you?" Kenny exclaimed.

Both men laughed at their little scripted play. Debbie, one of the counter girls, just raised her eyes to heaven with a silent plea.

Julian hurried up the street. He was both excited and concerned. *I hope Katy agrees to come,* he thought. *I'll just have to tell her it's important. And I need her support. Yeah, she's always saying that to me. Yeah.*

Julian mimicked Katy's tone of voice, "It's important, Julian. I need you to go with me. Behave yourself and act like a mature adult." So he sounded out, "Katy, this is important to me. I really need your support." It didn't sound all that convincing.

Katy looked up to see Julian coming through the door. "Hey," she said. "There's my honey pie."

Julian, deepening his voice by an octave, proclaimed, "Katy, I ain't your honey pie. I'm your man."

"Well, my big man, tell me how your day was."

Julian relaxed and answered, "Oh, good." He tried to sound casual when he added, "I ran into Sam O'Connor again."

"Really? Did you ask him about being shot?" Katy asked excitedly.

"Well, yes."

"And what did he say?"

"Well, he said it was a distraction then and it's a distraction now."

"What does that mean?"

"It means he doesn't want to talk about it."

"I think he's covering up something."

"No, he said it's not important. It just part of the story, and the events in each of our life stories are ultimately not important. I understood him to mean our inner life. Who we are is more important than the actual events, including getting shot."

"Well, this guy sounds like a real nut."

"You've mentioned that before, but I disagree. He's not. He's actually amazing, so calm. When I'm with him, I feel relaxed, and his eyes do this deep-pool thing that makes me happy just to see him."

"Oh my god! He's gay, and he's after you."

"No. No. It's not like that. And I don't think it actually works that way. He's married, has children, and he's invited us to come to his house and meet his wife, Amy, and have dinner with them Saturday night."

"That doesn't mean he's not gay. Anyway, what did you say?"

"I told him I'd have to ask you first, and then I'd call him. Look, this is really important to me. I need you to support me on this and just come. I'm sure we'll have a great time, and it's a good opportunity to meet Sam and his wife. Just say you'll do it."

Katy eyed Julian for a long moment and finally said, "Okay, but on one condition."

"Anything!"

"If it starts to get weird, we're out of there."

"It won't get weird. I promise. You'll really like them."

"I hope you're right. What do you want for dinner tonight?"

"Anything at all." And Julian heaved a sigh of relief. "By the way, what Beatle album has 'Across the Universe' on it?"

"*Let it Be.* Why?"

"Oh, it's Sam's favorite Beatle song, and I thought I'd give it a listen."

Chapter 21:
Dinner with the O'Connors

SAM DECIDED TO TELL AMY when he got home about the dinner invitation he had extended to Julian and his girlfriend. Something that Kenny had said about it all starting up again troubled him. He'd have to think about that later.

He found Amy in her studio working on a watercolor painting that she planned to submit to the New England Watercolor Guild Art Show. Last year her entry had placed third; the year before she had received honorable mention. Amy believed that this year she could take the top prize.

Painting had saved Amy's health and sanity, when their world had turned upside down eight years ago. In addition to her children, her husband had needed a tremendous amount of support. At first, for Sam, it had been just the physical challenge of recovering from the wound, but then had come the doubts, the moodiness, and eventually, the withdrawal from everything and almost everybody. Amy felt that Sam had lost part of his spirit that terrifying day in Minneapolis, and she was glad they had been able to regain a version of normalcy through their creative pursuits—he through his bountiful vegetable gardening and reading of poetry and she through her painting and teaching art.

Sam walked into the studio with a smile that pleasantly surprised Amy.

"Amy, my love, how are you?" he asked.

"Oh, I'm doing well."

Sam had a gleam in his eye as he bent over and gave her a kiss.

"Well, you seem light and happy tonight. Did something happen while you were in town?" Amy probed, trying to sound casual.

"Oh, I met a student from Amherst a few weeks back, a philosophy major. Anyway, we've met a couple of times at Kenny's café for coffee and for some philosophical dialogue."

"And," Amy observed, "you're enjoying it."

"Yes, as a matter of fact, I am."

"Male or female?" she asked pointedly.

"Naturally, male. I don't think females study philosophy anymore."

"Well, that's a very sexist thing to say, and I'm not taking the bait for your amusement."

"You sure? Looks like you're nibbling at it."

"Yes, Sam O'Connor, maybe a little," Amy sighed patiently. "So, what's he like?"

"Well, he's bright and of Irish descent for one thing, and he's got a lot of awareness. First, I saw him on the bus. Actually sat across from him. He's really got it. We've met twice"—Sam paused before continuing—"and I invited him and his girlfriend over on Saturday night for dinner."

"Well, it's wonderful that you can be so spontaneous, but what if we already had plans?"

"I knew we weren't busy," rejoined Sam.

"Yes, that's true, but it's always safer to ask first," Amy insisted, "especially if you don't want to have to order takeout."

"Point well taken, but it just came up. You're going to like them."

"Have you met the girlfriend?"

"No, I only know she thinks I'm a nut."

"Oh, how right she is! I like her already." Amy's voice carried a sense of satisfaction.

"Yeah, that's what I said. So what do you say? Can you make that wonderful spinach lasagna?" Sam smiled his biggest smile, hoping for the best.

"I'd be happy to. Sorry, sweetheart," Amy offered kindly as she moved closer to kiss him, "I didn't mean to give you a hard time about this invite. It's good to see you so cheerful about something besides the boys, the garden, and me."

"It's hard to keep down that inner bliss," Sam smiled again. "I can't explain it, but it feels good to be discussing ideas with a student again."

"Sam, it's easy to explain. You're a teacher. When you teach, you're in your dharma, and when you're in your dharma, you feel that all's right with the world. As you used to say, 'Your divine purpose is revealed and you feel the joy of the creation.'"

"You're as shameless as Kenny, using my own material on me," Sam countered with a grin.

"Feels pretty good to reverse roles," Amy said with some satisfaction.

Walking into the kitchen, Sam called back, "I'll pick up the boys at Edith's house, and then we can meditate."

"No need. The boys have their bikes, and they should arrive any minute. I'll clean up and be with you in ten minutes."

"Great. I'll just check in on the garden."

Julian and Katy arrived just before five as Sam had asked so Sam could show them his garden while there was still enough light. They used the tarnished but sturdy brass knocker on the front door, and in a few seconds, Sam opened it. He noted the autumn chill in the air as he ushered them inside.

"Welcome, Julian and . . ."

"Katy," Julian submitted. "Sam, this is Katy, and Katy, this is Dr. Sam O'Connor."

"Nice to meet you, Katy. Please come in, come in out of the cool air. And please, we have no formalities here. Call me Sam."

"Nice to meet you, Sam. Julian told me a lot about you," Katy greeted him.

"Yes, Katy, and I'm sure it was all good," Sam observed facetiously, looking at Julian with a grin.

Julian quickly added, "Of course, it was all good."

"Now we've covered that sufficiently, come meet my better half—and I do mean the better half. Without her, I'd have ended up as a crazy old fool sitting around a café all day long," Sam said, mischievously playing into Katy's fear.

"Amy, dear, our company has arrived," Sam announced as they rounded the corner into the living room.

Sam took Julian and Katy on a brief tour through the old farmhouse, and they were captivated by its exposed beams, built-in nooks, warmth, and charm. The O'Connors had refinished the structure's wide pine floors, now worn smooth and stained a honey gold. The day's last light shone gently through the western windows, tinting the rooms in soft rose. Practical artistry was in evidence everywhere, in the inviting colors of the walls and the welcoming arrangement of furniture. Someone had clearly invested him—or herself—lovingly in the design of every aspect of the home. When they reached the kitchen, they saw Amy. She had her apron on, and her hair was loosely bundled into a bun. She was stunning. "Welcome," she said as she wiped her hands on her apron and reached out to shake their hands. Sam looked proudly at his wife, reminding himself for the millionth time how lucky he was to be with her.

He introduced them. "Amy, dear, this is the bright lad I told you about, Julian Driscoll, and his charming friend, Katy."

"Pleased to meet you."

"Pleased to meet you also," replied Julian, trying to be his most polite self.

"Your home is so beautiful," Katy effused.

"Thank you, Katy," Amy said, appreciating the vibrant young faces before her.

Sam said, "All right, if you like the house so much, I'm sure you'll like the garden, particularly you, Katy. I understand you hail from a small farm in Vermont."

"Yes, I do. Did Julian mention that?" she asked, looking at Julian and then back to Sam.

"Actually, no, he didn't. I can tell by your complexion that you were raised on raw milk, straight from the udder, so to speak. And your accent, even though slight, speaks of Vermont."

Julian added with a wink, "See, Katy, I told you Sam had a bit of Sherlock Holmes in him." However, he was really thinking, *Please don't get weird on me, Sam, or it's going to be a really short evening.*

Sam looked at Julian and declared, "That's it. I'm taking off my cap and putting away my pipe for the rest of the evening. Now you must meet the rest of the household. Sam called out, "Josh and Paul, please present yourselves like the charming young chaps you are."

There was a scuffling and scampering sound in the hall before the two boys and a golden retriever appeared in the doorway. Tall and lanky, they seemed all arms and legs but for their striking eyes and amiable grins. Josh was just thirteen and favored his mother, while Paul, who was twelve, clearly favored his dad. Rufus, the dog, was all smiles and tail wagging, relishing the excitement.

"Josh and Paul, meet our friends, Julian and Katy."

"Great to meet you," Josh said.

"Yeah," added Paul. "This is Rufus."

Everyone paused to pet the squirming dog.

The two boys, along with Rufus, accompanied them on the rest of the tour of the property, highlighting their own points of interest, especially the two swinging chairs that faced each other on the back porch. Though the vegetable garden was well past its seasonal prime, the rich brown earth was still yielding some abundance: acorn and butternut squash and pumpkins. Sam, the steward of the fertile field, stood proudly and gratefully in his garden, explaining the logic of its design and the natural technologies he used to keep it free of pests. He broke a few acorn squashes from their vines while the boys pointed out the plots for which they were responsible.

"Let's go in and eat. I'm half-famished, and you must be also," Sam announced.

Twilight was fast approaching as they turned to mount the porch and reenter the house. Julian and Katy were seated at the table in the dining room, which was lit by the amber glow from a low-hanging chandelier. Sam kept them company while the boys helped their mother bring the steaming bowls of food to the table. Julian and Katy looked at each other thoughtfully, holding each other's hands and silently communicating their desire to have such a future for themselves.

Paul and Josh both had the gift of gab, and they told a number of stories, each funnier than the last. The group easily settled in, and at one point Paul inquired, "How long have you both been meditating?"

Before Julian could answer, Josh said with the authority of an old sage, "We've been meditating for years. We got walking mantras when we were five and a new mantra and sit-down technique when we were ten."

To which Paul added confidently, "It's a different mantra."

Sam jumped in, "Boys, actually, Julian and Katy have not started meditation yet."

"Oh," Josh responded then said helpfully, "You should let my dad teach you."

Paul added, "Yeah, he's the best."

"Thank you both for that grand endorsement," Sam told the boys. Looking at Katy and Julian, he remarked, "They are not prejudiced in the slightest."

Sam asked the boys to help clear the table and quipped, "I'll pay you five dollars each later for that plug. Now the four of us are going to talk in the living room, and you can watch your video. By the way, what are you watching?"

"*Indiana Jones and the Temple of Doom*," announced Paul.

"All right then, if you must see it for the sixth time," Sam added thoughtfully, knowing how much Amy disapproved.

"No, Dad. It's the eighth," Josh corrected him with delight.

Sam, feigning shock, said, "Don't tell your grandparents or your mother! Oh, I quite forgot, she's sitting right here." Sam and Amy exchanged looks. Sam smiled; Amy frowned. "Off with you before your mom thinks about it for too long."

Amy said to Katy, "Sam loves movies and passed it on to the boys. I swear if videos were around twelve years ago, he never would have gotten his PhD."

"Unfortunately, it's most likely true," Sam concurred.

Amy left the table to heat some water for tea, and Katy joined her in the kitchen to see if she could help with the dishes. The men were left at the table, and Sam suggested, "Let's head for the study, Julian. A hundred years ago, you and I would have retired to the library, drunk brandy, smoked cigars, and discussed the state of the world. Tonight we're going to the study to discuss the state of the world. Brandy, unfortunately, will not be served, and we are a nonsmoking facility."

Julian and Sam pushed their chairs away from the table, rose slowly, and made their way down the hall to Sam's study. Two walls were lined with books and one wall with family pictures. On Sam's desk sat a photo of Maharishi with a clean-shaven young Sam. A number of framed letters hung on the far wall, and Julian, curious, walked over to read them. "Wow! Look at these. I can't believe it!"

"After I was shot, I got many letters. These I liked especially," Sam offered.

Julian read each short letter out loud.

> Dear Sam,
>   Loved the book. Best wishes for a speedy recovery. Looking forward to your next one. A bit of advice—skip the book tour next time. Jai Guru Dev.
>
> > All the best,
> > George Harrison

Dear Sam,

Hope you recover quickly. We haven't read the book, but you can be sure, we will now.

Peace and love,
John and Yoko

Dear Dr. O'Connor,

Don't let the bastards get you down. Godspeed.

Sincerely yours,
Norman Mailer

"That's incredible!" exclaimed Julian.

"Well, writers and artists desire the freedom to express themselves more than anything else. When I got shot, many people felt it because they thought this could've happened to them. It's funny. As writers and artists, we all share the same consciousness. Something happens to one, and it happens to all of us."

"Sam," Julian jumped in, "you have a wonderful home, wife, children, and garden, and it looks like you had a great career as a professor. So what's next, or do you just hang out until it's over?"

"Ah, we're in the deep end of the pool, are we? So be it. Plain and simple, I don't know what's next."

"But you're this incredible man, with this fantastic mind. You have so much to give."

"Thank you, but let's talk about you."

"I'm not that interesting," Julian came back. "The conversation would last all of two minutes. But you! My god, you have letters from two of the Beatles and Norman Mailer on your wall. Who knows who else wrote to you? And I've been reading all kinds of articles that were written about you. Why in the world did you drop out for so long? I don't get it."

"It's not that hard to figure out. I was shot at close range by a former friend turned nut," Sam returned with some emotion.

"But people loved you, admired you," Julian pressed.

"Listen, Jules, the past is past. What we have is just this moment."

"I get the moment thing," Julian responded, "but you haven't answered my question. What are you going to do, besides dig for earthworms?"

"In the West it's all about doing, about activity, about progress. In the East it's about Being, silence, harmony. Maybe we ought to consider something more than doing and activity."

"I don't know about that, but suppose for the moment you're right. What does your life look like? What is your legacy? Are you satisfied with having written one successful book and then never being heard from again? Don't you have anything more to say?" Julian could not let up.

"I see you're having difficulty grasping my life. Let's just say I haven't dropped out, but rather, I'm working on a research project."

"Really?"

"Yes. I would say that I'm doing research in consciousness. You, me, everyone, we all have it. The Vedic teachings are definitely not averse to activity. Activity of all kinds is natural. However, they highly recommend being established in one's infinite source first and acting from there. It takes time to cultivate the nervous system to support the continuous experience of infinite awareness. However, once it's done, there's no end to what one can accomplish."

"So you're saying you've been on sabbatical these last eight years, working on the project of cultivating infinite consciousness?"

"Yes, I suppose I could say that, but I wouldn't tell too many people about it. It's not exactly an accepted Western concept."

"Yeah, I see what you mean. Well, that's actually pretty cool. You are Obi-Wan Kenobi after all, and you're going to save the universe, so to speak."

Before Sam could react, they heard Amy calling, "Sam! Julian! Dessert!"

"Yeah, I don't know if I'm comfortable with that handle, my young Jedi, and evidently our moment has come and gone. Shall we?" Sam got up and led Julian back to the dining room for their just reward—strawberry shortcake with or without ice cream.

"Julian, I've decided to start meditation," Katy announced without any prologue. "Amy was just telling me about some of the studies done on meditators and meditation's impact on students and education, and it sounds great. The student fee is only one hundred and twenty-five dollars." After a brief pause, Katy threw in, "Amy's available next weekend to teach us, assuming you want to join me."

"That's excellent!" Julian exclaimed, not really believing his ears. "But if we're going to learn, I was thinking that Sam would teach me. Okay, Sam?"

"Sure, that would be fine," Sam agreed, looking at his wife in amazement.

"Okay," approved Amy. "We need to go through all seven steps of the process." And Amy proceeded to outline the course and propose a schedule. "We can do the course right here," she concluded.

"Sounds perfect," said Katy. "I'm psyched!"

"Yeah, me too," declared Julian, astounded at his skeptical girlfriend's remarkable turnaround.

"Julian," asked Amy, "would you like some vanilla ice cream with that strawberry shortcake?"

"Definitely," Julian grinned. "I'm celebrating!"

On the way home, Katy was cheerful and animated. "I just loved Amy. She's phenomenal! And her children and the house! I've never met anyone like her. If meditation does that for a person, I want it."

"Well, you really surprised me."

"You don't sound too thrilled, Jules. I thought you'd be happy." Katie's tone registered some annoyance.

"Oh, I am. I'm wicked happy. Just kind of amazed that you are suddenly willing to throw caution to the wind," Julian conveyed carefully.

"It's true. I'm being impulsive, but I just can't believe these people. This family is so cool! So I'm in."

"Me too, Katy, me too," Julian confirmed quietly. He didn't tell her about his conversation with Sam. He didn't understand it, and he couldn't explain it.

Julian started to dream the moment his head hit the pillow. He was walking on the beach again with the most beautiful blue-green water lapping at his feet. He saw Sam before him on the beach, sitting with his legs crossed, looking out onto the shimmering waters.

As Julian approached, Sam turned toward him with smiling, dancing eyes. "Julian, not all is what it seems. Time and space is our playground, and in reality, it has no reality. All is well. No worries, mate." Sam began to hover in the air. He moved his legs into a full lotus position and flew off into the sky.

"Lucy in the Sky with Diamonds" began to play in Julian's mind, and with that, he dove into the warm and inviting waters.

Chapter 22:
The Appointed Time

JULIAN AND KATY ARRIVED AT the O'Connor home at ten o'clock Saturday morning with six pieces of fruit and a bunch of freshly cut gold- and rust-colored chrysanthemums, the gift of autumn. Both were as elated as they'd ever been. Spending Thursday and Friday nights with Sam and Amy hearing about Transcendental Meditation had been curiously fulfilling. Now they were actually going to learn the technique.

Julian and Katy climbed the farmhouse steps and lingered on the O'Connors' front porch for a moment before knocking. They both took a deep breath and allowed themselves to be absorbed in the sound of the wind rustling the few leaves still clinging to the branches of oaks and maples in the front yard. Then, without a word, they both turned toward the door. Julian raised and lowered the brass knocker a couple of times, and Sam came to welcome them.

The house was hushed and serene when they entered, and a faint odor of sandalwood incense filled the air. Sam greeted them warmly and accepted the flowers and the bag containing the fruit and white cloths that Katy handed to him. "I see you did your homework." Sam smiled and held up the bag. "Excellent! Leave your shoes by the door, and come on in and make yourselves at home in the living room. Amy is setting up a room for instruction."

Amy emerged barefoot from the meditation room and walked briskly into the living room. Instead of the jeans that were her usual attire, she wore a green mid-calf velvet skirt that flowed gracefully as she moved and a white embroidered tunic with full sleeves. She was radiant and beautiful. "So good to see you here today," Amy welcomed them.

"Thanks," Julian responded. "We're glad to be here."

"Yeah," Katy added, "we're pretty excited."

"I'll help Sam prepare your fruit and flowers, and then Katy and I will get started. Julian, Sam will take you upstairs for instruction. Katy and I will be in the meditation room," Amy explained.

Sam and Amy took the fruit and flowers into the kitchen. They washed the fruit and divided everything in two. They carefully placed the fruit, flowers, and cloth in two straw baskets. They returned to the living room and handed the baskets to their students. Amy and Sam gestured to Katy and Julian. The students rose from the comfortable couch into which they had sunk and followed their teachers to the instruction rooms.

An hour and a half later on the ride home, Julian and Katy couldn't get over how refreshing and relaxing meditation was. A whole new realm of inner experience had opened up for them.

"I swear, Katy, colors seem brighter," Julian observed.

"Yeah, I felt like I went so deep that I completely lost the sense of the room and my body," Katy enthused.

"I know what you mean. I lost track of my body for a few minutes. It was amazing! I can't wait to do it again," Julian declared.

"Amy told us to meditate again before dinner."

"This is pretty cool," Julian reflected, utterly content.

For the remainder of the short drive home, they drifted into silence, both enjoying a new feeling of tranquility. The rest of the TM course progressed smoothly. It was great to meditate with Sam and Amy, even for just the ten minutes during each lesson. By the end of the third night, they felt they understood the principles involved and were completely comfortable with the technique. They felt both light and joyful, sometimes to the point of silliness.

A few days later, on Thursday after class, Julian approached Dr. Harris.

"Hi, Dr. Harris. Good class," Julian remarked.

"Thank you, Julian. You look bright and chipper these days."

"Well, I started TM."

"Really? Is that so?" Dr. Harris responded energetically, trying to hide his displeasure.

"Yeah. Dr. O'Connor and his wife, Amy, taught my girlfriend and me. It was great, truly enlightening," Julian quipped, tongue in cheek.

Dr. Harris didn't get Julian's attempt at lightheartedness. "Well, everyone is entitled to make his own decisions. I personally wouldn't have made that one. I see you decided to ignore my advice about not getting involved with Sam O'Connor," the professor remarked.

"I didn't see it as going against your advice. I find the man fascinating. He's brilliant," Julian expressed strongly.

"I've already agreed with you about his brilliance, but in my opinion, he's also a loose cannon who threw away his intellectual gifts to chase a dream. However, I can see you're quite taken with him. I also see Sam has not lost his charm with undergraduate students. I tried to warn you, and now all I can say is good luck." Dr. Harris walked briskly out of the classroom, leaving Julian behind, alone and befuddled.

What the hell? Julian thought. *This guy's got a bug up his ass.* He let the matter go and trotted off to his next class.

Bob Harris, however, couldn't let it go. With each step, he grew angrier. Sure he had been sorry for Sam when he was shot so many years before. He had felt badly for him and his family. Of course, Sam's book went on to sell two million copies and was now in its tenth printing, not that he was counting. He had even heard that it had been translated into Russian, and the rumor was that all of the fifty thousand copies that had been printed had sold out in a week. *Perestroika, my foot! I'm going to warn the dean about this. Of course all he'll probably do is offer Sam his job back, not that he needs the money. I'm sure those royalty checks come in every month. But I must talk to someone, warn them that Sam O'Connor is teaching students to meditate. Who knows where this might lead?* He stormed off, not sure where he was going.

Julian wanted to find Katy and tell her about his conversation with Dr. Harris. He headed over to the Keefer Campus Center, where she would most likely be at lunchtime. He entered the snack bar and saw her sitting by herself with a cup of coffee and a turkey sandwich. She was lost in a book, Mary Oliver as it happened, a poet she had recently discovered. He quietly sneaked up on her, jumped over the back of the chair across from her, and landed with a bang.

"Oh my god!" she exclaimed. "Julian Driscoll! You big oaf! You startled me."

"Sorry," Julian stammered in between bouts of laughter. "It's just that you look so cute when you're startled."

"How about I just beat you to death with this book? Would I look cute then?"

"Well, you know, you're so beautiful, you would look cute."

"Julian, you're hopeless."

"Not as hopeless as Dr. Harris."

"What are you talking about?" Katy asked, still trying to regain her composure.

"Simply put, Bob Harris is an asshole," Julian stated.

"Julian, I hate that word. He's not. He's uptight and feels he's superior, but he's not what you just said."

"Oh yes, he is. Listen, I just finished class with him, and I went up to tell him that we started meditation and that Sam and Amy taught us. Gee, you'd think I'd told him I mugged his mother. Harris said, 'Well, if that's what you decided, I personally wouldn't make that decision. And you've gone against my advice.' "

"Well, he's jealous. He's so straight. I guess this somehow threatens him. I wonder why. Why does he feel so threatened?" Katy puzzled.

"I don't know. Maybe because Sam outshone him back when they were both young profs," Julian suggested.

"I suppose that could be it. So he's jealous. What can you do about it?"

"Nothing I can think of right now," Julian voiced.

"Maybe you should mention it to Sam," Katy proposed.

"Yeah, maybe I should," Julian agreed.

"Speaking of Sam, you know how you meet Sam on Fridays at the café?" Katy broached the subject seductively.

"Yeah," Julian returned cautiously.

"I was wondering if I could come with you," Katy ventured.

"Ah well, Katy, we discuss philosophical stuff. If you came, it would change it. We'd start discussing average rainfall and the various insects that invade tomato plants. So I don't know."

"Julian, I'd like to learn about philosophy. It's not fair that you get Sam all to yourself," Katy pressed.

"Just two weeks ago you thought he was a nut," Julian defended.

"Yes, and I was wrong. That was two weeks ago and this is now," Katy insisted, not backing down.

"Look, I prefer to go by myself, but I'll mention it to Sam on Friday when I go—by myself," Julian emphasized, looking directly into Katy's eyes. Instead of arguing, Katy kept quiet, and Julian felt his resolve weakening. He offered what he thought would be a satisfying alternative. "I have an idea. Why don't you call Amy and see if you can hang out with her?"

"I can't do that," Katy responded, clearly irritated.

"Why not?" Julian demanded.

"Because she'd have to ask me, that's why."

"Maybe she doesn't know that you'd be interested."

"Women know," Katy spoke in her this-is-the-end-of-the-discussion tone.

Julian sighed, realizing she was right. "I have it. Pick up a pot of mums and stop by on Saturday morning, or call her Saturday morning and say you'd like to stop by and drop off a gift. How can she say no to that?"

"Well, all right," Katy conceded. "That might work. I'll do it. You're off the hook for now, buster."

"Phew! Good thing too, because Friday night is coming up."

"Well, as we say on the farm, 'Don't count your chickens before they hatch, lover boy.'"

"They say *lover boy* on the farm?"

"The wives and girlfriends do," Katy came back with a straight face.

"Well, I do get points, right?"

Katy softened. "Yeah, Jules, you get points."

Chapter 23:
String Theory

SAM SAT HAPPILY NURSING A cup of coffee in the rear of the White Oak when he saw Julian making his way to the table. As Julian dropped his well-worn book pack onto a scuffed wooden chair, Sam greeted him enthusiastically, "Ah, Julian, another glorious day. Good to see you. I've ordered a cup of Joe for each of us and a couple of muffins. Okay?"

"Sounds great," replied Julian, settling into the chair across from Sam. His eyes reflected his eagerness for whatever the next step on this strange and satisfying journey might be. His chin held the first stages of a beard.

"How is meditation going?"

"Fine. I'm definitely enjoying it."

"And how was the week?"

"Great. This new experience of transcending is amazing. I'm pretty excited."

"Good for you. There is much to be enthusiastic about. I heard Katy called. So, the question is, should we venture back into suffering? Or we could pass the time reflecting on the goodness of the universe."

"Suffering might prove more interesting. So, let's continue what we've started."

Sam laughed. "As humans, we have the freedom to choose. So suffering it is. It's such a juicy, dicey subject, and we can approach it from so many tempting angles. Take Buddha. He declared that all life was suffering and then prescribed the way out. Or take Adam and Eve. According to the Bible, God expelled them from the garden of Eden and sent them out into a world where shame and suffering were to become commonplace. Most people would say that suffering is a fact of life, which means that philosophy must

175

come to grips with it. That includes concepts like hell. Hopefully, we'll be able not only to explain what's going on, but also to discover how to get out of suffering if that's possible." Sam raised his eyebrows.

"Well, it's a tall order no doubt, but I'm up for it. Let's have a go. By the way, where's Kenny?" Julian asked, looking around. "The café is sort of quiet today," he noted.

"Kenny is out on a few errands, and I wanted it to be quiet today."

"How does your desiring it to be quiet make it so?" Julian challenged, aware that Sam was often full of surprises.

"Well, we're going to talk about something important, and I thought it would be better if it wasn't so busy in here. Life is responding to my desire. It's really that simple," Sam explained.

"So you're saying that we're seeing a cause-effect connection here between your wanting things quiet and people deciding not to come in for their four o'clock coffee break." Julian's pursed his lips a little, and his voice reflected skepticism.

"Yes, exactly," Sam continued undeterred. "Life's infinite organizing power orchestrates a huge and complex universe with no apparent effort. Orchestrating an hour of quiet for two philosophers is not much of a feat from that perspective. As I said, even Kenny decided to run an errand or two. Besides, those people needing their afternoon coffee break are coming, only a bit later than usual. We only have an hour or so before they pack in, so let's get back to our topic. Have you heard the story about the snake and the string?"

"No, can't say I have," remarked Julian, still trying to take in what Sam had offered so matter-of-factly.

"It's an old Vedic story that Maharishi likes. It offers a powerful viewpoint on suffering."

"This string story is going to explain suffering?"

"It may, let's see. A man is walking down the path to his village at dusk. Earlier, someone had dropped a piece of string on the path, or we could say a length of rope. The light is growing dim, and the man spots the rope from some fifty feet away. From that distance, the rope looks like a large snake to him in the waning light. He becomes terrified and begins to scream, 'Snake, snake! A giant snake!'

"Villagers nearby hear him and come running. They too see a big snake. Deeply frightened, they start plotting how to get rid of it. One of the men carries news about the terrible snake to the village along with warnings. 'A gigantic poisonous snake is just a stone's throw away. Stay inside! Protect your children!'

"The villagers infer that if one snake is on the path, others must surely be in the area, perhaps lots of them. 'How frightening and cruel life is!' they cry out. Soon the news spreads to other villages. People now believe that the whole region is infested with huge deadly snakes and no one is safe. The story keeps widening its reach, enhanced by new 'facts,' growing scarier with each telling. After less than a week, the entire nation believes it is the victim of a virtual snake epidemic and that government action is required to deal with it.

"Concerned with the spreading panic, a wise seer decides to investigate. He walks to the place on the path where the first villager found the snake. He walks up to the snake, takes one look at it, and smiles. He calmly picks it up and declares, 'There's no snake. It's only a string, a piece of rope.' However, by now the whole country is caught up in fear and the suffering it brings, though no one is sure how or where the story started. In the great uproar, no one hears the wise man saying over and over, 'It's just a string. There is no snake.'"

"So suffering is just the result of a perception, or a misperception, that has no basis on reality?" asked Julian.

"My goodness, you are right on the number today." Sam raised his arms for a moment in a victory gesture. "Yes!" he exclaimed. "Suffering is the result of a biased perception. The intellect makes a mistake. It misinterprets events."

"And you're saying the whole world of suffering comes from that?" Julian asked incredulously.

"Precisely, and not only that, suffering has become the norm. A tradition of sorts."

"That doesn't make sense."

"All right, let's go into it a little deeper then. This point of view comes from the enlightened rishis' perspective. For them the truth is that only the Self, pure consciousness, exists. The only true interpretation of anything and everything is that it's all awareness. Nothing exists outside of this infinite unity, pure consciousness. And from this perspective, everything and everybody are also manifestations of pure, infinite awareness. It's like the ocean rising up in waves. Someone might be tempted to see the waves as different from the ocean. Yet the truth is the waves and the ocean are one and the same. For the person living in unity consciousness, everything is awareness.

"However, from the limitations of ordinary waking state, our perceptions tell us that differences dominate, not unity. And in those perceived differences is a lurking threat. You know, it's a jungle out there. That's why we're all taught that we best be careful lest something or somebody gets us. For some, that is the call for adventure. For others, it means sticking to the neighborhood your whole life. I know people who have lived in Greenwich Village their whole lives and rarely, if ever, leave."

"Everyone has their comfort zones, Sam, though that does seem a bit extreme. And besides, I'm sure you've warned your own children about the dangers of the world. That's sound advice, really."

"I don't know if it's sound advice or just advice. Growing up in the city, I was made aware of it. As for my own children, well, we try not to instill fear, nor do we cover up what's happening around them. One has to be practical in life, I agree."

"Anyway, why not just tell people that what they're experiencing is not real?"

"Wouldn't be very effective for one. You can't tell a person that his or her experience is not real, that his or her perception is not true. If someone is in a dimly lit room, they're in a dimly lit room. No sense arguing with them."

"Why not? People are always making judgments about other people's lives."

"That may be true. But this is not a judgment. The best way is to let a person experience it for him or herself. Everyone has the capacity to live in enlightenment. The rishis saw that. They also saw people can, through meditation, cultivate their own nervous system and would, over time, realize the reality themselves. Great insight, actually. Saves a lot of arguing."

Sam paused, studying Julian's face. "The Vedic rishis saw that bliss is the nature of reality, and everyone has the capacity to experience that themselves. Suffering then happens when we don't know who we are, unbounded infinite awareness."

"How has everyone been missing the boat on this for thousands of years?"

"Not everyone has been missing the boat, Jules," Sam said as he smiled. "For most people, our attention flows outward. For the enlightened, it's all about the Self. Every perception has a Self-referral reference, kind of like awareness meeting awareness. Before enlightenment, our intellect reflects our perception and thoughts if we're lucky, and that's not saying much."

"And if we're unlucky?"

"Then our perceptions and thoughts reflect our emotions. The problem here is that emotions are not very stable. Love someone one minute, hate him or her the next. That kind of thing. It makes for lots of ups and downs, sort of like riding a roller coaster through life. The intellect is more stable and offers a reasonable perspective on life. But the Self, being infinite, is infinitely stable and it's blissful. So if you could live life from this level, why not?"

"Bliss sounds good."

"Yeah. It's good. So the story of the snake and the string does help to explain suffering. Suffering is just a mistake. We've all made the same mistake, and we've been reinforcing it from generation to generation. It's the proverbial blind leading the blind, so everyone falls into the ditch."

"I get what you're saying, but it's too simple. Bad things do happen. There's the question of evil in the world. There's the question of crazy people like the guy who shot you."

"The truth is usually simple. And when you think on this some more, you may see just how profound it is. But putting that aside for the moment, yes, it appears bad things happen to people. But if everyone is shouting about the dangerous snakes slivering about, it creates an atmosphere of fear, tension, and even anger. All of this contributes to further discolor people's perception and makes everyone prone to making even more mistakes."

Sam sat back in his chair. "On a hot summer day, warm air rising begins colliding with cool air sinking. What happens?"

"A thunderstorm happens."

"Right. Moments before that first thunderbolt and the ensuing downpour, a certain tension gets created. You can feel it. The wind starts to pick up, the leaves on the trees begin to rustle, and the sky darkens. You can feel the storm about to happen. Then suddenly there's a flash of lightening, a clap of thunder, and then a downpour. And usually, as suddenly as it started, it's over. The atmosphere is cleansed, and the air is fresh. The tension has to be released one way or another. But what if there was never any tension created in the first place? What if that first guy recognized the string as a string? What if he picked up that string and put it in his pocket? And that was the end of the whole affair?"

"So you're saying if you could remove the first cause, the first misperception, then all the problems of suffering would just disappear?"

"Well, that's what Vedic rishis would say. And getting back to Albert, the guy that shot me, at one time he saw me as a friend, and then he perceived me as an enemy. If you have billions of people misinterpreting every perception, things could go wrong very quickly. Welcome to the world we live in."

"So how do we get out of it?"

"Don Juan says we make agreements about reality. There are individual agreements and collective agreements that make up reality. You want to change the world, change your agreement. Or another way to say that, change yourself and you change your perception. Maharishi offers TM and prescribes meditating twice a day. Just this is enough over time to, in William Blake's words, 'clean the windows of perception.' One person reaching enlightenment is incredibly significant. That person is established in the Self, and he perceives the world truly. And the world is changed to some degree. But when enough people wake up to who they really are, the world changes. The rishis saw by increasing awareness through meditation, you naturally increase perception. If we could actualize our full potential, then we would see the world differently, and suffering would fall away as darkness recedes before the light. The tradition of suffering would be no more. Remember, there is no snake, only a string. Maharishi's goal is to have enough people meditating and eventually enough people living their full potential so that the world changes for everyone. Suffering falls away, and people live happy, fulfilled lives."

"Sam, I get the principle, but it seems like too fantastic an idea. For all of recorded history, there's been tremendous violence, disease, famine, and cruelty."

Sam leaned forward again over the table and spoke in a soft but firm voice. "The world is suffering because the door to the infinite has been hard to find. We have all been too busy looking outward, in the wrong direction, for fulfillment. Maharishi has arrived with the key to open the door again. We don't have to worry about darkness. We only need to bring our inner light out. It's enough to do just that. The darkness will simply vanish. Maharishi is playing his role full out. So the question is, are we going to play full out ourselves and decide to go for infinity? I decided yes."

"Well, at the moment I'm leaning in that direction," Julian spoke hesitantly, overwhelmed by Sam's passion and vision.

"And for the moment, that's good enough. Now, let's look at one more interesting factor—attention," Sam continued, on a roll. "Maharishi emphasizes that whatever we put our attention on grows. If we focus exclusively on problems, they tend to multiply or get more complicated. If we focus on disease, it gets stronger, or we could say health gets worse. If we put our attention on health, that grows. If we focus on solutions, we are far more likely to find them. To seek knowledge or experience of the transcendent is to put your attention on the most comprehensive solution there is. From this viewpoint, attention is a key to enlightenment. It's also a key to success in the world. Attention is simply the flow of our awareness. Transcending twice a day expands your awareness and, therefore, strengthens your attention, so put your attention on the positive things you want or can accomplish. Meditators especially need to know about the power of attention so they don't create what they don't want."

"Like you wanted a quiet space to talk in today?" Julian smiled.

"Yes, but of course it could have been a coincidence that people were busy. Or it could be as simple as getting my wish. Or it could have been that Kenny needed to do some errands and didn't want his staff overrun without him here. Who can say? But it was quiet, and we were able to have a nice chat." Like an orchestra at the end of a symphony, Sam's voice softened, and his eyes took on a teasing glint.

"I don't really get it. I sense there's something more here," Julian challenged, remaining serious.

"Right you are. You see, we could be launching into a completely different discussion—how to fulfill your desires. However, now is not the time because soon lots of customers will be walking in."

Sam looked up. "And here's Kenny right on cue, which means it's time to settle up and go." He excused himself from the conversation, leaving Julian to mull things over in silence for a few minutes. He strode over to the counter and grinned at Kenny.

"Rachel tells me it's been very quiet since you and the Irish kid have been in," Kenny observed with a serious expression.

"Yes, I would say so. We could actually have a conversation."

"Well, Sam, I'm going to have to build you a private room so you won't be disturbed."

"That's good of you, Kenny, but not necessary. I like the charm of the place. It wouldn't do to be sitting behind four walls separated from the rest of the café."

"Sam, you kill me. I'm running a business here."

"And I'm ready to settle my bill," replied Sam.

"Are you talking about your tab or just your bill today?"

"Just the bill, thank you. You'll need the armored car standing by when I pay my tab."

"I'm glad you recognize that the amount of money you owe is worthy of an armored car."

"How much is my tab, by the way?" Sam inquired.

"Two hundred and fifty bucks, more or less."

"Oh. That's a lot of coffee and muffins. All right, be prepared for a windfall. I've taken advantage of your goodwill far too long. You know, your paying customers will be arriving any minute, so you'd best get ready for the rush. It's going to be controlled chaos momentarily."

Within moments, people came streaming in, and Kenny and Sam laughed loudly.

Julian was confused as to what he was seeing and let it go, but not before thinking to himself that those two were completely bonkers, which, of course, from some point of view, they were.

Sam and Kenny said their good-byes, and Sam returned to the table. Julian slipped his backpack over his shoulders, and the two departed together.

Just outside the café entrance, Julian turned to Sam and commented, "Sam O'Connor, you are an interesting and mysterious man."

"Well, Julian, I've been called worse. The bigger picture of course is that it is an interesting, curious, and mysterious world in which we live. See you next week?"

"Yes, next week," Julian confirmed.

"Coming alone or bringing friends?"

"I'm trying to hold off Katy. We'll see."

They parted, and Sam walked up the street, thinking, "My Lord, it is a wonderful world. I'm grateful, so very grateful, for all of it."

Chapter 24:
The Mystery of Enlightenment

ON THE FOLLOWING FRIDAY AFTERNOON, Julian showed up early to meet Sam. Sam hadn't arrived yet, but Kenny was there. He saw Julian come in and search the tables for his mentor. Kenny sauntered over and greeted him. "Hey, young Jules has made his appointed hour."

"Hi, Kenny," Julian returned a bit nervously.

"You're here early," Kenny remarked, looking at his watch.

"Well, I wanted to make sure I got a good seat. Hey, listen, I started TM almost two weeks ago," Julian shared.

"Congratulations and Jai Guru Dev," Kenny replied with rare seriousness. His hands pressed together, he bowed slightly to Julian.

"Do you do TM also?"

"Almost sixteen years. In fact, I've been meditating longer than Sam." Kenny grinned like the Cheshire cat.

"No kidding?"

"Yeah, I started an hour before he did," Kenny stated with a straight face.

"Oh, come on. That doesn't count."

"Of course it does. In the old days, if we were twins and I was born just minutes ahead of Sam, I, by custom and rights, would inherit everything and Sam nothing," Kenny rambled.

"Only if he didn't kill you first, like in a hunting accident," Julian countered.

"Barring acts of violence and murderous plots, I'd get the estate, and Sam would get nothing. So you see, I started TM first, and Sam followed in my footsteps."

"That's your claim to fame?"

"No, but it's an interesting fact. I'm his best and oldest friend. We're like brothers, well, more like half brothers. Same father, different mothers."

Sam entered the café at that moment, spied Julian and Kenny bantering, and made his way over. "Oh, is it the world according to Kenny?" Sam jumped in.

"Yeah, I was just educating Jules on some of the finer points of history."

"I see. Does it happen to include the story of the elder son?"

"Yeah. Well, it's a fact, inconvenient as it is."

"Yes, you see, Julian, on some level I owe everything to Kenny. He's a brother. No, we're actually more like half brothers. Same father, different mothers," Sam observed, unaware of the details of the previous back-and-forth between Kenny and Julian.

"I think I've been through this part of the story," Julian interjected.

"Fine, then let's move on. I see a table in the back just waiting," Sam agreed.

"Coffee and muffins coming up. I hope you brought a gold coin to settle your running tab," Kenny quipped.

"Short on gold, but I do have cash," Sam claimed. He reached in his coat pocket, pulled out a one-dollar bill, and waved it at Kenny. He put the dollar back in his pocket, grinned, and led Julian to a table in the rear.

"That's what you call cash?" Kenny said, addressing their backs, and made his way to the coffee counter.

"He's really a character." Julian rolled his eyes.

"Now that's an understatement if ever one was uttered. He is the character, and although at times I hate to admit it, Kenny's my best friend. Kenny has a way of keeping me straight, or my ego straight. He's helped me more then he knows. He's also as down-to-earth as they come and yet somehow a cosmic figure. He's my Han Shan, my Cold Mountain."

"Who?"

"Okay, here's a story for you. I'll have to give you the short version. Cold Mountain was a Buddhist monk, also well versed in Taoism, who worked with his best friend, Pick Up, in the kitchen of a prestigious monastery in China. They were totally enlightened, totally blissful, and totally irreverent towards the serious monks, the lazy monks, and the better-than-thou monks, including some of the abbots who ran the monasteries. People thought that they were crazy, just like some people in this town think Kenny's crazy. Anyway, this high government official is told by Big Stick, another enlightened one, that Cold Mountain and Pick Up are immortals disguised as paupers working in the kitchen of Kouching Monastery. This official decides to go visit the monastery. He walks into the kitchen with the monks of the monastery behind him. There he finds Cold Mountain and Pick Up talking and laughing. He bows to them, and it only makes them laugh louder. Cold Mountain says, 'If you didn't recognize Amitabha, Big Stick, why would you bow to us?' They both run out of the kitchen. I imagine they were laughing, and out of the monastery gates they go. You see, Julian, Cold Mountain and Pick Up's antics were enlightened antics. They were indeed both bodhisattvas. Cold Mountain then returned to the mountains and to his large cave.

"The story goes that the prefect, the high official, sent messengers with gifts who went to search for Cold Mountain and, after much exploration, found the cave where he was living. Cold Mountain, on being discovered, ran to the back of the cave and vanished into the solid rock. All of his poems were discovered. They were everywhere, inscribed on the walls, on large rocks, and even on the trees that grew outside the cave. There were over three hundred of them. No one ever saw Cold Mountain again. Fortunately for us, however, all the poems were recorded. Would you like to hear one?"

"Sure," Julian responded.

Sam looked into the distance and began to recite:

> *Who takes the Cold Mountain Road*
> *takes a road that never ends*
> *the rivers are long and piled with rocks*
> *the streams are wide and choked with grass*
> *it's not the rain that makes the moss slick*
> *and it's not the wind that makes the pines moan*
> *who can get past the tangles of the world*
> *and sit with me in the clouds.*

"Cold Mountain," Sam explained, "is an example of someone who absorbs his culture and the spiritual teachings of his times and then goes beyond them. He transcends all of it and then chides those who are still seeking happiness and fulfillment in ways that can't give either. Anyway, Kenny is a bit like this himself," Sam concluded.

"Are you saying that Kenny has a mountain cave retreat and composes poetry?" Julian questioned half seriously.

"Julian, you can't always take things literally, including religious texts. However, Kenny is very straight with people, very direct. Most people take him to be rude or insensitive, but I see him as refusing to go along with people's ego trips. He just short-circuits them. Sometimes even well-intentioned people have very large egos. Kenny sees right through them, and well, it's pretty funny when you know that's what he's doing."

Kenny appeared with coffee, cream, and some blueberry muffins.

"Oh great!" said Julian. "Thanks."

"You're welcome, kind sir, I'm sure. The muffins are yesterday's stales, but if you dunk them, they'll be fine." Kenny used his most formal tone of voice. He waved a napkin, bowed, and left.

When Kenny turned and left, Julian asked, "Are they really stale?" Picking one up, he noted, "They don't seem stale."

"No, they're fresh. That's classic Kenny. So, how's life?" Sam asked, moving on.

"Meditation is so cool. I'm really enjoying it."

"Good. And fair Katy?"

"Oh yeah, she's into it, loves it."

"Splendid! I'm thrilled to see that you both have started on the path. Of course, it's a pathless path."

"You like that theme. It's the subtitle of your book," Julian commented.

"It's an old Vedic idea. Maharishi gave a brilliant lecture on it: 'The Pathless Path Home.' I heard it and it resonated with me."

"What resonated?" Julian probed.

"That from one point of view, there is a path to enlightenment, but from another, the idea of a path is impossible. Remember, reality is different in different states of consciousness. Clarifying this is one of Maharishi's greatest contributions to philosophy and religion. The contradictions that are impossible to reconcile on one level of consciousness disappear from a different state of consciousness."

"I'm not following you," Julian confessed.

"Maharishi has reestablished the understanding and direct experience of seven distinct states of consciousness, all of which are the birthright of every human being. Each state has different physiological and perceptual or psychological qualities. It's easy to see that if we look at the differences between deep sleep, dreaming, and the waking state. In deep sleep, both body and mind are at rest. We have no awareness and, therefore no perception. Content-wise, it's a blank. When we move into the dreaming state, both mind and body become a little more active. We have some awareness or consciousness, and therefore, we do perceive some content, however strange and unpredictable. We could find ourselves in a large arena fighting bulls, and that's our reality at that moment. When we wake up from dreaming, our bodies become much more active, and we have much more consciousness or inner awareness available. We find ourselves back in more familiar realms—we're in our bed with the early morning light coming through the window—and our mental content expands and multiplies from there. Is that easy to relate to?" Sam checked in.

"Yeah. Sure."

"Good. Now let's take the fourth state of consciousness, transcendental consciousness, with which you and Katy are now becoming familiar. In this state, the body is resting even more deeply than it does during deep sleep—at least that's what the research tells us so far—but unlike deep sleep, our consciousness is fully awake. With the TM technique, we easily transcend all the levels of our waking awareness until we slip into pure awareness or transcendental consciousness.

"Welcome to the first stage of Self-Realization. Having gained that infinite reality, we come back to this." Sam waved his arm in a big half circle. "By the way, I think Saint Paul meant this when he said, 'I die daily.'"

"Are you saying," hazarded Julian, "that each time we meditate and transcend, it's the equivalent of dying?"

"Yes, in a manner of speaking, that's right. You see, Saint Paul was using a metaphor to describe transcending. Each time we transcend, we go beyond the body, mind, and ego and become one with transcendental or pure consciousness. We go beyond every facet of our individuality, so it's as if, as an individual being, we die. We are absorbed into perfect silence, infinite stillness, and our identity is now universal, unbounded. Even our breathing slows down to almost nothing. But then, quite naturally, we come out of that experience and back to our breath and awareness of our body, thoughts, and environment. As you can see, transcending is therefore very much like dying and being reborn. You have the technique for it now, and as you use it regularly, these experiences become clearer and clearer. They become self-evident."

"I sort of know what you mean, Sam, but it's not completely clear," Julian admitted.

"That's not surprising. For now it's enough that you meditate twice a day. Over time, clarity will increase. By establishing that meditation routine,

Katy and you are growing towards the fifth state of consciousness, cosmic consciousness, that we discussed during your TM course. Remember that eventually we come to a point where we never lose pure consciousness or infinite inner wakefulness. We have it during sleep, dreaming, and even life's most demanding circumstances. Each time we alternate the experience of pure consciousness while meditating with whatever we do during the day, we permanently stabilize our ability to engage in life with greater and greater values of consciousness. The stabilization or integration of pure consciousness grows automatically. That level of silent awareness becomes more and more present until it never goes away. Maharishi describes it as a perfectly natural process, as long as we continue to dip into pure consciousness every day, twice a day, and don't regularly exhaust ourselves. Using another vocabulary, we could say that in transcendental consciousness, the 'I Am' is awakened. In cosmic consciousness, we never lose it. We know ourselves as the Self that always is, beyond time and space altogether. We realize our cosmic nature."

"It sounds pretty fantastic, almost too simple for what it is. So would this be the goal of meditation? To know definitely who you are?"

"Strictly speaking, there are no goals. When seekers create goals, they try to define the indefinable. They remain in the realm of beliefs and concepts, and the transcendent is something that we can only be. We cannot know it intellectually. We become it. In truth, we already are that infinite being, only just about everybody has forgotten. That's why we sometimes call it a pathless path. We already are infinite and perfect. We already are what we are seeking."

"That's all fine, Sam, but as I see it, we're all disconnected and filled with insecurity."

"Well, Julian, I think you're catching on. Remember that the world looks different in different states of consciousness. When we don't experience our true, unbounded nature, we are left with the limitations of waking, dreaming, and deep sleep. When we step into life with limited awareness, we are easily overshadowed by whatever life sends us. Our mood, our level of fulfillment, goes up and down with life's tides. We could say that life sometimes seems to kick us around like a football. This feeling good one moment and lousy the next creates seekers out of us all. The ups and downs grow exhausting, discouraging, even depressing, and we start seeking lasting fulfillment. Fortunately, Maharishi has revived the knowledge and techniques that allow us to live our full, unlimited potential. Suddenly a new awareness, a new sense of life's possibilities, is created. That new awareness creates a new point of view, and the world shifts. When we learn TM and start to transcend, the world again shifts quietly."

Sam paused a moment before he continued. "Did you know, for instance, that it wasn't very long ago that people thought it was impossible to break a four-minute mile? No runner could do it. Why do you think that was?"

"Because they thought it was impossible."

"Right, but it wasn't physically impossible. It was a point of view that everyone shared. So, along comes Roger Bannister. He changed his point of view and set out to show the world that a runner could break the four-minute mile. And he did it. And once he did it, other runners could do it. Once a new awareness is created, everyone can share in it. It's a breakthrough. This is what I mean when I say awareness shifts. It happens to individuals and to whole societies. As awareness grows, understanding grows with it. Points of view change. What was impossible one moment becomes possible the next. Old beliefs are discarded, and new ones replace them.

"When people realize that they haven't even come close to tapping their true potential and it's possible to do so, a tremendous shift will happen, and the world will change. What we're calling enlightenment, a state of fully realized potential, will be seen as the new norm. Once that happens, it's a whole new ball game."

"I honestly can't see the world shifting like that. I can see certain people getting it, but that's about it," asserted Julian.

"It doesn't matter if you or I can see the larger, collective possibility. What matters is that we see the possibility of our own unfolding. The world will take care of itself. If we do recognize the possibility for collective transformation, we don't make it our goal. Having a goal outside of one's self creates a duality. The Buddhists have an expression: 'If you see the Buddha walking down the road, kill him.'"

"That seems rather extreme!"

"On one level, yes. However, what the Buddhists are actually saying here is that everyone has a Buddha nature. Everyone has Buddha potential. Everyone is in fact Buddha. Therefore, if you see Buddha as something or someone outside of yourself, as in Buddha walking down the road, then get rid of the thought and realize the Buddha within you. Own the infinite within. When there is only wholeness and you are that wholeness, when there is no separation, no difference between inside and out, when you and the universe are one, your enlightenment is the world's enlightenment."

"I can sort of relate to what you're saying, Sam, on some completely nonlinear level," offered Julian, "but my dad would call this crazy."

"I'm sure you're right, and he would be justified in doing so because he has no point of reference. Even though unfolding their full potential is everybody's birthright, few are ready to claim it. Most still have the hatcheck claim in their pocket. For the moment, they've forgotten all about it. They are so busy, so intent in wandering through the great museum of life, that they've forgotten who they are, as well as their hat. But it's all right. At some point, everyone remembers."

Sam continued, "In the East, more people appreciate the existence of higher states of consciousness. The knowledge is entwined in the culture. That doesn't mean that everyone born and raised in an Eastern country puts spirituality first, but in general, people have more respect for those who do. The culture supports reverence for the enlightened and those who seek spiritual perfection. The culture has a general acceptance that the enlightened serve a valuable purpose and that being around them opens up the heart and mind."

"That may be true," Julian said, "but in our culture, we need to be convinced scientifically, objectively. People here are very practical."

"Yes, and Maharishi recognized this. One of his other great contributions has been to define the states of consciousness he describes in scientific terms. He has inspired some fascinating research that has given us an increasingly detailed picture of the physiology of higher states of consciousness.

"However, people in the East are quite practical as well. They want a higher standard of living, better education and health, more comfort, just as we do here. It's only human to do so. Wanting enlightenment doesn't negate the desire for a good life, materially speaking. It's an unfortunate misunderstanding that gaining enlightenment requires abstaining from material pursuits or that only recluses can reach enlightenment. 'The road,' as Whitman said, 'is open to all.'"

"It's an interesting idea that science can verify the mystical notion of enlightenment," Julian remarked. "On the other hand, I think everyone likes mysteries. What fun would it be if scientists in white lab coats could explain all the mysteries?"

"If the scientist happens to be like Einstein, it might make it easier to swallow, but I agree. Scientists will undoubtedly be able to map the physiological parameters of the seven states of consciousness completely someday, but explaining the nature of consciousness is likely to remain a bigger challenge, something harder to prove with objective data. Lao Tsu said long ago, 'The Tao that can be told is not the eternal Tao.' Words cannot quantify or qualify pure Being. We have to become It. The mystery will continue, I believe. Scientists may have to enter the realm of pure subjectivity to know these states of consciousness themselves."

"From the standpoint of ignorance, enlightenment is a mystery. Could we also say that from the standpoint of enlightenment, ignorance is a mystery?" Julian inquired.

"Not exactly. From the standpoint of enlightenment, ignorance does not exist, separation does not exist. Beliefs, stories, opinions, attachments, and all the dramas that our inventive minds create are like a dream to the enlightened person. Therefore, he or she may at times find it mysterious that anyone still believes in the dream.

"However, from the point of view of those still on the path, those who still live in the world of dualities, the journey home to our true Self can be a grand adventure. In Joseph Campbell's *Hero with a Thousand Faces*, the hero's journey takes him to the source of his divine nature. He comes back with the prize of more knowledge, more awareness, and then tries to share that with the larger society so that everyone benefits from his journey. Myths and stories from cultures everywhere speak of this same journey.

"Read Walt Whitman's 'Song of the Open Road': 'Allons! to that which is endless as it was beginningless . . . To know the universe itself as a road, as many roads, as roads for traveling souls.' Whitman urges the reader to join him on this great journey, this grand adventure back home to the source. He writes,

Forever alive, forever forward,
Stately, solemn, sad, withdrawn, baffled, mad, turbulent, feeble, dissatisfied,
Desperate, proud, fond, sick, accepted by men, rejected by men,
They go! they go! I know that they go, but I know not where they go,
But I know that they go toward the best—toward something great.

Whoever you are! come forth! Or man or woman come forth!
You must not stay sleeping and dallying there in the house, though you built it
or though it has been built for you.

"It is a beautiful cosmic poem, and it's a grand journey whether it takes one or a thousand lifetimes to complete. But who's counting?"

191

Kenny walked to the back of the café and inserted his point of view: "Look, guys, if you're going to sit here all afternoon, you've got to help pay the rent. This is not a nonprofit, publicly funded business. How do you expect me to keep the doors open on a $3.50 tab? So how about a nice croissant, a slice of carrot cake, or New York cheesecake and more coffee?"

"Ah, Kenny, my dear friend, forever the businessman," Sam responded. "Julian, Kenny is an example of how to keep the world spinning yet not be in the spinning world."

"And Sam is an example of the gift of gab run wild. His father, Jimmy, used to say, 'He could talk the ears off a brass monkey.' I'm from the school that says that even the best description is a poor, shallow attempt to describe reality. Words are not of much benefit. Direct experience is the only way."

"What Kenny means is that he transcended and realized early on who he was. He skipped the description part, though not entirely of course, and went to the source."

"See? What did I tell you? He needs to explain everything." Kenny grimaced.

"As a teacher, it is my nature to explain. Kenny is a karma yogi. His nature is to do, to be active and yet nonactive at the same time, and if it includes hassling poor folks who are enjoying a private conversation, he'll do it."

"Well said, brother," Kenny offered ironically. "Sam's nature is to be a man of knowledge. That is, he goes deep into the mystery of life, understanding and reconciling all the opposites and apparent contradictions, and then attempts to explain it to people who don't have the foggiest idea what he's talking about. So what are you going to have? Cheesecake? Carrot cake? Croissants?"

"No sense in preaching to the choir, Kenny boy. I'm interested in those who are starting to think about joining the choir. However, now I'm thinking cheesecake. Yes, I'll take the cheesecake. Julian?"

"Yeah. Cheesecake is good," Julian added distractedly.

Sam added, "Put it on my tab, matey."

"On your tab, I could retire. Those royalty checks are still rolling in, I take it?"

"Yes. Sometimes they're big and sometimes small, but they're rolling. My publisher tells me my book is selling well in Russia. Imagine that."

"Well, to me it only proves that people everywhere will seek any port in a storm," Kenny observed and went off with a snort.

"Sam, I don't think Ken's a good advertisement for enlightenment."

"Well, God does have a sense of humor. Kenny is a New York City Irish American guy, and enlightenment doesn't change that. He's also a bit of an actor. Keep that in mind. Still, I know what you mean. Remember, on the surface, life is full of surprises and sometimes confuses the heck out of our expectations, including any expectation about how enlightenment ought to look. "

"I get that Sam. But still . . ."

"Let's just say, the enlightened uplift all those around them, each in their own way. If you could catch even a glimpse of the real Kenny, your point of view would switch."

"Well, honestly, he unnerves me. I don't feel a bit uplifted."

Sam laughed. "I don't want to push this too far, but let me assure you all is not what it seems. The sinners might be the saints, and the saints might be the sinners."

Sam paused then ventured, "Have you read Whitman?"

"No, I haven't," replied Julian.

"He's full of wisdom and consciousness, though not everyone approved in his day, approved of him or his poetry. He was a boundary breaker in that he went way beyond the norms of his day. I keep thinking to myself that I need to write a book on Whitman. He was like an ancient seer, seeing the unfoldment of cosmic evolution everywhere he looked. He wrote from an infinitely expansive awareness. I've been reading him now for perhaps twenty years, and he never ceases to amaze me."

"I'll definitely put him on my reading list. By the way, Katy asked me if she could join us on Fridays. I said I'd ask you."

"Fine with me. More the merrier."

"Thanks. I want to hold off a bit. It's going to break up the flow we got going here."

"Whatever you think."

"I don't mind chipping in on this stuff," Julian said, reaching into his pocket for a couple of dollars.

"What? And ruin the game Kenny and I have going. Not on your mother's life. The only thing you need to do is to keep meditating. Remember, it's effortless. See you next Friday."

"Okay. See you then." Julian grabbed his backpack and was off.

Kenny arrived with the cheesecake and coffees. "Where did the kid go?"

"Had a date and had to run," Sam replied. "Katy wants to come next week."

"Hey, buddy, I got news for you. Everyone's coming next week. You're blowing that boy's mind."

"No. He can take it. I'm just warming him up. Thanks for the coffee and cheesecake," Sam said.

"You're welcome." And the two friends drank their coffee and enjoyed each bite of the cheesecake and laughed out loud for what seemed like no reason at all.

Chapter 25:
Where Light Is Perpetual

JULIAN AND KATY SPENT A quiet night talking. Julian told her about his discussion with Sam on enlightenment. Katie sat, fully receptive, taking it in without questions. After dinner, they walked through the neighborhood holding hands, hardly conversing, enjoying the unusual silence between them. When they returned to their small apartment, they felt welcome by its warmth and light. Neither felt like watching the movie Julian had brought home. They read for a while, sprawled out on the bed, heads propped up against the pillows, with Katy's legs lying on top of Julian's. In less than an hour, they both dozed off.

Julian began dreaming. Once again he was walking on the beach in a luminous world. The white sand sparkled; the water was turquoise and clear, almost transparent, and spread before him without end. Something about the water filled him with immense joy. Small waves lapped at the shore, and the sound *aum* reverberated in his mind. He saw a figure up ahead, seated cross-legged and looking out to the infinite sea. Julian walked toward the figure and recognized Sam. When he reached Sam, he sat down beside him.

Sam spoke softly, "Hi, Julian. Good of you to join me."

"Hi, Sam. Good to be here, but where are we exactly? It looks like Saint Thomas, but I don't think it is."

"We're on another level of creation."

"I'm not sure what that means. Am I dreaming?"

"Yes, but it's no ordinary dream. You might call the dream you're having a lucid dream."

"Why do I keep having this same lucid dream?"

"Well, you've come to know that we can meet here, and besides, you like it here."

"It is so beautiful, and I do feel an enormous sense of peace."

"Human beings are complex. We can actually exist on different levels of the universe at the same time. We are, in fact, multidimensional beings."

"Is this like heaven?"

"Yes and no. This world is an expression of your highest vibratory rate. As you keep increasing that rate by enlivening your consciousness, you can experience even more luminous places or planes."

"But how is this like heaven?" Julian asked insistently.

"Well, there are actually seven heavens. This is one of the lower levels of heaven—not a bad level by anyone's standards. Still, as you proceed to higher levels, the light grows more brilliant, and the sense of peace, contentment, and happiness grow."

"Where are Amy and Katy in all this?"

"They're on different levels. Amy is learning to become a co-creator with God. She is bursting with creativity and discovering how she fashions her own world out of her divine nature."

"And Katy?"

"Katy is learning that to love is to nourish creation. The divine feminine nourishes every aspect of this endless creation with infinite love. Katy is learning to transcend judgment and give her love to all."

"What am I learning?"

"You're learning to trust your Self, your essence. You're learning to hear the voice of that divine impulse we call your soul and trust it, trust your inner wisdom and doubt your doubts. I learned those same lessons."

"How did you do it? I mean, how did you learn?"

"I remembered my Self, just as you will."

"Isn't it easier to just hang out here? Everything seems so clear. Why go back to the other world?"

"Being human takes a great deal of courage. It appears to us humans that we live in a dark world, far from the light of the Divine. Yet paradoxically, that is the world in which we can grow the fastest. We are confronted with not knowing who we are, and if we're lucky, circumstances are created that spur us on to discover who we are. Here, in this celestial world, we could sit for thousands of years and simply enjoy and not grow at all."

"But why not just stay here? This may not be infinite fulfillment, but whatever it is, I feel wonderful, blissful, and peaceful."

"If you stayed, eventually you would have a desire for even more happiness. It might take thousands of years in Earth time, but you would have a sense, however faint, that something is missing. The Creator has planted a desire so deep within us for infinite fulfillment to ensure that each and every one of us makes the journey home. You could say we are all cosmic children exploring the creation and ourselves. In the process, we've forgotten our cosmic status and feel quite separate from the divine essence that we are. The dream will do that. So until you and I awaken completely from the dream and realize our divine selves, the infinite wholeness within us, more growth is possible, and thus, staying here in this world is not possible."

"Sam, will I remember any of this when I wake up?"

"Not on a conscious level, but something of this dream will remain on the feeling level. That faint feeling will bring you some contentment and confidence. I won't remember clearly either. It's a dream."

"Sam, the water is so bright. It's shimmering with light."

"Yes, Julian. There is a world—in fact, many worlds—where light is perpetual, where everything glows with dazzling brilliance. Such places are beyond even what we think of as heaven, beyond space and time. We ourselves are light beings, expressions of divine light. Everything is made of light. Even the world of matter is all light. Remember, Julian, you are pure consciousness appearing as light, a light being. Nothing can ever harm or diminish you. You are infinite and eternal. Nothing can change that."

Sam smiled with the light of a thousand suns, rose into the air, bowed to Julian, melted into light, and vanished.

Julian awoke to find Katy still asleep and the bedroom lights on. He gently moved Katy's leg off his, found the covers, and pulled them up to just below her chin. Julian gazed at her. She looked so lovely lying there in deep slumber. He turned out the lights and rolled over, ready to fall asleep himself. Resting quietly, for just a moment he saw Sam's smiling face and a blaze of white light. Then he fell fast asleep.

Chapter 26:
The Theory of Relativity

JULIAN WOKE UP IN THE morning with the beautiful Katy in his arms. He recognized, as he often did, that this blessing could easily slip away. The world could swoop in and, in a moment, pull one of them elsewhere, and she would be out of his life. The fear of loss came and went, but for now, he was totally happy and he kissed her.

She stirred awake and returned the kiss before she muttered, "Morning breath! Oh my god!" She half pushed Julian away and ran down the hall to brush her teeth. Julian threw a pillow at her as she made the bedroom door.

"You see, just like that she's gone," he said to no one in particular. After a minute, Julian followed her down the hall. Naked and exquisite, Katy slipped into the shower while Julian brushed his teeth. Only a couple of minutes later, Julian tried to join Katy in the shower, but she was finished, her attention already shifting to the morning's next step.

"Hey! I thought you could wash my back."

"I'd love to, sweetie pie, but we've got to meditate, and I've got a few things to do before I leave to see my mom."

Julian's protest was for naught. His back not washed and his ego slightly bruised, he emerged from the bathroom to find Katy fully dressed and sitting quietly in meditation. He pulled on his jeans and T-shirt and joined her on the couch. When they finished meditation, they opened their eyes, looked at each other, and smiled.

Katy offered, "That was sweet." And Julian nodded in agreement.

Katy jumped up, ready to roll, and stated, "If you want a ride into town with me, we have to leave in twenty minutes."

Julian had other ideas, so he moved around in slow motion while Katy flew around the apartment getting her stuff together, straightening up as she went. "She is amazing," Julian reflected over a cup of tea.

Katy gathered her books, bag, and the repotted mum and announced it was time to go. She fired up the '69 Dodge pickup that her dad had given her two years ago and sat waiting for Julian. Julian came out the front door, walked reluctantly over to the truck, and put his knapsack crammed with books in the back. He opened the passenger door and got into the cab. Katy sensed his mood but didn't come to his rescue. Julian felt like an idiot and decided to act like one too.

"Katy," Julian started as he climbed into the truck, "I wanted to make love to you this morning, but the way you sprang out of bed and then leaped out of meditation and started running around like a rabbit, I didn't know what to think."

"Ah, Jules, you know I love you, but I can't have sex with you absolutely every time we feel like it. Besides, I'm going to see my mother."

"But your mother must know by now we're making love."

"That's not the point." Katy made a face of dissatisfaction and looked straight ahead over the steering wheel.

Julian knew that look and decided it was better to let it drop. Katie released the parking brake, pushed in the clutch, and put her in first gear. They rode in silence for the rest of the two miles to campus. When they arrived, Julian got out of the truck, retrieved his backpack, went around to the driver's side, and kissed Katy good-bye. "Have a safe trip."

Katy nodded, already thinking about the trip to Vermont. She yelled out the window as she rolled away, "I'll be back around eight. Good luck on your paper. Save some strength for tonight," and then beeped the horn.

Julian stood still for a moment, watching Katy depart. She drove down the road, swung a little to the right, signaled left, pulled a U-turn, and drove past him at an accelerated speed until she was out of sight. The day proved to be a long one for Julian, while for Katy, time flew.

Had Einstein been around, he might have commented, "It's all relative."

Visiting her mother meant a lot to Katy. Her two brothers, their wives, and her two-year-old nephew all lived close-by. Her father had died suddenly from a heart attack a year earlier. Her brothers worked the three-hundred-acre dairy farm now, though technically, Mom still owned it. As she pulled up the long, familiar drive to the house, shaded by large maples, her heart swelled with warmth and peace. Her mother, Annie, stepped out the front door and onto the wide porch to greet her. Katy was so excited to see her that she ran up the walk and scrambled up the stairs with the pot of mums in hand. They hugged and kissed each other on the cheek then went inside and down the hall to the roomy kitchen. Annie put the kettle on, and the two sat and talked about all the news, Katy's classes, and Julian while sipping on Red Rose tea with honey and fresh cream.

Anyone could see the roots of Katy's beauty in her mother. Though her skin had wrinkled and she was just on the round side, her features were still striking, and her face and blue eyes lit up when she spoke. Annie was loving, down-to-earth, and easy to talk to. Everyone who sat and chatted with her at that table felt it. She treated everyone with courtesy and respect as she lent a receptive ear. She was not too quick to give her opinion, and she encouraged her children to think for themselves.

Katy's brothers, their wives, and her nephew, Timmy, all came to the house for an early dinner. They enjoyed the sharing and teasing as always, and evening seemed to arrive suddenly. Her mother reminded her she had better get on the road to catch the last hour of daylight. With hugs and kisses, Katy parted. She realized how lucky she was to love her family so much.

Spending the day with her family and seeing the farm where she grew up often made Katy feel a little homesick. *Julian,* she reflected, *doesn't relate to farm life, cows, and the sweet smell of manure. Except, in a romantic way, Julian relates to everything . . . I wonder how he'd feel about cleaning out the barn?*

Julian spent part of the morning in the library but then decided to walk into town and over to the White Oak Café. He was half expecting to see Kenny but also just wanted a change in scenery. He walked into the café, found half the tables empty, and dropped his knapsack and coat at one of the empty ones. Rachel was at the counter and, recognizing Julian, said, "Hi" with a little bit extra of a smile. Julian grinned back, liking the recognition. Just then, Kenny came in from the back-room.

"Hey, kiddo. What's happening with you?"

"Oh, nothing much. Just wanted to take a break from the paper I'm writing."

"What ya having?"

"Coffee and a muffin sound good."

"Blueberry, cranberry, or almond. All fresh. "

"Blueberry."

"You got it. By the way, you're paying cash right?"

"Sure."

"Okay. I just don't want you falling into the bad habits of your mentor."

"Nah. That's your game. I'm a cash-paying kind of guy."

"Good man. You are definitely my kind of customer."

"Hey, Kenny, can I ask you a question?"

"You can always ask, but I can't always promise you an answer. Anyway, that's a buck seventy-five."

Julian paid the exact amount. Kenny thanked him and said, "I got the feeling what you want to ask is going to take a while to answer. You philosophy people are all the same. So why don't you have a seat, and I'll be over in a minute."

"All right, sounds good," Julian said, not knowing what he started.

Julian enjoyed his muffin and drank half his coffee before Kenny came around and sat down.

"So, young Jules, what's on your mind?"

"So much has happened in the past few weeks, my head is spinning. I don't really understand Sam in some ways. He's brilliant, that's pretty obvious. Had the makings of a great career and he dropped out."

"Is that a question?" Kenny paused. "Listen, Jules, life doesn't run on a straight track. And who's to say Sam's dropped out? Little early for that call. If anything, Sam's dropped in."

"What do you mean he dropped in?"

"Listen, kid, this whole world is about awareness. Sam is all about awareness. Out, in, these are just figures of speech. From your perspective, Sam dropped out. There are a few other people around here that think the same way. But from my perspective, Sam dropped into awareness. He couldn't have done that teaching, grading all those papers, and tending to his family. He needed the time to be unfocused. He needed to settle into his Self. Which he did."

"I don't get it."

"I see that. Let's just say for you to see it is probably not important. You have your own thing to do, and understanding what Sam has done might throw you off. So don't worry. Be happy. I like that song by the way. You want more coffee?"

"Yeah, sure. Thanks."

"You're quite welcome."

"Sam told me you're like Cold Mountain."

"You mean Han Shan?"

"Yeah, you know, Cold Mountain, a Buddhist monk."

"Sam's nuts. That guy is light-years ahead of me. Anyway, Sam knows too much. Hasn't worked a day in twenty years, and even then, it was just for the summer. Always reading, that guy, he wasn't always like that. When we were growing up, he was a pretty regular guy. Starting reading more as a sophomore in high school, always had his nose in a book, and it took off from there."

"You don't read?"

"I can read, but the only thing I've read is the paper."

"What books have you read?"

"This is getting a little boring. But if you want to know, I've read Maharishi's *Science of Being and Art of Living*. What Maharishi didn't put in there, he put in the Bhagavad Gita chapters 1–6. And I've read the trilogy."

"What trilogy?"

"The Lord of the Rings by J. R. R. Tolkien. That's about all anyone needs, really."

"Well, that's great, but you can't be serious." Julian chuckled.

Kenny, looking impatient, replied, "All right, I'm done with you for the time being. Got a business to run here. You better go read some more useless books, but when you get a chance, read the trilogy and *Dharma Bums*. And here's my last bit of advice for the day. Forget all about Kant and Descartes. Complete waste of time, ink, and paper."

"You've read Descartes and Kant?"

"Sam and I shared an apartment for a thousand years, and he had all these books lying around . . ."

With that, Kenny got up, bowed to Julian, and with a smile said "Namaste." Before Julian could respond, Kenny turned around and walked off. Julian sat there not knowing what just transpired. He drank his second cup, put on his coat, slung his backpack over his shoulder, and headed back to campus and the library, but not before Rachel called out, "Bye, Julian."

When Katy arrived home, Julian was heating up some soup and fixing a sandwich. "How was your day?" Katy inquired as she kissed a distracted Jules.

"Fine. Got some work done this morning. Walked over to the White Oak. Had a slightly crazy conversation with Kenny and haven't done much since. Kenny has that same sparkle in his eye that Sam has, and yet the two couldn't be more different. It's sort of odd, but then it isn't."

"Well, honey, you're not making much sense now. Any more soup?"

"Should be enough for the two of us," Julian said as he stirred the pot. "You want a sandwich? I'll put the toast down."

"Sounds really good. By the way, my mom and family send their regards. They'd like you to come up next time."

"Yeah, how is Mom? Nice she asked about me."

"Well, she knows you're important to me, and she's fine, really good actually," Katy added as she walked into the living room on her way to their bedroom to put her bag away.

"Sam told me yesterday that Kenny is like this mystical Buddhist guy Cold Mountain. And I guess I was curious about that. Anyway, I don't know anything about Cold Mountain, but Kenny is unlike anyone I've ever met, so maybe he is Cold Mountain," Julian half yelled.

"Julian, I have no idea what you're talking about," Katy called from the other room.

"Good, because I have no idea either," Julian called after Katy. As he reached to open up the cabinet to get the bowls for the soup, he thought to himself, *I guess it is all relative. It really is a point of view. Sam and Kenny have theirs, and I have mine.*

Katy came back into the small kitchen. "Hey, Katy, I just realized it's all a point of view, and everyone has one. And everyone's point of view is valid in a relative way. It's pretty amazing, and it's very cosmic."

Katy was hungry and distracted, and Julian's insight rolled off her. "That's good, honey."

Julian poured the soup, and Katy took the bowls to the table. Julian followed with the sandwiches. The two young lovers sat down and smiled at each other. In that moment, those smiles and shining eyes told a great story along with the billions of other stories also being told in that exact moment.

As the Vedic rishis say, "Purnamadah, purnamidam," meaning, "This is full and That is full. Fullness is all That there is."

And Jackie Gleason, a comic genius, would add, "How sweet it is . . ."

Chapter 27:
Mums, Tea, and Muffins

KATY ARRIVED AT AMY'S FRONT door early Sunday morning with two pots of mums in her arms. The yellows and purples were vibrant. On the porch she found two large pumpkins and a number of interestingly shaped gourds. Cornstalks were tied to the porch's two front columns. Morning light still illuminated the front door. All of this made Katy feel very much at home, reminding her of her family's farmhouse in Vermont.

Katy shifted her load and managed to knock on the door. She heard the dog barking inside and a tumbling and scampering sound making its way down the hall, a familiar sound. Paul and Josh flung the door open, and a few moments of chaos ensued as the dog leaped toward the door and the boys bumped into each other and stumbled, trying to contain their dog's effusive greeting. Paul shouted, "Mom, Katy's here!" Josh held Rufus in an attempt to shush the old fellow, who continued to bark, thrashing his tail enthusiastically.

Amy, in corduroy jeans and a green turtleneck, arrived just as things started to settle down. She welcomed Katy into the house. "Come in, Katy. Boys, let Rufus stay out. Sorry for the unceremonious greeting."

"No, it's fine. Really. There's so much energy. I love it! Here, I brought these for you." And Katie handed the potted mums to Amy.

"You shouldn't have. They're lovely. Thank you, Katy."

"You're welcome," Katy returned, feeling a bit shy.

Amy took Katy's canvas farm jacket and hung it in the hall closet bursting with winter coats. She then invited Katy to the kitchen, asking, "Cup of tea? Coffee? I just made some blueberry muffins."

"Sounds perfect, tea is fine. Thank you."

"Good. I'm glad you're here." Amy turned toward the boys standing at the foot of the stairs as if awaiting instructions. "Katy and I are going to enjoy a chat by ourselves now."

"Yeah, Mom, we know, time to get lost," Josh acknowledged.

"I didn't say that, Josh. Each of you grab a muffin and then off with you."

"No problem! We're outta here!" Paul declared, glad to escape before Amy thought about assigning any Saturday morning chores. He turned to Josh, "Let's take Rufus and make for the stream."

The screen door slammed, and the house settled into silence.

Katy remarked, "They're such great kids. You're so fortunate. Is Sam here?"

"Yes, we are. They're a handful, but in a good way. No, Sam is off to his cathedral in the pines as he calls it."

"Oh. I appreciate you having me over. Since Julian and I have started meditating, things are really opening up. I feel psyched, but I don't know where it's going." Katy was a little surprised to hear herself admitting this feeling of uncertainty.

"I felt the same way when I started to meditate. The uncertainty is perfectly natural. Nothing in life is certain anyway." Amy laughed. "And when old boundaries dissolve, new possibilities open up."

"What do you mean by that?"

"Maharishi likes to say that life holds infinite possibilities, so we should just pick something great to do and do it. He's always so positive, so encouraging. Sam likes to put it another way: 'Since we're all dreaming anyway, why not dream a bigger, happier dream?' "

"Well, Julian is a dreamer, that's for sure," Katy commented, rolling her eyes.

"Sam is also. He's definitely a philosopher and an idealist," Amy sympathized. "I've learned to be more grounded. Being a mom can do that. There are many reasons why I love Sam, and his being an idealist is one of them. Still, we had our challenges. And yet our love for each other sustained us.

"In terms of being a couple, Katy, remember that we evolve together and we evolve as individuals. Both are happening at the same time. So it's important that each person in the relationship supports the other. Maharishi once told us that the secret of marriage is to always say yes. He qualified it by saying if it's not a good idea, one can raise it for discussion later. And then he laughed. The point is that couples live for each other on the fine level of feeling, and it's important not to disrupt those feelings."

Amy paused. "I love Sam with all my heart, but we've had our share of ups and downs. Sometimes it's just the normal daily pressures of raising a family. Sometimes it's the difficulty of communicating about whatever is going on inside each of us."

"But your life looks so perfect," Katy protested.

"Our life is wonderful but keeps unfolding just like yours. Change is constant and inevitable. The idea is to be big enough to allow life to flow without resistance, to welcome change and be one with whatever is happening. Change is inescapable, and truly, we are not in control. Sam and I got a big lesson there." Amy looked down at the table and back at Katy.

"Do you mean when he was shot?" Katy blurted out.

"You know about that?" Amy asked, a bit surprised.

"Yes. Julian heard about the book Sam wrote and did some research at the library, looking up the news articles. He was stunned as was I when he came home that night and told me about all that had happened. We've been at the college for over three years, and no one's ever mentioned it. It's as if Sam is just forgotten. How did that happen?" Katy paused, refocusing on the shooting. "It must have been terrible seeing your husband shot. I can't imagine how you dealt with it. Julian has tried to bring it up to Sam, but he doesn't want to talk about it."

"Sam has come to a place of peace about the shooting, but it didn't happen overnight. It was a long process, and we each had to deal with it in our own way. As far as Sam being forgotten, I think he wanted it that way, and I'm not surprised he doesn't want to talk about it."

"Well, I guess it's understandable. But if you don't mind me asking, how did you deal with all of it?"

"Well, since you're interested, I'll tell you. Sam retreated—he went inward. He lost his ambition and became simpler. He started letting go of things, people, colleagues, friends—well, not true friends. He held on to a few of those. He meditated for long periods of time. Yet he was there for us still, in a quieter way. For the first year, I didn't understand what he was doing. I just thought he needed a long break and then he'd emerge, go back to teaching, and our life would return to normal."

"But it didn't return to normal?"

"No. Sam became very quiet and reflective. At some point, I just didn't understand what was happening to him. I began to feel I had lost the man I married. But I gradually began to see that he was working it all out. By questioning everything he knew, he was doing the inner work of sorting out what was true and what was false. So in time, I began to trust in him again, and once I did, our life came back, in a manner of speaking."

"Did you also go through something similar?"

"I did, only not as drastic as Sam. I left my teaching job officially the following June. Of course, I took a leave of absence in the fall for eight weeks. But once I resigned, I started my career as an artist. I needed to retreat into art and my creative side. It was therapy for me. I still took care of Sam and the boys and the house, but I also had those three to four hours a day to work in my studio. Sam's book really started to sell after he was shot. Funny how it happens that way. And of course, that gave us the financial support we needed to be freed from that level of responsibility, from working day to day. So we had the time and space to figure things out, to heal and grow."

"Did you continue to love one another through all that?"

"Yes," Amy said quietly. "Our love was the current in which we lived. But sometimes, when something is so constant, there are moments when you're not sure."

"You mean you took your love for granted? Do you think that most of us do that?" Katy asked with some concern.

"Unfortunately, yes, we all do that. We forget. We get busy. Overwhelmed at times and tired. So naturally, we forget our friends, our family. We forget God, forget who we are in the big picture, forget the big picture itself for that matter. And yet, in a way, that's what being human is about. Forgetting and remembering. Still, on some level, love continues to nourish us and connect us. When we love fully, we are in life fully and life is fully in us. Sam and I remind each other about love, what's important."

"That's so beautiful, Amy," Katy said with a sigh and then added, "Sometimes I see my whole life in Julian's eyes, and I think I'm so deeply in love with this man. Other times, all I see is that he's such a dreamer, and on a practical level, I can't imagine my life with him, and still I can't see myself without him either."

"Don't be concerned too much about the future," Amy smiled gently. "Stay in the present and allow life to unfold through you. Maharishi always encouraged us to keep meditating, and things will become clearer.

"Everything you need to know, Katy, is inside your heart. Our society doesn't support this idea very much. We strongly favor the mind and intellect. However, Maharishi used to tell us it's much easier for women than men to be in touch with their innermost feelings, that our nervous systems were more refined. He encouraged us to live from the finest level of feeling, but when we get stressed and tired, it's difficult to do that. But as you meditate more and more, Katy, you'll naturally be in touch with your deeper feelings, and that will make all the difference in your life."

Katy and Amy looked at each other. Katy felt a jolt of excitement rush through her with the realization that Amy was the wisest woman she had ever met. Her excitement led her to be a bit nervous and self-conscious, and she gushed a bit as she thanked Amy for having her over and stood up to leave.

"Listen, I should go. Thank you for having me over. I loved talking with you, and you've given me so much to think about."

"Come over anytime," Amy responded, smiling warmly.

"Really?" Katy asked, surprised, as she and Amy walked to the door.

"Yes, really." Amy laughed.

"Great! I will. Thanks again."

"I look forward to seeing you. Give me a call when you have some free time, and we'll see what we can work out. And I love the mums! They may show up in a painting soon."

"Fantastic! Bye. Give my best to Sam."

Katy felt elated driving home. *What an incredible woman Amy is*, she thought. When she got home, Julian was reading, still in his boxers and T-shirt.

"Hey, Jules," Katy called, bouncing in.

"Hi, Katy. How did it go?"

"Wonderful. Amy's amazing. She's gone through so much, and she's not bitter. Quite the opposite: she's so loving and kind. I felt totally relaxed with her."

"Well, remember, she's a married woman."

"You're such a jerk. Not everything is about sex."

"Are you sure about that?" Julian looked at Katy, grinning broadly.

"Yes," Katy spoke emphatically, "quite sure."

"I was only kidding, but you're acting like a woman in love."

"Maybe I do love her. She's fantastic."

"Well, remember, it was my idea to go visit," Julian came back.

"Julian, you get points for that."

"Can I cash those points in?"

"Yeah, lover boy, you sure can."

Katy moved toward Julian and bent over to kiss him. Julian pulled Katy gently onto his lap. The two lovers became absorbed in each other, with no hint of uncertainty in the air.

Chapter 28:
A New Life

*D*EVENDRA AND JYOTI ARRIVED IN *Allahabad with a letter of introduction from the raja for Professor Gupta. They found their way to the university, which had been established in 1875, only twenty-three years earlier. Devendra strode energetically through his new home, wearing his plain white cotton kurta and loose-fitting pants. Jyoti, in a bright yellow sari that had been a wedding gift, had to walk quickly to keep up with him. They had hired an ox cart to carry their simple belongings from the train to the professor's address, but they wanted to stretch their legs after the long train journey and feel the atmosphere of this ancient city that would now be their home. Devendra felt thrilled to be there, and thoughts about the city, originally called Pragya, circled through his mind. Allahabad was the very place where the god Brahma was believed to have made his first sacrificial offering after creating the world. And more, the great sage Bharadwaja had lived here almost seven thousand years ago in his ashram, before Pragya had become a city. Devendra was in heaven. The great epic, the Mahabharata, also spoke of Pragya. Lord Rama, hero of the Ramayana, had spent some months in the city, and Devendra was aware that his feet now touched the ground hallowed by Lord Rama's presence.*

"Jyoti, I can't believe our great fortune!" Devendra exclaimed. "We are in this holy city where the divine Saraswati herself joined the Yamuna and Ganges Rivers. We have come to live in such a sacred place!" Devendra practically shouted in his excitement.

"By our master's grace," Jyoti gently reminded him.

"Of course, by our master's grace." Devendra was quiet for a moment then shifted the subject. "How anxious I am to see my brother!"

"And I'm anxious to see my mother," Jyoti added.

"But I'm deeply happy to be with you, Jyoti," Devendra spoke tenderly, smiling at his bride, "to have you by my side as my beloved wife."

"And I feel such joy and gratitude that you are my husband and that we are in this blessed place together," Jyoti responded and squeezed his hand affectionately.

Two months earlier, the raja had sent word to his cousin Professor Gupta that Swamiji had a brilliant young disciple named Devendra, with a great capacity for research, study, and teaching. Devendra, the letter reported, was about to marry one of Swamiji's lifelong disciples, Jyoti—a kind, intelligent woman with a special gift for teaching children. Moreover, Devendra's brother, Balram, also a disciple of Swamiji, was an excellent cook with a good understanding of Ayurveda. Both Devendra and Balram would be leaving the ashram right after the wedding, and Swamiji was inquiring whether the good professor had positions on his staff for these three fine young chelas.

The professor smiled when he finished reading the letter. How does he do it? he asked himself. How does Swamiji know that I'm going to need an assistant and a cook? *He began to chuckle and thought,* I should really spend more time with him . . . but then, the accommodations are rather lacking. Still, I should get over it and go anyway. On the other hand, maybe I can ask my cousin to arrange a visit from Swamiji. Naturally, he'll invite me as well, and we can talk long into the night, drink tea, eat sweets . . . I must write to him to see if he'll do it.

However, the good professor never acted upon these thoughts despite his good intentions. Years before, when he was only seventeen, the professor had spent two months with the master. He was initiated into meditation and spent each evening discussing the voluminous Mahabharata, of which the Bhagavad Gita was only a small part. The master was impressed by the young man's intelligence and enthusiasm for knowledge and encouraged him to continue his studies. He told him he had strong potential to become a learned and respected scholar and teacher.

The idea took hold in the young man's heart, but he was wary of his father's likely displeasure. "What about my father?" he finally asked the master one day. "He is determined that I study military tactics and diplomacy so I can serve my cousin, the future raja, just as he has served his brother."

The master simply answered, "Everyone has his own nature and cannot ignore it. Everyone also has his own destiny, which is difficult to avoid. Your father's wish contradicts your nature and destiny. Hold on to the desire to become a learned man and professor, and let Mother Nature arrange the details. Your meditation will support a smooth transition from where you are to where you'd like to be."

Within a year, his own tutors spoke to his father on his behalf. Though he was a career diplomat, his father finally let go of his desire for his son to follow family tradition and recognized his potential to excel in the academic world. In the end, his father sent him to Oxford to study and was extremely proud of him. He realized that many of India's brightest young men were going to England to study. He also began to understand that this generation studying abroad would someday play a role in winning independence from England and forging a new united India. Suddenly, the boat carrying his son couldn't get to Liverpool quickly enough.

Now, nearly forty years later, Dr. Gupta had become the highly respected professor that Swamiji had foreseen. His considerable responsibilities at Allahabad University made him thankful to have an assistant and cook coming his way. "God be praised," he said to himself, placing his hands gently together and bowing his head in gratitude.

Balram had come to Allahabad early and had already been in the professor's service for weeks when Devendra and Jyoti arrived at the scholar's home. The professor's house was spacious and in good order. The main part of the house consisted of a large foyer, a reception room, a dining room, a large kitchen, and a washroom. It also contained a sizeable and brightly lit library with the professor's main study and office. Leather-bound volumes filled wooden shelves that lined two walls. A shaded veranda with a patio off the kitchen opened onto a beautiful garden filled with thriving flower beds and small trees laden with fruit. Ten-foot walls, surfaced with rose-colored stucco, enclosed the garden area. It was an enchanted place for Devendra and Jyoti, and they immediately fell in love with their new world.

The second floor of the house held the professor's bedroom, a guest room, and a smaller study and sitting room. A covered balcony outside the professor's bedroom and study overlooked the gardens. Two wings extended from the main house. One contained quarters for the housekeeper and her husband, the gardener, and the cook. The other wing contained a suite of three rooms that became Devendra and Jyoti's new home. Several old banyan trees sheltered the main house and, to some extent, the two wings from the hot Indian sun.

Balram ran to the front of the house when he heard the cart pull up. He flung open the door and rushed out to greet his brother and new sister-in-law. Everyone embraced warmly, overjoyed by the reunion. The professor was coming down the stairs when Devendra, Jyoti, and Balram entered the house flushed with happiness and excitement. They saw a somewhat pudgy man of medium height, dressed in an English-style suit. His hair had thinned, and what remained was white. He wore thick gold-rimmed glasses over his deep brown eyes, and the wrinkles around his eyes told the story of many hours of reading and thinking.

The professor greeted them warmly, and then excusing himself, he stepped outside for a moment to tell the oxcart driver how to enter the garden and where to deposit the young couple's belongings. He spoke in an authoritarian way and paid the driver a few rupees. He reentered the front hall of the house and turned his full attention to his new assistant and wife. "Please, let's sit on the veranda. Your brother, our illustrious cook, can bring us some light refreshments, and we can talk."

Balram went straight to the kitchen, and the professor escorted the young couple onto the verandah to a small round table surrounded by four wicker chairs. He gestured, inviting them to sit down, and began politely, "I trust you had a pleasant journey."

"Yes, our first by train," Devendra replied.

"The British, for all their mischief and meddling, have brought India a few good things as well, the railway system being one of them. I am very interested in India becoming independent, but I also admit some fondness for the British. I spent four years in Oxford, where I learned to admire their better qualities. Here in India, unfortunately, I find those qualities lacking most of the time."

"What are their best qualities, sir?" Devendra asked, surprised by his host's frankness.

"They have evolved an excellent legal code and a system of governance that maintains, for the most part, a good degree of freedom, justice, and social order—at least for their own citizens," Professor Gupta clarified. Quite used to lecturing, he continued, "They are also adventurous, courageous, and highly inquisitive. Hence, they have produced a host of bold explorers of the globe, the sciences, and knowledge in general. They are also inventive. Their naval technology and expertise alone has made them rulers of the high seas and taken them from that tiny island to continents across the earth. They can also be compassionate, imaginative, and passionate, and their history is full of magnificent writers and poets. Unfortunately, they also suffer from strong strains of arrogance, greed, and a belief in racial superiority. Consequently, simply exploring other continents has never been enough. Wherever the British go, they feel the need to subdue the people, profit grotesquely from their labor and assets, and impose their language and culture. They are deeply convinced that British culture is one of the few civilized cultures on the planet and infinitely superior. They are blind to their pride and prejudices, which also allows them to rationalize greed. These are fatal flaws that will in time be their own undoing."

Devendra waited a few seconds to be sure that the professor had rested his case then commented, "We've had little personal experience with the British, sir, and it sounds as if we want to avoid them."

Professor Gupta looked squarely at Devendra and spoke with great seriousness, "It is best to stay out of their way when possible, especially the soldiers and the businessmen. Those people will show you little respect or courtesy."

"How do you live this way, sir, caught between two worlds?"

"That is a direct question, and I shall give you a direct answer. The British are cordial to me because of my position at the university and my family connections. They respect those values. I have no idea what they say when I'm not present, nor do I want to know. I'm also respectful of them. However, I am firmly resolved to educate and influence our students to become the masters of India so the British will leave. We have a long way to go, but it will happen. Perhaps none of us will see it this lifetime, but history is on our side."

"How so?" Devendra probed, exhilarated by this open and lively exchange.

"History has proven that all empires have limited life spans," the professor replied. "Now, enough of this serious talk. Tell me how the master is."

The travelers' fatigue seemed to fade away, and the group talked for several hours, delighting in stories from the village and the ashram, cherishing the master's wisdom and laughing over Aseem's antics. Quite spontaneously, they forged a strong bond based on their shared experience of living with Swamiji and the love they felt for him. All felt thankful that the Divine Mother had arranged for their paths to cross.

Balram was elated to hear his brother's voice and laughter. He felt a strong desire to move out of his wing and in with Devendra and Jyoti. He missed his brother's company but had to resign himself to the fact that his brother was now married. Life had changed in this and so many other ways. Balram, listening to the conversation from the kitchen patio, also had to accept that as the cook, he was a servant, not a houseguest. He remembered Aseem's telling him that his path was through service and his situation here was a blessing, and he was comforted.

Devendra began accompanying the professor to the university daily. It was a short twenty-minute walk. Founded by an Englishman Sir William Muir, the school was originally called Muir Central College, but within four years, it became the University of Allahabad. The architecture, also a British creation, was a unique combination of Indian, Mughal, and Gothic. Devendra never failed to marvel at the campus's onion-shaped domes and towering minarets as they approached the university. He carried the professor's ponderous bag of books and discussed philosophy with him at every opportunity. At least twice a week,

Dr. Gupta invited him to sit in on his lectures. He taught in a dignified hall that held over a hundred students and was usually filled. The room seemed vast to Devendra, who occasionally envied the students with enough time and money to devote themselves to learning for several years. However, Devendra was most often grateful and inspired, moved by both the stately surroundings and the refined and lively atmosphere of an institution dedicated wholly to knowledge.

Devendra was also awed by his employer's command of language and erudition. Dr. Gupta could lecture with equal eloquence on Western and Eastern philosophy. However, after living so many years with the master, Devendra recognized that the lofty thoughts that the professor shared with his students were simply ideas for him, profound as they were, and not a product of his inner experience. Though this was a distinction that most students did not appreciate, it deeply affected Devendra. Professor Gupta was undeniably a great scholar and teacher, but the knowledge he shared with his students so brilliantly and eloquently remained in the realm of the intellect for him; he did not live it.

Devendra, having recognized this gap, wondered how it could be bridged. The academic world was highly structured, disciplined, and strongly invested in rational thought. Faith and spiritual matters were intriguing objects of study, and nothing more vital than that. Britain's secular approach to education had gained a strong influence in India, especially among those who wanted to make India an independent nation that could take its rightful place in the modern world. During his years at Oxford, Professor Gupta had become confident that the Western style of education, with its focus on reason, inquiry, and scientific investigation, was indeed what his fellow Indians needed to catch up with the European countries' western world. As soon as this generation of aspiring young people were properly educated, they could they take over the reins of government and get rid of the British.

Jyoti, with Professor Gupta's help, was hired to teach at a school for Indian children, whose fathers worked as middle managers for the British. Their regular income made it possible for these families to educate their children. A female instructor was highly unusual, but Jyoti was a skilled and experienced teacher. The children adored her, and the parents therefore accepted her. The mothers of those children were especially supportive and saw their own daughters' future in her eyes.

When Jyoti's mother, Poona, arrived, Professor Gupta received her graciously and ordered Balram to prepare a feast in her honor. The professor had never married. He loved his books and protected his time at home for research and study. However, much to his surprise, he felt an immediate attraction for Poona.

216

She was aware of this but knew her place and was careful not to jeopardize her daughter and son-in-law's position. Nevertheless, Poona and the professor quickly learned to admire and respect each other and enjoy each other's company. Within a month, Poona was in charge of the house, and she relished the opportunity to create a new level of orderliness.

Once in a while, the professor would ask Devendra, "Are you sure your mother-in-law is not British? Maybe in a past life then?" Both men would laugh. "See the way she orders everyone around? Including me at times! One has to admire her passion," he would say with a smile.

At first, all were content with their roles and the comfortable life they found in their new home. However, after about six months, Devendra began to recognize that he would never get the chance to teach since he lacked a formal education and academic credentials. At first, this was merely an observation, but it gradually developed into a major source of frustration. The professor was aware of Devendra's disappointment and knew it was almost inevitable in such an intelligent young man. He tried to alleviate some of Devendra's unrest by having him lead small discussion groups. Devendra proved good at it, and the students enjoyed their interactions with him. However, his desire for more authority and opportunities to teach did not diminish.

Meanwhile, Jyoti took to drawing. She kept paper with her and drew whenever time allowed. She started to create informal portraits of her students. One afternoon, one of the parents glimpsed one of Jyoti's sketches of her son, Ravi. Impressed, she inquired, "Do you paint?"

"Oh no, I just do quick drawings when I have the chance," Jyoti remarked, slightly embarrassed.

"I see. Well, you have a talent for it, that's for sure."

The next day, the woman returned with her son, carrying a canvas bag. Smiling, she handed the bag to Jyoti and offered, "A small present for you, to encourage your talent."

Jyoti, totally surprised, took the bag and opened it. It held brushes and a few metal trays with lids that contained, as her new patron explained, "Water colors. You can create beautiful paintings with these. They are easy to use and easier still to clean up."

"What a wonderful gift! How can I ever thank you?" Jyoti exclaimed.

"Someday, when you've had some time to practice, you could do a small portrait of my son," the mother suggested.

"I'd love to. Thank you again! I can hardly wait to try these paints. It was tremendously kind of you to think of me."

The mother spoke sincerely, looking deeply into Jyoti's eyes, "Well, as I said yesterday, it's obvious you have talent. I hope this puts you on a track to develop that talent to the full and share your special gift. Perhaps you will even gain some renown."

"My husband will most likely faint straightaway if I tell him that." Jyoti laughed.

"Then all the more reason to do it!" And the mother joined in her laughter.

The rest of the children arrived, and Jyoti bid good-bye to her new benefactor.

Like his brother, Balram also felt some restlessness and frustration with the limitations of his position. However, he had a different focus. He was strongly curious about and attracted to women. Devendra's obvious happiness with Jyoti definitely amplified Balram's interest.

Without knowing it, Balram's employer began providing him with a path of exploration. Now and then, the professor shared Balram's culinary skills with a colleague or friend who was entertaining for a special occasion. He would simply tell Balram that he would be spending a day or two at so-and-so's house to prepare a special dinner. Balram enjoyed the change in routine, and it gave him a sense of freedom. He soon learned that as curious as he might be about women, women felt even more so about him. He was handsome, well built, employed, lighthearted, and available. Busy as food preparation kept him, he found time to flirt with the female staff, something he found utterly natural. Eventually, a pretty housemaid pulled him into her quarters to make love. The experience was as fulfilling as he had imagined it would be. A new and unexpected door had opened for Balram, and he was highly inspired to keep it open. Very carefully and discreetly, he found more willing partners until his reputation as a lover as well as a cook became an unspoken but well-known secret among household help in the city.

Before Devendra, Jyoti, and Balram knew it, they had lived in Allahabad for two years. Each had adapted to circumstances that were, in almost every way, far from the simplicity of ashram and village life with the master. Each had accepted the limitations and embraced the possibilities of their circumstances. They had set unhesitatingly upon the paths of discovery that had opened before them though they held few road signs. None knew where life was headed, but few people really do.

Chapter 29:
The Gathering

A S SAM WALKED UP MAIN Street toward the White Oak Café, he could see that it was busier than usual. Once inside, he found himself in the midst of a lot of hustle and bustle. Kenny was distracted with all the customers and didn't notice his arrival. Sam ambled into the side room and saw Julian, Katy, and ten other students seated there. The tables were pushed together, and Julian motioned Sam to a chair. A mug of coffee and a muffin awaited him.

Sam greeted the group while looking at Julian, "Hi, everyone. Good to see you all."

Julian meekly acknowledged, "Hi, Sam. A few friends were interested in coming." Then he announced to the group at the table, "Hey, everyone. This is Dr. Sam O'Connor."

A flurry of hellos followed, and then everyone grew quiet. An uncomfortable silence filled the room. Sam easily broke it, suggesting, "Maybe we should introduce ourselves first—do the easy part before we get into an intellectual discussion. Let's have everyone give a first name and major. After that, I'll tell you a little about myself. Okay? Since Julian is the main culprit here, we'll start with him," Sam said, grinning at his young protégé.

The students introduced themselves, and Sam counted three education majors, two history majors, three philosophy majors, one psychology major, two literature majors, and finally, an accounting/business major. Sam raised his eyebrows. "Ah, Joe from accounting?" At which point everyone laughed. "I can plainly see the humanities being represented here, but I didn't expect the business department to be represented as well. Caught in my own bias already!" Sam laughed. "I'm very pleased you are here. The business community can always use some enlightened souls." Sam nodded appreciatively to Joe. "And naturally, the world is always in need of enlightened and educated people."

"Now, what can I tell you about myself that would be useful?" Sam pondered. "Well, as you may know, I was an assistant professor of philosophy at Amherst College when most of you were in elementary school. I live with my lovely wife and two wonderful sons in North Amherst. While I was in my PhD program, I was invited to join a meditation and philosophy course in Switzerland conducted by a contemporary master from India, Maharishi Mahesh Yogi. I was already practicing Transcendental Meditation, the technique that Maharishi taught, so it seemed natural to accept the invitation. It's not every day a yogi of some stature invites you to the Alps. Besides, I had just met my future wife a few weeks before, and she was attending the course, so once invited, it was an easy decision to go," Sam laughed affectionately, and everyone joined him.

He looked around at the group and observed, "I sense a few questions forming."

"Dr. O'Connor," a student named Mike began, "I understand from talking with Julian that you offered a course on consciousness at Amherst. He told me that the students learned TM and you looked at major thinkers in Eastern and Western philosophy in terms of consciousness. First of all, let me say, that was really cool. Would you tell us a little about that and why it drew so many students?"

"I spent three months with Maharishi, and believe me, that will change your point of view for a couple of lifetimes. Just before the course ended, he asked me to think about what I had learned and what I had experienced in meditation and to apply that to the study of philosophy. Maharishi felt that philosophy had lost some of its appeal because the source of thought— which he sometimes called pure consciousness—had disappeared from philosophical thought and experience. As a group, as a civilization, we had simply forgotten the basis of our own lives, pure awareness, and the knowledge of how to access it.

"This leads us back to the age-old questions that each generation asks itself, or should ask: Who am I? Who are you? What is all of this? Where did I come from and where am I going? The great majority of people just accept whatever their parents or culture or religion tell them. For them, it's simple. For the rest of us, these questions burn like hot coals in our minds, and we go off on a quest to find the truth. It is a noble adventure and a calling. First I joined the tradition of Western academic philosophers, a fine group of individuals, with great hearts and minds. Unfortunately, I didn't realize I had joined a club until I was out of it. Structuring the course on consciousness got me out of the club. I was attempting to do something innovative. Something that would have an impact on my students."

"What do you mean by club?" queried Sally, the psychology major.

"Successful researchers and academics know it's important to be on the cutting edge of their disciplines, whether it's science, music, art, business, or philosophy. In the case of physics, that edge is easier to define. These days you're either working on quantum physics or you're not. If you're a physics professor, you're either keeping up with the latest breakthroughs and theories or figuring out how to communicate them to your students or you're not. Once you're not, once you're comfortably teaching from the textbook, in my opinion, you've joined the club. Imagine the stuffiest British old boys' club you can: the overstuffed leather chairs, the heavy curtains on the windows, members sitting around swishing cognac and congratulating themselves on their imagined past victories.

"I don't mean to sound harsh, but life is always in the direction of growth, of more and more. Life is vibrant and full of unlimited possibilities. When you shut that out, life stagnates."

"But, Dr. O'Connor, you're describing the classic struggle between tradition and innovation. Not all tradition is something we should jettison, and not all innovation is successful," Mike argued.

"True, very true. New understandings and insights always build on or benefit from existing knowledge or traditional sources. A bedrock of cumulative knowledge underlies the appearance of all new ideas and innovation. So there's no argument there. Still the idea persists that if you're not living on the edge, you're taking up too much room."

Sam took back the direction of the meeting, wanting to share some basic information before more questions arose. "So, as I was saying, Maharishi challenged me to find the transcendent in Western philosophy. He assured me it was there, but without the experience of pure consciousness, the source of thought, it was almost impossible to identify, let alone understand. I began thinking about it and started finding the transcendental value almost everywhere I looked. It was exciting, very exciting. I realized that to make the course truly effective—which to me meant that it would produce real transformation in the students—the students would have to practice TM. This was the only surefire way I knew to give every student the direct experience of his or her infinite nature. Only this direct experience of the transcendent, the infinite foundation of life in each of us, would allow them to recognize the transcendent in the philosophers and writers we would study. Without that experience, it would all just be words on a page. I therefore made learning and practicing TM mandatory, and we set off to explore. The students began opening to subtler, more expansive levels of thought and to pure consciousness itself, their own unbounded being. It was a great process of self-discovery and very exciting for all of us."

Joe, the business major, stirred in his seat, "How does one quantify the success of the consciousness course?"

"Ah, Joe, spoken like a true bean counter," Sam said approvingly, to the delight of his audience.

"But seriously, if you mean, 'Has anyone from that group won a Nobel Prize?' Not yet. I can't account for all the students, but I do know a few went on to complete PhD programs, five students went on and became teachers of Transcendental Meditation, two became published authors, one is a distinguished painter, and two others founded successful software companies. However, that doesn't really get at the heart of your question, does it? That type of answer is very unsatisfying to the human spirit. Many Amherst College students go on to successful careers that never considered for a moment that meditation was important for their success. So how do we look at this question?"

Sally, the psych major, offered, "Since we're talking about inner development, if your students were happier with their lives and making a contribution to society, no matter how big or small, they would be successful, and meditation could be considered an underlying cause."

"Well, that's a good direction to pursue. What kind of study could you create to test the hypothesis that TM meditators live happier, more fulfilled and productive lives?"

Sally ventured, "A study could be done with a hundred of your meditating students from eight or nine years ago and a hundred non-meditating Amherst College students from the same period. A questionnaire could be put together that would attempt to quantify how satisfied the subjects were with their lives."

Sam added, "You could try to measure not only their inner life but also look at relationships, health, job satisfaction, contributions to the world at large, even happiness . . . could be interesting. Why don't you do it as an honors thesis?"

"Well, I just might. It's starting to sound intriguing," Sally responded thoughtfully.

"Great. Let me know if I can help.

"So Maharishi's technique of Transcendental Meditation allows the mind to turn within and effortlessly experience its source, the source of thought, our infinite potential. That process turns out to be equally natural and automatic. Someone just has to point the way. Devoting twenty minutes twice a day to experiencing the transcendent enlivens that unlimited potential and makes it available to us in everyday life, which in turn enhances absolutely everything we do."

The group was silent as they contemplated Sam's words.

"Any questions?"

"How do we start?" asked one student.

"You are a practical group. A course can always be arranged. My wife Amy and I are qualified teachers and can set up a course for those who are interested."

"Sam, why don't you address the college and bring the community up-to-date on your experience and thinking? I'm sure lots of students and profs would welcome the opportunity to hear you speak," Julian proposed. The other students nodded agreement.

"Sounds like a plot is being hatched," Sam laughed.

He caught sight of Kenny, standing close-by, busing a table and smiling with satisfaction. Sam could almost hear him saying knowingly, "It's starting up again, buddy boy."

"Well, I would have to be invited, and then I would have to accept the invitation."

"If we get you invited, would you accept?" Julian bargained.

"Possibly. It would be tempting."

Katy suggested, "We could start a petition and get hundreds of signatures and present it to the dean."

"Yeah," the others agreed, "that would do it."

Sam began to feel uneasy and grew quiet.

"I need to think about this. I'm not so sure the college would like me back on campus," Sam suggested.

"Of course they would!" several students said at once.

"Of course they would," Kenny echoed, smiling at Sam.

The students began talking among themselves, and Sam was left alone with his thoughts. As he sat among the animated group, he saw that he could once again be thrust into the world. He realized he was losing control, and he began to feel panicky like someone caught in a riptide current. He closed his eyes, slipped into the silence of his awareness, and began to watch the struggle taking place in his mind.

Kenny approached him, put a hand on his shoulder, and quietly whispered, "Nothing to worry about, brother."

Sam opened his eyes, turned around, and looked into Kenny's eyes. In his friend's happy, reassuring face, for just a moment he thought he recognized God. And still he whispered, "Easy for you to say."

Kenny laughed. "Remember, Sam, this is your dream." And he began to clear the tables.

The students started standing up, grabbing their backpacks, and saying good-bye to him. Sam nodded to each one. Julian and Katy were excited but did their best to tone it down in front of him. "Hey, Sam, if you want us to stop this, we will."

Sam looked at both of them and said, "No, it's all right. Let it play."

"You sure? You don't look too enthused," Julian observed.

"Well, honestly, I'm a bit shocked. I feel like a man enjoying a lovely, solitary walk in the woods, just enjoying the light, the colors, and the sounds, who suddenly finds himself in a busy, noisy village. I think I must have missed a turn."

"Sam," Katy spoke gently, "you have so much to give the world, and the world needs your inspiration."

"I don't know about that, Katy. There are plenty of people in the world more inspiring than me. Besides, the world forgot me, and it's been getting along quite nicely without me. I've been happy with my simple life. I guess I'm not sure where all of this is going, but let's not be too concerned about it," Sam added with a smile.

He thought to himself, *I feel like I'm being swept out into the ocean, far beyond the safety of the shore, but it is an infinite ocean, and after all, I'm rather fond of the infinite.*

"Okay. Good to see you both. Let me know how things go."

Katy said good-bye and walked over to speak with one of her friends.

"Julian, feel like taking a walk tomorrow?" Sam invited.

"Yeah, sure. I can meet you at two," Julian answered happily.

"Great, I'll see you at Amethyst Brook. I think it's going to be a nice day."

"Sounds good," Julian replied. "I hope today wasn't too much, Sam."

"No, it's fine. See you tomorrow."

Julian turned to look for Katy and strode off in her direction.

"Well," Sam said out loud to no one in particular, "I must go home and tell the missus of the house about my day."

When Sam arrived home, Amy was in the kitchen preparing dinner before the evening meditation. The boys were off on an adventure in the woods behind the house.

"There's my love, barefoot, pregnant, and in the kitchen. A wonderful Irish wife if there ever was one," poked Sam, wanting to see if Amy would take the bait.

Amy, having been through this routine more than once, saw the sparkle in her husband's eyes. She leaned provocatively against the sink. "Well, Sam O'Connor, I am barefoot in the kitchen, but you would have to be a lot more vigorous in your lovemaking if you want me pregnant."

"Madame, I can show you my vigor. Let's see, it's Friday. If I rest up a couple of days, I could be very vigorous by Monday night."

Amy now crossed her arms and tapped her foot as she teased, "Well, sir, I think you should be plenty rested as it is. How is it that your grandfather sired nine healthy children by thirty-three and you only have two in your forty-first year?"

"Well, you never saw my grandmother for one thing." Amy threw a damp tea towel at Sam, who ducked just in time. "And I think it might have been the whiskey."

"And," Amy continued, "there was no electricity and no movie videos to watch. I'm in bed alone often enough while you're watching *Indiana Jones* or *James Bond* for the umpteenth time."

"Quite right. My grandfather may have had fewer children if moving pictures with sound were available in County Claire. Without that, well, there wasn't much else to do, was there?" Sam moved in for a loving kiss and embrace.

When they separated, he asked, "How was your day?"

"Great, got some things done and worked on a painting. And yours?"

"Well, interesting. I went to the White Oak to meet with Julian, and to my astonishment, Katy and ten other students were there."

"Oh, that must've been a surprise. What happened?"

"After introductions, I gave a short talk on meditation and enlightenment, and it looks like they all want to start."

"That's great, Sam! You're teaching again."

"Yes, but it gets better, or worse, depending on your point of view. The students want me to come back to the college and give a talk to the community. They're going to start a petition." Sam watched Amy's face carefully to glean her response.

"Really? I'm thrilled!" she responded with total delight then probed gently, "But how do you feel about it?"

"I got nervous, even fearful. Of course, Kenny didn't make me feel any better when he said in his mysterious way, 'It's starting up again, buddy boy.'"

"Kenny said that?" Her eyes widened.

"Yeah, but the students were so excited I agreed to let them do their thing."

"Do you think the college will invite you?"

"Yes, I expect they will."

"What about your safety?" Amy's eyebrows knit with concern.

"I'm sure the college security team will have a plan."

"You did have a big day, didn't you?"

"Yes, I did. Yes, I did."

Chapter 30:
A Walk in the Woods

JULIAN SAT IN KATY'S PICKUP in the small parking lot at the entrance to Amethyst Brook, waiting for Sam. Considerable excitement had spread among the friends he had brought to the café. *It's funny that Sam has a certain effect on people,* he thought, reflecting on yesterday's event at the café.

Just then, Sam drove up and pulled in beside the truck. Closing the car door, he announced, "Great day for a walk, Julian. Good to see you."

"Likewise, Sam. I love these Indian summer days."

"Yes, they seem like a final gift before the cold and winter sets in. By the way, that was quite a gathering of friends you organized."

"Well, Sam, one thing led to another."

"Don't have to explain, Jules. I enjoyed it."

They started walking down the path.

Sam began, "We were in the midst of looking at suffering as I recall. The idea of life and death, health and sickness has troubled humanity forever. Sometimes these subjects are too big for a café. Grappling with these ideas becomes easier outdoors. Whitman loved being in the open air. The natural world softens our ideas and brings us more into the moment. I realized early one morning as the sun was just rising and all was quiet that the peace of the Lord is always present. When the noise of the world settles down, like the chatter in the mind, that peace is more accessible. Bliss is there, but activity covers it up. The suffering, the longing for love and fulfillment, cover it up."

"Is suffering a part of the plan?" Julian asked.

"Maybe. It's a good question. Let's look at this from another angle. Maharishi, true to the Vedic tradition, asks how a fish in the ocean can be thirsty. From the standpoint of unity consciousness, all is experienced as Self, infinite and eternal. Everyone and everything are the totality of Bliss, infinite awareness, and an expression or impulse of it, like a wave in that ocean of Bliss. Yet people suffer. Why?"

Julian thought for a moment. "Because people are unaware of the Bliss?"

"Good answer," Sam nodded. "From the waking state of consciousness, where almost everyone lives, we see the universe as infinitely diverse and dynamic. So we all have this agreement that we perceive and experience everything as separate and outside of ourselves, resulting in a perpetual state of duality. Once this duality is born then fear of the unknown, fear of the 'other,' arises, and in that sense, all the limitations and problems of the world arise.

"From the standpoint of duality, not knowing the other or what all this is," Sam said as he waved his arm in a sweeping gesture, "appears to be the source of suffering. Remember, Julian, the rishis were coming from the perspective of unity, where duality ceases to exist. The enlightened one is at home everywhere, deep in bliss with the knowingness that surpasses all understanding. So for them all is bliss, one without a second.

"Remember too that the world is as we are. Our perception of the world reflects who we are. Our beliefs, our stories, our expectations color our perception of the world. It's like having green glasses on. The whole world appears green. But then some kind saintly person gives us golden glasses to wear, and everything takes on a golden glow. The growth of awareness changes one's perception of the world.

"The rishis who lived in unity consciousness ceased to perceive duality. They perceived only Being and saw that everything was exactly as it should be. Hence, they did not suffer. However, for the man or woman in the waking state, with only limited awareness, duality dominates, not unity."

"Why isn't everyone born into unity instead of duality?"

"Another astute question. From the perspective of unity consciousness, everyone is that infinite consciousness. It's as if everyone already is enlightened, only they just don't know it yet. Yet the enlightened person certainly recognizes that most people have not awakened to the truth of who they are. Most people continue to engage in a world that is a dream, made of their own thoughts and emotions. It can be a good dream or bad dream, but it's still a dream.

"Why is everyone dreaming instead of waking up to the reality?" Sam continued as they walked down the path. "Most people are strongly attached to their dream, their version of reality, which makes it harder to remember their infinite essence. People want to dream, to create their life, to feel in control of their life. For all its drama, heartbreak, happiness, ups and downs, adventures, stories, romance, the world is a fascinating place. Our minds are always searching for happiness, for fulfillment, and so many elements of our stories appear to hold out the possibility of greater happiness. And so we go. This continues even for meditators and people seeking a more spiritual life. No one living life is immune from happiness. Maharishi stated it plainly in the *Science of Being*: 'The purpose of life is the expansion of happiness.'

"We call the energy that draws us to happiness *desire*. In the East, desire has gotten a pretty bad rap, because it appears to draw us away from wholeness, where lasting fulfillment lies, and into the entanglements of the world, where we can only find temporary happiness. However, on the other side of the coin, desire is not a bad thing. It keeps everything going, and most importantly, desire keeps us involved in that search for happiness that ultimately leads us to liberation from the dream. That continuum of desire for fulfillment eventually becomes the desire, conscious or unconscious, for enlightenment. All of us are compelled to figure out who we are and what this universe is, but with that, the journey home really picks up momentum."

Sam stopped walking, paused, and looked into Julian's eyes to gauge how he was responding before he continued. "All right so far?"

"Yeah. Sure."

"Okay, so we are born into a world afloat in other people's dreams—society's belief systems and judgments, our parents' and friends' and teachers' values and definitions of life—and we add more based on our own experiences. Desire governs our lives, and we seek knowledge, love, security, and happiness where we have come to believe we can find them. Teaming with ideas, our own and those of others, our intellects make a critical mistake over and over. Our intellects tell us that all this is real and therefore a real source of fulfillment. If we are fortunate, we do indeed find happiness, but most of the time, it doesn't last or feel like enough. We are aware of lingering empty spaces inside, and we go on trying to fill them with the stuff of life: adventures, relationships, new jobs, hobbies, ownership of this and that. The list is as endless as life itself. But life keeps changing, and as we say, 'The Lord giveth and the Lord taketh away.' Nothing is permanent, and that's our conundrum. Happiness here is fleeting, and we suffer because of our feelings of loss, our cycles of expectations and disappointments. We cling to those things that bring us the greatest happiness we think we can find, and we become afraid of change.

We keep grasping at the fleeting edge of all we desire because we do not own the permanent source of fulfillment inside."

"My dad loves his life. He loves his job, loves my mother, loves his friends," protested Julian.

"Yes, of course, many of us have that fortunate experience. Your father is living the good dream. However, even the good dream can come to an end: his firm is sold, his job becomes insecure, your mother grows ill, and friends and family move or pass away. My father, of course, is in the same spot, as is everyone."

Julian found himself growing unsettled thinking about his father facing those events. "That's a very negative way to go about looking at life, Sam. It takes away all the meaning and dignity from a person's life."

"Yes, I agree. No one wants to contemplate such things, let alone live through them. However, if we are honest here, much that one gains in life is often taken away or fades away. Still, men and women aspire to live life in fullness. For varying amounts of time, almost everyone succeeds. We are definitely here to know happiness, not just its loss. And a surprising number of people spontaneously open to the transcendent at least once or several times in their lives. It is after all where the mind, everyone's mind, wants to go. Even a brief glimpse of that infinite peace and fulfillment brings them a profound emotional satisfaction and sometimes initiates significant changes in their lives, though they can't explain it."

"But they can't hold on to it," Julian volunteered.

"On some level, they do hold on to it or integrate it, Julian, but it functions underground, so to speak. Everyday life is so busy. The mind is too dull or active, too hungover, or too pressured to maintain the transcendent continuously. But the memory of that experience is present in the mind and nervous system, and it can be enlivened spontaneously when the need is there. These experiences are forgotten on the surface yet not forgotten in our depths. This is the value of meditation. Regular experience of the transcendent cultivates both the mind and nervous system with the ability to live from that level all the time."

"What happens to those who don't find a teacher?" Julian pressed.

"The desire for enlightenment creates the opportunities for enlightenment. In time, everyone meets one or several teachers, depending on their desire to do so. Maharishi used to say that the river lays a pipeline to connect to the ocean. The enlightened overflow with compassion for those caught up in the delusion of duality and the suffering it brings. They want all to join them in the celebration of the infinite. History has recorded the words and deeds of some of these great souls from the past, and certainly, great teachers are with us today as well."

"So suffering plays a role in one's enlightenment?"

"Only in the sense that it creates the desire to be done with suffering and find lasting fulfillment. Of course, this is the viewpoint of the waking state where suffering definitely feels real. In the larger context of unity, no one suffers. When we finally live in that blessed state, even our personal history, no matter how traumatic it may have seemed at the time, carries no 'charge,' as psychology describes it. That so-called personal history, which we identified with, feels no more real than a movie we once saw or a book we once read."

"So is the universe for us or against us?"

"My personal sense is the universe or Life is for us, because we're a part of everything. But in another sense, the universe simply is, just as Being simply is. However, opportunities to awaken are everywhere, because the infinite is fully present everywhere."

"Let's say, for the sake of argument, you're right," Julian proposed. "The Self is beyond the pain of suffering, but I still don't fully grasp how suffering got such a grip on human life if it's a function of illusion."

"I promised you I would talk about my being shot, and here is a perfect segue that may help answer your question. When I was shot, I spun into a world of pain and suffering. Yet, even in all of that, as a conscious being, I was also able to transcend the pain and suffering and find my Self."

"How did you do that?"

"First, I was unconscious from the sheer shock of the shooting and loss of blood. Later, the doctors gave me morphine as a painkiller. Various other painkillers followed. Finally, I asked to stop them, not because I was out of pain, but because I was able to meditate. I simply transcended the mind and body and thus the pain. While I was meditating, I felt no pain. The suffering came later."

"What do you mean?"

"In time, my body healed, but my mind slipped into anxiety around what had happened. What if the gunman had succeeded in getting a third shot off? What if he had wounded or killed Amy? Why had this even happened? After all, I was a good person, doing something that was noble in some regards. And for that I get shot? I was unable to answer those questions, and I was also, for a time, unable to let them go. So I suffered."

"How long did you suffer for?"

"Off and on, for several years, the first year being the most intense. I felt raw fear for my wife, my children, and at times, for myself. There was always the possibility that someone would try again. I had to really grapple with that. I didn't have control, not that any of us do, but I was exposed to that truth in an undeniably brutal way."

"How did you reconcile that?"

"I'm glad you think I did. At some point I had to let go and realize that I was alive and my wife and family were fine. I also reexamined everything I thought I knew and began to discard all of it. I was in a crisis for sure at that point. Then I realized that through it all, the sun rose every morning and life was happening everywhere I looked. I took to the woods with *Leaves of Grass*, and I began to heal. I gradually forgot about the shooting. It began to seem like something that happened ages ago. I kept meditating, loved my wife and boys, did some gardening, and now I've met you."

"I feel like I should tell you that I spoke with Dr. Harris a few weeks back," Julian admitted forthrightly.

"Really? How is Bob?" Sam asked, curious.

"Well, he was not too happy to hear that you taught me to meditate," Julian answered frankly.

"I see."

Sam reflected for a moment and assured Julian, "Don't you worry about this, Julian. I'll talk with Bob. He's been laboring under some false concepts for a long time. I'll have a word with him."

"Katy thinks he's jealous of you and feels threatened in some way."

"I've been down this road before."

"What do you mean? Oh, wait a minute. Are you referring to Albert? You don't think Dr. Harris is like Albert?"

"No, Bob Harris is not like Albert. Albert was so far out of balance he became clinically disturbed, mentally ill. That's not Bob's situation. He is a good man. I'm sure I can talk with him."

"By the way, whatever happened to Albert?"

Sam spied the large trunk of a fallen tree and motioned for Julian to sit down. The bubbling brook flowed along in front of them.

"He's in a psychiatric institute serving time. Most likely, he'll get out at some point, but it will be some years from now. It took me over a year to visit him."

"Really," Julian exclaimed, "you visited Albert!"

"Yeah, how else was I going to forgive him?"

"You forgave him for almost killing you and Amy?"

"Yeah, you see, forgiving him liberated me, and I began to let go. The burden of being angry and outraged proved to be too heavy after a while. I was stuck, completely stuck. It's funny. Here I am a Catholic, and I have a PhD in philosophy. You'd think I would have known better, but I struggled with it."

"Sam, you're human, aren't you?" Julian responded with a slight smile.

"Yep, completely human, flesh and blood. But it took my old friend Father Mike Connelly to drive up from the city to visit me one day. I went to parochial school from kindergarten through twelfth grade. In fifth grade, Father Mike showed up straight from Ireland. He was maybe thirty-five at the time. He taught elementary school and later English and Latin. He even coached basketball. He also said Mass and heard confessions. Kenny and I were schoolmates, and as we moved up in grades, so did Father Mike. We had him for every grade until we were seniors. It was extraordinary. Naturally, he knew us inside and out, and my parents loved him, just adored him. They're still good friends to this day.

"So it was over a year since the shooting, and I was stuck in this funk," Sam continued. "One morning around ten o'clock, the phone rang. It was Father Mike saying, 'Sammy, me boy, I've just entered Hartford at a station filling up the petrol tank, and God willing, I shall arrive at your sweet farmhouse by noon. Put the kettle on for me, for I'm in need of a cuppa.'

"I replied, 'That's great, Father Mike, but as my dear sister, Susan, would say, 'What's the occasion?'

"Father Mike explained, 'I've been listening to Jimmy and Lilly describe your condition, and they can't agree if you're okay or not. Let's just say I'm coming to form my own opinion. And besides, it will be good to have a chat over a nice cuppa and see those beautiful angels of yours with me own eyes.'

"So I said, 'Okay, great. The boys will be home by half past two, so it will give us some time to catch up.'

"'Splendid,' he said, and then he added, 'I've met some pissed-off drivers coming through Connecticut. They'd as soon steal the sugar out of your tea as look at you.'

"'How fast are you driving?'

"'A good and constant fifty miles per hour.'

"'What lane are you traveling in?'

"'You know, I'm a middle of the roader.'

"'Now, Father, you need to stay to the right. Maybe then the other drivers won't seem as tight as a camel's arse in a sandstorm.'

"'Aye, Sammy, good advice, and it's a comfort to my heart that you haven't forgotten the good old expressions I taught you as a lad.'

"'Drive safely, Father. See you at noon.'

"Anyway, Father Mike arrived almost on the strike of twelve o'clock. I began, 'Father, did you move over to the right-hand lane?'

"'Only momentarily. I came up on some wide-arse big trucks and back to the middle I went. It was smooth sailing once I got through Springfield. People who live in the country are blessed. They're simpler folk, and their emotions run more even.'

"With that, we sat down, had our tea, and caught up on the news from the city. Then Father turned to me and said, 'So, Sam, tell me. How are you, really?'

"'Well, even though it's been over a year since that fateful day, all things considered, good.'

"'No, Sam. I want to know how you're doing.'

"He was giving me his unblinking full attention. His bright blue eyes were boring into mine—not in a threatening way, mind you, but in a compassionate, caring way. He's been doing that look for years. When I was ten, I would literally squirm in my seat. I remember sitting back in my chair, knowing it was useless to resist. I finally said, 'I'm not sure, Father. Some days I'm fine, others I'm bitter and angry.'

"'So,' Father Mike said, 'You're seesawing back and forth, huh? Is it like you're sailing your ship and you lost your course? Lost your bearing? Lost your compass?'

"'I guess some days you could say that.'

"Father Mike was quiet for a moment. 'Sam, what happened to you shouldn't happen to anyone on God's green earth. Yet it happens every day, even here in America. Violence of unspeakable horror is committed. It's bad enough to read it in the paper, but when that violence strikes you or someone you love, there are no words to express the anguish that one feels. One only wants to strike back, to hurt the person who perpetuated the violence that so deeply affected you. Naturally, we say it's only human to feel that.'

"Father Mike paused, took a breath, and exhaled. 'Sam, what did our Lord do when he was faced with this situation? He was arrested, stripped, lashed, tried, humiliated, made to carry the cross on which he was to be crucified. What was his crime? Preaching love and tolerance? Healing the sick? Raising the dead?

"'He was innocent, but this drama gave him the chance to teach all of us one more lesson. He had to demonstrate that lesson. It was, in a sense, a test for him, and in that, it became his greatest gift to all of us. In a word, he gave us the gift of forgiveness. Nailed to the cross, our sweet Jesus said, "Father, Father, forgive them for they know not what they do." What a stunner for the crowd gathered at the foot of the cross! Can you imagine it? Those eleven words. How precious a gift! I've repeated those words a thousand times or more.

"'Now, Sam, can you imagine if Jesus up on the cross started to curse the crowd, damn them all to hell? Who could have blamed him really? He was innocent. He didn't deserve to die such a painful, public, and humiliating death. It would have been completely human of him to curse out the lot, that crowd of savages. Only he didn't. If he had, his life and teachings might have been forgotten, or at best been a footnote in history. Instead, at that moment of pain, he looked at the people around him and offered forgiveness, asked his Father to forgive. That was, to borrow your oft-used term, a transcendental moment. It doesn't matter who hears that story. Everyone is moved. So the question for you now, Sam, is, have you forgiven Albert for shooting you, for trying to end your life and possibly your wife's life as well?'

"The question hung there for many seconds. I realized that I hadn't forgiven. Hell, I was still outraged that I had been shot by an old friend, for doing nothing more than writing a book and living my life. Had I robbed him, beaten him up, humiliated him, shagged his wife? Well then, I could see at least some reason why he shot me at close range. However, I hadn't done anything that I could think of. Was it past life karma catching up? Maybe, but that possibility didn't make me feel any better. So I had to answer Father Mike, 'No. I haven't forgiven him.'

"Father Mike simply replied, 'That's the crux of the matter. Until you forgive him, your wounds, those deep emotional wounds, won't heal. Sam, you'll forever be lost on the sea of life without a true bearing on how to get to the simple peace of God's grace.'

"I was stunned, Julian. I didn't know where to start. I knew he was right, but I didn't know how to do it. Father Mike, sensing my confusion, simply said, 'I'd love to see your garden and take a walk in the woods. I've forgotten just how beautiful this part of New England is.'

"He stayed the night with us and left for the city the next day. Nothing more was said about the shooting or my state of mind. That night I relayed to Amy all Father Mike had said. She listened quietly and affirmed, 'He's right.'

"I thought about it the whole next day," Sam paused and reflected.

Julian asked, "So what happened?"

"I forgave him."

"That's it? I thought you said you went and saw him."

"I did, but first I had to forgive Albert in my heart and mind. Then I flew out to Indiana and went to the institution where Albert was being kept. Face-to-face, with a glass partition between us, I forgave him."

"What did you say?"

"At first it was difficult to get Albert even to acknowledge that I was there. After a minute or two, I told him, 'Albert, it's difficult for me to be here, but it's also important that I am here. I can't figure out what I could have possibly done, or done to you, to make you shoot me. I've thought and thought about it, and nothing made sense, so I realized it was not personal.' At that point, Albert looked up at me. 'So I decided not to take it personally. That, however, only allowed me to stop hating you. Albert, I was just so furious that you tried to kill me and maybe my wife as well. I mean, didn't you see our two young boys sitting with us at dinner that night? Anyway, I finally realized that not taking it personally was not enough. It wasn't going to heal me. I needed to forgive you, so I came here to tell you, Albert, I do forgive you, you crazy bastard you.' Albert, aside from flinching a bit at the 'crazy bastard' part, sat unmoved.

"We sat for a few seconds looking at each other, and I said, 'Then as I thought about it, it occurred to me that we are part of each other's dream about life. You came to warn me, to show me what you were thinking, feeling, believing, and I ignored you. Everyone, it seemed, was listening to me, and who was listening to you? I continued to ignore you right up until the moment you shot me. I guess then you forced me to see you, if not hear you, but it was too late to serve any useful purpose in the dream we were acting out. Only recently I got that ever since we met in my home, I've ignored you. I had to forgive myself for that. Finally, I realized that from the level of Being, nothing happened. How can I forgive you and myself for something that never happened?'

"At that point, Albert looked at me and commented, 'Of the two of us, Sam, you're the crazy bastard. I'm locked up in here and you're running around out there, or according to you, maybe you're not. Doesn't make a lot of sense, does it?'

"And then it happened, Julian. I began to laugh, sort of chucking softly. Albert was looking me right in the eyes, and I laughed a little louder and harder. Then he began laughing, and we were both laughing, really laughing. It went on for a good minute or two. Then we both took a deep breath, and Albert spoke. 'Sam, I'm sorry for what I did, and you're coming here today is going to let me breathe a little easier. Have a safe journey home.'

"He got up and left, and just before he exited the visitors' room, he flashed me the peace sign."

With a grin, Sam added, "May his ass rot in jail forever and ever . . . only kidding. We occasionally write letters to each other now. I look forward to getting them. He's on medication, of course, which helps. People certainly have negative thoughts, sometimes murderous thoughts, but most don't act on them. Albert did. You could say he got lost in his illusions about the world far more completely than most of us when he bought that gun and shot me, maybe due to brain chemistry or some other things I'll likely never know about. The why doesn't matter anymore. I'm afraid to say it, but we're all crazy bastards to some extent, and to quote Mr. Lennon, 'We misunderstand all we see.'

"You see, Julian, I owe Father Mike big-time for that conversation. I don't know if or when I would have figured that one out without him. All of us need to forgive our enemies—and ourselves. Holding on to pain and anger keeps us in pain and anger. It's human to hold on to the pain of the past, but it's divine to forgive and let go."

"Amazing story, Sam. Thank you."

"Well, that's exactly what it is, a story. Anyway, suffering takes place in the mind when it is disconnected from its source. The mind then functions like a small island in a vast ocean. If we identify with the mind and its concerns and desires, the potential for suffering is ever present. When we begin to identify with pure awareness, the mind's stories lose their grip, and suffering loses its sharp edge and nasty bite."

"So it's all about awareness. It always sounds too simple, Sam."

"It is simple. Just be your big Self. Yeah, the infinite field of awareness is the whole ball game. When we are one with That, when we become fully merged with That, suffering ceases to exist. It's all Being, and all of this, each and every one of us, are expressions of That." Sam took a breath, "It's a big idea, even for us philosophers. And yet it's simple. Everyone wants to make it complicated. Just transcend twice a day and then plunge into activity. It all happens from there."

Sam looked at Julian as Julian looked across the field. The sun was warm on their backs, and there was a gentle breeze blowing into their faces.

"Shall we start back?"

"Sam, why don't we meditate for a bit and then head back?"

"All right, Jules, good idea. Let's sit comfortably and close our eyes."

As Julian started to meditate, Sam sat in silence.

Chapter 31:
The Petition

A S BOB HARRIS ROUNDED THE corner of the Robert Frost Library, a jeans-clad female student with long, wavy brown hair approached him carrying a clipboard. Smiling expectantly, she introduced herself. "Hi, Dr. Harris, I'm Andrea Wilson. Some of the students have gotten together to create a petition to bring Dr. Sam O'Connor back to campus for a public lecture. Would you like to sign?"

Taken totally by surprise, Professor Harris's face revealed his shock. "Did I understand you to say you want to bring Sam O'Connor back to campus for a lecture?" he asked incredulously.

Though somewhat taken aback by his response, Andrea still spoke with enthusiasm and delivered a resounding "Yes!"

"How could this possibly happen? Do you even know Sam O'Connor?" he probed with clear disdain in his voice.

"Well, two weeks ago, a bunch of us got together with him in a café in town," Andrea began to explain, trying to ignore the professor's scornful tone. "Dr. O'Connor was fascinating. Everyone who went that day has learned TM."

"Wait a minute," Bob Harris interrupted. "Sam taught you to meditate?" He narrowed his eyes and put one hand on his hips, as if bracing for the answer while he clutched his leather briefcase in the other.

"Actually, it was his wife, Amy. Sam taught the men, and Amy taught the women."

"I don't believe this," Dr. Harris almost hissed. "So now you want to bring him on campus?"

""Yes, he was a professor here some years ago," she added helpfully, seeming impervious to the professor's hostility.

"I know full well. I was one of his colleagues," Harris replied derisively.

"Then you know about him being shot and all."

"Yes, I know all about it."

"Good. Then you'll sign?" Andrea asked, proffering the clipboard and pen.

Recovering his professorial demeanor, Bob Harris questioned Andrea more calmly. "I need to know more about this. What is his topic? To whom is the petition going?"

"I don't know his topic, and we're not sure he'll accept the invite." Harris's mouth twisted in a sardonic grin as he shot back, "If I know Sam, he'll accept. He was never one to shun the limelight."

Andrea was growing more skeptical of the professor's motives by the second but remained polite. "I don't know. He seemed pretty reserved about the idea, the petition I mean. After we have several hundred signatures, the petition is going to the dean of students."

"And who is organizing this?"

"There are twelve of us."

"Including Julian Driscoll?"

"Yes, Julian arranged the meeting in the café. He and Sam are friends."

"I think I'll pass for the moment, Andrea." Harris asserted, trying to sound reasonable. "I'd like to confer with some of my colleagues, just to be sure this matter is being handled correctly."

"Oh . . ." Andrea stepped back, her face reflecting her disappointment.

"Thank you for the information. It's been most helpful," Dr. Harris concluded, then he abruptly headed for his office.

Harris felt aroused by a sense of righteous anger. Suddenly he was a man with a cause, headed for battle. He thought to himself, *So Sam's coming back to campus. We'll see about that. The last thing we need around here is another round of pop philosophy and Eastern mysticism masquerading as Western science, and I will do everything I can to stop him.*

Andrea spotted Julian at lunch in the student union. She carried her sandwich over and sat down to join him. "Hey, Jules," she jumped in, "I picked up another twenty-four signatures in front of the library in about forty-five minutes."

"That's great, Andy. We're over 150 for sure. I think we can get 250 by tomorrow."

"What's weird was ole Bob Harris wouldn't sign. He wanted to, and I quote, 'confer with his colleagues to see that this is being handled correctly.' He acted like a real jerk."

"Yeah," Julian agreed, "he seems to have a bug up his ass when it comes to Sam. I don't know why. Never mind him. I'm going to see Dr. Barnes after lunch to get his support. Maybe tomorrow afternoon we'll have enough signatures to make an appointment with Dean Griffin."

"Sounds like a plan." Andrea grinned. "Good luck!"

Bob Harris walked briskly to his office in Williston Hall muttering to himself. As he approached the building, there sat Sam O'Connor on a bench. Looking as if he was seeing a ghost, Bob stopped short and momentarily stared dumbly at Sam.

Sam rose to greet him. Offering his hand, Sam began politely, "Bob, it's been a long time. You look well." As he spoke, Sam noted to himself that Bob had grown bald and plump since he'd seen him last.

Bob nervously and tentatively reached out and shook Sam's hand. Seeing Sam and feeling his warm, strong grip made Bob feel a bit squeamish, almost guilty. *How very strange that Sam is here at this moment*, Bob thought. He raised his head slightly to regain his composure and replied, "Yes, Sam, it has been a long time."

"If you have a few minutes, I thought maybe we could talk in your office."

"Yes, of course."

The two men entered the building and moved down the hall in silence. Bob unlocked his office door, flicked the light switch on, and motioned to Sam to have a seat. He walked behind his large oak desk, covered by neatly stacked piles of books and papers, and sat down in a well-cushioned brown leather armchair. In that familiar position, he started to feel less unhinged and inquired, "So, Sam, what brings you here after all these years?"

"You may have heard that some students have asked me to come back to campus and give a talk," Sam broached the subject without hesitation.

"Yes. In fact, that just came to my attention. However, I have my doubts that the administration will support that request. They'll be polite about it, but I fully expect the petition to be declined. Maybe they'll offer you a faculty tea, that feels more appropriate." Bob's voice and face remained composed, almost expressionless, but Sam sensed the smugness behind the words.

"Nevertheless, with all due respect, I have the feeling that I am going to be asked back," Sam returned coolly. "If that happens, I'd like to know your feelings about it."

"My feelings?" Harris asked as he swiveled back in his chair. "Frankly, I can't imagine what you'd have to talk about that has any serious academic value—after all, you've been out of the classroom and research for almost a decade. Unless of course you've been writing and are about to publish another blockbuster of a book." Harris laughed, trying to mask his condescension with something light.

Sam shook his head no.

Sitting in his office full of reminders of his academic standing, Bob's confidence and self-righteousness returned in force. He couldn't resist further comment. "I suppose you could pull out the old material on consciousness and such and rehash it, but it's unlikely to hold much interest these days. Here it is 1986, and no one hears of the Maharishi anymore, and TM has largely faded from view. Not relevant, you see. The world has passed it by. If you were asked back, what in the world would you speak about? Tell your personal story about getting shot? Discuss giving up your profession?"

Sam smiled at Bob. "Well, Bob, I see you haven't lost your ability to belittle or your sense of superiority."

"Oh, come now. You're too sensitive. You always were. I simply can't imagine what kind of meaningful academic contribution you could possibly make."

"The discussion of consciousness is very much alive in academic circles," Sam retorted. "TM is still taught on many campuses, and Maharishi is still a world teacher with tremendous gifts to offer, including extensive knowledge of the Vedic literature."

"That may interest a few devoted souls," Bob countered, "but the world, as a whole, has moved on. Maharishi had his moment, as did you. You tethered your balloon to his. I hope you enjoyed the ride and found it worthwhile. I, for one, thought it was a ridiculous venture, a waste of your time and intelligence. I don't get it, Sam. If you had only stuck to academia instead of chasing clouds, you would have gained tenure and been teaching even now."

"I heard a different drummer. Life knocked on my door, and I answered the call. It was that simple for me," Sam offered patiently.

"Fine, but what did it get you? You lost your career and, in my mind, your credibility."

"I have freedom."

"In what sense?" Harris asked with annoyance.

Sam hesitated, took a deep breath, and settled back completely in his chair. "We had it wrong, Bob. We'd teach this stuff that we thought we knew and understood, but we never lived the teaching. We'd talk about Plato's dialectic and platonic forms or Schopenhauer's 'thing in itself' without having any experience of them, and then we'd punch the clock and go have a beer. Since that's what everyone else was doing, we thought that was enough. It wasn't and it isn't.

"I had to reexamine everything I thought I knew, what was true, what was false. And I found that life just is. At the most fundamental level, everything simply is—and then we place our interpretations, labels, and judgments on everything and everyone: good, bad, unhealthy, healthy, light, dark, good, evil, what have you—but everything and everyone simply is. So I understand that now. Doing so has left me in freedom. We can all live our lives on many levels, even from the level of Being. It's been an interesting journey," Sam concluded.

"Okay, let's say it's been an interesting journey. But I fail to see where it's gotten you. Really, you haven't changed a bit, still living in abstract realms, feeling above it all." Bob looked down at his desk for a second then raised his eyes to meet Sam's. His voice was openly angry now. "You say I'm superior! You are the one that always felt superior around here, not me. I confess to being a mortal. I will never see out of Socrates' or Plato's eyes. I make no such claims and never will. I get paid to teach. And I will have my drink at five o'clock, thank you very much. I deserve it."

"Bob, there is so much more than words in books. You can experience your universal nature as did the great teachers we claim to emulate. Without that experience, their words would never have ignited so many generations. They would have been empty of the power to inspire."

"But two thousand five hundred years later, we're still reading them," Harris rebutted. "We're still engaged, pondering, using our intellectual gifts to gain greater understanding."

"Exactly, but these masters spoke and wrote from the level of Being, and no matter how great one's intellect is, it is still limited and can't grasp the state of infinite awareness. But you or the custodian who takes care of this building can experience Being. You're still the professor, and he's still the custodian, but you're both living from pure awareness. Words in books can only do so much. To truly grow, we need both knowledge and the experience of our universal nature."

"Yes, I'm well aware of your theme of 'experience Being,' Sam, I just don't buy it. And it has no place in the academic world of knowledge. So if you're invited back to this campus, which I will oppose, you'll want to expound on the experience of this hypothetical universal nature?" Bob leaned forward on his desk, his whole body in alert mode.

"Yes, and I'll invite you to join me on the journey so you can find it yourself."

"Thank you. I'm content to read about it, think about it, and stay objective.

"I see little has changed for you."

"And for you as well." Dr. Harris relaxed and sat back in his chair then faced his adversary calmly. "You are an interesting man, I'll give you that. However, interesting doesn't get you to the podium and the opportunity to lure students into some kind of fantasy. You're a dangerous man, Sam. As far as I'm concerned, this meeting is over. It's been entertaining, but I have real work to do."

Sam stood, ready to leave, then placed one hand on Bob's expansive desk and stated, "Fine, but first consider this: almost all of humanity is living in a dream. For some, it's a good dream. For others, it's a nightmare. The dream is Plato's cave. We owe it to our students to help them wake up from the dream, to throw off the shackles as the hero in Plato's cave did. As a professor of knowledge, you owe it to your students to make the journey to self-knowledge before you stand in front of them and teach. Higher education should lead to higher states of consciousness, not just a diploma.

"While I was teaching the course on consciousness, you were so busy resisting everything that you missed the students' excitement, their bright, eager faces. You missed it because you were self-absorbed and, frankly, jealous. I invited you to learn meditation. I tried to become your friend, but you would have none of it. I'm sorry that ship sailed and you didn't step on board." With that, Sam turned and left the office, closing the door behind him.

Bob Harris sat quietly, listening to the sound of Sam's footsteps as he retreated down the hall. After a moment, he felt uncontrollable anger. He banged his fist on his desk and spoke fiercely to the emptiness of the room, "Damn you, Sam O'Connor! Damn you to hell!"

Julian arrived at Dr. Barnes' office and knocked on his half-opened door. The professor was at his desk and looked up to see him. "How can I help you?" Dr. Barnes inquired.

"May I have a word?" asked Julian.

"Yes, please come in and have a seat."

Struck by Dr. Barnes' warmth and openness, Julian entered the office and sat down in the armchair on the left side of his desk.

"I'd like to talk with you about Sam O'Connor," Julian jumped to the point. Dr. Barnes nodded his assent, and Julian narrated, "I wouldn't expect you to know this, but a few months ago, I met Sam O'Connor, on a PVTA bus, actually. He had long hair and a beard and wore work clothes. I thought he was a farmer or lumberjack at first. We noticed each other briefly—I'm not sure exactly why—but I didn't think about it again until a week later when I came across him on Main Street and said hello. We ended up sitting and talking over coffee and muffins at the White Oak Café and decided to start meeting regularly, every Friday. We talk about philosophy, but not like in a classroom."

"Tell me a little more about the meetings," Dr. Barnes encouraged Julian, settling back in his chair.

"Well, Sam makes things very intriguing, exciting. I don't know how to describe it, except I feel better, happier, after we finish talking."

"I see. Sounds like you're engaging in some stimulating conversations," Dr. Barnes commented, thinking that cafés can so often provide better environments for philosophical discussion than classrooms.

Julian paused, seeing Dr. Barnes lost in thought. When Dr. Barnes smiled, Julian resumed. "Anyway, my girlfriend and I went to his house for dinner. We were both so impressed with Sam, his wife and boys, their farmhouse, Sam's garden, everything. The whole evening was amazing."

"How are Amy and the boys?" Dr. Barnes asked with genuine concern.

"They're wonderful. My girlfriend, Katy, and I started TM, and we both love it. Then some friends wanted to go with us to meet Sam."

"At the White Oak, on a Friday?" Dr. Barnes smiled broadly.

"Yes, twelve of us showed up. Sam wasn't expecting it, but he was great. All of those students ended up learning TM with Sam and his wife, Amy."

"So Sam is teaching?"

"Well, at least since I met him. That's the reason I'm here. We want to bring Sam back on campus, Dr. Barnes, to give a lecture. It's been over eight years since he was here. He has a lot of valuable knowledge, and his angle on things is unusual. He kind of wakes you up and makes you question everything."

"Is Sam open to doing this?" Dr. Barnes sat forward, deeply interested in the answer.

"Well, when we first discussed the idea, he seemed surprised and a little uneasy. However, the other students were pretty enthusiastic, so he said if he were invited, he'd consider it. We started a petition to present to Dean Griffin, and we're looking for 250 signatures by tomorrow. Would you help us by signing? It would mean a lot since you're the department chair."

"I'd be happy to sign, but first let me say this. Dean Griffin and I were big supporters of Sam when he was on faculty here. I find your account of your relationship amazing, but as I think about it, it's only natural that Sam would meet a bright student like yourself and start to engage with you.

"We wanted him back, you know, after the shooting. We told him the door was always open. Dean Griffin called him a number of times as I did that first year. He really struggled after the shooting—can't blame him for that—and he made it clear that he was not ready. After a while, we both stopped calling, and I must admit, I lost touch with him. That was my fault." He paused, "But now maybe he's ready."

"I'm not sure if even Sam knows whether he's ready or not," confided Julian, "but if the college will have him and he accepts, it's a good first step."

"Yes, a good first step." Dr. Barnes agreed. "I'll happily sign, and I'll call the dean to alert him that you will want to meet with him soon."

"That would be great! Would you be at the meeting?"

"I could be."

"We'd really appreciate it." Julian looked down at his feet for a second, considering whether he should bring up his concern.

"What is it, Julian?" asked Dr. Barnes, sensing the student's hesitation.

"Well, Dr. Harris has been acting strange and almost hostile whenever Sam's name has come up. First, he warned me not to get involved with Sam, and when I did, he became quite upset. Today, Andrea Wilson was outside the library, gathering signatures. When she asked Dr. Harris to sign the petition, he asked a thousand questions instead. Andrea thought he seemed agitated by the whole idea. What's going on there?"

"I'm not sure, but we'll sort it out. Bob is a strong advocate of doing things by the book and not a great fan of change. This may have hit him like a bolt from the blue."

"I think it's more than that. He's upset that Sam's even talking to me and more upset that he has taught two TM courses to Amherst students."

"As I said, you can leave it to me. I've known Bob for many years. Now where's that petition?"

Julian left with one more key signature, somewhat relieved that Dr. Barnes was willing to talk to Dr. Harris.

Frank Barnes called Dean Griffin. "Hello, David? Frank here. Listen, a most interesting situation is brewing on campus. Got a few minutes?"

Chapter 32:
The Meeting

"HELLO, ADDISON? IT'S DAVID. I'VE just been in an extraordinary meeting with some truly inspired students."

"Anything to do with Sam O'Connor?" asked Amherst's president.

"Why, yes. You're either psychic or word has traveled at the speed of light." The dean laughed.

"Actually, neither. According to my secretary, Bob Harris and Tom Wesley have requested a meeting to discuss Dr. O'Connor's potential return to campus to address the college. Definitely took me by surprise."

"If you have a minute, I'll fill you in on what I know."

"Please, I'm all ears."

"Two days ago, Julian Driscoll, a fourth-year student and philosophy major, came to see Frank Barnes with a petition to bring Sam O'Connor back on campus for a lecture. Evidently, Sam and Julian connected a few months back, and they've been meeting weekly at a café in town ever since to discuss philosophy. One thing led to another, and Sam instructed him in TM, which shouldn't surprise you, knowing Sam."

"Really? Is that still around?"

"For Sam it is. Anyway, at some point, a number of students started showing up at this café to participate in the discussions with Sam, and they also learned TM."

"How many students are we talking about?"

"Twelve, at least twelve were in my office just now. They handed me a petition with hundreds of student signatures supporting an official college invitation to Sam to speak on campus. A number of faculty names are on the petition as well.

"What does Frank think about this?"

"He likes the idea as I do, at least in principle. We obviously have much to talk about."

"Fine. We can start discussing this at four o'clock in my office. I'll have Jane ask Harris and Wesley to attend, and we'll sort this out. Okay? You say there were twelve students?"

"Yes."

"Well, as long as Sam O'Connor doesn't come riding into campus on a white donkey, I think the school can handle it. Let's see where this goes. See you at four."

"Sounds good, Addison. I'll call Frank and let him know."

"Fine."

"See you soon," the dean signed off.

More than surprised, David asked himself, *What the hell is Bob thinking to go right to the president without checking with anyone else on this? I better call Frank.*

"Frank? David. You won't believe this one. Bob Harris has snared Tom Wesley, and we've been asked to meet with Addison at four today to discuss Sam coming to campus. I'll venture a wild guess here that they're both against it."

"I wonder what Bob has in mind. Addison doesn't suffer fools gladly," Frank pondered aloud.

"So he didn't come to you first then?" David checked.

"No. I wanted to contact him since my talk with Julian Driscoll, but I haven't had a moment," Frank explained. "Julian did tell me about a couple of sour interactions he had with Bob over the last few months concerning Sam," informed Frank. "That put me on alert, I must admit. I wonder what's going through Bob's mind."

"Well, Bob must have felt his concerns would have fallen on deaf ears with us, so he jumped right to the top to launch his protest. Interesting," David remarked.

"What does Wesley have to do with this? Science and philosophy teaming up?" Frank proposed skeptically.

"I don't know. It seems an unlikely alliance. Shall we walk over together?"

"Sounds good. I'll swing by your office, and we'll go from there."

"See you at three forty-five?"

"Yeah, see you then."

Both men hung up and were left alone to contemplate where all this was going. Dr. Frank Barnes and Dean David Griffin were in their early sixties and had spent most of their professional careers at Amherst College. They were highly regarded by both peers and students. They were also friends as were their wives. David was the taller of the two, with a lanky frame. He had not gained more than a pound or two in thirty years. The same could not be said of Frank. While he was energetic, he was also shorter by half a foot and generously proportioned. The two made for an interesting visual pair as they crossed the campus.

Dr. Addison Paul Stevens was a legendary educator, author, and administrator, having spent most of his teaching career at Harvard. He hailed from an old established family of Boston Brahmins. At nearly seventy years old, he looked like a benevolent aristocrat. His thick white hair had receded some but was still striking. His deep-set blue eyes were piercing and could twinkle in joy, shine in compassion, focus intensely, or command attention as circumstances arose.

All three men held Sam O'Connor in high esteem, and all had felt deeply shaken by his shooting. Each had taken turns calling Sam to inquire how he was and ask him if he wished to return to his position, and all were disappointed that Sam had refused them every time. In their hearts, the three educators now felt a sense of wonder and joy that a handful of students had somehow discovered Sam and engaged with him. The fact that Sam had touched these students in a personal way and inspired them to create a movement on campus seemed astounding from one perspective. Yet at the same time, remembering how Sam had electrified the students on campus nine years earlier, it was not altogether surprising that a new group of students who had encountered his personal magic were championing his return.

Frank and David strolled across the campus they adored in the last of its autumn glory. The maple leaves had fallen recently while the oaks held on to their rust-colored foliage. Many of the trees on campus were a hundred years old or more. Some of the brick buildings with granite steps were from the same vintage, all contributing to the campus' dignity, charm, and sheer beauty, especially in glow of the late afternoon sun.

As the two old friends ambled along, comfortable in the silence they shared, both anticipated the interesting but possibly divisive meeting ahead. When they entered Addison's reception area on the second floor of the building, they found that Bob Harris and Tom Wesley had arrived just ahead of them. The president's office was spacious, with a well-polished, hand-carved maple desk as its centerpiece. The desk stood before an array of large, colonial-style windows that stretched almost from ceiling to floor, allowing sunlight to pour in and providing expansive views to anyone looking out. The carpet was thick and rich with a reddish, golden hue. A couch and three upholstered side chairs formed a comfortable meeting area on the right side of the room; however, Addison intended to remain seated behind his desk, suggesting the formal tone of the meeting. Four chairs were arranged in a semicircle in front of the desk, with a fifth chair off to his right. Addison asked his longtime secretary, Jane Craymore, whose advice he had learned to trust, to attend the meeting as well.

President Stevens greeted each of the professors as they entered the office with a smile and a warm handshake. The professors in turn greeted one another informally and took their seats. Addison Stevens moved back behind his desk and began. "Gentlemen, let me start by summarizing what I understand this meeting to be about. Bob and Tom called my office earlier in the day requesting a meeting to discuss Dr. Sam O'Connor's possible return to campus to give a lecture." He faced Bob Harris and Tom Wesley directly and observed, "I take it from my conversation with Jane that you are not pleased about it. Shortly after your call, Bob, David phoned to tell me that he'd just had an exciting meeting with a dozen students. In just three days, they had collected hundreds of signatures on a petition to bring Dr. O'Connor back to campus. I then asked David to call Frank and invited them to join this meeting so we can sort this through."

"Addison, if I may," Bob spoke up.

Addison nodded his consent, and Bob started his carefully planned argument. "Sam O'Connor was perceived to be a valued member of this college when he was here. I say *perceived* because I believe that if he hadn't been shot and he had continued on faculty, his course on consciousness would have eventually failed to draw any attention, and his status among us would have faltered. I believe this because what he taught was not academically sound, regardless of its appeal. He mixed philosophy with pop culture, and if he had stayed on at Amherst, he would have diminished the college's reputation."

"Bob," David Griffin jumped in, "I couldn't disagree more. Sam had an incredible ability—a gift even—to connect with students and to use this ability to make knowledge relevant to their lives. You have forgotten perhaps how deeply news of his shooting affected people on this campus. People wept and prayed openly. Despite the fact that it was July and the college was in recess, do you recall how students, teachers, professors, and others from the community, including my daughter and myself, spontaneously converged on the Amherst Town Common? Addison was there as well as Frank. We all meditated and prayed in silence for his recovery, and then we sang. It was one of the most moving experiences I've ever had. Sam's connection with people was profound and important."

"I'll admit he was charismatic and popular," Bob responded." However, he was off course academically. His thinking was not rigorous, and he had given up on being a true academic."

"Are you drawing that conclusion based on his book on consciousness— the one that has been continuously in print and translated into at least twenty foreign languages over the last nine years? Or are you thinking of the course he taught?"

"Both. The book is hardly what you'd call a rigorous philosophical work."

"Do you understand," Frank spoke impatiently, "that his publisher asked him to write a book that would appeal to a larger audience, not just the philosophical community? Sam's book got countless people who live far from our ivory tower genuinely excited about philosophy. Some might think that's a miracle! His book has sold over two million copies. A book on philosophy! It's astounding! Academically rigorous or not, I'd be damned pleased if one of my books had that kind of impact on humanity."

"You cannot discount, gentlemen, that Sam was deeply caught up with the Maharishi," Bob asserted. "By choosing to join that group, I feel that he forfeited his rights and privileges as an assistant professor at this college."

Dr. Stevens stirred in his seat and spoke firmly, "Bob, that may be your personal opinion, but for the sake of this discussion, I want you to know that I sat in on two of Sam's lectures, and I found him stimulating and gifted. Moreover, the subject at hand is a single-guest presentation, not a faculty appointment."

This was not the reaction Bob had expected when he had rehearsed this moment. His voice wavered a bit. "I'm sorry if you find my assessment unjustified, but I stand by it. The guru's influence on Sam is certainly fine in his personal and spiritual life, but he brought it here to this campus. He tried to cloak it in scholarly thought, but he failed. At some point, the Maharishi tried to rationalize his spiritual message by using science. Suddenly TM was scientific. Out with the old, in with the new." Dr. Harris paused and nodded at Dr. Wesley. "However, Tom here has done some reviewing of the TM research, and he has found it lacking substance and real objectivity. Maybe you'd like to comment, Tom."

"Yes, well," Dr. Wesley began, "I'm not really sure why I'm here," he said, looking around at the others. "Bob stopped by yesterday with some of the earlier TM research and asked me to look it over and give him my opinion. I generally thought it was interesting but not conclusive. A lot more research would be required to validate the group's claims."

"And that's it?" asked Addison, looking at Bob.

"Look, the TM group has moved suspiciously from spirituality to science," Bob reasserted, growing irritated. "Their attempt to create what they call enlightened individuals everywhere was questionable, so they shifted their message to science."

Dean Griffin asked impatiently, "What does that have to do with Sam O'Connor speaking on campus?"

"Don't you see? Sam is meeting with students off campus, telling them who knows what. Who here has seen him lately? I just saw him three days ago. He was sitting outside my office. He looks like a madman with his beard, long hair, and work boots. Shouldn't we at least create a committee to meet with him, find out his intentions and what kind of a speech he wants to give? Are we going to give this man carte blanche to waltz in here and lecture us? What has he done that is academically credible in the last nine years? If you want to invite him to a faculty tea, I could support that," Bob concluded as he looked around at the others.

"Bob, you're jumping the gun here," Dean Griffin inserted. "You must know that we'll talk to him about his proposed lecture. Do we need a committee to do it? I hardly think so. This is not an inquisition. This man is a talented teacher. The students who met him are excited. I don't think a faculty tea to size him up is an appropriate approach with a valued former professor. Most of us are already well aware of his skill and knowledge."

"The students in my class are excited about ZZ Top," Dr. Harris rebutted. "Does that mean we should have them here for a lecture?" he asked sarcastically, throwing all caution to the wind. "I want to state for the record that I'm against it," he concluded.

Addison Stevens stepped in. "Thus far, you have not given us one substantial reason not to proceed, Bob. You are personally strongly opposed, that's clear. Can you give us any further reasons why you don't you want Sam O'Connor back on this campus?"

Bob closed his eyes for a moment. He tried to fight back the rising tide of anger welling up inside. Sam O'Connor was a bright burning star that had eclipsed him. For the two years that Sam was on campus, no one knew that he, Dr. Robert Harris, even existed. His envy had grown almost unmanageable. When Sam was shot, he was shocked and horrified at first, but those feelings gave way to a secret sense of relief and satisfaction. In truth, he felt vindicated.

"Bob, can you answer the question?" President Stevens demanded.

Bob opened his eyes, sighed as he exhaled, and in a steady low voice challenged the group. "Don't you see? Sam is going to deceive you all, cast his charm. His so-called philosophy is a danger to all that hear it. He is the Pied Piper for his so-called Age of Enlightenment. Fine, if that's his choice, but let him preach in the cafés of Amherst, not on campus."

"Frankly, I'm surprised at you, Bob. That makes no sense at all," Addison rebuked him and then spoke as if addressing an unruly child. "I ask you to keep in mind that Sam O'Connor was an esteemed member of our community. I don't know if he's coming back to campus or not at this moment, but if we decide to invite him, you will treat him with the same respect we treat all of our guest lecturers."

Bob looked around, dismayed that these bright men couldn't understand the points he was making. He took a deep breath. "Gentlemen, I say we agree to disagree about Dr. O'Connor." He looked at Dr. Stevens and asked, "Is there anything more we need to talk about now?"

Ever the politic mediator, Dr. Stevens, replied evenly, "No. Thank you for your time."

Bob got up, nodded at his colleagues, and walked across the room and out the door with as much dignity as he could muster. Once he departed, Tom Wesley tried to explain that he had known nothing about Harris' agenda and was sorry that he had gotten involved with it. He excused himself and hurried across campus back to his biology lab.

Jane Craymore and the three men remaining sat quietly. Jane shifted uncomfortably in her seat looking from face to face. After a moment or two, Addison broke the heavy silence. "Bob has obviously been under considerable strain over all this. I'm also concerned about what a public appearance by Dr. O'Connor might elicit. The world is a dangerous place for some, particularly pioneers of thought. I thoroughly support bringing Dr. O'Connor back on campus, but we have to realize that it is a responsibility to have him address the college community."

"Even provided that we agree to hold the lecture, we don't know if he will accept an invitation to speak," added Frank.

"True," acknowledged Addison, "but my hunch is that he will, and we have a petition here to answer. David, please call Sam, tonight if possible, and see if he's really open to the whole idea. I suggest you invite him to lunch, and I can drop in and say hello. In the meantime, let's look at the calendar."

Jane had the school calendar at the ready, and after scanning the busy campus schedule of events, she suggested, "How about Thursday, March twenty-third? It's the week before spring break. There's nothing scheduled, and it's just over four months from now. It would give us enough time to organize for the event."

After thoughtful consideration, Addison agreed, "Yes, we'd have enough time to do it properly." He then added, "You realize that we're going to need a security plan. If Sam agrees, no harm must befall that man while he's with us. David, assuming the lunch goes well and Sam accepts our invitation, will you see that our campus police and the Amherst PD are informed of the event? Ask them to put their heads together and design a security plan."

"Will do. We'll take every precaution. We're all on the same page there."

Frank Barnes, after sitting quietly throughout the meeting, now interjected, "I think Dr. Harris may be due for a sabbatical, but in the meantime, who's going to babysit him?"

"My god!" gasped Addison. "Why we should need to pose such a question, and worse yet have to answer it, is beyond me. Frank, if you find it necessary, I leave it to you to remind Bob Harris to live up to the high standards of this college as we plan and promote the lecture. I leave it to your discretion."

"Gladly. If he remains unconvinced, then what?"

"Then he'll answer to me personally," Addison added with a look of annoyance. "Let's see how events unfold and take it from there. David, keep me informed, will you? Thank you, everyone," Addison said as he rose, signaling the end of the meeting.

Striding back through the campus to his office, Dr. Harris contemplated protesting to the board of trustees and then thought better about it. "So Sam O'Connor the wonder boy has again successfully pulled the sheep's skin over everyone's eyes. Let him have his moment. What could possibly come of it? He'll most likely make a complete fool of himself, and those three brilliant men will have wished that they had listened to me," he said aloud to nobody at all.

Chapter 33:
The Plan

DEAN GRIFFIN CALLED SAM AT home that evening after the meeting in President Stevens' office.

Amy answered the phone. "Hello, the O'Connor residence."

"Hello, Amy? This is David Griffin."

"David! How great to hear from you!" Amy responded, smiling broadly.

"Good to hear your voice, Amy. It's been too long. How are you and the boys?"

"We're all doing well. The boys are growing like weeds. They seem to have an infinite supply of energy and an unlimited capacity for mischief. How about you David? How's your family?"

"We're fine, thanks, though I must say that growing older is not for the fainthearted." David laughed. "We're all thriving, really, and I should not complain. Amy, I hope I'm not being abrupt, but you probably heard from Julian that the college would like Sam to come back to campus and address the community. How do you think Sam will respond?"

"I can't speak for Sam, but if he wants to, I'd be all for it."

"I'm so glad to hear that! Is he at home? Can I have a word with him?"

"Yes. I'll call him. Wonderful to hear from you, David."

"The pleasure is all mine, I assure you. Thank you."

"Hold on. Sam!" Amy shouted down the hall. "Pick up the phone. It's David Griffin."

Sam looked up from the book he was reading and smiled. The moment of invitation was finally here. He picked up the phone on the table by the couch and said, "David?"

"Hello, Sam. How are you?" Sam could hear the smile in David's voice.

"Good. Very good, in fact. And you?"

"Well, thank you. Sam, I know this is a bit sudden, but I also know you've had some preparation, courtesy of Julian Driscoll and several other students. I'm calling with a proposal that I sincerely hope you will think over and accept."

"I rather enjoy thinking, so I see no problem there," Sam grinned as he spoke.

"As you know, some of your student friends here on campus circulated a petition to bring you back to campus for a lecture. What you may not know is that in just three days, they've gathered over three hundred signatures, including students, staff, and faculty. It was impressive. The college is responding to their effort—happily, I might add—by extending you an invitation to give a talk on philosophy and consciousness, whatever your latest thinking is on these topics. How does that sound?"

"You're right about the students. I knew a few weeks ago that this was coming. I wasn't sure about the administration's response, but now that I have it, I would be honored to accept."

"Fantastic! Are you free on Wednesday for lunch so we can talk it over?"

"Sure."

"Shall I assume you're still a vegetarian?"

"David, I've learned over the years to eat whatever mother serves. On the other hand, don't slaughter the fatted calf on my behalf."

"Got it! I'll make a note of that. One o'clock at my office?"

"Great!"

"See you then."

"Wonderful. Thanks for the call, David. I'm really looking forward to spending some time with you."

"'Bye for now."

"Bye." Sam hung up the phone and thought, *Julian Driscoll . . .*

"Amy!" he shouted down the hallway from his office.

"I'm in the kitchen, Sam."

Sam half ran toward the kitchen. Before he was through the door, he began, "David just asked me back on campus to give a lecture. Julian and his friends circulated that petition they told me about and collected hundreds of signatures. They presented it to the administration and voilà! An invite!"

"What did you say?"

"Yes."

"Oh, Sam," Amy exclaimed, throwing her arms around him. "I'm so proud of you."

"Then you want me to do it?"

"Sam, you've seemed so happy these past few months talking with students again and teaching. It's been wonderful to see. I know you have some important things to say, and I think you'll be brilliant."

"Well, we'll see," Sam said with a certain reserve. "I'm meeting David for lunch on Wednesday."

"Sam, did I ever tell you how much I love you?"

"Not lately." He grinned.

"Come, my dear hubby. Rather than tell you, let me show you," she teased. Amy took Sam by the hand and led him up the stairs.

Sam arrived at Dean Griffin's office just before one. The dean's secretary, Alice Stone, gray and motherly, welcomed him warmly.

"Hello, Dr. O'Connor. I'm truly delighted to see you again."

"Please call me Sam. The feeling is mutual. You look well."

"Thank you. How are Amy and the boys?"

"All doing just great, thanks."

"The dean is expecting you," Alice said. She dialed his extension to let him know that Sam had arrived. Seconds later, Dean Griffin opened his office door and waved Sam in.

"Sam, welcome. I must say it's marvelous to see you back on campus."

"Thank you. Things haven't changed much, at least on the surface." Sam noticed the dean's gray hair and the wrinkles around his mouth and eyes, but his eyes were as bright as ever.

"Well, some of us have grown a bit older." The dean chuckled a little self-consciously.

"Maybe in years, but you look well. There's an air of youthfulness and vitality around you," Sam shared with genuine feeling.

"Kind of you to say, Sam. I feel quite good actually. Life has been exceedingly good to my wife, Margaret, and me."

"You deserve it," Sam affirmed.

"I don't know about that, but I do feel fortunate, well deserved or not!" The dean laughed. "Speaking of family, I'm looking forward to seeing Amy and the boys again."

"The desire is mutual. Amy is anxious to see you as well." Sam abruptly changed the subject. "How are things on campus?"

"Good, good. However, I must tell you that the students have changed since you were on faculty. They're still bright and excellent, but we have more business majors and fewer humanities majors than nine years ago. They seem more practical and less idealistic than when you were teaching. The '80s are different from the '70s in that regard."

"Nothing wrong with being practical," Sam observed, "even though some philosophers have to learn that the hard way." He laughed.

"Speaking of which, the dining services have prepared a delicious lunch for us. You must have some old admirers on the kitchen staff." The dean beckoned Sam to a table set for two with plates covered by warmers. A pot of coffee was brewing on a side table. Sam sat down at the well-polished oak table, formally set with the college's best china. Both men lifted the warmers off their plates and enjoyed the tempting aroma of delicate herbs and spices rising from their plates. "I think you're right. I do have some fans in the kitchen," Sam said, grinning.

Sam was just about to take his first taste when he put his fork down on the table and broached the topic he had been thinking about since he accepted the dean's invitation. "Any protest from any quarter on my invitation back to campus?" he inquired.

"Well, yes, but only from a small minority of one. Other than that, people are interested in what you have to say. I don't know if you'll persuade them to your way of thinking, but they're clearly open to hear your arguments."

"Is Bob Harris that minority of one?" Sam asked directly.

"I'm afraid he is, but there's nothing to worry about, I assure you."

"I did stop by his office two weeks ago, and we had a chat," Sam informed the dean.

"Really?" The dean's face registered surprise. "How did it go?"

"It didn't go well, but at least I know where he stands," Sam revealed, looking a little grim.

"You know that in the academic realm, disagreements are inevitable and have gone on for centuries. We need to be able to agree to disagree and not take things personally. Unfortunately, in this case, Bob is taking it all personally, but don't let his feelings spoil the event."

"I definitely won't," Sam returned.

The dean continued, "You must know that you have a certain amount of personal charisma. That was obvious when you taught here, and the recent show of student support for your lecture tells me that nothing has changed. You seem to have ignited something special in Julian Driscoll and his friends as you used to do in your classes." The dean paused, watching Sam's face for some reaction. Sam simply listened attentively and acknowledged the dean's words with a nod.

"This gift you have attracts all types of people. Many admire you, but some don't. Some are angry and jealous as you learned with great pain. Adding to the mix, you challenge people to make room for new ideas, to expand their thinking and points of view—a difficult undertaking for anyone, educated or not." The dean shifted in his chair and noted that Sam remained fully attentive.

"You have a gift for inspiring change." Dean Griffin looked directly into Sam's eyes. "Your personality is disarming, charming really, in a way that makes it easier for most people to suspend their belief systems and listen to what you have to say. I know that you remain unattached to whether people buy your ideas or not. Otherwise, I would not be rooting so wholeheartedly for your return to campus. Nevertheless, I wonder whether real hostility, like Bob's, might be difficult for you since the shooting. That's really why I brought all this up. However, the fact that you went directly to Bob to confront him about his irrationality makes me feels easier. I'm glad you told me about the meeting. You have so much of value to say. I hope you won't be deterred."

"Maharishi is the one who has something important to say. Any part I have in this is quite small," Sam added calmly.

"I know you may have trouble hearing this, Sam, but I've been around long enough to understand how certain things work. Maharishi is brilliant, no doubt about it. He has changed how people view meditation and introduced the idea of enlightenment in a way that many people can grasp. But without individuals like you, his message would not reach as many people as he desires. He saw something in you just as I did when I hired you. I have the greatest respect for Maharishi, but he needs teachers like you who can talk to people, connect with them, and validate his ideas by adopting them into their own framework. You are a great representative of Western culture, as Maharishi is of his culture. Don't underestimate your value or your gifts," the dean asserted.

"Thank you. I appreciate your directness and your point of view," Sam observed, "but I don't fully agree. As I see it, without knowing what I was doing, I caught the tail of a tiger and went for quite a ride. I didn't intend any of it to happen, but it all happened anyway."

After a moment, David reflected, "I understand how you feel. Still, it doesn't take away from my argument. Your gifts matched up with a revolutionary idea whose time had come. We are looking at three components: who you are, the nature of the ideas, and the timing of their appearance. All three needed to come together, and they did."

"Perhaps, but my point is that I had very little to do with it," Sam maintained.

"Call it what you like, destiny or chance, but something real happened. People's lives were transformed in big and small ways when you taught here—in my opinion, for the better. And that's my point," he emphasized. "Education should be about just that: introducing ideas and changing lives for the better."

"Agreed," Sam pronounced, ready to change the subject. "What's next?"

"Food! Let's do this meal some justice as we talk!" Both men laughed and began to enjoy the feast and talk of lighter things. When they had happily consumed the main course and were taking a breather before turning to dessert, the dean got up and served their coffee. As he poured, he asked Sam if he had some ideas on what he'd like to present to the community.

"Yes, I've been thinking about it, of course. Consciousness will be the central theme, including a few highlights from my old course. I will definitely take into consideration the current student trend toward practicality. Actually, Maharishi always considered Westerners practical and tried to present his knowledge in practical terms. However, the theme of consciousness will remain central. The exploration of consciousness is the final frontier for humanity, and I will explain it as such. I'll use American writers and thinkers to ground all this for the students, to make it relevant and accessible. Who knows? Maybe some will even find it sensible." Sam chuckled softly.

"I've been spending a lot of time with Walt Whitman, and I'll bring in *Leaves of Grass*. Whitman, Emerson, and Thoreau were all familiar with higher states of consciousness. I'll have them jump in, so to speak, where appropriate, although I'll be concentrating on *Leaves of Grass*, especially 'Song of Myself.'"

"Sounds fascinating!" the dean jumped in, genuinely excited. "We're all in for a rare, expansive evening. By the way, I want you to know that my daughter, Katherine, my wife, Elaine, and I are still practicing TM twice a day. For me, it's a personal matter, and I'd like it to remain so. However, I do benefit from it significantly," the dean confided.

"Glad to hear it. How are Elaine and Katherine?"

"Katherine is extremely happy these days. She has a fulfilling marriage with a prof at Mount Holyoke in the earth sciences. He's a good man. She's also a mother, which makes me a proud grandfather, and Elaine is, of course, overjoyed to be a grandmother. I'm grateful they are all close by. Luke is six and Nancy is four."

"Congratulations! That's great!" Sam's face lit up as he acknowledged the news.

"Thanks. I must tell you how pleased I am to see you. I hope you know how much I and many others wanted you to come back to campus and continue teaching after the crisis in Minneapolis."

Sam was quiet, and he looked toward the windows and the trees swaying in the wind outside. After a few seconds, he turned his face back to David. "I'm aware of it, and I hope you understand that my refusals were no reflection on the college and the administration. I don't know . . . I just needed time."

"Well, I'm glad you're here now. I trust you to give an exceptional lecture. Would you send me a title and a short description for publicity purposes? We chose a tentative date in mid-March to give us enough lead time to arrange the usual—you know, promotion, security, that kind of thing. Does that work for you?"

"Fine, but what kind of security are we talking about? Calling in the marines?" Sam's expression indicated his dislike of the idea.

"Of course not, but you are our guest on campus, and we are responsible for your well-being. We need to take some precautions, and we'll coordinate our plan with the Amherst PD. We're not worried, but once the news gets out that you are coming back to Amherst to give your first public address in over nine years, well, it's going to be news. We need to handle it in a responsible way."

"I'll admit I wasn't thinking about any of that," Sam sighed. "In fact, it was far from my mind. But being practical has its place."

"Believe me, none of this is a problem. Just give your lecture and leave the rest to us," the dean concluded. "Now, let's move on to that dessert!"

"I'm for that." Sam laughed.

The conversation ceased as the two scholars turned their focus to the freshly baked apple pie. With astoundingly good timing, Dr. Stevens knocked on the dean's door just as they were about to dig in. He opened the door, and David and Sam both rose to greet him as he walked toward the table.

"Addison, nice of you to drop by," David greeted him.

"Dr. O'Connor, it is a great pleasure to see you back on campus," the president offered, extending his hand.

"It's a great pleasure to be seen, I assure you," Sam replied as they shook hands.

"Your timing is impeccable, Addison," David teased. "We're just starting on fresh apple pie and coffee. Will you join us?"

"Don't mind if I do. Thanks." David served Addison a healthy slice of pie and poured him a cup of coffee, which Addison drank black. As David busied himself for the moment, Addison paused and looked at Sam, thinking what a shame it was to have lost this man for nine years. Then he smiled and addressed Sam, "You look well."

"Amy trimmed my hair and beard last night, so that probably helps," Sam grinned.

"Have you decided to accept our invitation? We have a petition with hundreds of signatures on it to answer," Addison stated, looking back and forth at Sam and David with raised eyebrows.

"Why, yes, I have," Sam answered.

"Wonderful news! You have made me a most happy man," President Stevens shared with great warmth.

"No. Thank you, Addison, for inviting me."

David joined in, "Yes, it is wonderful news. Sam and I were just talking about the lecture. If I may summarize, Sam wants to talk about the American Transcendentalists and their relationship to the exploration of consciousness, with a particular focus on 'Song of Myself.'"

"Sounds fascinating," Addison commented enthusiastically. "I'm a lover of Whitman myself."

"I hope you'll find the angle I'm planning to present interesting," Sam remarked modestly.

"Knowing you, I'm sure you'll have us hanging on every word. I still remember the two lectures I sat in on when you were teaching the course on consciousness. They were brilliant and inspiring."

"Thanks for the vote of confidence," Sam returned in a quiet voice, somewhat taken aback by the president's unexpected praise. "I'll do my best not to disappoint."

The three men finished their coffee, and Sam thanked them both and prepared to leave.

"So good to see you again," Addison said graciously as they shook hands once again.

"Yes," agreed David, "just great to talk with you again after so long. I'll be in touch."

After Sam left, both men sat quietly for a moment. Addison spoke first. "David, we must make absolutely sure that nothing happens to Sam while he's on campus. It would be a tragedy too great to bear for myself personally and for the college."

"Nothing will happen. We'll take every precaution, I assure you."

Sam left the dean's office and walked through campus unrecognized. Unconcerned about security at first, Sam now began to think about it since the dean had brought it up multiple times. As he made his way to the Amherst common, he started to understand the dean's concern. Of course, the college would need to publicize the event. The local press would pick up on it, and he would have to tell his publisher, who would want to do even more promotion. Requests for interviews would start arriving, and people would start calling his home. With all the fanfare, who knew who might be attracted to the event and for what reason? Suddenly Sam started to feel uneasy about the whole thing. Just as that feeling bubbled up, he reached the White Oak Café. He swung the door open and saw Kenny standing behind the counter.

Kenny greeted Sam with a big smile. "Hey, what's happening, brother? You looked all cleaned up. Somebody die?"

"If you have a minute, let's talk in the back room."

"Sure, Sam, sure. Coffee?"

"Sounds good."

Sam sank into the only armchair in Kenny's small office. Piles of papers were stacked everywhere. He was always touched to see a photograph of Jimmy, Lilly, and Kenny together on opening day of the White Oak. The desk also held a picture of Sam and Kenny as eighteen-year-old new arrivals on the Amherst common.

Kenny came in with two mugs and two muffins. Sam moved some piles of papers to create a space for the mugs and plates, and Kenny plunked himself down at his desk and pushed the coffee and a muffin toward Sam. Both men just looked at each other for a moment, clearly happy to be together. "What brings you into town today?" Kenny asked, breaking the silence.

"First of all, nobody died. I had a lunch meeting with Dean Griffin, and President Stevens dropped in at the end. Amy felt I needed a haircut and my beard trimmed so as not to scare them off."

"Oh, probably a good idea, and?" Kenny inquired, lifting his hands upward. Sam grinned like a Cheshire cat.

"Well, you know about the petition that Julian and his buddies started. They gathered hundreds signatures and presented them to Dean Griffin—who had a meeting with President Stevens, and they agreed to invite me to lecture."

"Superb! I did hear a little about this. How's Harris taking it?" Kenny asked with his unfailing intuition.

"Why do you ask?"

"Just curious. He never liked you much."

"True. As a matter of fact, I went to his office last week. He was challenging as usual and utterly brazen about his negative opinion of me."

"Yeah," said Kenny. "Bob's most likely an alien. Could be a reptile."

"Kenny, sometimes I think you're a reptile."

"He probably needs more sun," Kenny decided.

"Can we move on? Here's the thing. I'm fine with the lecture, I'll enjoy it. But David brought up the idea of security, not once, but several times. He was almost apologetic about it. It's going to be a big deal. I hadn't considered it up until then. It made me start to feel a bit nervous about the whole thing."

"Well, when you think about it, they have to plan it out. They couldn't afford to look bad if something happened."

"You think something's going to happen?" Sam probed, disturbed by Kenny's response.

"No, I don't. Trust me. Absolutely nothing is going to happen. The place will be packed, not only with people, but with angels and devas. I'm willing to bet some of the old rishis even show up. In fact, I'll bet a certain number of muffins on it," Kenny maintained with a serious expression and twinkling eyes.

"Really? You think I'll attract that kind of a crowd?"

"You already have. There's only one consideration," Kenny said with a big smile. "That cosmic crowd isn't going through any security check."

Both men laughed hard and then harder as they began to play with the idea of rishis going through metal detectors.

"You know," Sam noted, "if people heard us talking this way, they'd think we were crazy."

"Well, I got news for you. They already think so," Kenny affirmed, and they burst into another round of laughter.

"It's funny," Sam continued when he caught his breath, "once you become aware of the divine nature of things, you become quieter about it. Plato mentions that you're better off teaching people with stories or myths. Jesus was always spinning stories. Whitman never explained *Leaves of Grass*. He let the poems speak to whoever could understand and was thrilled when someone got it. To understand what's really happening, people have to jump into the mystery."

"And what is really happening, if I may ask?" Kenny questioned with a lift of his eyebrows.

"Well, don't tell anyone," Sam whispered conspiratorially. "Nothing, nothing is really happening, but in the meantime, there's a lot going on."

"Oh," Kenny nodded, "I'm starting to come to the same conclusion."

"Anyway, we must keep up appearances that something is happening. Otherwise, people are going to get upset."

"Like Bob?"

"Yes, like Bob, but he was already upset."

"So," said Kenny, "back to the idea of security. If nothing is happening, why be concerned about it?"

"Well, this would be a tough one to explain to my parents or my in-laws. Let's just say, when a country creates a big army, there's an excellent possibility they will use it to fight a war. That's its purpose, after all. When the army appears, so does the enemy," Sam explained.

"Then you are saying that if the college had no security plan, you'd be safer?" Kenny squinted, trying to catch Sam's meaning.

"What I'm saying is that to be truly safe, we need to transcend duality, which makes us see some people as friends and others as enemies. We need to live from unity. Barring that, I'm saying that our attention and thoughts are powerful, and we should be cautious about planting seeds that we don't want to sprout."

"But what's the plan for your lecture?" Kenny pushed.

"I have no plan. That's the plan."

"Fine, but the college will have a plan." Kenny wasn't letting go despite all the good philosophy.

"Yes, but that's up to the college. For me, there's no plan."

"What?" Kenny raised his hands in a gesture of disbelief.

"Well, as we just agreed, nothing is happening, nothing has ever happened, and nothing will ever happen. Despite that, the show must go on," Sam contended with a wink.

"You're right. But best not to bring this up when you have your big night. Yeah, I'd leave the Mad Hatter routine at home."

"It is interesting though."

"Yeah," replied Kenny, "it's interesting. I'll give you that. But I still wouldn't mention it."

"You're right. I'll leave that part out. It would be a pretty short lecture anyway." They both shook with laughter again. When they calmed down, Sam shared, "I'm pretty excited to talk on Whitman."

"Well, buddy, I'll be there in the front row cheering you on."

"You better be! Damn the torpedoes! Full speed ahead!" Sam got up and punched the air forcefully.

"Aye, captain, full speed ahead!" shouted Kenny and stood up to salute Sam.

"At ease, sailor."

Once again, those in the bakery were treated to a rolling outburst of laughter from the boss's office. Carol, the head baker, said to no one in particular, "I think they're having way too much fun in there." The gods in the heavens agreed with her. The world of duality is awash in humor, an unlimited source of good jokes and inspired antics.

Leaving the café, Sam felt at ease. He walked up to the bus stop and hopped onto the next PVTA bus home. The bus would drop him off down the road from his farmhouse. Being a frequent passenger, he knew most of the drivers on a first-name basis.

"What's happening, Sam?" asked Sally, the day's driver, as Sam settled in.

"Hi, Sally, I'm going back into public life, ever so briefly."

"Oh?"

"I've been invited back to the college to give a lecture in mid-March," Sam shared freely.

"Fantastic! I'll be there. Mind if I spread the word?"

"No, not at all," Sam responded, noting that everything was already taking off effortlessly.

"Great!"

Within fifteen minutes, Sam was at his stop and walking home. Amy greeted him at the door.

"How did it go?"

"Good. Good lunch, good conversation."

"And?" Amy drilled with arms crossed.

"The dean is still meditating, and so is his wife and daughter, who, by the way, is married and has two children."

"Really? Nice! Okay, buster, quit stalling. When's the big day?"

"Mid-March, just before spring break."

"I thought it'd be sooner."

"Well, they need time for publicity, and there's the question of security."

"Oh, that question."

"I spent some time thinking about it and had a talk with Kenny. Everything will be all right."

"If you say so, but I think we should call my dad and get his input."

"That's fine. Give me a kiss, my love. I have something to attend to in my office."

As Sam entered his office, the *Tao Te Ching* was on a small table by his reading chair. He picked it up and opened to verse forty-four, which read,

> *Fame or self: Which matters more?*
> *Self or wealth: Which is more precious?*
> *Gain or loss: Which is more painful?*
> *He who is attracted to things will suffer much.*
> *He who saves will suffer heavy loss.*
> *A contented man is never disappointed.*
> *He who knows when to stop does not find himself in trouble.*
> *He will stay safe forever.*

Sam sat in quietly, contemplating the verse. The words would be rattling around in his thoughts for the next four months.

Chapter 34:
A Promise Made

*B*ALRAM WALKED TO THE LARGE *outdoor market near the center of Allahabad to buy fresh fruits, vegetables, herbs, and spices several days each week early in the morning. Occasionally, he went in the late afternoon to make some small purchases but also to socialize. As he moved through the stalls, carefully examining the produce, he was aware that many women followed him with their eyes and welcomed his conversation and attention. A few of the braver or more forward ones flirted or teased him. Jyoti grew embarrassed by all this when she accompanied Balram, yet she also could not resist teasing him and hinted that she was curious about his romantic exploits. Balram, however, felt modest around both Devendra and Jyoti, and he usually deftly changed the subject.*

Balram was fiercely protective toward Jyoti. A beautiful woman, she sometimes drew unwanted looks or comments. Balram always made it clear that he would not stand for it. Devendra, meanwhile, remained unaware of the happenings in the market since he spent most of his days at the university and many of his evenings reading and preparing notes for the professor.

The British had built a small military barracks near the market site. For the most part, the soldiers stayed away from the residents and out of their lives. Their simple presence was enough to remind people that the British were in charge. However, the soldiers did occasionally shop at the market, and one sunny morning, a young English sergeant noticed Jyoti as she wandered through an aisle abundant with fresh fruit. Her beauty caught him by surprise.

James Lewis Davis had been raised to see India's dark-skinned people as inferior and the English presence there as a civilizing gift. Despite this strong prejudice, he found that he could not forget Jyoti. As discreetly as possible, Sergeant Davis began to ask about her among the market's vendors. They told him that she was married and he must forget about her. Instead, the sergeant became obsessed. He started to note what days and times she shopped at the market and made sure he came when she was there. He watched her from a distance and fantasized about talking with her though he didn't speak Hindi and had no idea if she spoke English. The sergeant's obsession with Jyoti was strongly opposed to his belief in English racial superiority, a pillar of his self-esteem. This left him unsure how to proceed, and he held back from approaching her. The longer the young officer held back, the hotter his inner war of clashing impulses grew.

Neither Balram nor Jyoti were aware of James Davis's attention until one of the vendors confided to Balram that a soldier had made inquiries about her. Balram began to notice the officer's evident interest. He asked Jyoti to stay away from the market for a while and let him shop on his own. Caught unawares by the request, Jyoti hesitated for a moment and then refused. She had grown attached to the market's opportunities to meet with friends, as well as its tempting offerings—from aromatic spices to jingling bracelets and vividly dyed saris.

Balram went to his brother, ensconced in his books as always, and bluntly disclosed the situation. "A British soldier has been making inquiries about Jyoti at the marketplace. His interest appears more than casual and may even be dangerous."

"What? What are you saying?" Devendra jumped up from his desk, totally taken aback.

"I am saying that a British soldier is eyeing your wife like a jackal eyes a young female deer," Balram explained angrily.

"Then Jyoti must stay home," Devendra asserted firmly.

"I've asked and she refuses."

"She won't refuse me," Devendra declared adamantly. Knocked off center by the utterly unexpected news, he took a deep breath to calm himself. He left his study and strode out through the verandah doors to look for Jyoti in the garden, all the time contemplating how best to speak with her.

"Jyoti," he called, as he stepped into the garden, "please come inside. I need to talk with you right away."

"Coming," Jyoti responded. Pulling herself out of the meditative peace she often entered while painting, Jyoti put her brushes to soak in a container of water, blew on the watercolor painting to dry it quickly, and walked gracefully toward their rooms.

When she entered their sitting room, Devendra spoke immediately. "Balram just told me that a soldier has been following you at the marketplace. I want you to avoid the market for a while."

"Yes," Jyoti replied calmly. *She could quarrel with Balram, but not her husband.* "I will do as you request."

Devendra smiled his thanks and relief and said, "I hope all this will pass and we will not have to raise the issue again."

The small circle of the house and garden, lovely as they were, felt confining to Jyoti, so after two weeks, she confided to Devendra that she missed her trips to the market. "Why should a soldier be interested in me?" she insisted. "Though he means well, I think the whole thing is a product of Balram's imagination."

Devendra reacted gently but spoke with seriousness, "Balram has much personal experience in this area. If he says that a soldier is attracted to you, he most likely is. You are so beautiful, Jyoti. I am only grateful that this has not come up before."

"My beloved husband, you are the only one I care about. I never notice anyone else's attention," Jyoti revealed with unusual emotion.

Devendra smiled, noticing more clearly than ever how lovely she was.

"Good," he smiled. "This is how it should be. Come over here so I can see you better."

Jyoti slowly, shyly walked over, and Devendra picked her up by the waist. She wrapped her legs around his hips, and they kissed gently at first, then passionately. Devendra carried Jyoti over to their bed, and they made love with such devotion that they slipped into a sense of oneness. Afterward, as they lay quietly on the bed, a sense of peace and wonderment fell upon them like a soft blanket falling gently from the sky.

The next morning, Jyoti convinced Devendra to accompany her to the market and see for himself if she was in any danger. Devendra consulted Poona, and she agreed that assessing the situation for himself might be a good idea. In the end, they decided that all three of them—Balram, Devendra, and Jyoti—would go to the market on Saturday morning. The day was cool and clear, and the market was crowded. They spent nearly two hours shopping, talking, and enjoying themselves. They drank chai and ate some sweets. On impulse, Devendra bought his wife a sparkling garnet necklace. He loved her with all his heart and felt delighted to see her light up as he placed the necklace around her neck. She laughed and chattered away like a bird through the whole morning.

As they left the market and turned up the street to head home, they came upon three British soldiers leaning against a building, Sergeant Davis among them. Balram spotted the men first and put his arm out to stop the other two. Devendra quickly looked up to see why his brother had blocked them and saw the soldiers moving toward them. Devendra took Jyoti's hand and urged, "Quickly! Let's go back to the market." They turned around and started to walk away when the soldiers broke into a run and easily overtook them. Before they knew it, the soldiers stood directly in front of them, obstructing the street that led to the market.

Devendra and Balram dropped their bags to the ground and moved to protect Jyoti. Neither man was as tall or strongly built as the well-trained soldiers before them, dressed in boots and uniforms and armed with rifles. Devendra and Balram appeared almost fragile by comparison in their white kurtas, loose pants, and sandals. The English sergeant greeted them lightly, but his dark blue eyes were tense and hostile. "Top of the day to you," he greeted them with false friendliness.

They stood very still, their faces revealing their tension. James Davis felt confused by his strong, conflicted emotions as he finally stood before Jyoti. Assuming they knew no English, the sergeant found himself expressing his frustration by degrading Jyoti and her protectors in front of his men. "No need to get nervous. I just want to get a closer look at the young woman. Thought I might buy her from you. I'll pay a good price." He and his friends snickered, thinking the "joke" had remained untranslated.

Without letting the soldiers know that he understood English, Devendra spoke in Hindi to Balram: "This jackass wants to buy Jyoti. From the smell of them, I'd say they've been drinking. I want you to take Jyoti to safety. When you see the chance to go, don't hesitate. I'll talk to these devils and try to distract them."

"But what about your safety?" Balram asked anxiously.

"I'll be fine. Please do what I ask."

"I will."

"What the devil is he saying, Sarge?" asked the husky soldier with the ruddy pink face, slurring his words a bit.

"Don't know exactly. Don't speak that gibberish now, do I?"

Devendra had become almost fluent in English over the past two years, and he began to address the soldiers cautiously. "Gentlemen, we seem to have a great misunderstanding."

"Oh blimey, Sarge, the monkey speaks the King's English," the second soldier smirked and rubbed his hands up and down his rifle to intimidate Devendra.

"That's enough, Cahill. I'll take it from here. So you speak English. How did you learn it?" the sergeant challenged.

"I'm an assistant to a professor at the university."

"Oh, are you now? Think you're the big educated man, do you?" Davis, already flushed from drinking, grew redder with irritation.

"No, I'm just an assistant."

"But you have a beautiful woman there. Do you share her with this man?" Sneering, he pointed to Balram, and he and his cohorts chortled again.

Devendra swallowed his growing anger and answered carefully, "No, we're brothers. She is my wife."

"Well, I say she's going to become my whore!" The sergeant's voice was loud now, and his eyes flashed dangerously.

Devendra was losing his control. His voice trembled, barely containing his anger. "Sir, you are drunk, and your insulting behavior will not stand. I intend to lodge a complaint with your superior."

The two soldiers laughed at Devendra, but their faces and stance reflected hostility. "We can't have that, Sarge, now can we?" the burly soldier inserted.

Balram took the opportunity to move Jyoti to his side. He noticed that people from the market place were spilling onto the street. Some of the men were whispering and pointing toward them.

Sergeant Davis addressed Devendra scornfully, "You're not going to report me for two reasons. First, no one will listen to you, and second, I'll kill you if you do and nobody will care."

Devendra weighed the threat and, thinking quickly, tried a new strategy. "I believe Colonel Adams is your superior. To your misfortune, I met him recently." In truth, he hadn't met Colonel Adams, but Professor Gupta knew him and had mentioned him to Devendra. "How do you think he will take it if I tell him that you were drunk and disorderly and insulted and threatened my wife?"

"You're bluffing," the sergeant scoffed. "I don't believe you for a minute."

"I met him only last month," Devendra maintained his story, "and you would do well to believe me. There will be consequences, I can assure you."

While Devendra and the sergeant were going back and forth, about thirty men from the market had slowly and quietly encircled the small group. The soldiers started to feel edgy.

"I see," the sergeant responded, narrowing his eyes. "He's a young man to be a colonel, wouldn't you say?"

Devendra knew the sergeant was testing him but took a chance. "Perhaps."

"You are a liar!" the sergeant shouted.

Devendra let loose. "And you, sir, are an ignorant fool!" He turned to Balram and spoke urgently, "Take Jyoti to safety! Now!"

"What about you?"

"I'll be fine. Just go!"

The number of people surrounding them had grown steadily, and the soldiers realized that they needed to shift their attention quickly from Devendra to the *restless crowd. Sensing the opportunity, Balram took Jyoti by the arm, and they fled, weaving through and past the crowd and up the street away from the impending trouble. The soldiers placed their backs together in a defensive circle and moved to release their weapons. Devendra grabbed the sergeant's arm to prevent him from drawing his pistol. With that, the men from the market surged forward, armed with rocks and clubs. Devendra and the sergeant struggled with the gun. Suddenly it went off, wounding the sergeant in the thigh. The crowd beat the other two soldiers to the ground and took their rifles. Devendra dropped the gun and looked around in horror at the chaos that had descended.*

Meanwhile, the barracks had been alerted, and twenty armed soldiers were running up the street. The men from the market dispersed almost instantly, but not before the soldiers opened fire. Two Indians were shot and killed; three others fell wounded. Devendra escaped down an alley, unable to believe what had just happened. He thought of his master and prayed, "Blessed Swamiji, I need your help as never before. Hell has just broken out all around me. Jyoti is in danger, as are Balram and myself. Please, master, help us."

Devendra ran back toward the professor's home and met Balram and Jyoti just before they reached the door.

Balram took his brother by the arm and looked at him with both sadness and fear. "Brother, we heard gunshots and screaming."

"Yes, more soldiers came. They fired into the crowd, and some people in the market have been killed," Devendra disclosed, trying to catch his breath.

"What about the soldiers who accosted us?" Balram questioned.

"Dead or wounded, I don't know. Quickly now, we must go inside."

Jyoti started weeping softly; she knew everything was about to change, and she was afraid.

"Come, Jyoti," Devendra said gently, taking her hand. "Everything will be fine. The professor will know what to do."

Hearing their voices, Dr. Gupta, who had been anxiously awaiting their arrival, came to the front door. He had heard the gunshots and screaming from his study. When he saw them on the porch, he felt relieved, although the relief proved fleeting.

"What happened?" the professor probed, looking at each of them for an answer.

Devendra spoke, "Sir, please, let's go inside, and I'll tell you."

The four of them headed for the sitting room, where Poona quickly joined them. For the next ten minutes, Devendra explained their interaction with the three intoxicated British soldiers and the street battle that followed. The professor posed a few questions for clarification, but for the most part, he let Devendra give his account.

Afterward, he sat silently for a few minutes. Then, both sad and serious, he spoke, "My friends, this is a serious affair. The British have informants whom I'm sure they are interviewing as we speak. They will thoroughly investigate what just happened, and the path will lead them directly to you."

"Good," commented Devendra, "then they will know we are innocent."

"No, they will not come to that conclusion," Professor Gupta observed quietly.

"What about the fabled British code of laws?"

"Devendra, they don't apply to you or your brother. You are Indian and not British. Three soldiers have been wounded or killed by a mob, and you'll be seen as the ring leader."

"I was defending my wife, and I never instigated the crowd's anger!" he protested.

"And you had every right to do what you did. Nevertheless, the British will come after you. Therefore, Balram and you must pack a few things and escape from the city. I'd say you have less than an hour. Poona, you and your daughter must also leave. The British will surely want to arrest and question Jyoti. Pack a few things, and I'll take you to the train station myself. I'll give you enough money to get back to the safety of the master's village."

"Balram and I will also go back," Devendra jumped in.

"Sadly, my friend, that is not possible. Balram and you must head north into the mountains until this all quiets down."

"How long will it take before things quiet down?"

"A year or two if we're lucky. I will do what I can to make sure that the authorities know what actually happened, but they will hunt for you anyway."

"A year or two?" Devendra shot back, astonished.

"Yes, at least."

"The British will find out that you are from Swamiji's village and that your wife is there. The master and the raja will use their influence to keep Jyoti and Poona safe, but they cannot protect you and your brother. If you choose to go, they will use informants to tell them when you get to the village and then send soldiers to arrest you. No, safety lies for you in the north, in the Himalayas. I know some people who will smuggle you out of the city at dusk. You must get ready to meet them. They will take you to Rishikesh, a village in the Valley of the Saints. There you will be among friends, for many know the master. Take a few minutes with

your wife. Poona, gather some things for the trip. Balram, pack some food and clothing. Everyone, get ready so you can all fly to safety," advised the professor.

"Indrajit!" the professor summoned his gardener, who came running.

"Good man, take these rupees and find Rudra and his son. Tell them I'm sending two friends who must leave town tonight and not be seen by anyone. They must take the travelers as far as Rishikesh. Ask Rudra to bring me a letter from Devendra confirming their safe arrival. When he returns with the letter, I'll give him five silver coins.

"Go quickly, and when you return, if anyone comes asking questions, tell them I'm away and will be back in two hours." The professor looked at his loyal gardener and said, *"Thank you, my friend. Once again, you are a man I can trust. I shall not forget your friendship and loyalty."*

Devendra and Jyoti walked out into the courtyard. Jyoti wept openly. Devendra took her in his arms and held her closely. He spoke softly but clearly from the depths of his heart. *"Beloved Jyoti, I don't know how this will end, but I want you to know that I love you with all my heart. These last two years have been the happiest of my life."*

"My dear husband, my time with you has been sweet, almost beyond imagining, but now I feel so ashamed. I am full of regret and guilt. This is all my fault. I was so stubborn and selfish. I should never have insisted on going to the market. It seemed like a small thing, but it has changed all our lives forever."

"Gentle Jyoti, this is not your fault. Your desire to visit the market was innocent. You cannot possibly be responsible for what happened. The devils disguised as British soldiers envied our happiness and wanted to destroy it. Surely this injustice will not stand. Everything will work out. Most importantly, you and your mother will be safe with the master."

"And what about you, wandering the Himalayas?"

"Balram will be with me. We'll be safe."

"You'll come back to me?"

"Yes, I promise you before God. I will find you wherever you are, no matter how long it takes."

"You promise that you will hold me in your arms again? You promise before God?"

"Yes, I swear it. Even if it takes a lifetime or more, I'll find you."

They kissed and held each other until the professor called out, *"We must fly!"*

Devendra and Jyoti strode swiftly back into the house. Professor Gupta gave Devendra a leather pouch full of rupees and a small purse with silver coins that was easy to conceal.

"*Trust Rudra, but don't trust him. Keep the silver hidden from him or he will kill you while you sleep. He's a good man to a point, but a smuggler after all. He's tough and dislikes the British, and he will get you to Rishikesh. God made all types of men for just these occasions. I will take the women to the train station and see them onto the train. At dusk, go to the western gate dressed like the poor pilgrim you are about to become. Take nothing that indicates that you are educated and literate. Rudra will look for you. Wear this yellow shawl as a sign to him, and have Balram wear this red one. Rudra and I have a prearranged understanding. You're not the first person Rudra has smuggled out of the city at my request. Indrajit has gone ahead of you to tell Rudra or one of his people to be on the lookout for you. He'll tell you what to do and how to find the caravan. Follow the instructions precisely. He'll stow you both in some secret compartments in his wagon that he will cover with barrels of cooking oil tied into place. When you are far enough outside the city, the wagon will stop and you can come out of hiding.*

"*Once you are beyond the outskirts of the city and the sun has set, you should be fine. One more thing, don't speak English during this journey, and don't talk with the others in Rudra's company. Now, one last warning," the professor spoke sternly. "If the British catch you, you'll be dead by morning." The professor paused and took a breath. Now he expressed in a soft, somber voice, "Devendra, you have been a son to me these past two years. I will miss you and pray for you. Why this has happened will become clearer in time. Now, I must go." The professor hugged Devendra briefly, which was very unlike him, then hastened toward the door.*

"*Thank you. I'm so sorry for all the trouble. I'm forever in your debt," Devendra called after him.*

The professor paused in his steps and turned back toward Devendra. "Nonsense! You are not at all in my debt. It's the damn British, not you, that are the cause of these problems. Someday they will leave India with their tails between their legs. Someday they will leave India to India. Godspeed." The professor turned toward the door again and left the room.

Balram looked at his brother and saw the pain and uncertainty in his face. "Devendra, you will see her again. We'll manage this and all will be well, with the grace of God and Swamiji."

"*I hope you're right, brother," was all Devendra could muster.*

Colonel Adams visited Sergeant Davis at the barracks infirmary three days after the incident. Davis was resting in a cot, his thigh heavily bandaged. His face, normally reddened from the hot Indian sun, looked pale from loss of blood, but the doctors assured the colonel that as long as the wound did not become infected or gangrenous, the sergeant would be up in two weeks and ready for duty in three months.

"Sergeant Davis, are you resting comfortably?" the colonel asked politely but stiffly.

"Yes, sir. Thank you, sir," replied the sergeant, surprised and pleased by the colonel's visit. Perhaps the colonel saw him as a hero.

The well-polished colonel remained standing, tapping his baton on his open hand. He turned his sharp blue eyes directly toward the patient. "Well, you won't be after my visit. What a bloody mess you made! We had three days of rioting over this incident. What a bloody mess!"

"But, sir, my men and I were ambushed," Davis sputtered in shock.

"So you say, but we know that's not the whole story. Our official investigation interviewed numerous witnesses, all of whom say that you and your men were drunk and that you harassed and insulted a man, his wife, and his brother. In fact, everyone agrees that you threatened them." The colonel paced back and forth in front of the bed then declared angrily, "Frankly, you behaved despicably. You're a shame to your uniform."

"Well, sir, I did have a drink. However, I was doing my duty and investigating possible agitators against the Crown," the sergeant protested rather meekly.

"I see. An interesting statement that is fully at odds with everyone else's. Just what in God's name gave you the impression that they were agitators? Nothing! Nothing! How dare you lie to me?" the colonel fumed. "Every witness contends that you had been stalking the Indian woman for some time, even though you were repeatedly informed that she was married. Then you insult the woman and her husband and actually ask to buy her? You must have been mad, man!

"Unfortunately for you and your men, an Englishwoman witnessed the whole incident, and she happens be related to a prominent government man in Delhi. Several respectable Indian merchants told the same story, as did the university professor who employed the man and his brother. I'm well acquainted with him. He is first cousin to the raja. You can't lie your way out of this one, Davis. You disgust me!"

Davis was stunned. He lay quietly in his hospital bed, trying to shield himself from the colonel's outrage.

The colonel stopped pacing and pressed on. "Look at me, sergeant. Don't dare look away. Now I'll tell you what's going to happen next. You will be stripped of your rank, court-martialed, and cashiered. You will likely serve a prison sentence that includes hard labor, but that will be determined at your hearing. Whatever *happens, know that five Indians are dead and six wounded because of your drunken, immoral, irresponsible behavior."*

"What about the brothers?" the defeated Davis asked, wanting assurance that they would share the pain. "What happens to them? After all, one shot me, and they both fled like the criminals they are."

"It's none of your damn business, Davis." The colonel returned sharply, almost pounding his baton on his palm. "You ruined their lives as well as yours. Just be grateful we don't hang you as we might have to if we find them." The colonel briskly turned around and left the room.

Davis simmered in fear and anger, hating the Indian man who shot him and his whore of a woman who had led him on and driven him half-crazy. That the military would blame him for this was absurd, disgraceful, and un-British!

Davis was court-martialed and dismissed from the British service but pardoned from serving hard labor. He returned penniless to civilian life in England, with a large black mark on his record and nothing to show for his years in India but pain and disgrace. His heart hardened with anger and resentment. He plotted his revenge as he slowly drank himself to death.

Devendra and Balram disappeared into the Himalayas. The British abandoned their pursuit in less than a year, hoping the populace would forget the incident as well.

Many months passed. Devendra was heart broken with all that had happened, and his separation from Jyoti was too much to bear. Balram did his best to buoy his brother's lagging spirits, but to Devendra's mind, his situation seemed impossible with no way out. In his despair, his body grew weak, and in the cold of the mountains, he became ill. Balram took care him with steadfast devotion, but he didn't have the healing life-giving herbs he knew his brother needed. After five days and nights of fever and chills, Devendra—intent on Jyoti and the life he had just lost—passed away quietly, leaving Balram beside himself with grief and rage.

Balram's grief almost did him in as well, but his anger at all that had transpired kept him alive. He was determined to see Jyoti and his master again. So three months after Devendra's passing, Balram made the long journey south from the mountains he now despised. The monsoons forced him to seek shelter and hold up until they passed. Many people along the way were kind to him and offered him shelter and food. After nearly six months, he arrived at the outskirts of the village. Balram had aged and was greatly weakened by the loss of his brother. That weight was almost too much to bear, and as he approached the village, he dreaded having to tell Jyoti the news. The thought of it stopped him in his tracks, and he decided to find a cool place to sit and rest. He saw a banyan tree with its mammoth trunk and sturdy limbs and knew it would be a safe place to close his eyes and sleep.

Balram found a comfortable nook between two massive roots and the trunk of the tree. He sat down and quickly fell asleep. When he awoke, there was an old man with long graying hair and an even longer beard, dressed only in a loincloth, sitting in front of him, gazing at him with compassion and concern. Balram sat up a little and said, "Namaste."

The old man bowed his head and returned the greeting.

"I can see that you have journeyed far and have suffered much," said the old man in a kindly tone.

"Yes, I have," Balram mumbled quietly.

"Suffering is a mirage. It is something that exists only in the mind. That may not be of much comfort now."

"You're right. I can take no comfort in those words. If you knew all that has happened, you might not be so quick to say such things, old man," Balram said with an unusual lack of respect.

"I do know all that has happened, from your flight from Allahabad to the loss of your brother."

Balram was so startled by what was said he thought he was dreaming.

"You are dreaming. The whole world is dreaming." Balram sat up a little straighter, realizing he was in the presence of a holy man.

"My name is Aditi. I have been wandering in this world for hundreds of years. My friend, life is forever going forward. Your life, your brother's life, and your sister-in-law's life will go forward as well. God never deserts his devotees. In the midst of all of your emotions, remember the truth. Your brother's soul is Divine and Eternal as is yours, as is everyone's." Aditi looked deeply into Balram's eyes. "Your desire to be with your brother and his desire to be with you and Jyoti will be fulfilled. Now, dear friend, I must be going." The old man stood up in one fluid movement. "Namaste," he said as he bowed to Balram, and he silently walked away.

Balram sat in wonderment for a moment before he remembered Jyoti. He quickly got to his feet. He felt stronger and lighter. He walked briskly for nearly another half hour until he reached the village. He knew he'd find Jyoti at the school, and he made his way slowly but steadily to the small stone and plaster building. Jyoti looked out the window and saw a beggar walking toward the school. She looked more closely, and something in the man's gait seemed familiar. As she studied the man for a few moments more, she realized it was Balram. Without thinking, she ran out the door to meet him in the dusty street. As she embraced him with great happiness, she looked into Balram's weather-beaten face and his eyes. From the deep sadness she found there, Jyoti realized that Devendra had passed away. Her happiness abruptly fled, and overwhelming shock and despair flooded in. Grabbing on to Balram, she sank to her knees, dragging him with her. Jyoti was beside herself with grief. Balram sobbed and kept whispering into her ear, "Sister, it will all be all right. We will all be together again." Jyoti clung to Balram as a drowning person clings to anything floating while lost at sea.

Meanwhile, all the children had filed out of the one-room schoolhouse. Confused and saddened, they formed a protective circle around their teacher and the strange man and witnessed their despair.

Maharishi opened his eyes and marveled at Nature's infinite organizing power. *Nothing remains undone*, he thought, *down to the last detail.* Witnessing the joy of the reunion of these two souls now called Sam and Amy, Maharishi laughed softly and whispered to himself, "Jai Guru Dev."

Chapter 35:
The Activity of the World

ED SANDERS RECEIVED NEWS OF his son-in-law's willingness to lecture at Amherst College with surprise and delight. He had frequently urged Sam to capitalize on his name and fame, arguing, "Sam, you have the world's attention. If you don't yet feel comfortable getting out in front of people and lecturing, then write another book. Jack Abrams figures, conservatively, that your next book would sell half a million copies. Think what that would mean in terms of financial security for Amy and the kids."

Sam had responded with equal frequency, "It's not happening. I don't have anything new to say, and I'm never going to put a book out just for the sake of selling half a million copies. Somewhere down the road, I may write another book, but not now. Please let it go, Ed."

"I'm only thinking about your interests and the welfare of my daughter and grandchildren. I trust you know that," Ed inevitably yielded, more than a little deflated.

"I hope you don't believe what you just said—the security of your daughter?" Sam would counter indignantly.

"Sorry, Sam. Lawyer training. I get it, really. When you're ready, you're ready."

Thus the conversations went, both parties withdrawing into their own thoughts at that point.

When Amy called to tell her dad about Sam's invitation to lecture at Amherst, Ed Sanders enjoyed a moment of relief and inner triumph. The long period of Sam's mourning or healing or whatever he had been doing appeared to be ending. He expressed his happiness enthusiastically to Amy and then, after only seconds, automatically switched from father to lawyer.

"Amy, I need to call Jack Abrams in New York, and I need to call the college. Who do I speak to there?"

"Dad, don't get ahead of yourself, or Sam for that matter," Amy insisted.

"Fine, but who do I talk to at Amherst?" he demanded as if Amy hadn't spoken.

"If you must," said Amy, "start with Dean Griffin."

"All right. Do you think Sam will do some interviews? We have a guy at the *Times* who would jump at the opportunity." Ed was already in high gear.

"I don't know, Dad. We haven't gotten that far. We just found out. I was just calling to share the news. I also wanted to tell you that the college is working up a security plan along with the local police department. Would you be willing to take a look at it?"

"Oh, I'm sorry. Of course, Sam's safety comes first. Yes, I'll review it." Ed thought for a moment and added, "We might want to hire a private service as well."

"I don't know if Sam will agree to that," Amy stated with some force.

Ed continued, virtually ignoring his daughter's input. "Amy, what if Angel wasn't on that tour you took? No, an extra person or two is not asking too much. We don't know what kind of person this event will attract."

"Dad, whatever you do, you'll need Sam's approval, and it has to be low-key," Amy emphasized. "We don't need guys with sunglasses and Uzis. It's a college campus after all."

"I understand your concern. I'll make some inquires and keep you both in the loop," he agreed, considering this a generous concession. "You and Sam have final approval, I promise. Okay?"

"Okay, Dad. Just keep us informed at every step and before you sign any contracts. We appreciate your excitement and support, but please remember that this is Sam's life and mine. Don't go overboard," Amy stated firmly, knowing that her father had no concept of her definition of overboard.

"I promise," Ed confirmed, his mind already ten steps ahead.

"Okay then," she replied a little dubiously. "Love to Mom. Bye, Dad."

"Love you too, honey. Bye."

As they hung up, Amy wondered how Sam would take all this. She knew he valued simplicity, and Ed's promotional energies could get seriously out of hand.

Ed Sanders had worked hard his whole life, and he hated to see missed opportunities or unexpressed talent. He was the kind of man who could have ninety-nine wheels spinning and feel greatly distressed if the hundredth sat idle. Despite his conversation with his daughter, he immediately began to ponder how to get the most traction out of the new turn of events. *Maybe we can do Harvard, Yale, and Princeton,* he thought. *Maybe Sam will write that next book after all. That would be terrific.* He picked up the phone to call Jack Abrams, Sam's publisher in New York. For Ed, this was such an obvious thing to do that he never considered consulting Sam first.

Busy as he was, Jack Abrams took Ed Sanders' call immediately. He had worked with Sam enough to recognize that the man had something special, something beyond being a talented writer and teacher. Despite his youth, Sam was inspiring and inspired. He was one of the few people Jack had met in his long career in the world of media and publishing who was authentic. Jack had been waiting for Sam to discover his next step for some years and much more patiently than Ed. He was curious to see what developments Ed wanted to discuss.

Jack picked up the phone, and the two men exchanged brief, polite greetings. Then Ed jumped directly to the point, "Listen, I'm calling with good news."

"I'm all ears, Ed."

"Sam's accepted an invitation to speak at Amherst College. This could be the start of the next big step."

"Wonderful! You have my attention. Tell me more." Jack's gray eyes lit up, and he sat straight in his swivel chair.

"Now I don't want to overwhelm Sam. You remember he's not big on promotion. In fact, he doesn't know that I'm calling you, but I thought we could put our heads together and get the word out. If it's a fait accompli, he's more likely to go along with it. So how about that guy at the *Times?* Think we can get a piece into the Sunday magazine?"

"I think it's an excellent possibility." Jack turned his chair around and gazed through his office window over the bustling streets of New York. His imagination was full on. "I'm also thinking about *60 Minutes.*"

"Really? You think that's possible?"

"Anything is possible, Ed. I learned that from Sam. Listen, Morley Safer owes me a lunch. I'll call him. You know Sam is still a best-selling author with an international audience, and his life makes one great story: he studies with the Maharishi and teaches meditation, a crackpot fundamentalist shoots him in a Midwest Barnes & Noble, he drops off the world stage for nine years, and now he's suddenly reemerging. What more could a journalist ask for?

Not to mention that Sam is handsome, charismatic, and has a wonderful young family. This makes the story even more compelling. It's the boomer's generation of the new American apple pie. I honestly think *60 Minutes* will go for it." Jack Abrams paused and took a deep breath. "But the question is, will Sam?"

"He will if he has any sense," Ed responded impatiently, "but I don't always understand how his mind works. To tell you the truth, I'm not sure even Amy does. However, I'll ask and get back to you."

Ed hesitated before hanging up the phone and checked, "It would be a friendly interview?"

"That's what I would expect, but it's *60 Minutes*, and no one can guarantee the content. I'm sure they'll try to challenge him, but nothing Sam can't handle. He's not some sleazy politician after all, and the people over at *60 Minutes* were sympathetic about his shooting as I remember."

"All right, but I hope they'll go easy on the far-right Christian angle. We heard from many, many Christians who were horrified by the shooting, including the shooter's minister," Ed pointed out. "That might be a good thing to mention.

"One more thing. If we go forward, I need to review the contract to make sure there is no ambush," Ed demanded in an aggressive tone of voice.

Taken aback by Ed's forcefulness, Jack reminded him calmly, "You know how much I respect you and Sam. I have always looked after Sam's best interests, and rest assured I will continue to do so. Of course, you can review any contract involved. My legal team and their counterparts in whatever companies we engage with will draw up the contracts. You can look them over and negotiate any necessary changes with the legal teams before anyone signs anything." Jack stopped, waiting for any rebuttal from Ed. There was none.

"But we're getting ahead of ourselves. Let me pitch the idea to Morley and I'll get back to you. Don't start the clock yet, Ed," Jack advised, chuckling.

"He's my son-in-law," Ed countered, a little offended.

"Oh, in that case, you should double the rate!" Jack laughed.

"You know, I anticipate a new book from this, which is another reason I contacted you."

"I was wondering about that from the moment you called. That's one exciting possibility, and we'll do whatever we can to support it," Jack reacted with sincere joy.

"Thanks, Jack. Let's talk again very soon. And hey, we want that piece in the *Times*!" Ed was too energized to end the conversation.

"I'm on it. Take it easy. This is only the first phone call. We're just getting started. By the way, when's the big day?"

"In mid-March."

Jack flipped the pages on his desk calendar. "Let's see. That's a little less than four months away. I'll get the engines running right away." If Ed could have seen Jack's eyes, he would have recognized that his fertile mind was already alive with ideas.

Satisfied for the moment, they said their good-byes, hung up, and began moving in their own directions. Ed Sanders found himself daydreaming for a minute or two. *If Jack Abrams can get Sam on 60 Minutes, I'll take back every bad thought I've ever had about the guy. I wonder if Mary and I could be worked into the interview. We could take the family angle. There could be footage of the boys playing with the dog, maybe Mary and me sitting on the porch of the farmhouse. Our friends would be green with envy. Who ever thought that my son-in-law would be on 60 Minutes?* Ed sat down and briefly relished his fantasy.

Snapping back, he consulted with his company's media relations expert for about ten minutes. Next, he phoned David Griffin. When the dean's assistant put Ed through, the dean greeted him warmly. After the introductory exchange, Ed informed Dean Griffin that he was acting as Sam's legal counsel and wanted to go over the security plan among other things.

No one had warned the dean that Sam's father-in-law would be directly involved in the lecture, and the news unsettled him a bit. Nevertheless, he tried to be helpful. "Our campus police will be working with the Amherst PD on that. You can certainly review the plan, and we'll welcome your input."

"Thank you," Ed replied. "We may want to hire some private security as well."

"Well, why don't we let the college's team work on the plan, and if you feel we need something more, we can discuss it then. Anything else?"

"We'd like to sell Sam's book *Consciousness* at the lecture and keep the proceeds," Ed claimed though he did not have Sam's knowledge or approval.

"We propose buying Sam's book at the wholesale price through the bookstore and selling the book to help cover the extra security cost."

"Let's put it down for future discussion," suggested Ed, knowing he was on thin ice without Sam's consent. Then he batted another ball into the park.

"We want the recording rights, both audio and video, to belong exclusively to Sam and his publisher."

"The college usually records such lectures and makes them available in the library for the students and the faculty," the dean returned, beginning to lose patience.

"We can arrange to furnish the library with several copies, but we'd like our own team to record the lecture and keep exclusive distribution rights." Ed couldn't let it go.

Clearly offended, David Griffin spoke firmly, "May I remind you that this will be an academic presentation at a college, a seat of higher learning, and not a concert at the Boston Garden? I suggest you write up what you want, and I'll discuss it with our legal department. Does Sam know about these conditions?"

"No," Ed admitted. "Sam is so easygoing. He needs people to watch out for his well-being. By the way, we're working on an interview with *60 Minutes*. Any objection to their filming on campus if they choose to?"

"You are making this into a circus. *60 Minutes?* We'll discuss it."

"Could be great publicity for the college," Ed pushed.

"Please, just put all your requests in writing so we can consider them thoroughly. Anything else?" inquired the dean, anxious to end the obtrusive conversation.

"No, that's it for now."

"Good day then."

"Good day."

"Interesting, interesting," David Griffin said to himself after hanging up, "*60 Minutes.*"

Ed Sanders called his wife at home. "Mary, you won't believe this, but Jack Abrams thinks he can get Sam on *60 Minutes.*"

"Really?"

"Yes. He seemed confident. He knows Morley Safer personally and is going to lunch with him to pitch the idea. Isn't it great?"

"I don't know," Mary expressed thoughtfully. "Sam and Amy have been so happy away from the limelight all these years. And there's the boys' safety to consider. I don't think they'll go for it."

Surprised at her lack of support, Ed contended, "This could give Sam a big career boost."

"He left his career behind in Minneapolis."

"I understand that, but he's decided to speak at Amherst in March, and *60 Minutes* is going to want to be there."

"Well, maybe if we could get Ed Bradley. But I don't know, darling. When are you coming home?"

"I could be home by three. Call Amy and ask if we can come for dinner. I'll raise the idea with Sam while we visit."

"Okay. You can discuss the idea but, Ed, dear, try to be tactful. You don't want to push Sam so hard that he retreats back into his lovely home," Mary advised her husband.

"Yes, but I'll have a better chance of convincing him in person than over the phone. I wish sometimes he was just a little more normal. A normal person would jump at this chance," Ed lamented.

"But, darling, if Sam was normal, *60 Minutes* wouldn't be interested in him, would they? He wouldn't have met Maharishi, written a book, or been shot. No, dear, the world is interested in Sam because Sam is not normal. He's extraordinary. And I suspect that after you've been shot at close range, normal is out the window altogether anyway."

"I see your point, but do you see mine?" Ed pressed.

"No, not at all, frankly. It's not one of your better arguments, dear," Mary maintained.

"All right, I'll drop it. See you at three. Would you pack me an overnight bag?"

"Of course. Bye."

Mary hung up and dialed Amy. "Amy, darling," she greeted her daughter, "it's Mother."

"Hi, Mom."

"Hi, sweetheart. How is everything?"

"Well, now that you've called, I'm a bit concerned since Dad called too, not more than an hour ago."

"Dad and I would like to come out and have dinner with you tonight. Will that be okay?"

"Now I'm really getting concerned."

"Now you know how your father is. You won't be surprised if I tell you that he's all fired up over Sam's lecture at the college. He wants to discuss some ideas on how to promote it."

"I don't like the sound of that, and Sam's going to like it even less. I asked Dad not to go overboard," Amy declared, obviously irritated.

"Your father has some good ideas, and it would be nice if you would both keep an open mind about them. People pay a lot of money to talk to him," Mary reminded her daughter.

"Honestly, I never understood that."

"That's not kind. Your father is an excellent lawyer."

"Fine, Mom. Come to dinner. Can you be here around six o'clock and we'll eat at six-thirty?"

"Could we stay over? We'd leave first thing in the morning. Would that be too much of an imposition?"

"No, that's fine. See you at six?"

"Yes. Thank you, darling. Bye for now."

Sam was in his study, and Amy walked down the hall to tell him the news.

"Mom and Dad are coming for dinner."

"Really? Seems pretty spontaneous for them. What's happening?"

"I told my parents that you accepted the invitation to speak at the college. Evidently, Dad's charged up about it and wants to be involved in promoting it," Amy divulged, carefully monitoring Sam's face for his response.

"It's a pretty low-key event," Sam said with a shrug, "and the college will promote it within the Five College area. I imagine it will draw a few profs and students from Mount Holyoke, Hampshire, Smith, and UMass. Besides, the hall's not that big."

"Well, honey, you know Dad. He's thinking big. He's the guy who made partner at age forty as we know all too well."

"Oh, God, not the 'made partner at age forty' routine again," Sam groaned. "I have a sinking feeling I'm in trouble here."

"Just hear him out, okay? His intentions are good, even if he sees the world through very different lenses than we do. Just listen politely and don't dismiss his ideas right away." Amy was almost begging Sam to be patient with her father and keep the peace.

"All right, I'll do my best. You know I called Jimmy and Lilly and told them. They said, 'Great. If that's what you want to do, then we're happy.' That's it. Simple."

"Well, fine and dandy, but your father is not my father. On the positive side, Dad did negotiate a good book deal for you."

"Yes, and he made partner at age forty," Sam teased.

"Exactly. They're arriving at six, and dinner is at six-thirty."

"Got it."

Ed and Mary arrived right on time. The November evening air was crisp, and a bright half-moon lit up the sky. Paul and Josh heard them pull up and ran out the front door, excited to see their grandparents—no surprise since Ed and Mary were smitten with them.

"Hey, Grandpa! Hey, Grandma!" the boys shouted and stood by the car, waiting for hugs. Rufus, ever present, pranced around the car, tail wagging.

By now, Sam and Amy were in the entryway and welcomed them in. There were more hugs all around, and the family migrated toward the living room. After making sure her parents were comfortably settled on the plump couch and had drinks in their hands, Amy announced that dinner would be ready shortly and exited to the kitchen.

"Great! I'm starving," proclaimed Ed. "What's for dinner?"

"Acorn squash from the garden, tofu steaks, whole wheat rolls, parsley potatoes, and steamed broccoli—and peach cobbler for dessert," Sam informed his father-in-law.

"Sounds really healthy as usual," Ed commented politely, but with an edge of sarcasm. Then he turned toward Sam. "Amy called me about the lecture at Amherst. Congratulations! How did the invitation come about?"

"I met a few students in town, and one thing led to another," Sam explained vaguely, clearly not eager to share the details.

"Oh, what thing led to what thing?" Ed probed.

"Dad taught them how to meditate," offered Josh.

"Really!" replied Ed, his face reflecting surprise.

"Yeah, and they liked it so much, they started a petition and circulated it around campus and got hundreds of signatures," added Paul.

"Yeah," continued Josh, "and they took it to the dean. The dean took it to the president, and they decided to invite Dad. Right, Dad?"

"Yes, that's about right, boys," Sam replied, laughing.

"This is marvelous, Sam," Mary said with genuine sincerity.

"I think it's wonderful also. Who knows where this will lead?" Ed ventured.

"I don't think it's leading anywhere," Sam reacted sharply. "It's just one night."

"Well, Sam, honestly, I think there's an opportunity here. We could get you back on the circuit. Yale, Harvard, and Princeton for starters would want you. Maybe you'll even find yourself motivated to write the next book," Ed pressed on.

"Ed, let's talk after dinner. Boys, grab your grandparents' bags and take them to the guest room. I'm going to check and see if Amy needs some help," Sam informed them. "Why don't you relax after your drive? How about something to drink? Tea? Coffee?"

"A cup of tea would be fine," Ed replied.

"Water is fine for me, dear," answered Mary.

After Sam served the drinks and left the room, Mary told her husband frankly, "I think you need to do a better job in warming him up, or there's no Ed Bradley in our future."

"I know. I was just testing the waters." Ed frowned and then complained, "I'd love to come out here just once and be served a good steak."

"Better let go of that. It's never going to happen." Mary smiled maternally at her husband.

"All right, let's relax for a moment and then go eat our tofu steaks," Ed replied gloomily.

Paul, Josh, Amy, and Mary chatted throughout the meal. The two men were attentive but quiet. Ed was thinking about how stubborn Sam was and that he should have gotten back in the saddle a long time ago. *Who takes nine years off at a time when they should be building a career?* Sam was thinking that Ed would take over their lives if he let him; maybe they should have moved to New Zealand.

The peach cobbler was served warm with a scoop of vanilla ice cream. Everyone savored every bite. Paul and Josh giggled as they licked their plates clean then helped Amy clear the table.

"Okay, boys, off to your homework. Grandma and I will finish up," Amy addressed her sons then turned to her husband. "Sam, why don't you and Dad go talk in the study?"

"Okay. Ed, would you like some tea?" Sam asked pleasantly.

"Anything stronger? Cognac maybe?" Ed requested hopefully, feeling a need to bolster himself for the conversation to come.

"Well, I do keep a little apricot brandy around for my father's visits. Will that do?"

"That would do fine. Thanks," Ed smiled.

"All right, just give me a minute and I'll join you in the study."

Ed strolled down the hall, entered the softly lit room, and lowered himself into the well-worn small couch across from Sam's desk. He was surrounded on two sides with floor-to-ceiling books while over Sam's desk hung framed letters from John and Yoko, George Harrison, and Norman Mailer. Ed shook his head in disbelief. Who gets letters from icons and then lives like a hermit?

Sam came in with two glasses of brandy and handed one to Ed. He brought his chair from behind the desk so that Ed and he could talk without a desk between them.

"I love your study, Sam," Ed reflected, looking around. "There's great peace here." Ed sat quietly for a moment, sipping his brandy and allowing his eyes to take in the impressive contents of the walls and bookshelves. Finally, he came back to his central intent and began. "By the way, did you keep all the other letters you received? That was quite a list as I recall: Ted Kennedy, Donovan, that guy from Aerosmith. Could be important for your biography some day."

Sam remained silent and expressionless.

"I'm so glad you've decided to get out into the public realm again. You have so much to offer."

"Thanks. It will be interesting for me," Sam answered noncommittally.

"Right. Hey, I took the liberty of calling Jack Abrams to tell him the news. He was quite excited. Got a little carried away," Ed disclosed cautiously.

"Really? How so?"

"Well, you know Jack. He thought he could get a story on you in the *Times*."

"Knowing Jack, that seems rather tame," Sam observed.

"Yes, well that was just for starters. He also brought up the idea of a spot on *60 Minutes*."

"*60 Minutes?*" Sam looked startled.

"He's having lunch with Morley Safer, and he said he'd bring it up."

"You told him it was out of the question, right? I'd never subject myself and my family to that kind of intrusion," Sam protested, dangerously close to anger.

"Honestly, I thought it was a good idea," Ed confessed.

"Oh, Ed!" Sam crossed his arms defensively, and his eyes knit in concern and frustration.

"Hear me out. The world is interested in you. You wrote a book on philosophy, and against all odds, it became a best seller. Large numbers of people learned about philosophy, who would never have done so otherwise. People learned TM, and that was good. You've got letters on the wall from two of the Beatles and Norman Mailer for God's sake! You dropped out after the shooting, and people want to know what happened to you. *60 Minutes* is a perfect forum for letting them know. It could be inspiring. You could talk about the book you're writing."

"I'm not writing a book," Sam shot back.

"But you might, and that show would be great publicity. With that kind of exposure, your book would sell half a million in hardback easily. More importantly, you'd be back in the game." Having pleaded his case, Ed leaned back on the couch and waited.

"I know you have trouble understanding this, but I don't want to be back in the game. That's not the direction I want."

"But why not?" Animated, Ed sat forward again, his face suffused with excitement. He held his ground, unwilling to take no for an answer. "You have a lot to offer the world. You're an original thinker, and the world doesn't have many of those. If you wrote a new book and gave lectures, you could have a powerful influence on people everywhere."

"Maybe that's not what I want to do," Sam countered, fending off Ed's energy.

"Like it or not, Sam, people listen to you. You have a gift. I suspect you were born with it, and sooner or later, you will have to share it."

Sam stayed quiet, arms still folded across his chest, surprised by his father-in-law's vision of his potential and his willingness to reveal it. It stirred something inside, something that had been coming up since that first conversation with Julian at the White Oak. As Sam quietly reflected, Ed continued.

"It's true, Sam. You have a gift, and it's a terrible thing to waste a gift. Besides, what would Maharishi do?" Ed played that card before he even knew he had done it.

"He'd most definitely take the interview."

"So there you go."

"Ed, I'm not Maharishi," Sam declared strongly. "Maharishi has a clear mission to spread his knowledge far and wide. It's the engine that drives his life. I have no such sense of mission."

"But you're one of his teachers. Don't you share the same mission?"

"Yes and no. I can only do what I know is right in any given moment, and I don't think that *60 Minutes* is the right thing to do at this point."

"So you might consider it at a later time?"

"I don't know for sure, but maybe."

"What if we could get Ed Bradley to interview you? I think you two could have great chemistry together," Ed asked hopefully, holding on to any thread of possibility.

Sam chuckled. "Yeah, maybe we would."

"Okay, we'll put it on the back burner for now," Ed finally conceded but quickly moved on to his next project. "Now what about this new book?"

"Well, I am thinking about writing a book on Walt Whitman," Sam disclosed with a teasing grin.

"What does Whitman have to do with anything?" Ed looked frustrated.

"A lot in fact. If transcending is to take hold here in America, we need some Americans we can look to who experienced transcending and were transformed by the experience. Whitman is just such a man. Part of my talk at Amherst will focus on him."

"Then that's perfect, Sam. I read a little Whitman in college, but I never really understood him."

"You're not alone. He was writing from an enlightened consciousness, and that's been overlooked by nearly everyone." Sam relaxed now that the conversation was back on his own turf.

"I knew you had it in you." Ed's voice carried a flavor of victory. "By the way, I spoke to Dean Griffin today."

"Oh?"

"I told him we want the recording rights to the lecture you're going to give," he conveyed bluntly.

"Why do we want the recording rights?" Sam solicited patiently.

"Because of intellectual copyrights which guarantee that the profits from this go to you, if there are any."

Sam sighed. "I'm not doing it for the money," Sam explained as if he was talking to a child.

"I know. That's why I'm here to take care of that aspect. I'll also be reviewing the security plan and maybe hiring a private firm," Ed informed Sam.

"I appreciate your interest in helping, but really, this is a low-key affair, and I don't want it turned into a Broadway production."

"I'm your father-in-law and your lawyer. I'll handle this, and you think about your lecture and that book," Ed contested strongly.

Sam was learning again what Amy had learned countless times over the years. Ed Sanders tended to hear only one voice: his own. "Listen, I think it's a little early to be worrying about intellectual copyrights," Sam maintained, trying to insert his viewpoint one more time.

"No, it isn't too early," Ed declared with certainty. "Your original ideas on Whitman could be the basis of the new book. We need to protect those ideas so no one else uses them in their book. Your next book will likely make a lot of money because your name is already established. So it isn't too early." Ed paused for a second then admitted, "I have some people at the firm working on it already."

"Ed," Sam protested, "I have to tell you that I find all of this very discouraging, draining even. It takes the joy out of the whole event for me. I flourish in simplicity. I live from inspiration, not calculation. I'm not interested in making things so complicated, no matter what the financial repercussions are."

"I'm sorry, but this is the world we live in," Ed pronounced with conviction.

"You must understand. I don't live in that world."

"You're wrong, you do live in it. You have a family and a house to maintain. College expenses for the boys will be coming up before you know it." Ed's mind held no room for argument.

"Some things you understand, and some things you don't," Sam observed a little sadly.

"All right, for argument sake, let's say you don't live in the same world that I do, but Amy, Paul, and Josh do. I understand that you don't like complications. All I'm asking is that you let me take care of the complications and you do what you do best."

Sam sighed, wanting to end what he saw as a go-nowhere conversation as soon as possible. "Look, I want final approval on everything. If I disagree with a proposal, you will drop it without argument. Agreed?"

"Agreed." Feeling triumphant, Ed tried to hide his smile.

"Listen, I appreciate your good intentions," Sam added.

"I love what I do, and I'm happy to do it for you. And for whatever it might mean to you, I'm proud of you."

"Thanks. Nice of you to express that." Sam had had enough. The conversation made him feel tired. "I'm going to check on the boys and Amy now." He stood up, shook Ed's hand, and escaped from the study.

Both men went back to their worlds, both seeking more expansion, more fulfillment in their own ways. Ed sought to manifest his vision of life in more activity, drama, and creative and profitable ventures while Sam sought more stillness, awareness, inner freedom, and inspiration. Both men were doing exactly what God intended.

Chapter 36:
The Holidays

IT WAS A WHITE CHRISTMAS, six inches of fine, light snow having gently fallen on Christmas Eve. The snow clung to the green boughs of the tall pine and hemlock trees, outlining their beauty. The still cold of the morning gave way to warmth and activity inside the O'Connors' home. The boys awoke early since they were in charge of sorting out the colorfully wrapped presents. Boxes of all shapes and sizes encircled a seven-foot evergreen sparkling with tinsel, lights, and angels with wings and trumpets. Paul and Josh, in thick socks and red flannel pajamas, piled the presents in four groups then dashed upstairs to wake up their parents.

"Merry Christmas, Dad and Mom!" the boys shouted as they burst into the room.

Sam and Amy sat up in bed, sleepy but smiling, and returned the greeting. "Give us a few minutes and we'll be down," Sam told them.

"Okay, we'll put the tea kettle on."

Sam and Amy heard them run down the hall and bound down the stairs. "Wow! Did we have that kind of energy when we were their ages?" Sam wondered out loud.

"I'm sure we did," Amy answered, "but it's getting harder all the time to remember what that feels like."

"All right then, we better try to keep up. By the way, Merry Christmas, honey." Sam kissed Amy on the cheek.

"And Merry Christmas to you, Sam." Amy returned the kiss and spoke, smiling gently, "You know I don't want to get all sentimental, but I'm thrilled to see you happy, I mean really happy, these past few months."

"Well, my darling, I'm glad I could accommodate you. I guess it's the ebb and flow of all things. I appreciate your being so patient with me. You must be an angel."

"It wasn't always easy to watch you go through what you did, but thank you for the acknowledgement. Anyway, I'm just glad the joy came around again. The angel part, I'm not too sure about."

"Well, it's difficult to see oneself, and from where I'm standing, you look like an angel." Sam kissed Amy. "Amy, darling, it takes a lifetime to live a life with the ups and downs included. I wonder how anyone can get through it all. Maharishi said once, 'The best blessing of the Creator is the ability of humans to forget.' I guess that's why we can all get through it. We just forget." Sam stirred to sit up in bed. "Now, however, the ritual of Christmas morning awaits, and we best get going."

"Yes, can't keep the munchkins waiting for too long." Another kiss and out of bed they climbed.

The O'Connors settled down around the tree near their respective pile of gifts. Paul, being the youngest, opened the first present; Josh opened the second, followed by Amy and then Sam. This pattern continued until all the wrappings and ribbons were undone, the boxes opened, and their contents fully appreciated, with a flurry of oohs and ahs and thanks given and received. Even Rufus, the dog, received a toy and a fresh marrow-filled bone from the butcher, which he worked on, grinding his teeth for the remainder of the day.

When the living room was awash with wrapping paper and empty boxes, Josh and Paul withdrew to their bedrooms to explore in private their new books, video and music tapes, pajamas, shirts, and board games. Sam and Amy went upstairs, took showers, dressed, and meditated. Refreshed, they went down to the kitchen, where they would spend most of the day, and started cooking breakfast. Amy worked on the fresh fruit salad while Sam mixed pancake batter and mashed overripe bananas, adding them to the mix. The grill, blackened along the edges, was placed on the stove top, neatly covering two burners. Sam greased it with ghee that Amy had made the day before and lit the burners. Amy heated the maple syrup collected from the maple trees surrounding the farmhouse the previous March. She squeezed fresh orange juice, poured coffee for Sam, and made tea for herself. She called the boys, who once again sprinted down the hall at top speed, jumped down three stairs at a time, and slid into their chairs. Breakfast was alive with laughter, silliness, and family jokes, and hearty appetites were fully satisfied.

All of the grandparents, Susan, Kenny, and his new girlfriend, Mona, came in the afternoon to share in the evening meal. Jimmy and Lilly always brought a Christmas ham—Virginia baked, of course. Ed and Mary always brought a small, twelve-pound baked turkey with ample gravy. Sam and Amy prepared the mashed potatoes, the sweet potato casserole with a melted marshmallow topping, broccoli au gratin, fresh cranberry sauce, bread stuffing, whole wheat dinner rolls, green beans, and a mixed-green salad. Kenny brought napoleons and cheesecakes for dessert; Sam made more coffee to accompany them. By the time they finished dessert, everyone was beyond stuffed. As they put down their forks, there was a pause in the conversation, and the company of celebrants viewed the table's empty bowls, plates, and glasses with a hearty sense of fulfillment. Another Christmas dinner vanquished.

Jimmy and Lilly usually stayed three nights. This Christmas they were pondering retirement and thought of moving up to live next to Sam and Amy. They agreed to meet with a builder who was an old friend of Sam's. They loved the idea of leaving the city and living next to their grandchildren, but they were also concerned it might be too quiet for them to sleep. They also worried about adapting to a slower pace of life. This amused Sam, who had long ago learned to relish the silent nights, barring the summer's hoards of chirping crickets, and enjoy the fresh air and spacious countryside. To help relieve one of their concerns, Sam and Amy bought them two small sound machines. When plugged in, the machines produced white noise—a soft, soothing background sound that masked the deep silence of the night.

On Christmas night, Jimmy and Lillian climbed into bed, said their prayers, kissed each other good night, turned off the light, and switched on their sound machines. They went right to sleep and slept like babies through the night. Jimmy didn't even get up to use the bathroom in the middle of the night—not once. He generally made two regular trips to the bathroom every night. In the morning, he awoke feeling chipper and refreshed.

He remarked at breakfast, "You know, I haven't slept this well in ages. I didn't even get up once to use the john. When was the last time that happened, Lil? Maybe a hundred years ago?"

Lillian responded, "At least a hundred, if not more."

"You see, I had no idea that this thing, you know that noise machine, could help to shrink a guy's prostate," exclaimed Jimmy.

Lillian gasped. "Mother Mary of God, James, that's a heck of thing to be talking about at the breakfast table and in front of the boys. You should be ashamed!"

"Yeah, Dad," chimed in Susan. "You should be ashamed," she echoed, shaking her head from side to side.

"Now, now, Susan, don't you worry about nothing, honey," Jimmy assured her, patting her on the hand. Then he turned to Lil. "There you go again. The heart, the liver, the prostate—they are all the same, woman. Parts of God's design, not mine, and the boys should know what they'll be up against as they get older."

"For mercy's sake, James Patrick, they're only eleven and twelve. What do they want to know about the problems of an older fella for?"

"I'm interested," volunteered Josh.

"I'm not, if it's disgusting and involves blood," Paul commented.

Amy, listening patiently, finally said, "Dad, let's do this discussion later, unless we can also discuss our monthly cycles."

"Oh, Mom," said Josh and Paul with faces of exaggerated disgust.

"Oh, heaven forbid, no! Let's not get into that. That's private and should be kept so. All I was trying to say was that I slept well," Jimmy corrected himself.

"And for that we're grateful, Dad," concluded Sam.

For New Year's Day, the O'Connors had a standing invite in Concord for a party hosted by Ed and Mary. Sam felt reluctant to go. He had managed to avoid the event for five years running after the shooting. After that, he conceded, but only after Amy threatened him with dire consequences if he continued to stay home. Therefore, on New Year's Eve, all four O'Connors dressed a bit more formally than usual. Sam put on newer jeans and his newly opened beige cotton crew sweater. Amy made him leave his work boots at home and put on a pair of shoes she had picked out for him. The boys both wore corduroy pants and new checked flannel shirts. Josh's shirt was a cranberry check, and Paul's new shirt was an evergreen check. Amy put on a new, delicate floral-print dress that hung below the knee with her mid-calf leather boots. She decided to wear the pink shawl that Sam had given her for Christmas. There were a few minutes of high-energy chaos with the boys running to and fro between their rooms and the waiting minivan for forgotten items before the O'Connors finally got under way for Concord.

It was cold and gray, but there was no traffic, which is always a relief to a former New Yorker. They arrived ahead of the other guests so they could help with last-minute details. Ed and Mary were happy to see them, especially Josh and Paul.

"Come in, come in. Welcome!" Ed greeted them merrily and ushered them in. Sam noticed Ed's penny loafers, argyle socks, pressed gray slacks, white dress shirt open at the collar, and tailored navy blue blazer and felt momentarily conscious of the jeans he was wearing. He casually looked down at his new shoes and felt better. Ed, meantime, noticed Sam's attire and thought, *Good Lord, will I ever live to see this man dressed for any event besides raising a barn.* He failed to notice Sam's new shoes.

"Happy New Year!" announced Josh and Paul, almost in unison.

"Happy New Year, boys! And to you too," Ed proclaimed, addressing Amy and Sam.

"Happy New Year, Dad," returned Amy, giving Ed a warm hug.

"Happy New Year, Dad," offered Sam and shook Ed's hand vigorously.

"And a great New Year it's going to be!" Ed replied, winking at Sam. "Thanks for coming out, Sam. It's good to have you here."

Mary emerged from the kitchen, wearing an apron over a classically styled black cocktail dress. "Oh, boys, I'm so happy you're here," she exclaimed, pulling the boys into her soft, grandmotherly embrace. "So happy you're here too," she told Amy and Sam as she released the boys.

"Happy to be here," Sam spoke politely, not really sure if he meant it.

Amy looked at Sam and caught his tone. "It's wonderful for all of us to be here, Mom," Amy spoke emphatically and hugged her mother.

Mary hooked her arm into her daughter's and led her toward the kitchen. As they walked, she confided, "Your father is all hyped about Sam's lecture. It's driving me a bit crazy."

"Well, Mom, Sam has a theory that people are always doing exactly what they want, irrespective of what it looks like. Knowing Dad, he's thoroughly enjoying himself. "

"No question he's having a good time. I'm talking about myself."

"I thought you'd be used to Dad in overdrive after all these years. Isn't he this way about everything?"

"We'll talk about it later," Mary ended the brief discussion and then asked, "Does Sam really believe that? How would he explain all those poor starving people in India? Do they really want to starve?"

"He does believe it, but those kinds of details may be tough to explain. When you have an hour or two, why don't you ask him?" laughed Amy.

"Maybe sometime, but not right now with his lecture coming up," Mary replied vaguely. Arm in arm, they entered the kitchen.

"It wouldn't be a bother. I'm sure Sam would welcome the question," Amy urged.

"Well, not today. Too much to do, and I want to celebrate the New Year. Can you believe it's 1987? My, my, time is flying by."

When the women left the front hall, the boys scampered into the den with a video of *Star Wars* in hand contributed by their grandfather. Ed and Sam carried the family's coats to a spare bedroom upstairs. When they were by themselves, Ed disclosed, "A writer from *The New York Times Magazine* will be up in a few weeks to interview you. His name is Justin Waterhouse. He did an article on you after Minneapolis. It was a good article, very fair and supportive of you and your work. He'll be bringing a photographer, who'll want to take some photos of you, Amy, the kids, the farmhouse, the college, and so on."

"No pictures of Josh and Paul. None!" Sam spoke forcefully.

"It's a family story," Ed pressed.

"No, Ed. That's an absolute no."

"Okay, I understand. No pictures of the boys. I'll make that clear. Anyway, they'll be staying at the Lord Jeffrey Inn. Justin wants to talk with a few students. What's that kid's name? You know, the one that got this started?"

"Julian. Julian Driscoll."

"That's right. Anyway, he'll want to interview him, maybe the dean, a few faculty members, maybe a few folks in town, like Kenny. Sound okay?"

"Yeah, sounds fine," Sam concurred, feeling otherwise.

"Good. Later, in March, they'll come back and attend your lecture, and then he'll write the article. If all goes well, it should be in print by mid-April. How's the book coming, by the way?"

"I'm still thinking about it," Sam conveyed abruptly.

"Oh well, that's good. Got to start somewhere, and thinking is a good place to start." Ed wanted to ease the obvious tension between his son-in-law and him, but this was not his field of expertise. He just kept pushing instead. "How about the lecture?" asked Ed.

"I'm working on it," replied Sam curtly.

"Oh, excellent. Look, this guy's going to write an outstanding piece, and when your next book comes out, the publicity will give it a tremendous boost. Now, that's a good thing, isn't it?"

"Yeah, sure. It's fine, Ed," Sam contributed without enthusiasm. "I just want to leave Josh and Paul out of it."

"I understand, Sam, no pictures. Is it all right if they're mentioned in the article?"

"It's okay. I'm sorry to come across a bit uptight on this issue."

"Nothing to apologize for, Sam. They're my grandsons as well. I don't want them in harm's way, not that I think they'd be in any danger whatsoever."

"I'm sure it will be fine. So who's coming to the party?" asked Sam, trying to switch gears.

"Some of the people Mary works with from the Historical Society, a few partners and juniors from the firm, a number of neighbors, and a young professor and his wife from India."

"Really? Where is he teaching?" Sam inquired eagerly. "You never mentioned him before."

"That's because I don't know him well. He and his family just moved in around the corner in August. He's at Tufts, I believe. Teaches political science. He's around your age and has three children, two girls and a boy. Mary wanted to invite them, and I thought it was a great idea. We knew you and Amy would be pleased to meet them." Ed was hoping for approval and got it.

"Thank you, Ed. That was very considerate," Sam acknowledged.

"You're welcome. You see, I'm not that bad a guy, contrary to how it seems at times."

"For the record, I never thought of you as a bad guy—a little aggressive maybe, but not a bad guy."

"Coming from my son-in-law, I'll take that as a compliment. But just to clear the record, what you call aggressive, I call assertive, and it comes in handy in my line of work."

"I'll take the aggressive-assertive part under consideration, but yes, it's a compliment. You've been very helpful to the family and me over the years. I hope you realize I'm grateful," Sam conveyed.

"I've tried to be helpful. This may surprise you, but people pay me big bucks for my advice," Ed added as if to convince himself. Then he finally moved on. "Listen to me going on. There's a party about to happen."

"Yeah, we better get down there," Sam said, relieved, and they went downstairs.

The guests began arriving, and within a half hour, twelve couples had made their way up the front walkway and porch stairs and through the thick oak front door. Once inside, Sam was in charge of their coats, and Ed was in charge of their drinks. Mary and Amy laid out the dining room table with scores of hors d'oeuvres—from stuffed mushrooms to shrimp cocktails to mini-wieners. Josh and Paul, for all their mostly vegetarian upbringing, loved those little hot dogs.

The Indian couple arrived with their children, which surprised Ed. "Happy New Year to all of you," he welcomed them.

"And to you, my friend. Thank you for inviting us to the festivities," Professor Gupta shared warmly. The professor had thick brown hair and warm large brown eyes and sported a well-trimmed goatee. "Let me introduce you to my wife, Rita, my elder daughter, Ramani, my younger daughter, Neela, and my son, Vijay. Children, this is Mr. Sanders, our host." The children all smiled shyly, a bit awed by the grand house and their presence at an adult gathering. The children were dressed like typical Western kids.

"Nice to meet you, children. Let's go down the hall to the kitchen"—Ed pointed the way—"where you can say hello to Mrs. Sanders." The Gupta family followed Ed to the kitchen, where they exchanged cheerful New Year greetings with Mary. Ed turned to the children. "My grandsons, Josh and Paul, are here. They're in the den watching *Star Wars*, and I bet they'd be happy for you to join them. How does that sound?" he suggested.

The children looked smilingly at their parents for approval. When they nodded positively, the three broke into even bigger smiles and scampered off in the direction of the den.

Ed continued, "I want you both to meet my daughter, Amy, and my son-in-law, Sam."

"We are looking forward to meeting them," Professor Gupta replied. "From what you told us on the phone, we have much in common."

"I'm sure you do. Come with me and we'll look for them."

They made their way to the spacious living room, brightly lit by a large crystal chandelier hanging in the center of the room. Holding drinks and hors d'oeuvres in their hands, the guests were chatting animatedly; some were standing and some were sitting on the thickly cushioned couch and chairs. Sam and Amy stood in front of the fireplace, enjoying the fire dancing on the logs and talking with the next-door neighbors, Jim and Sally Borden.

"Allow me to interrupt," said Ed, "and introduce you to Dr. and Mrs. Gupta from India." After polite greetings, Ed skillfully led the Bordens away to join in on another conversation, leaving the Guptas and O'Connors together.

Sam and Amy noticed how refined this striking Indian couple was. The professor was tall and slender, wearing a white turtleneck sweater and dark trousers. His wife wore a graceful emerald green silk dress with matching shoes. Her dark hair was lustrous and long. She was adorned in a gold necklace, matching bracelet, and ruby ring on her right hand and a wedding band on her left. Amy suddenly felt underdressed in her calico dress, shawl, and boots. Sam jumped in, smiling warmly. "So nice to meet you both. Where in India are you from?"

"Allahabad. We're both from Allahabad. Do you know where it is?" Hari Gupta inquired.

"I know it's on the Ganges River and near the site of the Kumbha Mela," Sam returned.

"Very good! Most Americans have no idea," the professor laughed. "As a whole, Americans are not big on world geography. However, my wife and I have an interest in India."

"Yes, we heard. Mary told us you are both with Maharishiji. We are also meditators."

"TM? You do TM?" Sam asked, astonished.

"Yes. My grandfather knew Maharishi's master, Guru Dev, and Maharishiji has stayed at our ancestral home. He initiated us when I was nineteen and Rita was seventeen. Our marriage had been arranged a few years earlier, and we married two years after our initiation. I continued my studies, as did Rita, and received my PhD at twenty-six."

"And I became an MD at twenty-seven," inserted Rita. "Maharishiji encouraged both of us to study."

"That's incredible!" Amy said.

"Which part, Amy?" Sam asked, amazed by what he had just heard. "The Guru Dev part, the Maharishi part, or the PhD-MD part?"

"All of it," Amy declared. "And you live just around the corner?" Amy checked.

"Yes, I'm afraid so," Rita said. "It's a friendly town but difficult to know the neighbors."

"It takes time. I'll introduce you to the Unitarian Universalist minister, Bob McCall. That community is going to love you," Amy assured them. "But please, tell us more about your family."

The professor began. "You see, my great grandfather was the last raja in a long line of rajas in the area near Allahabad. My great-great-uncle was a professor at Allahabad University and began teaching there just a few years after the university was founded in 1892. I'm following in his footsteps. He taught philosophy, but in his heart, he was a political scientist. He worked, in his own way, for the liberation of India from the British," Professor Gupta explained with clear pride.

"I hope you won't find this intrusive, Sam, but I feel as if I already know you," the professor continued hesitantly. "I was aware of your shooting and prayed for your recovery. I had read your book and felt somehow close to you as a fellow professor and meditator. Rita and I arranged a month-long Vedic ceremony, a *yagya*, for your swift and safe recovery."

"Well, thank you. I'm honored you would do such a thing for me," Sam observed quietly, obviously moved.

"You're quite welcome, I'm sure."

Amy asked Rita to go into the kitchen where they could talk more comfortably, away from the noise in the living room. Sam likewise invited Dr. Gupta to go into the library to talk.

"I'm fascinated that you were initiated by Maharishi and that your family had ties with Guru Dev," Sam remarked.

"Well, for us, the fascination is that Maharishiji has become so popular in the West, particularly in America. The teaching is universal, as you know, but his ability to help people of so many diverse cultures accept this has been remarkable.

"He first came to stay with us in 1957. Even then, he was bright, blissful, and optimistic. He had been teaching meditation in different parts of India and noted that everywhere he went, people benefited quickly. This was so for everyone who learned, educated or not, and irrespective of religion or caste. Everyone transcended effortlessly. Looking back now, I can see that the foundation was being laid for everything that followed."

"Do you feel that he is your personal guru?" Sam asked respectfully.

"Yes, of course. He is my personal guru, but he is also a world teacher. He has the capacity to be both, which is very unusual—even by guru standards." The professor chuckled. "When Guru Dev passed, Maharishiji spent two years in silence. In my opinion Maharishiji became like Guru Dev in that he radiated bliss and silence. What struck me was his great happiness, but also his knowledge and insight into the Vedas was tremendous. He really is a great rishi."

"Well, I heard once," Sam added, "that a reporter asked Maharishi what some of Guru Dev's greatest accomplishments were. Maharishi apparently replied, 'He made me.' Now I'm beginning to understand that statement."

"The transformation that Maharishiji experienced was the fruit of his total devotion to Guru Dev," Dr. Gupta observed then changed the focus of the conversation. "I understand from your father-in-law that you are coming out of retirement and speaking at Amherst College."

"Yes," Sam confirmed. "I'll be speaking in March. Ed is a promoter at heart," Sam said with a sigh.

"Everyone needs a little promotion now and then." The professor laughed. "Rita and I would very much like to attend the lecture."

"Really? That's very kind of you."

"Nothing to do with kindness. I'm genuinely interested in what you have to say. After all, almost nine years of virtual silence must have gestated something profound in a man such as yourself. Am I right to make that assumption?"

"God only knows. I think it will be at least interesting, but significant I can't guarantee. At any rate, I'd be delighted to arrange VIP seating for you and your wife and would be truly honored to have you both there."

"The honor will be all ours."

In the kitchen, Amy told Rita how beautiful her dress was. Rita confessed to maybe being overdressed. "Hari encouraged me to wear this dress. He likes it." Amy shared that in Western Massachusetts, where they lived, people generally dressed very casually.

"It was a bit of a struggle to get Sam to wear his new shoes rather than his work boots," Amy explained.

Both women shared a laugh. "Husbands can be worse than the children. They're very stubborn about certain things," Rita acknowledged. Amy nodded in agreement, thinking, *You don't know the half of it when it comes to Sam.* Amy and Rita then moved to sharing their experiences with Maharishi. Rita eventually mentioned Sam's upcoming lecture. "Hari and I are both thrilled to learn that your husband will be coming out of retirement to speak at Amherst in March." Rita paused then plunged ahead. "I hope you don't mind my asking, but as a wife, I wondered if you were nervous about Sam's safety? We were so concerned when we heard about the shooting. Hari and I went straight to the temple and prayed to Ganesh."

"Thank you for your prayers," Amy said sincerely. "Sam is not concerned about security, and the college is putting together a security plan for the evening. To tell you the truth, nothing much ever happens in Amherst. I'm not worried," Amy affirmed. "Well, maybe a little," she owned up.

"Maybe a little concern is prudent in this case. But I think all will go well," Rita spoke reassuringly. "Maharishiji will know about the lecture, and I expect that he will have his complete attention on Sam that evening. Under the master's umbrella, Sam will be safe. I'm certain of it," Rita proclaimed convincingly.

"I don't doubt Maharishi, and I hope you're right," said Amy softly, betraying her apprehension.

Later, as the O'Connors drove home along Route 2 in silence, the clouds were breaking up and the moon was almost full, its soft light illuminating the landscape. The boys were sleeping in the backseat. Sam said, "You know, we should plan a trip to India someday."

"Yes, we should," replied Amy. "We would both love it."

"Yeah, who knows what we might find?" Sam murmured.

"You mean like inner peace and enlightenment?" Amy was grinning.

"Yeah, well no. We can find that here. The richness of the culture, the incredible temples, the Vedic knowledge and ceremonies would be enough for me. Well," Sam daydreamed out loud, "I suppose you can always throw in a few holy men and wandering sadhus for effect." They both giggled.

"Maybe when the boys are older, we can go."

"Yeah, when they're older," Sam said, trailing off into silence.

Chapter 37:
The Divine Artist and the Lover of Art

THE HOLIDAY AND JANUARY TERM break had come and gone. Julian arrived back in Amherst a day ahead of Katy and two days ahead of classes. On impulse he decided to ring Sam. On the third ring, Sam picked up.

"Hi, Sam, it's Julian. I just got back into town."

"Nice to hear from you, Jules. How's everything?"

"Good. Great even. Hey, are you busy this afternoon? I thought maybe we could meet at the White Oak."

"Sounds good. I haven't been out of the house in days. Does one o'clock work?"

"Fine for me."

"Good. We can have a little lunch. All right, see you then. Thanks for calling."

"Oh, sure. Looking forward to it. Thanks, Sam."

"Bye for now."

"Bye," answered Julian. He sat for a moment just thrilled to be able to connect with Sam and be treated as a friend. He decided to head over to campus, work at the library for a couple of hours, and then move on to the White Oak.

Sam walked through the familiar door at the café, leaving the cold behind. The extra warmth of the ovens hit him first, followed by the smells of coffee and baked bread.

"Kenny around?" he asked Rachel, who was dressed in jeans and a long-sleeved T-shirt with a green apron over the top. She was youthful, bright, and pretty.

"No, Sam, he's gone to the bank and had a few other errands to run."

"Okay. I'm meeting Julian, and we're here for the tomato basil soup with the accompanying slices of peasant bread and butter and a chunk of cheddar. Coffee afterwards."

"Okay, Sam, I'll get it started. Am I putting this on your tab?" she said with a smile.

"Why not? While the cat's away, the mice all play," Sam replied with wink.

The café was quiet for the lunch hour, but then it took a few days when the students came back from the winter break before they started heading into town in earnest. Sam selected a table in the back. He hung up his coat and wool cap on one of the wooden pegs just as Julian rounded the corner into the dining room. Sam turned to greet him, and the two hugged with affection, happy to see one another.

"I just ordered the peasant lunch for two. Rachel's getting it ready, followed by coffee. Sound good?"

"Yeah, definitely."

"Good to see you. How were the holidays?"

"Fine. Let's see, went to Jersey to see my folks and younger brother. Then I made the trek to Putney, Vermont, to see Katy and her family. Next to Boston to see some friends there, and here I am. And yours?"

"Well, it gets a bit hectic with Josh and Paul all pumped up for Christmas. Then my folks and sister came up for Christmas dinner and stayed for a few days. Amy's parents came out for Christmas dinner as well. And Kenny and his new girlfriend, Mona, joined us for dinner and wandered back a few times over the holiday week, and some other friends came over for a holiday party, and finally we made the trip to Concord for Amy's parents' New Year's Eve party. And then it's over. I'm grateful for it all and especially happy when it's over. Then we can collectively turn inward to hibernate for the rest of the winter."

Rachel called Sam and Julian up to the counter to pick up their order. "Thanks, Rachel," Sam said.

"You're welcome. I'll bring your coffee over in a bit?"

"Perfect. Julian, how about a couple of blueberry muffins with the coffee?" Sam asked, turning to Julian.

"Sure, why break up a perfect record," Julian replied with a smile.

Sam nodded in agreement.

"No problem," responded Rachel.

"Thanks, Rachel," Julian added, noticing how especially beautiful Rachel looked. *So many fish in the sea*, he thought as he carried his soup, bread, and cheese back to the table.

The soup was delicious and warming. Sam loved dunking his buttered bread into the soup and sopping it up.

"So," Julian ventured, "where does God come into all of this?"

"My, you like big subjects. Hmm, God. Well, Maharishi talks about two aspects of God. One, unmanifest, omnipresent, infinite, and the other in a personal manifested form, He or She, Almighty Father, Divine Mother, and it goes from there. The manifested form of God has one foot in the Absolute level and the other in the finest relative level of creation. There He or She resides. All, by the way, is in *Science of Being*.

"This whole notion of God is the crux of the mystery we're all grappling with. Yet there are a thousand paths up the mountain. So one of the many possible approaches is coming to terms with the awe and grandeur of the creation. Here we are, born into a beautiful world, a blue pearl of a world in an infinitely expanding universe, filled with an infinite variety of life-forms on an incredible number of levels. It turns out, no matter which way you go, microscopically or macroscopically, you end up in infinity. What cosmic awareness comes up with that? God? From the Vedic standpoint, the creation is born from the level of pure, infinite awareness or, as a physicist might say, the unified field. It's so incredible, it's beyond our comprehension. We're left in awe, bafflement, and admiration. Sometimes I stand on my back porch at night with all the lights out and look up at the stars and the Milky Way, and I think, we're living on a small planet, floating in space, as a part of a galaxy that can't be measured in any meaningful way, in a universe made up of thousands of galaxies. This level of expansion is indeed mind-boggling."

"So are you saying God is beyond our comprehension and all we can do is contemplate God with no means to reach him?"

"Julian, this is a subject that men and women of much higher status than I have struggled with for thousands of years. I have no expertise here. I was just commenting on the incredible expanse of the creation and hadn't even gotten to the Creator as such." Sam paused. "There's a little verse from Saint John of the Cross entitled *The Sum of Perfection* that may help us get out of the corner we've painted ourselves in since knowing God in the sense of knowing *XYZ* may not be possible. So here it is:

Remember the Creator,
Forget the creation,
Study the Life within
And reach Love's summation.

"So we're probably going to have to leave our intellects at the door on this subject and go with our heart's knowingness instead," Sam proposed.

"Okay, I agree. This is more a matter of the heart than the head."

"Good. Maharishi has repeatedly stated that Transcendental Meditation is not a religion in any sense of the word. But he continued, that doesn't mean we're not fond of God. So from the Vedic perspective, Maharishi tells a delightful little story that can help us in reaching God. It goes something like this:

"There was a man who went to an art gallery every day. Without fail, the man arrived in the morning and walked through the gallery, studying and enjoying the magnificent paintings hanging on the walls. He left quietly just before closing time only to be back the next morning. Weeks went by, and the man's appreciation of the subtlety of the paintings, along with the mastery of each brush stroke, the palette of colors, shading, and use of light was astounding. The artist working in a back room studio started to become aware of the man's presence and appreciation. Occasionally, he looked around the half-opened door and saw the man. A few more weeks went by, and the artist was aware of the man going from room to room and the delight his paintings were giving. Then he left the door of his studio a little more open so he might get a better glimpse of the man.

"This went on for another few weeks. Finally one day, the artist felt he just had to meet this admirer, and he strode out of his studio into the gallery and introduced himself and shook the man's hand. Both the master artist and the man who so deeply appreciated the creations of the master were very happy to be meeting. It was a cause of celebration, and a certain unity was struck between them.

"Like that, as a person meditates and grows naturally in awareness, he or she begins to see more and more beauty in the world around them. As they begin to experience more subtle states of inner awareness, they grow in their perception so that the more refined levels of the creation can be perceived. The more refined the perception, the more joy experienced by the perceiver. Finally, the growth of perception reaches the finest level of creation where a golden light emanates from every object. The joy has now become bliss.

God, like the artist, becomes aware of this person who so deeply appreciates his creation and who is in fact experiencing waves of bliss with every new perception. This stirs God's heart, and he comes to shake hands with the devotee. The cosmic meeting is so joyous that the devotee's heart merges with God and the two become One.

"Love is what brings us home, Jules. But until our heart can stir tidal waves of love, becoming One with God remains an abstract goal. Here's something I like from the *The Cloud of Unknowing*:

> *All rational beings possess two facilities: the power of knowing and the power of loving. To the first, to the intellect, God who made them is forever unknowable, but to the second, to love, He is completely knowable.*

"This theme of love is a common thread amongst all of the world's religions. And to love is very natural for people. Yet this divine love, which has the power to create unity with God, is beyond mere human emotions. It comes from another level. All humans can access and develop that level. That ability is baked into the cake. Whether people decide to do that is another matter. Like transcending, the development of the heart is very natural. But it is something that needs to be cultivated. A small puddle cannot rise up in tidal waves, only an ocean can do that."

Julian sat, quietly absorbing Sam's description. He was looking at Sam and thinking, *I can't believe I met this guy on a bus.*

Rachel arrived with coffee mugs and muffins.

"Oh, Rachel, just in time to rescue us mere mortals from flying too close to the sun," Sam joked.

"Anything you say, Sam," she remarked, knowing Sam and her boss, Kenny, to be cryptic and untranslatable.

"So, Julian, let's have a sip and a dip and get back to earth."

"Thanks," Julian replied, adding sugar and cream, stirring his coffee, and taking a first long sip.

"While you were describing all of that Sam, I could feel my awareness really expanding."

"Yeah, contemplating God and infinity can do that. It's very humbling. Puts one's life in perspective. We're all like ants on an elephant's arse," Sam casually commented, breaking the muffin in two and dunking half of it in his coffee.

"It's a good story, the artist and art lover."

"You should have seen Maharishi tell it. Very beautiful. I've done it little justice in comparison. So, Julian, I'm working on my lecture for the college community as well as outlining a book I want to write. We might have to skip a few Fridays, okay?"

"Sure. That's exciting, Sam. A new book?"

"I decided to do the book on Walt Whitman. Or it's decided to be written. Anyway, it's in the works. But please not a word to anyone."

"All right, mum's the word."

"Thanks."

Kenny came in with his winter parka zipped and buttoned up tight. He stomped his booted feet a couple of times. Rachel said hi and told him Sam and Julian were there.

Oh, the two Irish American intellectuals are here, Kenny thought as he rounded the corner.

"Kenny, my friend, companion, and mystic," Sam nearly shouted as he saw Kenny.

Julian turned around in his chair to see Kenny walking toward them.

"Well, boys, how are things? Cold enough for you?" Kenny asked with a smile.

"Nice and warm in here."

"Yeah, feels good in here," Julian agreed.

"So what's the topic of today's discussion? Still into suffering?"

"No, Kenny, we've moved on to God."

"God?" Kenny shook his head slowly. He looked at Sam as he sat smiling and then at Julian.

Julian offered weakly, "Yeah, God. You got to start somewhere."

"You can't talk about God. Of course, you can talk about anything you want as long as you understand that talking about God is pretty futile."

Julian, finding a little more conviction, replied, "Everyone talks about God, Kenny."

"They sure do, and I can tell you talk is cheap."

Sam saw where this was going. "Kenny, dear brother, what would philosophers and theologians do if we couldn't talk about God? Are you trying to put us out of work?"

"It depends on how you define *work*. Work is an activity that is productive in nature. Talking about God is never productive. Better to experience God. Once you do, there's nothing to talk about."

With that, Kenny abruptly turned around out of the dining area, around the corner, and into the kitchen. Sam and Julian watched him go.

"You know, Jules, Kenny makes a good point."

"But, Sam, as a teacher, you know these things have to be talked about."

"True. But there comes a time when talking is over and experience must begin. We're back to the idea of knowledge and experience. Both are necessary for enlightenment."

"That's becoming pretty clear, Sam. But Kenny just seems so extreme. He told me he's only read three books. The only books worth reading are the Bhagavad Gita that Maharishi translated and commented on, *The Science of Being and Art of Living*, and the Lord of the Rings trilogy."

"Well, I know he likes those books, but he's also into Jack Kerouac, Gary Snyder, and Allan Watts amongst others."

"Really? Then why would he tell me he only reads those books? And then he told me to forget all about Kant and Descartes."

Sam started laughing. "You know, Kenny and I shared an apartment for years. Whatever I was studying he read. He particularly disliked Kant and Descartes. Who knows for sure what he was after, but he was trying to make a point that you have to start at the beginning. Maharishi has put transcending and experiencing pure consciousness back on the map. One time early on, someone at a lecture was introducing Maharishi. This very intelligent man was saying something to the effect that as a teaching organization, we don't need books, we don't need buildings. Transcendental Meditation gives any man or woman the direct experience of the fourth state of consciousness, pure consciousness. Books can't do that. Buildings don't matter.

"Maharishi sat listening and turned to the man and said, 'Maybe we could use one or two books, maybe a few buildings here and there,' and started to laugh. So shortly after that, it was arranged that Maharishi have some time to write *The Science of Being and Art of Living*. Which he didn't actually write. Rather, he dictated the book into various tape recorders in various rooms in a house high up in the mountains over a few weeks time. Remarkable by anyone's standards."

"Okay, fine, but where does the trilogy come in?"

"I take it you haven't read it?"

"No."

"It is a great gift of imagination and knowledge, filled with archetypes galore that speak to people everywhere. Jung explained that there are universal archetypes that exist in the collective unconscious of humanity. Both terms he coined by the way. So if writers can tap into those universal archetypes, they can, in effect, reach their readers on a deeper level by enlivening their unconscious consciousness. Tolkien did that superbly well with the trilogy. Jung really latched on to something there in understanding myths and stories. Joseph Campbell has taken up the sword and has really created a new field of study. Fascinating."

Julian sighed and looked at Sam. "Sam, if you don't get back out there and start teaching again, it will be a damn shame."

"Whoa, Jules, whoa. It can't be as it was before. This idea of recreating the past or holding on to the past won't do. It's all about the flow. Life flows. Evolution flows. It's important to not get stuck."

"All right, I guess." Julian sat dejected.

"Hey, Jules, you got me doing a lecture, and now I'm writing a book. That's pretty good."

"Yeah, that's true."

"Good. God is patiently waiting for us to be one with him or her again. In the end, it's not about much else, but we just can't tell everyone that. It would be very confusing, and people would get pissed off. Everything and everyone is fine. It's all good."

"It's all good," Julian repeated.

Sam and Julian finished their coffee, which had turned lukewarm. They looked at each other in acknowledgement and got up to put on their winter coats and wool caps. Sam put a few dollars in the tip jar and thanked Rachel and the crew. Kenny came out and bid them farewell.

The cold, dry air hit the back of their throats as they sauntered up the sidewalk, Julian turning left and Sam right. With a nod they parted, each on their own way home.

Chapter 38:
The Lecture

ALL THE PREPARATION HAD BEEN done. In the Five College Area that was Amherst, the buzz was audible as word spread that Dr. Sam O'Connor was breaking his silence after nearly nine years and that he would be giving a lecture on Thursday night at Amherst College. Posters were put up around town, and the college sent out VIP invitations to some of the deans at the other schools. Ed Sanders signed off on the security plan, but he insisted on having a private bodyguard onstage with Sam. The college reluctantly agreed. Sam strongly disagreed, but he went along with the plan.

Amy gave Sam a haircut and trimmed his beard a few days before the big night. She also took him down to the Hampshire Mall and JCPenny and insisted he buy a new tweed jacket, shirt, and pants for the lecture. Sam agreed reluctantly to the demand.

When Ed saw his son-in-law on the eve of the lecture, he couldn't help but comment with his hands on his hips, "Why, Sam, you clean up well." Sam frowned.

But when Mary said, "How handsome you look, Sam," he smiled self-consciously.

Amy had her parents and Sam's for dinner. Sam ate little and was distracted through much of the meal. The three women noticed, but the men were too busy eating and talking to one another to see Sam's mood.

Before Sam and Ed left, Amy asked Sam at the door if he was all right. Sam nodded yes and kissed her.

"See you at the hall" was all Sam offered as he left the house.

Sam and Ed drove the fifteen minutes pretty much in silence after Ed's failed attempt to engage Sam in conversation. As Ed parked the car, he looked at Sam and said, "You'll be fine." Sam nodded and got out of the car. Sam felt quiet and calm, but there was also a tinge of nervous anticipation. He was aware of Bob Harris's challenge that he was no longer academically relevant. He also realized, though, that he didn't have to stay within the confinement of academia. He was a guest lecturer, not a professor on a tenure track. He had thought about the lecture for months and, for the most part, had structured it in his mind. So without notes, except for the quotes he would read and his worn copy of *Leaves of Grass* in his jacket pocket, he walked up the hill from the parking lot.

They arrived at the Buckley Recital Hall forty-five minutes early. Amy, the two boys, and Jimmy and Lilly would travel in one car, and Kenny would drive with Susan and Mary Sanders. Julian, Katy, and the other ten students were seated in the second row. The first row was reserved for Sam's family, Kenny, his publisher, the Guptas, and assorted deans from Amherst College, UMass, and Mount Holyoke, Smith, and Hampshire Colleges. The President of Amherst College, Dr. Stevens, would speak a few words of welcome before introducing Sam. A few of Sam's friends from the TM movement, including David Roberts, were also there, dressed in cream linen suits with accompanying cashmere scarves. Amy, Josh, and Paul went to greet them.

"Jai Guru Dev" was given as a warm greeting exchanged by all. "Sam is thrilled that you are here," she told them with genuine sincerity. Amy also felt proud to introduce her two sons to these special guests. She then invited the three teachers to meet the Guptas and the family.

By ten to seven, the hall was packed and noisy. But not everyone in attendance came through the front doors and walked through the metal detector as Kenny had predicted. Unseen and unknowable by the audience at large, the hall began to fill with angels, some curious gods, and a gang of rishis. With that distinguished group was a large man with a felt hat, long locks, a full beard, and sparkling blue-gray eyes.

A little after seven, President Addison Paul Stevens climbed the stairs to the stage and walked over to the podium. The crowd quieted down.

"I would like to welcome everyone to what shall prove to be a night extraordinaire. For tonight we greet the return of one of our own professors after a long unscheduled sabbatical. Our speaker tonight held this campus spellbound with excitement with his visionary course on consciousness just over ten years ago. Next came a best-selling book, a lecture series, and a book tour that ended tragically, but not fatally. When the word of the event in

Minneapolis came back here to this community, we were stunned, in shock. Many, upon hearing the news, went to the common and held a candlelight vigil and sang songs of sadness and hope. I, too, went to the common along with Dean Griffin. We were greatly saddened, and both of us prayed that this young man shot at close range would not pass from the world so soon. We prayed for his wife and children and for his mother and father. There have only been a few times in my life that I had been moved in such strong terms. This is the first time that I have spoken publicly about my feelings that night. I can do so because this young professor survived.

"He became a symbol of universal brotherhood amongst teachers, authors, musicians, poets, and artists that demand the freedom to express their thoughts, ideas, art, and music without the threat of backlash from those who are less tolerant and narrow in their views. He didn't set out to become such a symbol, but it happened nevertheless, and the world became a better place for it. It gives me great pleasure and honor to introduce to you Dr. Sam O'Connor."

A thunderous applause erupted as Sam walked out on the stage. Everyone in the audience was on his and her feet. The angels were twirling, the gods rolling, and the rishis were hooting and hollering. Sam shook Addison's hands, and then both men embraced.

As the crowd quieted down, Addison continued, "Sam has been in relative silence for the last nine years. We have asked him to come back to campus on many occasions. But it took a handful of students to accomplish what we couldn't. As I reflected on that, it made a great deal of sense to me. Dr. O'Connor loves to teach because he loves students. It took meeting one of our brightest, Julian Driscoll, and his circle of friends to encourage Dr. O'Connor to agree to speak tonight. A few months ago, twelve students appeared before me in my office presenting a petition with several hundred signatures, which urged the college to invite Sam back to campus for a lecture. I didn't have to be asked twice, and I received the news with great pleasure that Dr. O'Connor had agreed.

"After the lecture, there will be a reception for Dr. O'Connor in the Hampshire Room for the faculty, deans, and special guests. Light refreshments will be served, and all are welcome. So, with no further ado, I turn the podium over to Dr. Sam O'Connor. Thank you."

The applause almost lifted the roof. The great sense of joy and happiness in that moment reached the highest heaven. Sam was visibly moved and stood in front of the podium thanking everyone for such a warm welcome. The audience quieted down. Sam exhaled loudly.

"I'm tempted to quit while I'm ahead." Laughter erupted. "No, seriously, thank you, President Stevens. Listening to that introduction, I realize I probably should have called you from my hospital bed and asked for a raise." More laughter.

Addison replied from his front-row seat, "And you would have gotten it!" and another round of laughter swept the hall.

Sam looked over the group and saw a sea of smiling faces full of anticipation. He turned to Mike Smith, his bodyguard, sitting on a chair next to his not ten feet away, looking like a Boston bouncer with dark shades on. Sam looked at Mike as Mike looked out into the audience. As Sam looked, not saying anything, people began to nervously laugh.

Sam finally said, "This is my brother, Mike. He didn't get as much attention as I did growing up and insisted upon being onstage with me tonight." Everyone applauded Mike. Mike smiled for the first and only time that evening, and he nodded and waved weakly to the audience.

Again the room grew quiet.

Sam began, "The *Tao Te Ching*, authored by Lao Tsu, begins this way:

> *The Tao that can be told of is not the eternal Tao.*
> *The name that can be named is not the eternal name.*
> *The nameless is the beginning of heaven and earth.*
> *The named is the mother of ten thousand things.*
> *Ever desireless, one can see the mystery.*
> *Ever desiring, one can see the manifestations.*
> *These two spring from the same source but differ in name;*
> *This appears as darkness.*
> *Darkness within darkness.*
> *The gate to all mystery.*

"This verse from the *Tao Te Ching* is a fine translation by Gia-Fu Feng and Jane English. So we are going to talk tonight about something we can't talk about. Once we acknowledge we can't talk about it, we're free to spend the whole evening talking. There is no direct translation for the *Tao* in English. Just like the word *dharma* in Sanskrit, there is no good English word that gets at the meaning. So we must talk about it. The Tao and dharma are similar in meaning, however. They are likened to that which upholds evolution, maintains the equilibrium of all things. They have a certain flow. The Tao flows, universal dharma flows in an evolutionary way. Once a person, community, even a nation, is established in the Tao or in the dharma, the goal of evolution can be easily attained. Harmony and peace are upheld. Advances in knowledge and culture are made. How, you might ask? I hope by the end of the evening, you'll have a feeling for it. There is a mystery to all of this, a mystery that is worth our attention.

"So, let's first begin with what is meant by evolution. The principles of physical or biological evolution have been talked about for over a hundred years. A conversation started by Darwin. These evolutionary changes, as such, are due to environmental conditions or stresses. The DNA mutates over time, allowing the organism to change to meet the demands of the environment. So that's one kind of evolution. This kind of evolution doesn't necessarily make the organism better in any moral sense but allows change to be structured at the fundamental level of the DNA so the organism can adapt, and its odds for surviving as a species increases.

"Now, when we think of evolutionary ideas, for instance, we think of ideas that are unfolding in a progressive way. When considering the Tao, or dharma, and the flow of each as evolutionary, the implication is that there is a progressive unfoldment taking place. But where is it taking place?

"The idea that there is spiritual evolution is something old and new. Spiritual means nonmaterial. In a material universe, what could possibly be nonmaterial? This is a confounding topic to those who study physical science. It's a little like the person who's looking and looking for their glasses only to realize they're wearing them. Consciousness, or awareness, is what you are listening to me with now. Awareness is so basic to our lives because it's the basis of our lives, and being such, it is hardly considered. It is just a given in many people's minds if they ever consider it at all.

"Our perceptions, our thoughts, our feelings, our bodily sensations are experienced because we have awareness. Everything we experience, we experience because of consciousness or awareness. Consciousness is life, and as we shall see this evening, everything in the material creation has its source in consciousness. In order to understand ourselves and the world around us, we have to understand the nature of consciousness.

"The problem for those of us in the West is that we have few, if any, experts on consciousness at this time in history, so our eyes have turned to the East. His Holiness Maharishi Mahesh Yogi hails from the Shankara tradition of knowledge and holds the keys to that tradition. Why is this point important? In India, who your spiritual teacher is is of the utmost importance. The tradition of spiritual knowledge is very important. Not that long ago, who your father, grandfather, and great-grandfather were was considered to be of great importance. Nowadays, in this country, we hardly know who our own great-grandparents were. That tradition for most of us is gone.

"As I was saying, Maharishi hails from the holy tradition of sages, which Shankara is a part of. Shankara is considered a great saint in India, and he is credited with the revival of Vedic knowledge in his day. The Vedas are the world's oldest known collection of knowledge that dates back to who knows when. Some date the *Vedas* back twenty-five thousand years. Maharishi tells us they are as old as creation itself. For many thousands of years, the Vedas were passed down, strictly as an oral tradition, and then at some point they were written down. The Vedas describe the manifestation of the whole creation, the maintenance of it, as well as the dissolution. The Vedas describe the creative impulses, or laws of nature, that govern creation as well as the seven states of consciousness that man and woman have the capacity to experience and live. The knowledge is quite extensive, and if you were to settle in and read the entire literature of the Vedas, it could take years and years to read it, let alone understand it. There are many aspects or parts of the Vedas, and so it is organized by the primary Vedas and the supporting Vedas. Tonight, we want to discuss a part of the Vedas called the Upanishads. The Upanishads are more accessible for most of us than, let's say, *Rig Veda*. The opening verse of the tenth mandala of *Rig Veda* goes like this:

> *The great fire in the beginning of the dawn has sprung aloft and issuing forth from the darkness has come with radiance. Agni, the bright-bodied, as soon as born, fills all dwellings with shining light. When born thou, O Agni, art the embryo of heaven and earth, beautiful, born about in the plants; variegated, infantine, thou disperses the nocturnal glooms, thou issues roaring loudly from the maternal sources.*

"Agni is an ancient god, predating Brahma, Vishnu, and Shiva. The Vedas, it should be noted, predate Hinduism by many thousands of years.

"Now, let's go back to the Upanishads. The Upanishads are a collection of wisdom stories created by the great rishis of old to help those on the path to enlightenment. They are fantastic to read. They are bold. They describe the Supreme Reality and state it as fact. The Self, large *S*—non-changing, pure, eternal, infinite, unbounded—is described as the source of creation and the source of the Vedas."

The rishis roared with approval, some blowing conch shells like trumpets, some roaring like Agni of old—a spectacle that no one in the audience saw or heard.

"From time to time, there are great souls born who have the capacity not only to understand the essence of the Vedas but to live the fullness of their precious knowledge. Shankara was one such person. Guru Dev, Maharishi's master, was another, and Maharishi himself is in that category. In the East, it is not enough to know the Vedas. The bar is set higher than that. One must live the Vedas. That is, one's awareness must be so refined and yet so full that one simply becomes the embodiment of the Vedas. Or, in other words, a PhD is good, but in regard to the Vedas, it's not worth much. For this knowledge, one must be fully enlightened before one can represent that tradition of knowledge. Fortunately for all of us, there has been a tradition of knowledge handed down from master to disciple. The Shankara tradition, though it is over 2,500 years old, is still currently in a state of revival by the grace of Guru Dev and now Maharishi.

"In order to preserve the knowledge in a useful form that would benefit the people, Shankara created four seats of learning, or Maths, in the four corners of India. Jyotir Math in northern India is the principal seat, and the Shankaracharya of the north is the head of the tradition. The system to select a new Shankaracharya is rigorous. You can't just know the Vedas—you must also embody the *Vedas*. You must be learned and you must be fully enlightened. For one hundred and fifty years the principal seat at Jyotri Math was empty. Just empty. To get the full impact of what this means for the people of India, it would be as if there was no one worthy to be the pope in Rome and the papal seat was empty for one hundred and fifty years. Imagine such a thing!

"Guru Dev, Brahmananda Saraswati, was a great saint and recluse. It is not possible to tell his story tonight in any detail, for time won't allow it. Maharishi also makes the point, when considering the life of Guru Dev, or any other enlightened individual, that it is not the events of the life that are important. These souls live on a much deeper level, and the real story of their lives is on that deeper level.

"Having said that, Guru Dev left home as a boy of nine years old to find an enlightened teacher so he might find his own enlightenment. Eventually, he found his master. He was one of the youngest disciples, but also one of the most advanced. He became enlightened at a young age, maybe around twenty-one years old. He left the ashram with the permission of his guru and lived alone in various caves in Uttar Kashi. Later, he was to meet his old master again at the great Kumba Mala in 1906. He would have been around thirty-six years old. His master recognized the great state of enlightenment that Guru Dev was living. He was initiated into the order of the sanyasi. Sanyasis are a special group of monks who wear orange robes and who live a reclusive lifestyle. After this, he lived alone in solitude and in silence for forty years. It took another twenty years for him to be persuaded to become the Shankaracharya of Jyotri Math. The story is that a group of men just picked him up and put him on the throne before he could change his mind and bestowed upon him the crown and scepter, so to speak.

"Maharishi had a chance meeting with Guru Dev a few years before. He had said, 'He was fond of visiting saints.' Just one look that lasted for the briefest of moments as some headlights illumined Guru Dev's face while he sat on an upstairs patio was enough for Maharishi to end his search for his master. It just took an instant.

"Guru Dev told him to finish college. 'But how will I find you again?' Maharishi asked. To which Guru Dev assured the young man that he would, and not to worry. Maharishi enrolled in Allahabad University, where my good friend Dr. Gupta taught."

Sam nodded to his friend in the first row, who raised his hand over his head to acknowledge the recognition. The doctor bowed his head and placed his hands in a prayerful form to Sam in gratitude for the honor.

Sam continued. "So, Guru Dev became the Shankaracharya. Since this is a really big deal, many people in India were aware of it. With college over, Maharishi inquired as to where Guru Dev was and he went to Jyotri Math. Maharishi spent the next thirteen years as Guru Dev's personal secretary. Which means, in one sense, he's on a thirteen-year internship, doing anything and everything for Guru Dev. Missing meals, missing sleep—anything that Guru Dev needs to get done, Maharishi is the man he turns to. For Maharishi it was pure bliss. He's said that, 'I wanted to tune my mind to his mind. I wanted to be able to anticipate his every thought and desire. I wanted my breath and his breath to be one.' I'm sure there are a few professors here that would like their graduate students to have even 25 percent of that effort and devotion." The audience laughed and smiled among one another. Dr. Harris, sitting on the right of the auditorium toward the back, frowned and muttered to himself, "Very charming."

Sam continued. "In May of 1953, Guru Dev passed, and Maharishi's world was turned upside down. Maharishi's devotion was so great that when Guru Dev's body was lowered into the Ganges River, Maharishi dove overboard and accompanied the body to its resting place on the riverbed below, bowed to his master one more time, and surfaced. Maharishi then retired to the Himalayas and sat in silence for two years.

"Guru Dev was concerned with the suffering of people everywhere, and that must have been on Maharishi's mind. A thought started coming to him to go to southern India to visit a holy temple. He mentioned this thought to another saint who was sitting next to him. The man replied, 'Just ignore it. Maybe it will go away.' A few days later, Maharishi reported that it was still there—this same thought. The other saint counseled, 'Why leave this sacred place and travel out into the mud of the world? You are better off staying here.' Another few days passed. Maharishi reported the thought was still persisting. 'What to do?' he asked. The other saint sat quietly for a while and said, 'Maybe you should go to this holy temple to get rid of this thought and then come back here as soon as you can.' Maharishi agreed, and he left and has not been back to the seclusion and solitude of the Himalayas since.

"In southern India, in the town of Trivandrum, a stranger approached Maharishi and asked him did he speak, meaning, 'Are you in silence?' or 'Can you speak?' Maharishi answered, 'Yes, I speak.' The man asked if he would give some public lectures. Maharishi replied, 'What would I speak on?' The man assured him not to worry and told Maharishi that he would call on him the next day. Maharishi had written down seven titles for seven consecutive evenings. The man said, 'Good. You just need to show up, and we'll do the publicity.' And he started to leave, at which point Maharishi said 'Wait. Please leave me a copy of the titles.' Thus, we have the birth of the TM movement.

"You see, Maharishi emerged after thirteen years with Guru Dev and then two years of silence in the Himalayas as a man transformed. Brahmachari Mahesh, as Maharishi was known, was given the title of Maharishi, which means Great Seer, after he began teaching in India.

"He began to teach a simple, easily learned technique that allows the student to transcend effortlessly to the source of thought, to pure consciousness, or the Self. Self with a capital S. That, my friends, changed everything, because suddenly people everywhere—regardless of belief, religion, background, male or female—could learn to transcend and experience the fourth state of consciousness. Busy, practical people can now learn Transcendental Meditation and practice it twice a day for twenty minutes and receive great benefits. For thousands of years only monks pursued meditation, and now people who are not monks can learn this meditation, which he originally called "a simple system of deep meditation", and start on a path to enlightenment. Quite miraculously, householders were no longer blocked from the path to Self-Realization. Somewhere in the first two years of teaching TM, Maharishi realized that if he was to go to the West and the people there were to adopt TM into their lives, it would cause India to sit up and take notice, and teaching in India would go much quicker.

"So this is the short version of Maharishi's story and how the TM program has found its way to Great Britain, France, Germany, and the US. In 1958, Maharishi landed in Hawaii before it had even become a state. Imagine. I was perhaps nine years old when Maharishi stepped off that plane with all his possessions in a simple cloth suitcase, not even sure if there would be someone to meet him. I'm telling you all of this because the lineage that Maharishi belongs to is important. In India, it's important to know the lineage of the Master. It brings confidence in the teacher and confidence in what you're being taught. So we have in Maharishi the Holy Tradition of Masters that goes back to Shankara and, back from there, to the great Rishis of the Vedic tradition.

"Maharishi has brought many gifts with him and he gives them out rather freely. From a philosopher's point of view, he has given us a tremendous gift in his description of the seven states of consciousness and in the two simple statements from the Vedic perspective, which are 'Knowledge is structured in consciousness' and 'Knowledge is different in different states of consciousness.'

"So there are the three states of consciousness that we are all familiar with: waking, dreaming, and the state of deep sleep. We experience each state within a twenty-four-hour period. We wake up each morning and attend to our days and even attend lectures like this in the evening. A few will begin to experience the deep-sleep state of consciousness while I speak, and when you start to snore, your neighbor sitting next to you will give you a poke."

The audience began to laugh softly. Susan, sitting in the first row, turned to her father, Jimmy, and said, "Yeah, Dad, no falling asleep," as she gave him a soft, playful poke with her finger.

"If you sleep quietly, though, you may experience the next state of consciousness and begin dreaming, hopefully a happy dream of some beautiful place, a beach perhaps, with calm turquoise waters lapping on the shore." Sam smiled at Julian, who stirred in his seat and brightened as he looked up at Sam.

"We know that each of these states of consciousness have unique states of physiology. And if you were wired for an EEG by a scientist sitting in the next room, he could, by looking at your brain waves, determine which state of consciousness you were in without taking a peek at you. Each state of consciousness has its own unique physiology.

"Like that, the fourth, fifth, sixth, and seventh states of consciousness have their own unique state of physiology. There are two professors at Maharishi International University who are presently involved in pioneering research on the physiology of enlightenment. They are effectively creating a map from an objective standpoint of recording the physiology parameters of enlightenment.

"Back to Maharishi. Maharishi arrived in the US in 1959. Eisenhower was president. And Maharishi talked about the simple technique of Transcendental Deep Meditation and how, in just a few minutes, the mind settles down and experiences the fourth state of consciousness. As a culture, we have no reference point for this transcendental consciousness, and being a practical people, we ask collectively that 'If I should experience this inner state, what's the benefit?' My father, who has been a businessman his whole life, likes to say, 'You don't sell the steak, you sell the sizzle.' And he was in the bakery business!" Sam looked down and smiled at his father. "So, Maharishi caught on quickly. 'I've come all this way to talk about enlightenment, and the people here want to talk about sleeping better, having more energy.' So for a number of years, all he talked about was transcendental consciousness and the benefits of experiencing TC. Transcendental consciousness, by the way, is transcendental to the other three states of consciousness. It is beyond waking, dreaming, and deep sleep. Its nature is pure silence, pure awareness. It is unbounded, infinite, and beyond—or transcendental to—creation. In this sense, it is a spiritual, nonmaterial state of being.

"Maharishi talked about experiencing the kingdom of God, which Jesus had made reference to, and that once you have this experience over and over again, then, as Jesus put it, 'All else will be added onto you.' The Upanishads describe transcendental consciousness as the infinite source of the whole creation. Everything, the whole infinite diversity, springs from That. So deep within all of us, beyond our thoughts, feelings, and egos, there is this infinite state of pure awareness, which is the source of creation. So when Jesus says, 'First ye seek the kingdom of heaven within,' the state of transcendental pure awareness, 'then all else will be added onto you,' he knew what he was talking about. However, almost nobody else at the time understood him. Maharishi has said one of the big obstacles in speaking and teaching this kind of knowledge is that the master speaks from his enlightened level of consciousness, but the student can only hear from his or her own level of consciousness. This gap can only be filled in by the student rising to enlightenment." Dr. Harris squirmed in his seat, suppressing his desire to yell out his disgust with what he was hearing.

Sam began to walk around the stage as he was warming up. Mike, the bodyguard, felt dismayed when Sam left the relative security of the podium, and he began to be extra diligent as he surveyed the audience for a threat of any kind.

"As Maharishi experienced life in the West, he realized people here were so practical, he began to encourage scientists to look into TM and begin to quantify the effects on mind and body. And he began to talk about the benefits of TM in terms of increased energy, clearer thinking, and better health. Slowly the idea of 'The kingdom of heaven is within' was replaced by the application of science. After all, Maharishi conceded, we live in an age of science. Not everyone in the early days was ready to grasp the nature of consciousness. Fortunately for all of us, Transcendental Meditation produces experiences quickly.

"After some time, some of the meditators began having experiences of cosmic consciousness. If transcendental consciousness is the fourth state of consciousness, then cosmic consciousness is the fifth state. As one meditates regularly, twice a day, the silence of pure consciousness begins to be more established so that even when one is not meditating and is in day-to-day activity, the silence of pure awareness is not lost. The identification of the mind with one's thoughts, feelings, and actions gradually shift to the realization of that inner silent level of awareness. 'I am That' declare the ancient Upanishads.

"The experience that meditators started having was that they were witnessing their thoughts and actions. It's a very natural state to experience. Maharishi comments that once established in cosmic consciousness, one now has access to one's full potential. Once cosmic consciousness is fully established, the fullness of the infinite awareness is never lost, even in deep sleep or in the dream state. Waking, dreaming, and deep sleep continue, but now on the basis of pure awareness. So I'm sleeping, but I'm also awake in my pure awareness. So part of me is asleep and part of me is awake. The naturalness of this state of CC cannot be emphasized enough, although I realize it sounds pretty abstract.

"So meditators, having this experience of CC, began to notice that their perception of the world was deepening. That is, the five senses became enlivened. Colors became brighter, sounds clearer, taste and smell stronger, and touch more intense. This development continued so that the celestial world that is all around us began to be perceived." Dr. Harris uncrossed and crossed his legs and had an exasperated look on his face. Mike was beginning to zero in on him.

As he walked around on the stage, Sam waved his arm around and looked up to where the rishis and angels were assembled. The angels felt a thrill and the rishis roared their approval and Sam smiled broadly.

"So with this new level, Maharishi began speaking about God consciousness, the sixth state of consciousness. Here he described that the sense of sight, for example, can become so refined that the finest aspect of the object can be directly perceived. We know from quantum mechanics that everything that appears solid is, in fact, not solid. Everything is, on some level, a whirl of high-energy particles. Like this, the experience of the sixth state of consciousness is that the finest relative value of the object is light. Light is the first manifestation of the creation. The person in God consciousness, GC, perceives the shimmering golden light in every object he or she sees. There is a great joy in every perception. Every sight, sound, touch, taste, and smell brings great joy to the person experiencing God consciousness. It is on this level, the finest level of the relative, that God resides. Maharishi was fond of saying that 'God has one foot in the absolute and one foot in the finest relative level of creation. In God consciousness, one literally has the experience of shaking hands with God.'" Sam nodded and smiled at Julian.

"You might think that no more development of consciousness is possible. Meeting God with full awareness and with the fullness of love that one must have, how does one top that? Because no matter how great that experience is, and I imagine it to be a pretty great experience, there's another step. From there, Maharishi spoke about the seventh state of consciousness. This is the ultimate flowering of human awareness, the goal of evolution. Unity consciousness is described as when the Self that was established in cosmic consciousness cognizes the Self, or pure consciousness, in every object perceived, and then unity is born. The infinite Self has realized that all is infinite Self and that it has always been so and it shall always be so. Everywhere a person living from UC goes, he or she is at home, for everything is the Self. Here, every perception brings great bliss, tidal waves of bliss. Everything is known. There is nothing left to know. One only now floats in the bliss of pure consciousness. This is the end of the Vedas, The Vedanta. These souls who live in unity are a great blessing to life and to all of us. These are the saints of the world who people have revered for ages on end.

"The Upanishads are the stories of unity, the stories of the Self. Every age has those precious souls who are so close to enlightenment they fall into it and then give some expression to it. In the East, history has recorded many such souls, and yet in the West we also have such souls. So let's take a ten-minute break, and when we're all back, I'd like to talk about one such soul and the beautiful poetic expressions that he faithfully recorded for all of humanity."

The audience clapped wildly, and then many got up and stretched and wandered up the aisle to attend to this or that. Sam walked offstage with Mike. Mike met briefly with one of the Amherst College security guards and mentioned the agitated behavior of a guy dressed in a tweed jacket and bow tie, sitting on the right-hand side of the auditorium toward the back on the aisle. Then he joined Sam backstage. There was a pitcher of water and two glasses waiting on a small table. Sam poured a glass of water for each of them. Mike took the glass and sipped the water. He then said, "That's some pretty heavy stuff you're throwing around. I'm following it some, but I don't get it entirely, man."

"The experience of transcending is the important thing. First time you sit and learn TM, you'll experience transcending, and you'll know exactly what this is all about."

"You think I can learn TM?"

"Without a doubt, you and everyone else can learn and get the benefits and be on the path to enlightenment."

"Well, that's cool, man. I'm going to check it out."

"Good, man."

"One more question. Why would some bastard shoot you? I know lots of guys who could use a good beating and a couple who deserve to be shot, but why you?"

"I wish I could answer that, Mike. Must be something left over from a past life."

"Well, it certainly ain't from this life from what I can tell."

Just then, Josh and Paul came running over to Sam and gave their father their full-bodied hugs. "Dad, you were great. Really. Grandpa didn't even fall asleep, and Susan never took her eyes off you."

"Thanks, guys. Grandpa didn't fall asleep. Amazing! I think Susan gets this stuff on some deep level."

Amy walked over and kissed Sam. "You're brilliant. I don't know how you do it. Everyone is so excited, they're practically drunk. It's just wonderful. Sam O'Connor, I love you."

"And I love you, my darling." And they kissed. "Let's see if I can pull off this next part."

"You'll be fine."

"Dr. O'Connor, I'm going to start flicking the house lights so people will start taking their seats in the next couple of minutes," said a student wearing a headset.

"Okay, thanks. So, all of you, back to your seats. Another sip of water for me, and on with the show and all that rot."

The hall began to settle as people found their seats. The person sitting next to Dr. Harris was given a new seat, and unbeknownst to the professor, a plainclothes detective now occupied that seat. Mike and Sam walked back onto the stage. Mike saw Detective Coles in position and felt better. The audience was quiet, and the air was filled with anticipation. Sam began.

"I was just talking to my brother, Mike, backstage, and in all fairness to you, I'm really giving you an awful lot to think about tonight. So I want to remind you that speaking of pure awareness, transcending, and enlightenment is not the same as directly experiencing it for yourselves. If none of you had ever tasted a strawberry and I stood here and described to you the sweetness, the juiciness, that incredible strawberry flavor, it doesn't really do you much good. But if I could give each of you one strawberry, the moment you bit into it, the moment you experienced it, you would know. So TM, transcending, pure awareness, and enlightenment are just like that. You experience it, you got it. No more words are necessary. But words are fun. If you liked the strawberry, you might find yourself telling others all about it.

"Spiritual evolution is constantly going on. All of us are wired to seek more and more. All of us seek more happiness, more knowledge, more experiences, more things, more and more in the hot pursuit of happiness. It's just the way it is. What we really seek is infinity. More and more and more, eventually ending up coming face-to-face with the infinite. But there's a catch with that plan of just going after more and more and coming up to the infinite. That is, it can't be done on a practical level. The mind, for all its brilliance, is also limited and will stay on this path forever unless there is some inner awakening, some feeling that there must be something more. After all, how many things can I have? How many houses? How many trips to the mall? How many wives, husbands, children, dogs, cats can I have? And in the end, did it make you truly satisfied and happy? At some point, the journey must take an inward turn. Why? Because infinity is within. It is closer to you than you are to yourself. The crux of the mystery . . .

"Regardless, evolution is always happening. In fact, as I mentioned before the break, there are some souls born so close to enlightenment that they seem to fall into transcending or experiencing pure awareness in a spontaneous manner. For most of us, we need to learn a technique, like TM, to order to experience pure awareness. Once you begin having the experience of transcending, suddenly you understand when you read or hear other people describing it. It's exhilarating. Knowledge is structured in consciousness. Learning for Plato was a 're-membering.' Knowledge for the rishis was a 're-cognition,' or a cognizing of something that was already present in consciousness. All knowledge is already structured in consciousness. Consciousness has many layers to it. Knowledge is also different in different states of consciousness. When we are unaware of this, then we are faced with all kinds of seeming contradictions, particularly when going into the mysteries or spiritual or religious texts. And sometimes, even the poet, writing from his or her level of consciousness, offers up contradictions galore.

"I have been reading Walt Whitman's *Leaves of Grass* for over twenty years. I read parts of it every day. I've even taken Walt's advice on how to read it. Read it outdoors in Nature. So I have a spot on my property, back in a wooded area, where nature has placed a large stone near a small stream, where I take my *Leaves of Grass* and read it out loud. Oh yes, Walt advises to read it out loud. The way the Vedas are chanted out loud by the pundits, I read *Leaves of Grass* the same way.

"I have read a number of books on Whitman and his life over the years. The best of them speak to his transformation of consciousness. If one doesn't get this transformation, then the full gifts of the *Leaves* will never come forth. Walt Whitman was a large man for his day. Remember, people were all smaller a hundred years ago. Not Walt, he was six feet tall and about two hundred pounds. He was a newspaper man, a reporter, and an editor living in New York City. He had a bad habit of not paying much attention to time, tended to be late, and tended to take afternoons off. Sounds as if he might have made a great professor." The crowd laughed, and the professors in the audience smiled and shook their heads.

"He was not a brilliant writer, as newspaper men go, and he tended to be fired frequently. By all appearances, this didn't bother him much. We know he was intensely curious as a child, and he never lost that innocent curiosity as an adult. This, I think, served him well. He didn't have much use for the overly intellectual stuffed shirts of the day. He loved being with the simpler people, the blue-collar workers of the day. He sensed their common humanity and deeply felt their goodness. Once, after being fired from a job, he was offered the editorship of a newspaper in New Orleans. This was to be the great moment he was waiting for.

"All of his life up to this point, he lived on Long Island, Brooklyn, and Manhattan. Then he was about to see America. Without this opportunity, he would not have become America's poet. In 1848, he traveled by train, stagecoach, and river ferry to New Orleans, a journey of perhaps six weeks. He stayed in New Orleans less than four months and traveled back to New York City via the Mississippi, the Great Lakes, and Hudson River. So, as Maharishi might say, he went from here to there and back to here again.

"What happened to Whitman, though, in these six months was astonishing. From a number of accounts, he experienced periods of 'mystical spiritual illumination.' Or what I would call experiences of transcendental consciousness or pure awareness. These experiences continued over a period of a few years. In any event, when he arrived back on the streets of New York City, he was a man transformed. Many of the people he knew noticed the transformation. For the first year after arriving home, he worked as an editor of the Brooklyn Free Press, then he operated a printing press and did some freelance writing and even worked as a house builder. Sometime in June of 1853, Whitman had another transcending experience, and sometime after that, he began his great work, *Leaves of Grass*.

"What is remarkable about *Leaves of Grass* are the many parallels with Eastern philosophy, mainly with the Upanishads, which Whitman has no knowledge of. There is a story that Emerson sent Thoreau to Brooklyn after *Leaves of Grass* was published in 1855. Thoreau asked Whitman, 'Have you read much of the Hindus?' 'No,' Whitman replied, 'tell me about them.'

"Experiencing pure consciousness is a universal experience, open to everyone at any time. Whitman's experience was so complete, he was able to give expression through poetry to those experiences and his transformation.

I've been reading the original 1855 version of *Leaves*." Sam held up the book. "In this edition, republished in 1959, Malcolm Cowley gives an excellent introduction that I would encourage you to read. The first edition of *Leaves of Grass* appeared as a collection of thirteen poems. The first poem is 'Song of Myself.' It is the longest poem in the edition and the one we'll talk about for the rest of the evening because it is truly remarkable. Over the years, Whitman added more and more poems to *Leaves*, but the 1855 edition is the first sprouting. Maharishi likes to say, 'The whole tree is contained in the first sprout.' It just needs time to unfold. I'm going to read excerpts from this poem as time allows. Remember, as I read, it is my contention that Whitman is an American rishi giving us a wisdom story about enlightenment. So let's begin . . .

> *I celebrate myself,*
> *And what I shall assume you shall assume,*
> *For every atom belonging to me as good belongs to you.*
>
> *I loafe and invite my soul,*
> *I lean and loafe at my ease . . . observing a spear of summer grass.*

"Whitman begins his great poem telling us he celebrates himself. Not the small self, not the personality of Whitman, but the larger Self, the Self that is equated to the soul. From this level, a spear of grass is in itself a whole universe. He's not in a hurry to tell us what he has learned. Indeed, the poem goes on for 1,334 more verses. But he tells us right from the beginning that what he has discovered and what he assumes you also shall assume. For this is not just to be Walt Whitman's discovery, but your discovery as well.

> *Stop this day and night with me and you shall possess the origin of all poems,*
> *You shall possess the good of the earth and the sun . . .*
> *There are millions of suns left,*
> *You shall no longer take things at second or third hand . . .*
> *Nor look through the eyes of the dead . . . nor feed on the specters in books,*
> *You shall not look through my eyes either, nor take things from me,*
> *You shall listen to all sides and filter them from your self.*

"Whitman wants the reader to experience for him or herself 'the origin of all poems'—the source of thought, pure consciousness. By doing so, you'll possess 'the good of the earth and the sun,' and to reassure us, he tells us, 'There are a million suns left.' He's also telling us there is much more to life than we take there to be. Imagine the audience in 1855 for whom Whitman is writing. The Civil War is only five years off for one thing. In 1855 he only sold a handful of copies. In his lifetime he may have only sold several thousand copies. In any case, Whitman wants us to know that spending time with *Leaves of Grass* is spending time with him. He once remarked in reference to *Leaves*, 'You don't touch a book, you touch a man.' By spending time with him, you will not take things first- or secondhand, but you will know things through your Self, as he has done.

> *I have heard what the talkers were talking . . .*
> *the talk of the beginning and the end,*
> *But I do not talk of the beginning or the end.*

"Whitman, like all of us, has been caught up in the maya or illusion of the world. He makes it clear he rejects what all the talk is about.

> *Knowing the perfect fitness and equanimity of things, while they*
> *discuss I am silent, and go and bathe and admire myself.*
> *I am satisfied . . . I see, dance, laugh, sing;*
> *As God comes a loving bedfellow and sleeps at my side all night*
> *and close at the peep of the day,*

"Here, Whitman is describing the joy and freedom of the Self. And there is a reference to witnessing sleep. When pure awareness is established, one is awake while sleeping . . . one witnesses sleep. He continues.

> *And leaves for me baskets covered with white towels*
> *bulging the house with their plenty,*
> *Shall I postpone my acceptation and realization and*
> *scream at my eyes,*

"Maharishi described how, in the state of cosmic consciousness, Mother Nature automatically arranges everything one needs. 'No worries,' as they say Down Under. Life's infinite abundance becomes clear. So things have changed for Whitman. His life is different from before. His needs, as he has expressed here, are taken care of spontaneously.

"In the next verse, he makes a list of things—the latest news, his dinner, his associates, looks, loss of money, family problems, mood, both good and bad.

> *They come to me days and nights they go from me again,*
> *But they are not the Me myself.*

"How marvelous!" continued Sam. "Most of us identify with our moods and what is happening in our lives as who we are. 'I'm in a bad mood,' one might say, or 'The boss ignored me today at the meeting, and that bothered me,' or 'I'm sick,' 'I'm tired,' 'Nothing's working.' Sound familiar?

"Here, Whitman acknowledges all of that, but he sees these things coming and going. And then he states that 'They are not the Me myself.' Note here the *M* in *Me* is capitalized. He is making a great distinction, not unlike in the Upanishads, where the *S* in *Self* is also capitalized. Next he goes on to describe the state he's in.

> *Apart from the pulling and hauling stands what I am,*
> *Stands amused, complacent, compassionating, idle, unitary,*
> *Looks down, is erect, bends an arm on an impalpable certain rest,*
> *Looks with its side curved head curious what will come next,*
> *Both in and out of the game, and watching and wondering at it.*
> *Backward I see in my own days where I sweated through fog*
> *with linguists and contenders,*
> *I have no mocking or arguments . . . I witness and wait.*

"The chaos of life pulls and hauls at us today as it did in Whitman's day. He is above it or has transcended it. He's now amused, complacent, full of compassion, restful, unitary, and curious. He sees the path he has taken . . . labored through the fog . . . dealt with the speakers of the day who claimed to know and didn't. But he himself will make no arguments. And then comes 'I witness and wait.' Witnessing again. And then he invites us also to experience the transcendental, in the next verse, as he himself had experienced.

> *Loafe with me on the grass . . . loose the stop from your throat,*
> *Not words, not music or rhyme I want . . . not custom or lecture,*
> *not even the best,*
> *Only the lull I like, the hum of your valved voice.*

"So here we go. 'Loose the stop from your throat.'" Give me not your words, music, customs, and not even your best. Whitman wants something beyond all of that. The lull . . . the hum . . . maybe like this . . ."

Sam stood, put the book at his side, closed his eyes, and started to chant,

"aummmmm . . . aummmmm . . . aummmmm . . ."

After the reverberation stopped, he opened his eyes. The audience sat perfectly still as the rishis nodded and smiled, shaking their heads with approval.

"*Aum* is the sound of the universe collapsing back in on itself. The universe transcending . . . going beyond itself back to its infinite source from which it sprung. Now the next four lines are commonly misunderstood.

> *I mind how we lay in June, such a transparent summer morning;*
> *You settled your head athwart my hips and gently turned over upon me,*
> *And parted the shirt from my bosom-bone and plunged your tongue to my barestript heart,*
> *And reached till you felt my beard, and reached till you held my feet.*

"I think, for many years, these four lines have been thought to be some kind of seduction scene. It is nothing of the sort. Whitman experienced what they call in India Shakti—or kundalini—as he was transcending. Kundalini sometimes comes during a particularly clear experience of transcending. It can begin as a trickle of energy from the base of the spine, and it can suddenly start pouring up the spine and seem to explode on to one's consciousness. It can sometimes feel as if it is coming from the soles of one's feet and pouring upward. As the Shakti merges with the awareness, the individual awareness expands to infinity, and then the experience begins to dissolve. One slowly begins to reenter one's consciousness, and as that happens, peace, joy, and even feelings of great bliss are experienced. And the next part of the verse is the key to this insight.

> *Swiftly arose and spread around me the peace and joy and knowledge that pass all the art and argument of the earth;*
> *And I know that the hand of God is the elderhand of my own,*
> *And I know that the spirit of God is the eldest brother of my own,*

339

And that all the men ever born are also my brothers . . . and the
women my sisters and lovers,
And that a kelson of the creation is love;

"Whitman is giving us the insight to the crux of all mystery, that deep within, all that we desire already exists. And all the activity of the world can't get at it. Why? Because it lies transcendental to the world of activity. After this intense experience of Shakti, Whitman says, 'Swiftly arose and spread around me the peace and joy and knowledge that pass all the art and argument of the earth.' This is one of the great expressions of truth in the Western world. God is my elder brother, and all men and women 'ever born' are also my brothers and sisters. And that love supports all of creation. Whitman has had a good experience, as we might say, in the TM movement. Without this experience, this clear and powerful transcending experience, *Leaves of Grass*, may have gone unwritten.

"From this point on, Whitman is reborn in spirit. The very next line concerns the childlike innocence of the enlightened.

A child said, What is the grass? fetching it to me with full hands;
How could I answer the child? . . . I do not know what it is any
more than he.

"Maharishi has said this about cosmic consciousness: that it is a state of half enlightenment. That is, the Self is known, and that is enough for a man or woman to be enlightened. But the experience is 'I know my Self, but what is all of this?' Whitman uses the grass as an analogy. He continues in the next fourteen lines to say, 'I guess it's the flag of my own disposition . . . it's the handkerchief of the Lord . . . the grass itself is a child . . . it's a uniform hieroglyphic.' Here's a man who has, just a few lines back, told us, 'Swiftly arose and spread around me the peace and joy and knowledge that pass all the art and argument of the earth,' and now he doesn't know what this handful of grass is. He knows his Self, and yet he doesn't know what all this other stuff is. This is a classic expression of cosmic consciousness. Now begins the journey to Unity. The rest of the *Song of Myself* is about this journey, and Whitman intends to take us on this journey with him. He even gives us the instructions to carry the *Leaves* with us and escape outdoors and read it out loud.

"The Vedas are chanted out loud, and people sit and listen. Certain Puranas, which are epic Indian stories, are read out loud, and still today,

340

people will come and sit for seven days straight to hear certain stories. Why? Because certain sounds, like in the chanting of Rig Veda, have a resonance in people's awareness that enliven that value of pure consciousness. Certain stories resonate on an archetypal level and elevate one's awareness to a cosmic level. Whitman intends, without knowing about the Vedas or Upanishads or the Puranas, for his *Leaves* to have the same effect on his readers.

"So what is the path to Unity from Cosmic Consciousness? It is the path of refinement of perception, which creates a feeling of devotion and deep love. Every day the world appears more beautiful, more radiant, and more vibrant. Every day one falls in love with the whole world. One begins to see the divine everywhere and in everyone. There is an expression in India and some Buddhist countries, and the expression is *Namaste*. Upon greeting or saying good-bye, one brings the hands together as in prayer, slightly bows, and says, very simply, 'Namaste.' What does *Namaste* mean? It means, 'I bow to the divinity within you.' I think Whitman would have liked the word.

"Also, the journey to unity involves integration. For Whitman, this is a key concept. The Self is established. Now we need to bring the Self and the apparent non-Self together to create unity. Everything needs to be integrated into the infinity of the Self. And thus, Whitman's lists. This man is not an egomaniac as some felt he must be. This is a man on his way to unity. And he must bring everything into his Self. Whitman witnesses all and then becomes all.

"I want to read some bits of verses here and there. Line 126:

> *I am not an earth nor an adjunct of an earth,*
> *I am the mate and companion of people, all just as immortal and*
> *fathomless as myself;*
> *They do not know how immortal, but I know.*

"Whitman goes on from line 140 to 250 describing various scenes and people, and then comes this verse:

> *What is commonest and cheapest and nearest and easiest is Me,*
> *Me going in for my chances, spending for vast returns,*
> *Adorning myself to bestow myself on the first that will take me,*
> *Not asking the sky to come down to my goodwill,*
> *Scattering it freely forever.*

"This is a cosmic man, living a cosmic life. Then he goes right back into another long list of things that he needs and we need to integrate as part of our Self. Verse 15 is 75 lines long and ends like this:

> The city sleeps and the country sleeps,
> The living sleep for their time . . . the dead sleep for their time,
> The old husband sleeps by his wife and the young husband sleeps
> by his wife;
> And these one and all tend inward to me, and I tend outward
> to them,
> And such as it is to be of these more or less I am.

"Here's Whitman after going on for seventy-five lines about everything under the sun. 'All of these tend inward to me and I tend outward to them.' The integration of all things, all the opposites and all the parts, is absolutely necessary to create the state of unity. For unity to happen, everything must be cognized in terms of the Self in order to be at One with the Self. Whitman is an American rishi who has stumbled into enlightenment. He is so clear about his experience that he created this poem, "Song of Myself." This is not just a poem, but a map to the highest enlightenment.

"Whitman wants us to stay encouraged so he talks directly to us in a close and intimate way.

> Do you guess I have some intricate purpose?
> Well I have . . . for the April rain has, and the mica on the side
> of the rock has.

> Do you take it I would astonish?
> Does the daylight astonish? or the early redstart twittering
> through the woods?
> Do I astonish more than they?
> This hour I tell things in confidence,
> I might not tell everybody but I will tell you.

"Whitman is creating a close personal relationship with you, the reader. The master creates an intimate relationship with his student because he has realized his own Self, but you have not realized yours. So the master must create some confidence in you. Whitman does it by establishing that he knows something you don't and then says, 'This hour I tell things in confidence, I might not tell everybody, but I tell you.' He's hooking your attention. Just as Don Juan told Carlos Castaneda a good teacher must do to his disciple.

"So, Whitman has your attention. You're open, you're listening. So now I'm going to read all of verse 20, and then we're going to have to stop for the night."

Some in the audience shouted, "Don't stop!" The rishis hissed and booed.

Sam continued, "All right, maybe I can also read the last verse of the poem.

"So after 387 lines, he's got you warmed up. Remember there is another almost one thousand lines to go. He's taking you on his journey in the hopes that it has become your journey too. I think Whitman sensed he was writing this for a future generation. I know he hoped it would be for his own, but except for a handful, it was lost on the masses. He never really seemed discouraged by that. He knew what he had created. He knew it would stand the test of time. He knew, I believe, that some yet-unborn generation would get at his words, get at the meaning.

"So the last two lines of verse 19 and then on to 20. There is so much left to read and talk about. But the hour is getting late. Perhaps we can arrange another evening?"

President Stevens said to Sam, "Why don't you go another half hour?" A roar of approval erupted.

"All right then," Sam replied. "Dare I tell you I'm working on a book about Whitman?"

Dr. Harris turned to the man sitting next to him and said, "I knew it. I knew it! He's plugging a new book. Always promoting himself." Detective Coles looked at him for a long few seconds and then looked back at the stage.

"Yes. Walt has been misunderstood for long enough. I'm just going to read now for a little while from the poem . . . a verse here and there. Maybe part of a verse, and we'll extend the night a bit and wind our way to the last verse. I'm grateful to all of you and the college for being with me here tonight, for giving me the opportunity to share *Leaves* with you in a new light."

Everyone clapped, and some stomped their feet in approval. Sam began.

This hour I tell you things in confidence,
I might not tell everybody but I will tell you.

"Verse 20:

Who goes there! hankering, gross, mystical, nude?
How is it I extract strength from the beef I eat?
What is a man anyhow? What am I? and what are you?
All I mark as my own you shall offset it with your own,
Else it were time lost listening to me . . .

In all people I see myself, none more and not one a barleycorn less,
And the good or bad I say of myself I say of them.
And I know I am solid and sound,
To me the converging objects of the universe perpetually flow,
All are written to me, and I must get what the writing means.
And I know I am deathless,
I know this orbit of mine cannot be swept by a carpenter's compass, . . .

I know I am august,
I do not trouble my spirit to vindicate itself or to be understood,
I see that the elementary laws never apologize, . . .

I exist as I am, that is enough,
If no other in the world be aware I sit content,
And if each and all be aware I sit content.

One world is aware, and by far the largest to me, and that is myself,
And whether I come to my own today or in ten thousand or ten
million years,
I can cheerfully take it now, or with equal cheerfulness I can wait.

My foothold is tenoned and mortised in granite,
I laugh at what you call dissolution,
And I know the amplitude of time.

"Whitman is establishing himself as timeless, and because he tells us that
he and we are in the same boat, we are also timeless beings.

"Verse 21:

> *I am the poet of the body,*
> *And I am the poet of the soul.*
>
> *The pleasures of heaven are with me, and the pains of hell are*
> *with me,*
> *The first I graft and increase upon myself . . . the latter I translate*
> *into a new tongue.*
>
> *I am the poet of the woman the same as the man,*
> *And I say it is great to be a woman as to be a man,*
> *And I say there is nothing greater than the mother of men.*

"He raises up the status of women here. Remember we're in 1855, women are second-class citizens. They can't vote. They can't own property. Whitman is carrying heaven and hell with him. The joy of heaven needs no translation, but the pains of hell do. The question of suffering and death, Whitman must grapple with that.

"Verse 24:

> *Walt Whitman, an American, one of the roughs, a kosmos,*
> *Disorderly fleshy and sensual . . . eating drinking and breeding,*
> *No sentimentalist . . . no stander above men and women or apart*
> *from them . . . no more modest than immodest.*
> *Unscrew the locks from the doors!*
> *Unscrew the doors themselves from their jams!*
>
> *Whoever degrades another degrades me . . . and whatever is*
> *done or said returns at last to me,*
> *And whatever I do or say I also return . . .*
>
> *I believe in the flesh and the appetites,*
> *Seeing hearing and feeling are miracles, and each part and tag*
> *of me is a miracle.*
>
> *Divine am I inside and out, and I make holy whatever I touch*
> *or am touched from;*

The scent of these arm-pits is aroma finer than prayer,
This head is more than churches or bibles or creeds.

"Whitman states his divinity here. He is saying that the Self is more glorious than all the churches' bibles, prayers, or creeds. The Upanishads would agree. Verse 8 of the Isa Upanishad goes like this:

The Self is everywhere. Bright is the Self,
Indivisible, untouched by sin, wise,
Immanent and transcended. He it is
Who holds the cosmos together.

"Back to the *Leaves*, verse 25:

Dazzling and tremendous how quick the sunrise would kill me,
If I could not now and always send sunrise out of me.

We also ascend dazzling and tremendous as the sun,
We found our own my soul in the calm and cool of the daybreak.
My voice goes after what my eyes cannot reach,
With the twirl of my tongue I encompass worlds and volumes
of worlds.
Speech is the twin of my vision . . . it is unequal to measure itself.
It provokes me forever,
It says sarcastically, Walt, you understand enough . . . why don't
you let it out then?

Come now I will not be tantalized . . . you conceive too much of
articulation.

Do you not know how the buds beneath are folded?
Waiting in gloom protected by frost,
The dirt receding before my prophetical screams,
I underlying causes to balance them at last,
My knowledge my live parts . . . it keeping tally with the meaning
of things,
Happiness . . . which whoever hears me let him or her set out in
search of this day.

346

*My final merit I refuse you . . . I refuse putting from me the best
I am.*

*Encompass worlds but never try to encompass me,
I crowd your noisiest talk by looking toward you.*

*Writing and talk do not prove me,
I carry the plenum of proof and everything else in my face,
With the hush of my lips I confound the topmost skeptic.*

"The Katha Upanishad, verse 8:

*The Truth of the Self cannot come through one
Who has not realized he is the Self.
The intellect cannot reveal the Self,
Beyond its duality of subject and object.
Those who see themselves in all
And all in them through spiritual
Osmosis to realize the Self themselves.*

"Whitman has realized the Self. Its truth is self-evident. He confirms it with just a look. He wants you to set out on a journey with him.
"*Leaves*, verse 33:

*Swift wind! Space! My Soul! Now I know it is true what I
guessed at;
What I guessed when I loafed on the grass,
What I guessed while I lay alone in my bed . . . and again as I
walked the beach under the paling stars of the morning.
My ties and ballasts leave me . . . I travel . . . I sail . . . my elbows
rest in the sea-gaps,
I skirt the sierras . . . my palms cover continents,
I am afoot with my vision.*

"And what a vision! He goes on for over four hundred lines. Again remember all must be reconciled and cognized as the Self. And then we come to verse 44. Here he says,

It is time to explain myself . . . let us stand up.
What is known I strip away . . . I launch all men and women
forward with me into the unknown.
The clock indicates the moment . . . but what does eternity indicate?
Eternity lies in bottomless reservoirs . . . its buckets are rising
forever and ever,
They pour and they pour and they exhale away . . .

"Verse 45:

See ever so far . . . there is limitless space outside of that,
Count ever so much . . . there is limitless time around that.
Our rendezvous is fitly appointed . . . God will be there and wait
till we come.

"So after Whitman shares with us four hundred plus lines on all the parts per se, he states that time is eternal and space is limitless or unbounded. And that we are all preceding to God, but not to worry because God will wait until we arrive.

"Now on to verse 46. We're getting close to the end of the poem.

I know I have the best of time and space—and that I was never
measured, and never will be measured.
I tramp a perpetual journey,
My signs are a rain-proof coat and good shoes and a staff cut
from the woods;
No friend of mine takes his ease in my chair,
I have no chair, nor church nor philosophy;
I lead no man to a dinner-table or library or exchange,
But each man and each woman of you I lead upon a knoll,
My left hand hooks you around the waist,
My right hand points to landscapes of continents, and a plain
public road.

Not I, not anyone else can travel that road for you,
You must travel it for yourself.

It is not far . . . it is within reach,

Perhaps you have been on it since you were born, and did not know,
Perhaps it is everywhere on water and on land.

Shoulder you duds, and I will mine, and let us hasten forth;
Wonderful cities and free nations we shall fetch as we go.

"Whitman is consciously putting you on the path. Maybe you're already on it and didn't know. He wants you to be conscious of all the wonders of the universe, but he also assures you, you are as wondrous as anything you might take in.

Long enough have you dreamed contemptible dreams,
Now I wash the gum from your eyes,
You must habit yourself to the dazzle of the light and of every
moment of your life.
Long have you timidly waded, holding a plank by the shore,
Now I will you to be a bold swimmer,
To jump off in the midst of the sea, and rise again and nod to me
And shout, and laughingly dash with your hair.

"Whitman is telling us there is so much more potential than you are living. He wants to 'wash the gum from your eyes' so you can see for yourself the dazzling light that surrounds you. In the sixth state of consciousness, God consciousness, the light of the celestial world is open to your perception.
"Verse 48:

I have said that the soul is not more than the body,
And I have said the body is not more than the soul,
And nothing, not God is greater to one than one's-self is, . . .

And I call to mankind, Be not curious about God,
For I who am curious about each am not curious about God,
No array of terms can say how much I am at peace about God
and about death.

I hear and behold God in every object, yet I understand God
not in the least,
Nor do I understand who there can be more wonderful than myself.

"Remember, Whitman is referring to the cosmic Self here, not the personality.

> *Why should I wish to see God better than this day?*
> *I see something of God each hour of the twenty four and each*
> *moment then,*
> *In the faces of men and women I see God, and in my own face*
> *in the glass;*
> *I find letters from God dropped in the street, and everyone is*
> *signed by God's name,*
> *And I leave them where they are, for I know that others will*
> *punctually come forever and ever.*

"Here's a man who is established in God consciousness. With every perception, there is God. And yet there is something more. How is that possible? Because, even with God everywhere, he or she still creates a duality between Self and God. Unity wants nothing but unity. Infinity wants infinity. Brahman wants Brahman. How can one talk about infinity and eternity? We're back to Lao Tsu's opening verse, 'The Tao that can be told is not the eternal Tao.' And so it is for Whitman. 'He that is not curious about God.' He that has gone on and on naming everything and claiming them as part of his Self. Now, if Whitman had not written verse 50, we'd be stuck in GC. Not a bad place to be stuck, but not the unity we seek. Notice how, after Whitman has given us page after page of incredible description, that in the next few lines, he now has no words to describe what he's experiencing. There is no describing it. Brahman is, infinity is. Notice the struggle with it, but then notice the sleeping as a metaphor for transcending and being absorbed in the infinite.

"I'm going to read all of verse 50, 51, and finally verse 52, and we'll close out the evening.

> *There is that in me . . . I do not know what it is . . . but I know*
> *it is in me.*
> *Wrenched and sweaty . . . calm and cool then my body becomes;*
> *I sleep . . . I sleep long.*
>
> *I do not know it . . . it is without name . . . it is a word unsaid,*
> *It is not in any dictionary or utterance or symbol.*
> *Something it swings on more than the earth I swing on,*

To it the creation is the friend whose embracing awakes me.
Perhaps I might tell more . . . Outlines! I plead for my brothers
and sisters.
Do you see O my brothers and sisters?
It is not chaos or death . . . it is form and union and plan . . . it
is eternal life . . . it is happiness.

"Verse 51:

The past and present wilt . . . I have filled them and emptied them,
And proceed to fill my next fold of the future.

Listener up there! Here you . . . what have you to confide to me?
Look in my face while I snuff the sidle of evening,
Talk honestly, for no one else hears you, and I stay only a minute
longer.

Do I contradict myself?
Very well then . . . I contradict myself;
I am large . . . I contain multitudes.

I concentrate toward them that are nigh . . . I wait on the door-slab.
Who has done his day's work and will soonest be through with
his supper?
Who wishes to walk with me?
Will you speak before I am gone? Will you prove already too late?

"Whitman has proven his enlightenment to us in many marvelous ways. He has established the Self, pure consciousness. He established the Self in activity. Living in cosmic consciousness has established God is everywhere—God consciousness. And he has grappled at coming face-to-face with the infinity of the Self—something that can't be described by words, Unity Consciousness. Now, he's back with us and challenges us to be done with our supper and walk with him.

"Last verse, verse 52:

The spotted hawk swoops by and accuses me . . . he complains of
my gab and my loitering.

I too am not a bit tamed . . . I too am untranslatable,
I sound my barbaric yawp over the roofs of the world.

The last scud of the day holds back for me, it flings my likeness
after the rest and true as any on the shadowed wilds,
It coaxes me to the vapor and the dusk.

I depart as air . . . I shake my white locks at the runaway sun,
I effuse my flesh in eddies and drift in lacy jags.

I bequeath myself to the dirt to grow from the grass I love,
If you want me again look for me under your bootsoles.

You will hardly know who I am or what I mean,
But I shall be good health to you nevertheless,
And filter and fiber your blood.

Failing to fetch me at first keep encouraged,
Missing me one place search another,
I stop somewhere waiting for you

Sam closed the book and slipped it into his jacket pocket.

As Sam read the final verses, the rishis began to chant in unison some ancient verse of the Vedas. The mantras they recited together in the gayatri rhythm began to have their effect. As Sam read, the angels and the gods began to close their eyes out of a reverence for that which was taking place. Their rarified and purified energy began to enliven all that were fortunate enough to be in the hall.

As Sam read, it was as if the words on the pages of the *Leaves* began to lift and float into the air. As more words were liberated from the paper, they began to swirl together and dance about the auditorium like hundreds of swallows flying in union.

As Sam continued, more and more words became liberated and were swirling about in a tighter and tighter concentric circle. The words falling in upon themselves . . . pulsating . . . transforming into a ball of whitish-violet light. The words, the letters, then light . . . the rishis chanting, Sam reading. The audience was completely silent, not a thought arising. All eyes and ears were upon Sam.

As he read, all the words of the song left the page and merged into the circle of light as it moved around the great hall like a life-form, dancing and swirling. As Sam came to the end of the poem and the last word left the page and joined the massive ball of light, the light began to collapse on itself. The light became smaller, denser, and began to gather up its energy into a bright small, tight, sphere.

As Sam finished, the powerful ball of light, with the power of a thousand suns, a point of intense radiance, moved to the highest point in the back of the hall. As Sam closed the book, the rishis finished their verse and sat in silence with eyes closed. The energy was palpable to all. Susan squirmed in her seat. The TM teachers, Amy, Kenny, and the Guptas, were sitting with eyes closed. Even Bob Harris was left without a thought and absorbed in silence. As the book closed shut, the fiery pearl of light rushed at Sam, rushed at everyone simultaneously, and exploded into white light. All were touched. The many had become one, and there was silence and then there was riotous joy.

Sam slipped the *Leaves of Grass* into his tweed coat pocket. With hands together, with fingers touching just below his beard, he closed his eyes and bowed deeply at the waist and said "Namaste." Everyone in the hall, as if on cue, rose to their feet and, with hands together as in a prayer, bowed and said, "Namaste." And then came the applause, the shouts, the stomping of feet.

As Sam looked up, all of heaven was revealed—the angels, the gods, and the rishis were revealed. He saw them all. He then looked down and saw his wife, children, parents, sister, and best friend in the front row smiling up at him. He looked up once again, and all of heaven descended upon him.

Epilogue:
I Stop Somewhere Waiting for You

ON A BEAUTIFUL SUMMER MORNING in late August, almost eighteen months after his lecture at Amherst College, Sam was out in the garden early while the rays of the sun were gentle and friendly. His wife and children, asleep in their beds, were dreaming of other worlds. Jimmy was awake, resting in the bed he shared with his wife, wondering about this new world in which he found himself. Lillian was up and in the kitchen making the morning coffee. Susan was asleep but began to stir as the enticing aroma of freshly made coffee wound its way from room to room.

Sam was pleased with the garden, all the plants so vital and heavy with fruit. He was also pleased with his new book, *Walt Whitman: An American Rishi*, soon to be published and distributed worldwide. On impulse, he decided to take a walk in the forest surrounding the Quabbin Reservoir. He jogged briskly to his truck in the driveway, got in, and drove off. Within fifteen minutes, he parked in a small turnoff just before the gate and began a solitary descent toward the water below.

Sam reflected that some fifty years ago, the Swift River was dammed and the valley flooded. The four towns that had been there for over 150 years were dismantled and the buildings displaced. The dead in the cemeteries were dug up and moved to higher ground and the trees cut down to make way for the deepening waters to come. Sam remembered the flooding of the Swift River Valley as a dramatic lesson in letting go of the known and embracing the mystery to come.

As he sauntered slowly down the path, he marveled at how nature had renewed herself. The forest was silent, full, dynamic, and aware. He came upon a stream and, further down, a large stone wall and partial stone dam

355

that blocked the cool flowing watercourses, creating a large pool of clear, calm water. A grist mill once stood there. Men worked in the mill crushing wheat and barley. For a moment or two, he contemplated the wondrous handiwork of men long forgotten then noticed a man sitting on a large stone gazing out over the still pool.

The man had a big frame, long hair that swept his shoulders, and a full beard that graced his strong, handsome face. A wide-brimmed hat set off his sparkling gray eyes. Sam walked toward the man and offered a greeting. The man seemed surprised to be seen but quickly accepted Sam's presence and smiled.

"People don't come this way often, and few appreciate this natural stone wall and the function it once played," the man said. "It's as if nature herself constructed this wall, and I suppose she did."

"I only come here myself once in a great while now," Sam mused. "I came more frequently at one time, and I've always felt attracted by this wall and this particular spot. I saw a bobcat not that long ago right up on that ledge," Sam pointed. "He stood there for several minutes. I admired him. Perhaps he admired me. After a short time, he turned and trotted off."

"Bobcats have a unique beauty," the stranger observed. "I'm grateful that bobcats are still here."

"Would you like to stroll with me down to the water's edge?" Sam suggested.

"Yes, I should like that very much."

As the two men walked along, they must have appeared to be brothers to anyone fortunate enough to witness this meeting of souls. They had a similar gait, stature, and ease, and they moved at precisely the same pace.

"I saw you speak some months ago now at the college," the bearded man shared.

"I thought I caught a glimpse of you at the end there," Sam recalled.

"Yes, that was quite the ending." The man laughed heartily. "Some of the rishis are still talking about it."

"Really?" Sam was genuinely amazed.

"Yes, I think you delivered a bit of surprise, even for them."

After a pause, the tall stranger began a story, something at which he was particularly good. "When my life ended, I came to a place not that different from here. The sky was a radiant blue, the forest healthy and vibrant with color and scent. The air felt alive. I wandered about, with no sense of time of course, until I came to a clearing. The clearing held a small hut with a fire burning in a shallow pit. A man sat before the fire with his eyes closed. As I approached, he was as still as a mountain. I sat down across from him, folded my legs, and closed my eyes as well.

"In only seconds, I was completely absorbed in a space that had no beginning or end. Eventually, I opened my eyes. Whether a minute in human time or an eternity had passed, I could not say. The man sitting across from me looked right at me as if waiting for a sign. We sat that way for a bit. When I asked him how long we had both been sitting there, he laughed. He started with a giggle, but it rolled into a wild gale of a laugh.

"Once he calmed down, he said, 'My dear friend, there's no way to answer that because we are now outside of time and space.' He seemed to know what he was talking about, so I let it drop.

"'My name is Whitman, Walt Whitman,' I told him.

"'Yes,' he replied, 'and you may call me Bhrigu.'"

Sam interrupted. Awed, he checked, "You mean the Bhrigu? The great rishi Bhrigu?"

"I suppose he's one and the same," the stranger assured him. "This Bhrigu started to review my life and my works. He nodded and smiled repeatedly, appreciating everything I had experienced. No judgment, only appreciation."

The two men were approaching the reservoir. They stopped to admire the serene beauty of the green-tinted water lapping against the stony shore. The bearded stranger motioned to a rock forgotten by a glacier long ago, and the two ancient friends sat looking out over the water's expanse.

Whitman continued, "We sat for a long while after that in silence. Then Bhrigu began to explain that, though it sometimes it takes a little while after the passage from one world to another, I'd soon begin to remember things from my life. When a memory or image arose, he instructed, just be with it and let it go. 'Keep doing this over and over until all the impulses cease,' he advised.

"'All right, fair enough, seems simple,' I thought. So I began. I closed my eyes. My awareness became enormous, transparent, and images came and went, like waves in the ocean of this inner spaciousness. Though my eyes remained closed, I suddenly noticed a pyramid before me, not unlike what the Egyptians built. As I gazed, it dissolved and there sat the most beautiful woman I ever had the grace to behold. She smiled, and her radiance illuminated thousands of universes. Then she spoke. 'Your goodness is complete, and you are the master of all you see.'

"Instantly, I knew myself as infinite, present everywhere, a continuum of vastness in which there is no sense of inside or out, only Being—being Itself.

I had hints of this in my human life. I had visions, and some lived and some faded away. I realized I sat before the mother of the creation and she was blessing me. She smiled one more time and entered into my Being, or I entered hers. It's hard to say because at this point there was no two, only one."

Sam listened raptly. Whitman revealed, "Sam, there's a mystery here I can't say too much about. It's bigger than *Leaves* or the Veda or all the holy books put together. That mystery is all around, everywhere to be found. It's within you and within everyone, but most people go on missing it. They cover up that which is true and real with the story and events of their lives. Everyone is chasing illusions, and still everyone is fine. That's also part of the mystery.

"Keep one foot firmly established in Being, Sam, and the other gently touching the earth. When you have a chance, to speak, speak from there. And, Sam, when you have a chance to talk or lecture, do so. While you're here, participate. Don't go out of your way to do it, but follow the inspiration and opportunity when they arise. When someone knocks on the door, answer it. After all, you're as much a doorway to the mystery as anyone."

Whitman looked at Sam, and Sam looked at Whitman and they both smiled. They were one mind. Words seemed almost irrelevant, but the gray-eyed poet went on talking. "I know for certain that you already know the mystery. You don't need my encouragement, but people need yours. Their minds are so busy. They have too many thoughts, too many emotional storms to contend with. The peace of the Lord is in and around them every moment. God is in and around them every moment. Keep them encouraged, open, seeking, aware. You have a gift for it. The sound of your voice is enough to pull the greatest cynic out of his mind and into his heart. That's a start enough for anyone.

"And by the way, you did great honor to my *Leaves*," he acknowledged.

"The honor was all mine," Sam returned. "*Leaves of Grass* has stirred many a heart. You know millions of copies have been sold since you passed."

"So I hear. It's done some good then."

"I'd say a world of good, Walt."

Again, they sat silently for a few moments or a thousand years. This time Sam broke the silence, confessing, "I've had a similar dream of Mother Divine. I think she was surprised when she saw me."

"Hah! You have a knack for being surprising," Walt quipped.

Both men began to chuckle. Their chuckling swelled into full-bellied laughter that reached the highest heaven. With that, whatever had been left undone was complete.

Acknowledgements

First and foremost, I want to thank my wife, Kay, for her constant love and support. I stumbled a number of times in this undertaking and she was always there to help me get on my feet again. She readily discussed with me the development of the story and gave me some important insights in the process. I also benefited greatly from her careful reading of the manuscript. Without her I might not have completed the writing of this book.

Also I want to thank my sons, Michael and Jon, for their support in writing this novel. They were the inspiration for the story for I wanted them to know the importance of this time in my life. Starting TM at 19 in 1974, going to teacher training, meeting Maharishi, studying at MIU, meeting so many great people and making so many good friends --- it truly was a golden time. And I'm glad that so many others like me caught the wave.

My dear friend, Dami Kirk, began telling me twenty-five years ago to start writing. He bravely labored through the first draft and was constantly encouraging through the process. Over the years and particularly as young men in our twenties, Dami and I have had some similar conversations on evolution and enlightenment in diners and cafes along the New Jersey shore. I'm grateful to him for his help and our unique friendship.

My editor, Cynthia Lane, really pushed me to get the second draft I'd sent her into shape. Cynthia is a special person in my life, as she initiated me into Transcendental Meditation. After not having seen each other since 1982, I found Cynthia on a Google search for 'editors' twenty-five years later. I wrote an email to her asking if she was the same Cynthia Lane I knew from Cambridge, MA and Fairfield, IA. She replied that she was. Thus our friendship was renewed. Thank you, Cynthia, for all your help and love.

After working intensely with Cynthia for nine months, I let the manuscript rest for six months before I picked it up again. I decided to rewrite it once again and I spent another six months on it. Finally satisfied with the writing, I asked Mary Ann Palmieri to serve as my copy editor. She diligently corrected my grammar, pointed out some inconsistencies and encouraged me to rewrite a few passages for clarification. She also urged me to get the manuscript to the publisher and "to stop sitting on it." I'm grateful to her for the confidence she instilled in me as a new author.

I want to acknowledge my readers who gave me helpful feedback along the way: my sister, Kim Barry, my friends Dr. Joel Silver, Dr. David Haight, Dr. Philip Tomlinson, David Bornstein, Josh Roberts, my nieces Heather Wight and Sophie Stone. Thank you one and all.

A very special thanks to Jerry Jarvis for his careful reading of Chapter 38, *The Lecture*. He made several good suggestions on the earlier history of the TM Movement. Jerry is a great man and teacher who was a role model for me as a young TM teacher. His love of knowledge, his devotion to Maharishi, and his compassion for everyone is inspirational.

Lastly, I want to thank my friend, Kristin Stashenko, for the beautiful watercolor painting that serves as the cover of the book. You can see more of her work at her website, www.kristinstashenko.com.

Also, many thanks to the staff of Xlibris for their help, patience, and professionalism in producing the final book version of *The Best of All Possible Worlds*.

THE AUTHOR

Steve began Transcendental Meditation in 1974. Impressed by his experiences and the knowledge of spiritual evolution as described by Maharishi Mahesh Yogi, Steve became a teacher of the TM program in 1976. He attended MIU in Fairfield, Iowa, graduating with a BA in Philosophy in 1981. He met his future wife, Kay, at the university. They were married in 1982. Over the next 24 years Steve and Kay started and ran three different businesses while raising their two sons in New Salem, MA. They currently live in Wellfleet, MA. This is his first novel.

CPSIA information can be obtained at www.ICGtesting.com
Printed in the USA
BVOW07s0755180713

326192BV00002B/560/P